From Indigo Sea Press
By Bud Fussell

Shepherds
Mixed Emotions
Redemption?
Serenity
Whirlwind

indigoseapress.com

Scoundrel

By

Bud Fussell

Sepia Books
Published by Indigo Sea Press
Winston-Salem

Sepia Books
Indigo Sea Press
302 Ricks Drive
Winston-Salem, NC 27103

First Sepia Books edition published December, 2015
Sepia Books, Moon Sailor and all production design are trademarks of Indigo Sea Press, used under license.

For information regarding bulk purchases of this book, digital purchase and special discounts, please contact the publisher at indigoseapress.com

Cover design by Tracy Beltran

Manufactured in the United States of America
ISBN 978-1-63066-206-6

CHAPTER ONE

The rolling hills were beautiful at that time of year. The trees had traded their spring and summer green for spectacular shades of red, yellow, and orange. Those that still held on to their tan and brown leaves added just enough contrast to create God's perfect palate. Added to that, the sky was deep, deep blue. Contrasting to the puffy white clouds, it defied an artist's imagination.

While the view from any of the hilltops was amazing, one hill was slightly higher than the rest, and that was the one Raymond was going to prepare for Jake's funeral. From there one could take in the breathtaking panorama of miles and miles of Big Jake's ranch and the magnificent view of the main house. It was what Jake had asked for when he made Joey promise to bring him back to Cana for burial. He would be buried next to Leann.

It was ironic Raymond and Sue were on the hill together. When he was alive, Jake had been adamant about keeping the two apart. They sat beneath a huge sycamore silent for several minutes as they absorbed the peace and beauty of their surroundings.

Both wanted to bring up a subject they hadn't talked about before, but neither wanted to be the first to speak. The mood and circumstances of the afternoon brought it to the forefront of their minds. Now that Jake was no longer an obstacle, each of them wondered what would happen next in regard to their relationship.

Finally, Sue couldn't hold back any longer. Reaching over, she placed her hand on Raymond's. "Have you had any thoughts about what is going to happen with us? Are we going to go on the way we have for years, or are we going to make changes in our lives that will let us include each other more? Thanks to your pa we are both pretty wealthy now. If we want to join forces and combine our land, we can become real important to a lot of people. Besides, I love you, Raymond."

He didn't say anything for a minute or so; then replied, "I don't know. Pa had such a hard time about you and me being together I still feel kind of uncomfortable about doing something I know he wouldn't like. I've been thinking about it, but I just don't know. I guess I feel guilty."

Changing the subject, he said, "We'll talk about it later, okay?" Then he said, "It's getting pretty late, so let's wait 'til tomorrow to start setting things up. We still have enough time."

As they started to leave, Asa and Thomas rode up. Before any of them could say anything, Raymond turned toward Sue and with his back toward the others, he mouthed the words, *"I love you, too."*

Asa was the first to speak. "Mr. Raymond, is there anything we can do to help you? Master Jake was like our family, and we wanna help you get things ready for his burying."

Thomas added, "It don't matter what you want us to do; we just wanna do something for Master Jake."

"Okay men, I can use the help," Raymond replied, "but it's so late in the day now that I've decided to wait 'til in the morning to start setting things up. Come on back then, and we'll get started. Pa really loved you two, and he would be happy to have you help with this last thing for him."

Asa and Thomas were two of the first four slaves Jake bought when he and Josiah went down to Dayton several years before. Jake saw potential in the two right away and not only made them supervisors, but went back to the slave market and bought women to be their wives. Later, he gave all of them their freedom. In addition to the humane treatment, Jake worked out a deal for each of them to get one hundred and sixty acres through the Homestead Act, plus he gave each of them one hundred and fifty acres when he freed them. Jake's help and influence pretty much propelled the pair into positions of respectability among the citizens of Cana. Not many colored folks had that standing around the area. The fact that Jake owned practically the entire town of Cana and most of the land around it didn't hurt either.

Cana might have been called a town, but it was actually just a little community located in the southwestern part of the country. It was made up of a few families who sharecropped the land surrounding the town. They were a blend of native westerners and easterners who had tried unsuccessfully to cross the country from the East to California. The unbearable conditions on the trail – extremes in temperature, sickness with no doctors available, and the constant threat of being attacked by outlaws and Indians—made the trip harsh. Many simply didn't have the heart to continue and just gave up, ending their trip in Cana.

There were other towns located in strategic areas on the edge of Big Jake's land made up of similar people. Cana, however, was where Jake grew up and it was a special place for him.

It was not on the trail to anywhere. One had to be going there intentionally, so the large crowd converging on the town was a big deal. Folks in that part of the country had never seen anything like it, especially for a funeral. Jake had done big things in life, and it was only fitting the celebration of his life be marked by the huge ceremony planned to honor him in death.

Big Jake had amassed a fortune; the largest part made up of the huge amount of land he owned. Jake himself probably hadn't known exactly how much he had. Some estimated around 765,000 acres. His ranch was actually larger than the State of Rhode Island. In addition to the land, he had thousands of heads of cattle, sheep, hogs, and hundreds of horses. He was a major grower of cotton, citrus fruit, rice, peanuts and sorghum. His lumber business had become a large part of his enterprises.

Thanks to a few savvy individuals whom he had trusted to look after his interests, he was one of the richest men in the country, if not the richest. His large family was a big help, but the major part of his labor force was made up of black slaves, a few people of mixed race and several white indentured servants and their families.

Since he was really old, Jake's death was not a surprise to anybody. But it's always hard to lose a parent even though you're expecting it. It was recorded that Jake had fathered thirteen children: twelve sons and one daughter by four different women. Two of the women were white slave girls whom Jake later set free, but who stayed on with him and his two wives. Many people thought several of his mixed-race and white slaves were actually his offspring, but no one ever spoke of it. Jake was too powerful for most people to cross, and the average person thought twice before meddling in something to do with him. It was none of their business, anyway.

Jake's favorable name was achieved in a large part through the influence of his business associates, and this drew many people, but the prominence of his son, Joey, was the main reason for such a huge turnout for the funeral. It was unlikely that many people knew anything about Jake's life before he came back to Cana, but once he got back, he made a huge impact on the whole region. His life, for the most part, consisted of trying to outsmart, out-maneuver and con his way to the top, but much of this took place before he returned.

He didn't always have such a favorable reputation; In fact, he had a very poor one until late in his life.

***

From a very early age, Jake was what might be called a scoundrel. He wanted a lot, but was not willing to work for it. If he could con somebody in order to get what he wanted, it was all the better. He would often cheat or steal to get whatever it was he wanted.

He loved his mother and was content to let her do nearly everything for him. He was happy to stay in the house with her most of the time. She loved him, too, and it was easy to see that he was her favorite.

As a young man Jake had overheard his pa speaking to his brother, Eph.

"Son, I told Perry Jordan I would buy that big Hereford bull of his, and I want you to ride over to Sparta to get him."

Eph jumped at the chance to go. "Okay Pa. I'm glad you're sending me. When you sent me over there last fall, I found a nice little sixty-acre spread I think I can get for a really good price. If I can get it right, do you think I should buy it?"

"Well, I don't know why you would want a spread all the way over there, but you know what it is. Can you afford it? If you can and if you like it that much, I guess I would go ahead and get it."

Eph felt better having talked to his father about the deal. Also, while in Sparta he had struck up a conversation with cute little Maggie Thompson, and was anxious to see her again. He just hoped she wanted to see him too. Accomplishing all these things, plus the distance to Sparta, it would be at least two days and possibly three before he would get back home.

Jake was always plotting how he could do something to make a big score, and this fit perfectly into his plan. His jealousy of Eph caused it to not matter that it involved stealing from his own brother. All he could see were dollar signs. Conscience never entered into it. While Eph went to Sparta, Jake would go to Bradon.

Eph had been in Bradon a couple years earlier, and during the course of business he'd run into Don Payne who was talking about wanting to sell a nice piece of land he had.

A fellow named Gerald Hall wanted it, but never seemed ready to close the deal. Eph became interested in the property, and convinced Don to sell the land to him. Don didn't know Gerald very well, but he did know Eph and knew he had a spotless reputation. Eph was also very charismatic, and this made Don comfortable in selling to him. The two had also had a couple of minor dealings in the past.

At the Bradon Bank, Eph arranged for a loan to pay Don; then went to the Land Office to get the deed. From there he headed home. When he got home he put the deed in a drawer in his room with some other papers where he was sure it would be safe.

Every time he had a chance, Jake would go into Eph's room and rifle through his things. After Eph's trip to Bradon he found the deed. Notes Eph had made contained the names of Don Payne and Gerald Hall. Jake kept that information in his head until he found the best time to use it.

As soon as Jake knew Eph was on his way to Sparta, and far enough away not to come back for something he might have forgotten, he saddled up and headed for Bradon. He wasn't sure exactly where he was going, but he figured Gerald Hall was the one he would try to find.

He went to the Land Office, asked where Gerald lived and rode out there. Gerald lived about four miles outside of Bradon, and when Jake got there he walked up on the porch and knocked on the door. A stern looking middle-aged man answered and didn't say anything at first; he just looked at Jake. Jake asked, "Are you Gerald Hall?"

Gerald said, "Yeah."

Then Jake said, "I'm Jake Isaacson from Cana. I think you know of my brother Eph. Can I come in and talk to you for a minute?" Gerald opened the screen door and gave Jake a hand-signal to come in and offered him a chair.

"How Can I help you Mr. Isaacson?" Gerald asked.

"Well, Mr. Hall, I guess I'll just cut to the chase. Do you remember a couple of years ago when Mr. Don Payne had a piece of land for sale that you wanted and he sold it to my brother, Eph, instead?"

Gerald said, "Yeah, I was disappointed when I didn't get it. That property borders this farm, and that would have made my place just exactly the size I wanted it to be. Why are you asking about it?"

Jake continued, "My brother asked me to come here for him. He is a proud man and is embarrassed to face you. He wanted me to tell you that if you still want that land, he will sell it to you for what he paid for it. He has over-extended himself and prays you still want it. I have brought the sale papers with me, and we can make the deal right now. I have my brother's power of attorney, so I can sign for him."

Jake had copied the papers he found in Eph's room, and he presented them to Gerald.

He wasn't totally convinced by Jake's story, but wanted the land. Since the papers looked authentic, he decided to accept the deal. "Okay, I'll take it. Are you sure you can do all the paperwork for your brother when we get to the land office?"

Jake assured him he could. "Besides, I have a letter from my brother authorizing me to act for him. I also have a copy of the power of attorney, so there should be no problem."

Everything went well at the Land Office, and Gerald gave Jake two bags of gold to pay for the land. "I'm sorry your brother is having problems," he said, "but I appreciate his sending you to do me this very big favor. I was really disappointed when I didn't get the land when it was for sale before. I have heard your brother is a good man, and this confirms that in my eyes. Please give him my best regards." They said good-bye, and each went on his way.

Jake was ecstatic as he mounted up and started home. He had just executed the cleverest deal anyone could imagine. Eph had probably bought the property to use after their dad's death, but Ike was still a relatively young man. More than likely, Eph wouldn't make a trip over there until after Ike's passing. In the meantime, Jake had two bags of gold, and plenty of time to figure out how he would handle things when that time came.

His deep-seated jealousy of Eph made this deal that much sweeter in his warped mind.

When he got home from Bradon, he went immediately to see his mother, and took her into his confidence. He was such a *mama's-boy* he couldn't wait to tell her he had completed a big deal, but he didn't go into much detail, and didn't mention that it affected Eph.

Then he couldn't stand it any longer. He had to tell her what he did. "Ma, you might not like it, but I sold Eph's land in Bradon."

"You what?"

"Yes ma'am, I sold it."

"Whatever possessed you to do something like that?"

"Ma, I'm so tired of you and Pa thinking everything Eph does is so good. Maybe not you so much, but in Pa's eyes, he can't do anything wrong. Y'all act like I can't do anything except hang around the house. I just thought if I could do something big on my own, it would make me feel better and this is what I did."

"Honey, you did wrong, and I believe you're gonna get in big trouble over it."

"Please don't say anything to Pa about it, Ma. I'll try to work something out, but please don't tell anyone, especially Pa."

"Okay,. But I hope you know what you're doing."

Jake hid the gold in the barn under some old trunks and stuff. No one ever went near that area except to pile on more old junk to be stored.

For the next couple years Jake felt good about his life. He and Eph were even getting along a little better than usual. Things were going smoothly until the day Eph had to go to Bradon. Ike wanted him to go over there to look at some livestock.

When Jake heard that, his heart nearly stopped. Panic set in. *What am I going to do?* He decided to offer to go himself on the pretense that he just wanted to help out his brother. "Pa, why don't you let me go to Bradon for you? I don't have too much to do right now, and Eph's busy on the new barn. Why don't you let me go?"

Ike smiled at that. "Son, that's nice of you, but I'm not sure you would know the difference between a cow and a goat. No, I had better send Eph. This job requires someone who really knows their business when it comes to livestock, and I'm happy to say there aren't many better than Eph."

Jake spent the next few hours trying to come up with an excuse to keep Eph away from Bradon, but nothing logical came to mind.

Eph got up the next morning, had breakfast with his mother and got an early start on his trip. Jake tried to convince himself Eph would be so busy with their pa's business he wouldn't have time to visit the property, but deep down he knew Eph would go by, since he would be so close.

Eph's father was very proud of him. No matter how hard he tried to show love equally to both sons, it was clear he loved him more than he did Jake, and Jake felt that.

Eph was popular with the other young men his age, and the young ladies all seemed to notice him. His thick red hair was appealing to them. He didn't try to encourage their attention, but he didn't discourage it either. He dated some, but not a lot. He didn't have a steady girlfriend.

Most of his time was spent outside. He never had a gun, but he was an expert hunter honing his skills with the bow and arrow until the bow became almost an extension of his arm. He could kill a deer easier than any of his buddies and his ability to do things with a knife was amazing.

From time to time he would ask Jake to go hunting or fishing with him, but Jake always found an excuse not to go. Sometimes, when Jake would refuse Eph's invitation, Eph would call him *"mama's boy"* or "sissy" and tease him. That only kindled Jake's resentment.

Ike loved to eat wild game, and Eph made sure his dad was never without some. He saw to it there was always venison available as well as buffalo. Rabbits and squirrels were frequent dishes along with just about anything else that roamed wild.

When Eph wasn't out hunting, he was usually working on a project outdoors. He would build things, or chop firewood or anything else he could find to do outside. This greatly pleased his pa and their bond was very strong.

***

After a couple days in Bradon, Eph started home; a man on a mission. The journey seemed to never end. Finally, spotting his house, he spurred his horse on. Jumping off his horse, he hit the ground running. "Where's Jake?" he yelled to his mother as he entered the house. He was in such a rage he was shaking all over.

"In his room." She'd never seen Eph so upset. His demeanor frightened her. Wondering what was wrong, she followed him to Jake's room.

Charging into Jake's room he didn't say a word when he saw him. In a split second he hit Jake flush in the face, breaking his nose. Blood squirted everywhere. Eph jumped on top of him, beating him unmercifully and shouting, "I'm gonna kill you for what you did, Jake."

"Ma and Pa might be blind to your sneaky ways, but I'm not. I've overlooked your sorry life ever since you were little, but this is too much. I'm gonna take everything you have; starting with your miserable life."

After the first two or three blows, Jake was out cold and couldn't hear anything, but Eph kept ranting as he pummeled Jake's face

Becky was screaming and trying to pull Eph off, but he was too strong.

Ike heard the racket and came running, and he, too, was unable to get Eph off Jake. Finally, two of their workers came in, and between all of them they were able to pull Eph away. He was like a madman. He was shaking, and they could see the rage in his eyes.

While Ike and the two hired men held on to Eph, Becky tried to minister to Jake. Eph kept trying to get at Jake and kept yelling, "I'm going to kill you, you thieving snake. I'm going to kill you." It was a terrible situation.

Becky was just beside herself as she looked at her baby and tried to clean him up. Jake was out cold, so Becky sat in the floor and cradled his head in her lap. She blotted his bloody face with a warm, wet rag and applied as much pressure as she dared to his broken nose. All the while she kissed and whispered to him, even though he couldn't hear her.

Ike was a little calmer about the whole thing, thinking that Eph would soon cool off, and things would get back to normal. Of course, at that point neither knew why Eph had gone so crazy. Becky thought about the Bradon land deal, but didn't say anything.

Just to be safe, Ike had his men stay in the house the rest of the day with instructions to absolutely not let Eph get near Jake. Eph was still saying he was going to kill him.

Later that afternoon, Ike spoke to Eph. "Son, what got into you to make you whip your brother like you did? I've never seen anything like it. When you calm down some, I think we need to talk. Eph, I'm asking you to not go after Jake again, if for no other reason, it upsets me and your ma and you know how your ma is. This has about made her sick."

Nobody was hungry for supper. Becky was so upset she probably couldn't cook anyway. If anybody got hungry, they could find something to eat in the kitchen without any problem.

Eph went down to the creek with a fishing pole to try to cool off some, and the two hired hands went on back to the bunkhouse. Eph couldn't seem to get in the mood to fish when he got to the creek and didn't even gather any bait. He just sat on the creek bank, thinking.

When Eph came back up to the house, Ike and Becky asked him to sit down and tell them what was going on.

Eph didn't say anything for several seconds and then started telling what happened in Bradon. "Pa, do you remember me telling you about a man named Gerald Hall? He was the man that wanted the land I bought from Don Payne. Remember?" Ike said he did. "Well I ran into him at the Bradon stock sale the other day and he told me how sorry he was that I had to sell my land, but he was sure glad that I chose him to sell it to. I asked him what he was talking about, and he told me an unbelievable story."

"He told me about Jake coming to him with papers saying I was overextended and was having a hard time, financially. Jake told Gerald I was too embarrassed to face anyone about it, and I had asked him to see him for me. He had with him a bill of sale, power of attorney papers, and the deed to my land. All those papers were forged, and he must have stolen the deed out of my room."

"Pa, I really wanted that land. I worked hard, saved my money, and felt really lucky to get it, and then my low-down brother stole it from me. Gerald said he paid Jake in gold the amount I paid for the property. I've got to find out if Jake still has it, and if he does, where it is. I may have to beat it out of him. I'll tell you this Pa, this is not over by a long shot."

Ike said, "Son, if what you're telling us is true, then I can see how you would be so mad, but Jake is your brother and you're gonna have to try and work something out with him. I don't know what at this point, but you can't attack him again. That's not going to help anything. It's hard to believe Jake could do this to his own brother."

Becky told him, "Eph, you nearly killed Jake. How could you do that to your brother? I know he did wrong, but he's still your brother."

"Ma, you keep him away from me."

It was hard to tell which disturbed Ike and Becky most; the fight or what Jake did. It seemed that Jake's deed bothered Ike more than the fight. Of course, Becky knew all along about the land deal.

They asked each other, "What are we going to do about this?" After what would have been suppertime, they went out on the porch and talked. They threw some thoughts out to each other and finally decided that it would be best to have Jake leave for a while until things cooled down.

"Ike, do you remember my cousin, Josiah Taylor over in Mercer? Maybe we could send Jake over there to stay until Eph gets over this. What do you think?"

"I think that might be a good idea, but first, we have to get the gold back from Jake, if he still has it. Eph will never cool off if he doesn't get it back. Since you're closer to Jake than I am, you find out where it is, and be sure you get it back."

Unbeknownst to everybody but Jake, Becky knew exactly where the gold was. She told him what she and his pa had decided, and to get the gold from the barn.

Jake protested. "Ma, I shouldn't have to give that gold back to Eph. I think I deserve to keep it. I earned it when he beat me up. I'm gonna keep it."

But Becky prevailed and he went to the barn. When he came back to the house, he only had one bag instead of the two. "Ma, here's one bag. I'm gonna tell Pa and Eph that I spent the rest."

They argued about it, but Becky finally relented and went along with his lie.

The next morning Ike sent Eph into town to pick up supplies. Such a trip normally took at least half a day, and of course, Ike knew it. The trip was just an excuse to get Eph out of the way until Jake left.

As soon as Eph left for town, Becky and Jake packed his things. Writing a letter to her cousin, she introduced Jake and asked if he could stay with his family for a little while.

Before he left, Jake went to the barn and got the other sack of gold. Then, when Ike gave him a sizeable amount of cash to last him until he could find a job, he really did have a large sum of money.

Not saying a thing about having the gold. He just took the money and said, "Thank you Pa." He shook his pa's hand and hugged him. Then he hugged and kissed his mother, and mounted up. Heading east, he rode in the opposite direction from Eph.

***

About dinnertime, Eph returned from town. His mood seemed a little better, but he didn't have much to say. If he noticed that his brother was gone, he didn't let on, going about his business as always.

A short time later, Ike caught up to him. "Since things are so volatile right now between you and your brother, me and your ma, and Jake felt like he should leave for a while. Son, I think it will be best if you don't know where he is going, so please don't ask me or your ma to tell you."

Eph replied, "That's fine with me. I don't want to know, and I don't care where the little lowlife is going. I just hope he stays gone."

CHAPTER TWO

The long trip to Mercer was more of an ordeal than Jake had expected. It was a little more than one hundred miles from Cana, and the terrain was rugged. Large creeks had to be crossed and part of the way was hilly, almost mountainous. It was hard for the paranoid mama's boy.

He had never hunted or fished, so he didn't know how to fend for himself in the outdoors. But the mama's boy had brought enough provisions to last him for the whole trip. It was a good thing he'd spent time in the kitchen with his ma. At least he could cook. As a result, he didn't go hungry on his trip.

Afraid someone might rob him, he avoided towns as much as possible. After all, he did have a lot of money with him. He was riding one horse and leading a mule and another horse with all his supplies, so he had a legitimate reason to be afraid. And he didn't have a gun. He was lucky to get through each day without being robbed.

The country was brutal, and for the most part, so were the people.

Of course, there were good people, too, but they stayed on their farms working, raising their families and minding their own business. These were not the people Jake ran into on the road.

The third evening he came up on a pretty little stream and decided it was a good place to camp for the night. It provided good, fresh water for him and the animals, and the countryside was beautiful. Picking up some rocks from the creek, he made a circular fire pit. A large dead oak tree had fallen nearby, and he broke off limbs to make kindling for his fire. Before starting his supper, he laid out his bedroll, making a nice place to relax after a hard day's ride.

He fried some salt pork, added some beans to the skillet when the pork was about done and boiled some coffee.

After he ate, he cleaned the skillet and packed everything away except the coffee pot. He pulled his bedroll over to a stump, and leaned up against it to enjoy another cup of coffee. He sat there thinking how peaceful it was. His thoughts drifted to home. He missed home, especially his mother. He thought about Eph, and how he had nearly killed him. *I'll never be able to go home, at least not as long as Eph is there.* For an instant, Jake felt a pang of guilt for stealing his brother's property, but the guilt didn't last long. He had been cheating people all his life, and he was hardened to it. He dismissed it from his mind.

On the verge of dozing off, he heard one of the horses whinny. With his heart beating in his throat, he sat up and looked around, but couldn't see anything in the dark, but he remained alert. He didn't know what he would do if someone came into his camp.

A voice said, "Howdy."

Jake jumped and managed to answer "Howdy."

The stranger asked, "Mind if I have some of that coffee?"

"Sure," Jake rinsed out his cup and refilled it for the man. He seemed pleasant enough at first, but things soon started to get a little tense.

The man looked over everything intently. "What's in the packs on the mule?"

"Just provisions," Jake answered.

"What's the horse carrying?"

"Same thing," he said.

The man got up and walked toward the animals." Well, I wonder what kind of provisions you're carrying. You don't care if I have a look, do you?"

Jake didn't know what to do. The man was carrying a gun and he looked like he knew how to use it. He started rifling through the bags on the horse, and when he didn't find anything that interested him, he moved over to the mule.

Jake had not put the gold or the money in such an obvious place as on the pack horse, but he was terrified the man would soon come over to him. He knew if that happened, the man would more than likely kill him. He was frantic, but tried his best not to show the fear that consumed him.

Just then another voice boomed through the darkness. "Hello in the camp."

Jake tried to steady his quivering voice. "Hello."

"Mind if I come in?"

Jake was thinking whoever it was had to be better than who was already in the camp. "Not at all. Come in."

A giant of a man walked in and introduced himself. "Hi young fella, my name is Jack Self, and I own all the land around us. I've been having trouble with wolves killing some of my cattle so me and some of my boys are staying out a few nights to try and kill the wolves."

"We're camping just a little ways from here. You can't see it in the dark, but it's right over that knoll there. I figure two camps are too many for a wolf hunt, so I'd like for y'all to come stay at ours. We'll help you tear down and move."

Jake jumped at the chance. "Okay, that's fine with me," and started putting out the fire. He rolled up his bedroll, and gathered up everything else he had unloaded and was ready to move.

The stranger said, "I've got to go. Thanks for the coffee." And he left.

Jake felt a huge sigh of relief. When all his gear was packed, he and Jack rode to Jack's camp, where they spent the night. Jake felt safe there, and was thankful to be alive.

The next morning he figured he was just about half way to Mercer. That meant another three nights sleeping in the open.

Alone with his thoughts as he rode in the direction of Mercer he pondered the scare he'd had the night before. *I'll sure be glad to get to Mercer. I figure I'm lucky to be alive after last night. Man, it's a good thing Jack came when he did or there's no telling what would have happened. I think I'll try to spend the night in a town every night from now on. I'll try to find a rooming house to stay in. This campin' sure ain't no fun, anyway. Besides, I don't want no more experiences like I had last night.* So after an uneventful day, that's what he did the fourth night.

After traveling alone for nearly a week, Jake was getting a little more self-confidence, and some of his paranoia was leaving him. He felt that he could take care of himself, if he could just stay alert and out of the way of people who were obviously trouble-makers. It had finally sunk in that everyone was not out to get him, and he was starting to get a little excited about reaching his cousin's place. It was now into the fifth day, and by the end of the next day he should be in Mercer. But today, it looked like Buffalo Creek would be the place to end the day, and if they had a hotel or rooming house, then he would stay there for the night.

As he rode into Buffalo Creek about an hour before sundown he noticed a sign on a small inn. *"Perkins House."*

The inn was once home to Mrs. Perkins and her family. She was married to John, and they raised two children there. The children grew up, married and moved away. Five years ago John got consumption and died a year later.

Their house was a large structure with several bedrooms and a large front porch with rocking chairs which looked inviting when you passed. John always kept it up very well and at one time it was the showplace of Buffalo Creek.

When John died, Mrs. Perkins had nowhere to go, and with the kids gone, she converted the house into an inn.

Jake dismounted and went in, and luckily she had a vacancy. After Jake paid for the room he took his animals across the street to the livery stable. After that he came back to the inn and went up to his room to rest before he ate supper.

It had been a long day, and he was tired and hungry. After he cleaned up he went to the small café next to Mrs. Perkins'. He ordered a steak and a cup of coffee, and could hardly wait for his food to be brought out. While he sipped his coffee, he looked around the dining room.

"Hey Jake. Whatta you doin' over here?" a voice asked.

Jake whirled around. Three feet from him was William McClain, one of Eph's friends from Cana. William just happened to be in Buffalo Creek on business, and was at the café eating supper, since it was the only place in town to get any food, except for the saloon.

"I had to come over here on some business and thought I would grab a bite before I went to my camp," William said. "Have you been here long."

"Naw, I just got in this afternoon."

"Listen Jake, I'm camped just a couple of miles outside of town. Why don't you come out and spend the night with me?"

"I've already checked in and paid for a room over at Mrs. Perkins', but I appreciate the invitation."

He was thankful that he didn't have to spend much time with William, because he didn't want him to know any more about what he was doing there than was necessary.

William asked him again, "Whatta you doin' up this way? I didn't think you ever strayed very far from home."

"I'm on my way up to Sheridan to visit my Pa's brother and his family. My uncle is sick," Jake lied. "I guess you heard about Pa breaking his leg. Well, naturally he can't travel. Since Pa's laid up, Eph has to run the farm, and that leaves me."

William said "I'm sorry about your Pa. Is there anything I can do?"

"No, thank you," Jake answered. "Eph has things well under control, and Pa is mending just fine, but I appreciate your offer to help. If my uncle is doing better when I get there, I won't stay long. Pa just thought I could help with the farm work until Uncle Lawrence gets back on his feet. Hopefully that won't be long."

A waitress brought Jake's food, and William said, "Jake, it looks like they brought my food, too. It was really good to see you, and I'll see you back in Cana", and with that he went back to his table.

Jake was bothered because he knew his lies were not convincing, but he had to think fast when he encountered William. Hoping the bruises on his face had healed enough that William hadn't noticed them, Jake wished he hadn't said his Pa broke his leg. His brother's friend was such a good man he would probably make sure that there was nothing he could do to help at the farm. If he went there, he would naturally tell the family that he'd seen Jake at Buffalo Creek. Likely he would mention Jake had said he was on his way to Sheridan. Jake knew Eph would pick up on that, even though they didn't have any folks in Sheridan. Buffalo Creek was on the way to Mercer, and that was the most logical place Jake was headed.

Oh well, he thought, *there's nothing I can do about that now.*

He was a long way from Eph, so he settled down to enjoy the thick steak, and then went to his room for the night.

***

Jake woke up to loud thunder. It was still dark outside. He stayed in bed and watched the lightning light up the sky, trying to guess what time it was. After what seemed like forever, he heard the clock downstairs chime five; almost time to get up. Rain beat on the windows, evidence that the storm was getting worse. He wasn't going to start out in this weather. Only a day or two from Mercer, he didn't have to be there at any certain time. The storm gave him a good excuse to sleep late, so he turned over and went back to sleep.

The rain was still pouring down when he woke up two hours later. He got up, stretched, and looked out the window. The wind was so strong the rain was going sideways. Until the weather cleared, he was stuck in Buffalo Creek.

He washed his face, got dressed, and went downstairs. "Good morning Mr. Jake." Mrs. Perkins gave him a cup of coffee. When he tasted it he thought it was the best coffee he had had, maybe ever.

"This is real good coffee, Mrs. Perkins. It may be the best I ever tasted. You ought to taste the stuff I've been boiling in camp."

"Thank you. I've had a lot of practice making it. You're not going to try to travel in this weather are you?"

"No ma'am. I guess I'll stay here until it clears some". He finished his cup and asked for a second, then asked, "Is there any place in town where I could get some breakfast?"

"Why yes. The café where you ate supper last night serves breakfast".

"Thanks". He finished his coffee and headed to the café. The walk was covered, so he walked over to the cafe and ordered a steak, some eggs, potatoes, and coffee. It was delicious, and he ate every bite. The storm was still raging when he finished eating, so he went back to the inn. Since the weather was so bad, Jake didn't want to get out, so he stopped downstairs for a while and visited with Mrs. Perkins and then went to his room and took a nap.

By the time it cleared up, it was nearly noon. He decided since he'd already lost a half day, it wasn't worth starting out so late. He couldn't reach Mercer by dark, and would have to camp in the open, and he didn't want to do that. He hung around the inn for a while, and then took a walk through town.

Buffalo Creek was bigger than Cana, but it was still tiny. Jake guessed there might be five hundred people who called it home. While exploring the town he came upon a general store and went in.

"Howdy, stranger, what can I help ya with?"

"Nothing right now. I just want to look around a little."

In a minute, Jake found a large can of peaches. He paid the clerk and asked, "Can you open these for me?"

"Sure can." And he took some kind of tool and opened the can.

While walking around the store eating out of the can and sipping the juice, he saw a section with books for sale. Looking through the selection, he found two books to his liking. One was a book on animal husbandry. Jake was fascinated with different breeding techniques. The other was a book written by a fellow who had recently started a new religious movement over in Fayette, New York. The book was called *The Book of Mormon.*

After a lazy afternoon of doing nothing, Jake bought the books and went back to the inn. He thumbed through his new books until it was time for supper, he ate at the café again, and then retired to his room for the night.

The next morning he got up early, and was anxious to get on the road. He had only one cup of coffee with Mrs. Perkins, went to the café for breakfast, and came back and packed up his things.

When he got everything loaded onto the animals, he paid the hostler, told Mrs. Perkins goodbye, and hit the road, hoping it would be his last day of travel.

He was in a good mood today. He'd had a full day of leisure and two nights of comfortable rest. Apparently that helped his attitude as well as his body.

At the end of the day, Jake would meet his mother's first cousin, making him Jake's second cousin. Whatever number cousin he was, Jake just wanted to think of him as family

He had a lot of questions as he rode along. *Will Josiah be tall or short? Fat or thin? Will he be easy to get along with? Or will he be hard to deal with?* Having never seen Josiah, Jake was conjuring up images of what he would be like.

Jake had thought about these things before, but now that he was getting closer, he was starting to get a little excited. Josiah was two years younger than Becky, so how would he act? What would he be like?

It was getting dark when Jake saw some lights in the distance. It had taken longer than he'd expected to get from Buffalo Creek to Mercer. He knew it was too late in the day to go to Josiah's, so he headed directly into town to find a room.

He found a rooming house on the main street. "Do you have a room for tonight?"

"Yeah, I can put you on the second floor"

Jake said, "That'll be okay. How much?"

"A dollar."

"Is there some place I can get something to eat?"

"Yeah, we serve food here if you want to eat here. We serve supper and breakfast for an extra seventy five cents."

"Okay, I'll do that. Where's the livery?"

"Down at the end of the street."

"Okay, let me take my animals down there and I'll be right back. What time is supper?"

"In about fifteen minutes"

"Okay." He hurried and took his animals and returned to the inn just as supper was being served.

Jake took a seat just as the food was being passed and it was delicious. While he and the other guests were eating, he asked, "Does anybody here know a man named Josiah Taylor?"

One man said he did and gave him directions to the Taylor's farm.

The next morning he was up at daybreak, nervous, but excited. He ate breakfast, loaded his animals and set out toward Josiah's.

CHAPTER THREE

Jake hadn't gone more than two or three miles from town, when he came up on a large entrance with a sign over it, J-T (pronounced J Bar T), and he knew he was getting close. The man who gave him directions had said J-T was the name of Josiah's ranch. Cattle were grazing on both sides of the road, but no buildings or people were in sight. He guessed the main house would be ahead if he kept riding. As he rode on, for probably another mile, he saw large flocks of sheep, and he thought to himself, *Ranchers in my part of the country would never mix cattle and sheep on the same land, but what do I know? I'm not a rancher.*

Approaching a flock on the right side of the road, he noticed a young girl nearby. He rode over to her and asked, "Is this Josiah Taylor's place?"

"She didn't answer. She just nodded her head.

"My name is Jake Isaacson and I'm Josiah's cousin from over in Cana. I'd like to see Josiah if I could."

She said "Wait here, I'll be right back," and she took off running. In a little bit he saw her coming back, and she had a man with her. He supposed the man was Josiah.

It was indeed Josiah, and he rushed to meet Jake warmly. "Jake, it's good to meet you. C'mon, follow me up to the house."

It was a short ride to the house. Jake dismounted, wrapped the reins around the hitch rail and followed Josiah into the house. When they were seated at the dining room table, Jake told him the story of how he and his brother were not getting along. and his family all thought it would be better if he left home for a while to let things cool down. He made sure he didn't tell why they weren't getting along. In fact, the way he told his story it seemed as if Eph was at fault. Then he produced the letter Becky had sent with him, to give to Josiah.

My dear Josiah,

This is my youngest son, Jake, and I wish for you to make him welcome in your home for a little while. There has been tension between my two boys lately, and Ike and I feel that it will be to everyone's advantage if Jake can spend some time with other members of our family. He is a good boy and is certainly willing to work and help you do anything you wish for him to do. Please accept my thank-you for receiving him into your home.

I would love to see you, but I understand that you are busy and the distance is great. Please keep us in your heart and think of us occasionally.

Your loving cousin
Becky

After Josiah read the letter, he looked up at his cousin's son. "You are welcome here, Jake. Your mother is my favorite cousin and I've missed seeing her for many years. You favor your mother in a lot of ways. You have her eyes."

They talked for a long time, just getting acquainted. Jake told him about his family, and then Josiah told Jake about his.

Josiah and his wife had five children, three boys; Buck, Ray, and Eddie, and two girls; Leann and Raelyn. Buck was the oldest, then Ray, and then Eddie. Leann was born next. She was eighteen years old, and Raelyn was seventeen.

The ranch was 14,000 acres. Cattle and wool were the primary products, but there were money crops as well; wheat, corn, soybeans, and cotton. The work force was made up mainly of slaves. They provided the labor needed to grow and harvest the crops, and they also did the sheep shearing. With help from slaves, the girls looked after the sheep, and the sons looked after the cattle.

After their *get acquainted* session, it was dinnertime. The boys, Leann, and Raelyn had come in, so everybody was there. Jake thought about his mama's cooking while he stuffed himself at the table.

After dinner Josiah had Jake saddle up and he took him around part of the ranch, to show him some of what was there. The ranch was so large it was impossible to ride it in one afternoon.

"This is real interesting, Josiah. I like what you've showed me, and I especially like what y'all are doing with your animal breeding. That's always been my favorite part of farming."

They got back to the house late in the afternoon, and Etta had another big meal almost ready.

After supper Josiah gave Jake a minor shock. "In the morning you can go out with Ray and Eddie and help them with the branding. We have a lot of calves that are ready, and it will be a good time for you to learn how we do it at the J-T."

Jake had known he might have to help at Josiah's, but he'd thought maybe he could hang around the house and help Etta. He was in for a rude awakening.

Branding cattle was not a fun job. It was hard, hot work. Not only was it hot being around the fire, it was hard *bull-dogging* the calves to the ground.

Every few days Josiah had Jake doing something different, and he was learning quite a bit about ranching. He actually enjoyed spending time with Leann and Raelyn, while they looked after the sheep.

After a week or two Jake was starting to get used to farm work and the outdoors, and he was beginning to like it.

Physically, Jake was a good specimen. He tolerated the physical work without complaining in order to get to something that he enjoyed. He was splitting his time between the cattle and the sheep, and whenever he could, after supper each night, he read the book he bought on animal husbandry. Between the book and the hands-on experience he was getting, he felt that later on he would be able to help improve the quality of newborn calves and lambs through cutting edge breeding.

Josiah had noticed that Jake seemed to have a knack when it came to knowing what to do in certain situations connected to breeding.

He had been there for about a month when Josiah came to him one day. "Jake, just because we are cousins, there is no reason for you to work for me for just room and board. What do you think will be a fair wage for me to pay you?"

Earlier, Jake had thought there was no telling when or if he could ever go back home, and had decided he would just stay on Josiah's ranch indefinitely.

After Josiah asked him that, Jake said, "I would like to work out something that would enable me to buy that vacant house down by the river. I would also like to buy a few acres, and maybe a few heifers, if I can use one of your bulls as breeding stock, until I can get my own bull."

"Sounds good, Jake. I'll agree to that." And they negotiated a fair wage.

After work each day, Jake went down to the river house to fix it up enough to move in. He had a great deal of experience doing house cleaning and other household chores, so he was very much at ease with that work. There was no well, but there was a spring about two hundred feet from the house. He thought he would build a spring-house, and that way he would not only have good water, but refrigeration as well.

When the house was livable, he moved his few belongings into it. Josiah, Etta, and the sons and daughters pitched in and helped him build a few things that he needed, such as a bed, a chair, a table, and some benches. They had some extra items stored in their barn, including a wood cook stove, and they gave those to Jake. He set up housekeeping, and was fairly comfortable. It wasn't a fully furnished house, but he had the bare necessities. It was okay for a single guy who was gone all the time, except at night.

Now that he had moved, Leann and Raelyn started coming around to check on him, and he enjoyed being with them, especially Raelyn. He had started to notice that Leann did little things to indicate she was interested in him. He liked her, too, but he really had his sights set on Raelyn, even though she was younger. Both girls had observed birthdays since he arrived, so they were now nineteen and eighteen years old, and at that age they were considered adults. They were plenty old enough to marry, but neither one was serious about any of the young men in the area.

Jake had now been working for Josiah for three months, learning quite a bit about livestock. He was also learning quite a bit about growing crops, especially the crops that were being grown to feed the animals. He studied his animal husbandry book so much, he could almost recite it. He was so fascinated with raising animals, and was starting to get ideas about doing some things on his own.

Doctor Stanley Wells was a Veterinarian and a regular visitor to the J-T. He had become a good friend of Jake's, explaining what he was doing when treating an animal, and showing Jake how to do them. They had long conversations about breeding methods, nutrition, and other things needed for successful breeding.

Doc had become interested in the artificial insemination of animals, and he and Jake spent much time discussing it. Jake had an insatiable thirst for learning new and advanced methods in animal breeding. Between his picking Doc's brain and studying his book, he was becoming quite an expert.

***

The river house and the fifteen acres included with it was really close to the boundary of Josiah's land and far enough from the main house, Jake could leave and go to town or other places without Josiah or anybody else knowing he was gone, not that anyone would care. But Jake was starting to hatch some ideas in his devious mind, and didn't want to have to explain anything to anybody.

He had made up his mind to try to buy some land of his own to use as a place to start a herd of cattle. If it was big enough, he would also start a sheep operation. He still had most of the money that Ike gave him before he left home, plus the bag of gold that wasn't returned to Eph from the land sale that started the whole mess. There was enough to buy a sizeable farm plus some livestock if he could figure out how to get some free from Josiah. It would not be good if Josiah knew anything about it, so great care was used to not do anything that would give his plot away.

It was on his mind every day when he was working. More and more he was having to spend time with Leann and Raelyn, helping with the sheep. He looked forward to going to work, just so he could see the girls, especially Raelyn, but he was crazy about both of them.

When he tired of reading the animal husbandry book, Jake would read some in *The Book of Mormon*. From time to time, whenever he went into town, he would pick up literature at the town hall about this movement. It was called the Church of Jesus Christ of Latter-day Saints. The believers were called Mormons, because they believed in *The Book of Mormon*, which they claimed was divinely inspired. After having translated it from golden plates, Joseph Smith and five other associates founded the Church of Jesus Christ of Latter-day Saints.

Jake was becoming more interested in the movement than he probably should, but he told himself that if God inspired it, then it was good enough for him. He thought that his pa, Ike, would be proud of him because Ike was a staunch, God fearing man, and had tried unsuccessfully over the years to instill his beliefs in Jake.

But now Jake had found something that fit into his way of thinking, in certain areas. For instance, he noticed that many of the Mormons he read about, had more than one wife. This was certainly not allowed in Ike's narrow belief, but Jake liked the idea of being able to have two or three wives. He overlooked the fact that polygamy was not a part of the Mormon doctrine, and was practiced by only a few. He figured if it was good enough for some, then it was good enough for him. Leann and Raelyn were the only two girls he knew, and he liked both of them, in fact, he thought he might even love Raelyn, but it was not the time to take on any wives. Maybe a little later, but right now he had things to do, and didn't want anything to interfere with his plans.

***

Six months had passed since he arrived at Josiah's. He was working every day, and managed to pay Josiah for the house, land, and stock without delving into any of the money Ike had given him.

Josiah had sold him six heifers, nine ewes, and one ram. By using a bull from Josiah's herd, four of the heifers were pregnant, and his ram had six of the ewes pregnant. Josiah had loaned Jake one of his slaves to help look after the stock, and that was a big help to him.

One day Doc Wells came out to Josiah's ranch to help with the birthing of some lambs. "Hi, Doc."

"Hi, Jake. How's it going?"

"Okay. Listen, I've got something I want to talk to you about. How about stopping back by when you are ready to leave?"

"Okay, I shouldn't be too long. Where will you be, here at the barn?"

"Yeah"

"I'm just gonna be a couple of hills over, so there'll be no problem getting back."

"Thanks, Doc."

When Doc finished he rode over to see Jake, and Jake asked him for a favor. "Doc, I know you travel around these parts all the time and know just about everything that's going on, right?"

"Yeah, I guess I do."

"Well, here's the favor I want to ask of you. I'm interested in buying some land for myself, but I don't know the people in the area like you do. I'm wondering if you would keep your eyes open for a nice tract that I might could buy. I don't plan to quit working for Josiah. I just want a place where I can establish a nice herd and a decent flock of sheep and maybe move over there at some point. I am not ready to tell Josiah yet because he might take it the wrong way. He's been good to me and I don't want to hurt his feelings. Would you do this for me?"

Doc said, "Yeah; in fact, I know of a place right now that may be for sale. I'll check it out the next time I'm in that vicinity. It's not too far from here. From what I hear, the folks want to sell out and move to California. There have been rumors of some people finding gold out there, and these folks want to go out and try to find some for themselves. I'll let you know."

"Thanks," Jake said. "Please be sure and keep this between you and me, okay?"

"You bet," answered Doc, and he left.

Jake was feeling really good about what had just happened. Maybe he will be able to get his own place earlier than he expected. Hopefully Doc wouldn't be too long getting back to him. He was anxious to see the place. Thinking to himself, *If a family is living there now, then there has to be a house and maybe a barn. If they're going to California, then they can't carry too much with them, so they might sell me some of their furniture and other stuff at a good price.*

Excitement was mounting. There were so many things running through Jake's mind right then that he hardly knew what he should do next.

He was brought back to reality when he saw Leann coming toward him.

"Hey," she said.

"Hey, yourself."

"Whatta ya doing?" she asked.

"Not much," Jake replied.

They made small talk for a few minutes, and then she asked, "You know, the sheep shearing is coming up. Has Pa told you what your part in it is going to be?"

"Naw, he hasn't said anything yet, but I'll ask him when I get a chance."

This would be his first shearing since he arrived at the ranch. Actually his first shearing ever. The slaves did most of the actual shearing, but Jake knew there had to be more to it than just cutting the wool off the sheep. He was anxious to know because when he established his own flocks, he would need to know these things.

He called on a middle-aged slave named Miles to help him out. Estimated to be around fifty-five years old, he had been with Josiah since his early twenties. Josiah looked at him almost as a family member. He helped Leann and Raelyn with the flocks and they loved him to death. They confided in him, probably more than they did Josiah.

Miles seemed to like Jake, and was more than glad to tell him all he knew about shearing. Jake was getting a free education in ranching at Josiah's expense.

Miles said this was the time to shear the sheep because the weather was warm. The warm weather brought out the oils in the coat and helped lubricate the shears, producing a more even coat. Because the coat needed to be clean, a clean mat was used for the sheep to stand on. Miles emphasized the importance of keeping the coat all in one piece, and not to go back and shear it a second time. He had been building some shearing platforms that allow the sheep to stand with their head secure while being sheared. This also got the sheep up off the ground, making it much easier on the shearer.

After the shearing, the wool was stored in a cool, dry place before taking it to market. It needed to be tied with paper twine, so the most valuable part of the wool was toward the outside.

Jake was fascinated with Mile's gentle demeanor and the expertise he had. If a person couldn't understand after hearing Miles explain something, then that person simply wasn't too smart. The whole process sounded to Jake as though it was really hard work. He was glad the slaves were going to do the shearing. He just hoped that Josiah would have something fairly easy for him to do.

Between twenty and thirty men would be shearing. Figuring fifteen to twenty sheep per man, per day, Jake figured it would take ten days to two weeks to finish. That was a lot of wool, and it would take several wagons to get that much wool to market.

The shearing started a week later. Slaves were doing most of it, but sometimes Buck, Ray or Eddie would take over and rest them for a little bit. Jake's job was tying up the bundles of wool and putting them in the storage building. It was hard work, and the smell was terrible. The long summer days seemed even longer. The tremendous amount of work was being crammed into a short period of time.

Each night when Jake went home, he stripped down, jumped into the river, and soaked for a long time, trying to get the sheep smell off. It seemed as if the odor was always in his nose.

The shearing was finished in two and a half weeks. Josiah, his boys, and Jake loaded the wool into four wagons and started hauling it to the market in Mercer. It took three trips to get it all there.

At the conclusion of each trip the receiving clerk at the market would have them unload the wool. He would weigh it and give Josiah a receipt to keep until the last trip was complete. When all the trips had been made, Josiah presented his receipts to the cashier and was paid after the weights were verified and other paperwork reconciled. After the third trip, while the market people were figuring everything up, they went to eat dinner at the small café in Mercer. While they were eating, Jake saw Doc Wells pass by the window.

"Doc Wells just went by"

Buck said, "Yeah, his place is just up at the end of the street."

"Josiah, when we finish eating, do you care if I go up to Doc's to say hello?"

"Go ahead. We have to go to the general store for some things and then back to the market to collect for the wool. We'll meet you back there in a little while.

"Hi, Jake. What brings you to town? It's good to see you."

"Hi, Doc. I'm here with Josiah and his boys. We finished bringing the rest of the wool in today. I've got to meet them back at the market in a little while. I just wanted to come see what's going on with you."

"I'm glad you're here. It saves me a trip out to the J-T to see you. I talked to the man I told you about, the one who is going to California, and he said he would. like to talk to you about his farm."

"Really? Tell me a little bit about it and when can I see it." Doc said. "First of all, the farm is four hundred acres and has a house, a barn, a smokehouse, a good well, ten hogs, and about a hundred head of cattle. The man's name is Ben Green, and he's anxious to talk to you. I told him that I would tell you, just as soon as I saw you. I have to go back out there this afternoon. What do you want me to tell him?"

"Ask him if I can come out Sunday afternoon," Jake said. "I have to work every day until then, but I can go out Sunday."

"All right," Doc said. "I'll tell him."

Jake said, "Today's Wednesday. Are you going to be around town on Friday?"

Doc said, "As far as I know now."

Jake said, "I have to come in for Josiah on Friday, so I'll stop by, and you can tell me what Ben said then, okay?"

"That's fine. For what it's worth to you, I can tell you he's really anxious to get started to California. He figures he has about three more months of warm weather before winter starts. He would like to be in some part of the country that's warm in winter if he hasn't made it to California yet. If you or someone else doesn't buy him out soon, he'll probably just wait until next year to go, and who knows, he might change his mind by then. If I were you, I would get out there as quick as I could. And Jake, I don't know what Ben wants for his place, but as bad as he wants to get rid of it, it wouldn't surprise me if he let you have it for fifty cents an acre."

"Okay," Jake replied. "Doc, ask Ben something else for me. Ask him can I come out Friday afternoon, if I can work it out. I can't say that I will, but I would like to. If he doesn't care if I just drop in on him, If I can't I'll definitely be out there on Sunday. You'll need to tell me how to get there." After Doc gave him the directions, Jake went back to the market. Josiah was just finishing up. His payment for the wool was being counted out to him. Jake couldn't help but see all the money. He didn't know how much it was, but it was a huge amount. It was just another tidbit he stored in the recesses of his mind. Already he'd seen big money change hands at cattle sales, and now this. *Boy, this ranching is fun,* he said to himself.

On the ride back to the J-T, Jake forgot all about the shearing and hard work he had been through. Josiah and the boys were talking about the good price they got for their wool this year, but Jake pretty much tuned them out. All he had on his mind was the farm that he was going to look at; and maybe buy. If he could get it for fifty cents an acre, he wouldn't have any trouble paying cash for it, and he hoped he could buy the stock at a good price, too.

When they arrived at the ranch, Jake took the wagon to the shed and unhooked the team. Walking out of the shed he raised his hand, said "So long" to everybody, and went straight to the river house. It had been a long day.

He fried some potatoes and streaked meat, and boiled some coffee. Putting the meat on some biscuits Etta had given him, he felt like he was having a feast. *Boy, that streaked meat and biscuits really hits the spot*, he thought after his first bite. The potatoes were unusually good tonight, and even the boiled coffee tasted good. In fact, the whole world was good.

The next morning was spent cleaning up after the shearing. The slaves did most of the work. All the platforms had to be scrubbed and then picked up and put in storage. Then they had to scrub the floor.

Jake and Josiah's boys had a lot to do, too. They had to wash out the four wagon beds where the oily, smelly wool had been. The wool was oily, and it made the wagon beds oily and hard to clean. They used lye soap, but it was still hard to cut through the oily mess.

Finally, they finished, and went to the house for one of Etta's big, delicious dinners. Everyone was in a good mood, and they all had a good time. Even Buck and his brothers talked a little. A couple times Buck was seen smiling.

Leann and Raelyn were especially playful. They giggled and a few times they would brush against Jake. Once, Leann put her hand on his forearm. Another time Raelyn playfully socked him on the shoulder and Jake was starting to get ideas about them.

After dinner, Josiah said before everybody left, "Listen to me for a minute y'all. Since the shearing went so good and we got such a good price for the wool this year, all y'all can take off 'til Monday."

That, of course, didn't include most of the slaves. They would have to keep an eye on the herd and the flock, but Miles and some of his men who did the shearing were given time off as well.

They finished out the day, Thursday, just killing time more than anything else. After dinner, Leann and Raelyn went back to the flock, and Jake went with them. Sitting in the shade of a large sycamore tree he watched the sheep. They were funny looking without any hair, but Jake thought they had to feel better, as hot as it was. As he watched he envisioned the sheep growing more hair, and realized

Josiah would make another big profit next year and the year after, and the sheep would do all the work. The thought only made him more anxious to establish his own herd.

The day finally ended. The girls put the dominant ram inside a small corral at the pasture, so the flock wouldn't run away, and the three of them went to the main house. Jake then headed back home after picking up the customary leftovers that Etta had saved for him to have for supper.

After he got home he ate just about everything she gave him except for three biscuits, and didn't even leave room for dessert. The three biscuits would be saved for breakfast in the morning.

He went to bed when it got dark and fell asleep thinking about the farm he was going to see the next day. He slept like a log until daylight woke him up.

Jake got up, put on his clothes, and started a fire in the cook stove. He put a pot of coffee on to boil, and fried up some eggs and streaked meat, and heated up the three biscuits he saved from supper. When he sat down to eat, he thought to himself, *What a great day this is going to be.* After he finished eating, he washed his face and brushed his hair the best he could. The only mirror he had was a small piece of one that he had found, so he couldn't see himself very well, but he did what he thought was an adequate job. Looking as nice as possible was important to him when he met Ben Green.

Doc was right, Jake thought. The farm he was going to see was not far from Josiah's ranch. If one went the back way from the J-T to the main road to Mercer and then turned right onto Redding Road, Ben's road was only a half-mile down. After a pleasant four-mile ride, he came up on a sign that read, "Green Farm," and turned onto the dirt road. In a few minutes he came to a nice, well-kept house. He dismounted and knocked on the door.

A reasonably attractive woman came to the door, and Jake removed his hat and introduced himself. "I'm here to talk to Ben Green about his farm. Is he here?"

"Oh yeah, Doctor Stanley Wells talked Ben about you. He will be back in just a little bit, if you want to wait. One of our cows became fresh last night, and he's gone down to the pasture to check on the calf."

"Can I get you a glass of lemonade?"

"Yes ma'am, that would be real good," Jake nodded.

He stayed on the front porch while she went to get the lemonade. When she returned, he took the glass and sat on the steps to wait for Ben. He'd gone about his business as usual, not knowing Jake would be there.

When Jake finished his lemonade, he asked Mrs. Green, through the front door, "Is it okay if I look around some."

"Yeah, that will be all right."

He sat his glass on a small table next to a chair, put his hat on and walked down the steps. His stroll took him around the barn and the smokehouse, which seemed in good shape. In the barn he noticed there was a good deal of hay. *Ben's idea to go to California must have been sudden. He wouldn't have filled the barn with hay if he knew he was leaving.*

Looking in the smokehouse, Jake saw quite a bit of meat. Even if it was left over from last winter, there might be enough to last him all the coming winter. That was good, but it was none of his business. He certainly wasn't going to bring it up to Ben.

Hoping he could make the deal, Jake finished his walk and went back to the house and sat on the porch. In a few minutes he saw someone riding toward the house. Thinking it must be Ben, his heart started to beat faster.

Ben looked serious when he rode up. Dismounting, he looked Jake up and down. "Can I help ya Mister?"

"I'm Jake Isaacson." Doc Wells told me you are wanting to sell your place here. He said he had talked to you about me"

"Oh yeah. I wasn't expecting to see you 'til Sunday," Ben replied.

"Well, that was what I thought when I talked to Doc, but my boss gave me the weekend off, so I came early," Jake said.

"You mean Josiah?" Ben asked. "He's a good man. Doc said you're some kin to him. That right?"

"Yeah, we're cousins. Why don't you show me around the place and tell me something about it. Everything I've seen from here looks like you have taken good care of it. Why are you wanting to leave?"

"Come on; we'll talk while we ride."

They mounted up and headed down the road to where Jake had seen the Green Farm sign.

Ben said, "The road we're on just about splits the four hundred acres right down the middle. The river borders the farm on one side, and good grass grows all the way to the border on the other side.

Turning right at the sign, they went in the opposite direction of the river. As they rode, Jake was thinking just how pretty and rich looking the land was, and the healthy cattle he saw. They passed a couple of small spring-fed creeks that provided plenty of water for the stock on that part of the farm away from the river. The river provided plenty of water on the other side.

"Why are you wanting to leave such a good farm?" Jake asked again.

Ben said, "I got a letter from my brother, who lives in Oklahoma. He is planning to move his family to California, and wants me and my family to go with them. My brother knows a man who was out there a year ago. According to him, people are starting to find gold. He told my brother you can get rich if you can find a good spot and stake a claim. I've always wanted to do something like that. I've never been anywhere farther than about fifty miles past Mercer. Me and my wife talked it over and decided we were going to pack up and go."

Jake asked, "What are you going to have to get for the farm, and what comes with it?"

Ben sat tall in his saddle and looked directly at Jake. "The land and the buildings, of course, but the stock is a separate deal, unless you want to buy them in addition to the farm. I'm asking seventy-five cents an acre, and twelve dollars a head for the cattle. I also have ten hogs, and we can work something out on them. The hay in the barn stays, and maybe some of the meat in the smokehouse. We will take as much of the meat as we can as part of our provisions. We will take what furniture we can, but you know you can't put much on a wagon, so most of that stuff will stay with the house. How does that sound to you?"

Jake frowned. "I don't know. I'll have to think about it. Seventy-five cents is more than I had planned on, and twelve dollars a head is a little much for me. I'll think about the farm, but you might have to try and sell the cows to somebody else in case I can't buy them. I'll come back in a few days and let you know something."

Ben said, "It's a fair price, so think hard on it. It's doubtful you can find any other place this nice for this kind of price. I hope you will take it."

Jake had seen all he needed to see and was dying to close the deal, but he told Ben he would be back on Sunday afternoon with his answer. They said goodbye, and Jake left.

Heading for the river house, all he could think about was the farm and the price Ben was asking for it.

Doc had said he could probably get it for fifty cents an acre, but Ben had asked seventy-five cents. Jake thought the cattle would be part of the deal.

He was disappointed. He had hoped to close the deal while at the farm. Wishing he could talk to Doc Wells about it, Jake mulled everything over, finally deciding Ben was just trying to get as much as he could for his place.

Having made up his mind to buy the farm, even if he had to pay Ben's asking price, Jake wondered if Ben would be willing to negotiate. Waiting a couple days was a smart move. On Sunday, Jake would ride back to the farm, see Ben, and make him a counter offer.

One thing Jake wasn't sure about yet was whether or not he would pay Ben's price for the cattle. He would give that more thought in the next day or two. Assuming there were a hundred head, he would need another twelve hundred dollars. That would eat into his money more than he wanted it to.

After breakfast the next day, Jake went down to the river bank and sat on a log for a long time, thinking about the farm and what he could do with it. Since he had become so very good at breeding techniques with sheep and cattle, he wanted to make the connection between successful breeding and monetary success.

After a while he went back to the house, scratching around inside until he found some paper and a pencil. Back outside, he listed every kind of scenario he could imagine, and when he finished one, he scratched through it and put down another one. This was more than just buying a farm to Jake. It was a reconciliation between the cost of the farm and livestock, and how much money would be left for other necessities. He worked so hard at it that he finally used up all his paper and had to stop, but before he did, he thought he had come up with a very good plan.

***

On Sunday, Jake left the river house about mid-morning. He headed to town first, hoping to talk to Doc before going on to Ben's, but Doc wasn't there.

Jake had some time to kill, so he went to the little café down the street from Doc's. Since it was Sunday, there weren't many people there. Most people ate dinner at home after going to Church. Jake spoke to the lady who owned it and ordered a steak. He didn't know any of the people there, and only knew the owner to speak to, so after his food was brought, he ate in silence. He took his time eating, and after a refill on coffee, he got up, paid his bill, and left for Ben's place.

As he approached the Green farmhouse, Jake saw Ben outside with a young boy that looked as if he might be around eleven or twelve years old. He hadn't been at the farm on Friday, and Jake hadn't given any thought to Ben and his wife having any kids. Obviously they did.

Jake rode up and nodded to Ben and the boy, "Hello there."

Ben said "Welcome back. Get down and let's go up on the porch. By the way, this is my boy Tommy."

Jake dismounted and greeted Tommy. "Hi". Then he and Ben sat down. Before they started talking, Ben said, "Tommy, how about going around back and helping your mama shuck that corn she's working on."

"Jake, have you made up your mind about buying the farm?"

"Well actually I haven't, 'cause I just don't think I can afford seventy-five cents an acre. Also, if I were to buy the land, I would want to have some cattle, but twelve dollars a head is just more than I can handle."

"How close are we?"

Jake said, "I have been trying to figure out a way to make this work, and I feel that I could maybe pay you forty cents an acre, and about nine dollars a head for the cattle. I have the money with me, if you want to deal."

"Jake, I don't have very much money. I'm going to have to depend on what I get for this farm to take me to California, and I don't see how I can take what you've just offered, but I'll tell you what I'll do. I'll let you have the whole farm for fifty cents an acre, if you will take all one hundred cows for ten dollars apiece, and I'll throw in the ten hogs for free."

Jake took out one of the pieces of paper that he had scrawled on at home, along with the pencil, and looked down, pretending to be figuring out something. He thought his insides were going to explode, but he couldn't let Ben know how thrilled he was.

In a minute or two he looked up at Ben. "Well, it's really going to strap me, but I guess I'll take it. When do you want me to take over?"

Ben said, "We can be gone before the week's out. Is that all right?", "The end of the week is fine. Can you make out a bill of sale? If you can, I'll pay you after we sign it, and if you see you will need more time, that will be okay, too."

They shook hands on the deal and went into the house for some paper so Ben could write up the bill of sale.

While he was writing, Jake added up the price of the farm and cattle. He started counting out the money and said, "I come up with one thousand and two hundred dollars. Is that what you get Ben?"

"It is" Ben nodded as he finished the bill of sale.

They each signed it, then shook hands.

"Ben, would you mind going over some of the day-to-day routines used to operate the farm?"

"I don't mind at all."

While Ben was showing him some of the routines, Jake realized he was going to have to have somebody to help look after the place as long as he was working for Josiah, and he asked, "Ben, do you know anybody who could keep an eye on the place while I am working?"

"No, I can't think of anybody, Jake."

Jake now had his first problem as a landowner, and he was going to have to think of something.

"Ben, I wish you and your family well on your journey. I'll be praying for your safety."

Ben said, "We are going to my brother's first, then both families will be making the trip together. We think it will be safer to travel together. I just hope we can get to Oklahoma before my brother gives us out and goes on without us. That is one reason I wanted to sell this place so fast."

They shook hands one more time and Jake left. On his way back to the river house, he felt like king of the world. He had his own property, but he also had a problem. Somebody had to look after his place while he was working, and he didn't know how he was going to find somebody without Josiah getting wind of it. Somehow he had to figure out something before he went to Josiah's for work the next morning.

CHAPTER FOUR

Sunday night was a sleepless one for Jake. He had bought a farm without realizing somebody other than him would have to work it and look after things. He didn't know enough about farming to run his on his own, even if he could afford to quit his job at Josiah's; which he couldn't. He figured he could handle the ins and outs of cattle buying and selling, but he knew practically nothing about raising crops. Knowing what crops to raise; some for silage, some for food, and some for market, didn't help, since he had no idea how to do it.

Secretly, he'd had thoughts of someday becoming a large landowner with hundreds, maybe even thousands of heads of livestock. Those people were called land and cattle barons, and he wanted to be one. The Green Farm was his first step.

As he tossed and turned he wondered if one person would be enough. Doubting it, he figured it might be necessary to find two or three people to work the place.

Jake couldn't sleep. He kept thinking if the averages held true, his four pregnant heifers should produce six calves, making twelve heads from Josiah's cows. Add those to the hundred head he bought from Ben, and he was getting off to a pretty good start.

Sheep usually had three to five lambs, so if the six pregnant ewes averaged four each, that would be twenty-four sheep, plus the two that weren't pregnant and the ten from Ben. That was very good.

All those thoughts running through his mind, and still he didn't know what to say to Josiah. Originally, he didn't want Josiah to know about the Green Farm, but near dawn Jake decided to level with him, hoping they could work out some kind of agreement.

Wrapped up in his own world, Jake wasn't aware that over the last several months, Josiah had been very impressed with his expertise in breeding and nutrition. He was becoming more and more dependent on him for the future success of his cattle herd and sheep flocks.

While Jake was trying to decide what to say to Josiah, Josiah was trying to come up with a plan to keep Jake on at the ranch, in the event he ever decided to go back home. Little did Josiah know he might need that plan in just a few hours.

Jake didn't fix any breakfast when he finally got up. He boiled a pot of coffee, thinking Etta would have biscuits left over from breakfast at the house. Kind of nervous and not very hungry, the strong coffee satisfied him.

Saddling up, he left the river house for Josiah's, hoping for a good outcome from their conversation. He dreaded it, and yet, he was excited. Saying the right things was important to convince Josiah that Jake could work for him and operate the Green Farm at the same time and that he could still be a big, big help on the ranch. Needing to be sure Josiah didn't think he was trying to go behind his back and pull something on him, he was going to try something that he wasn't used to; he was going to try to act humble.

When he got to the J-T house, Josiah's family was just finishing breakfast and starting to get ready for the day. The girls were just about ready to leave for the flock, and Buck and his brothers were getting up from the table. Josiah and Etta were still sitting there drinking coffee. When Jake came in, he said, "Good morning."

Etta said, "Good morning, Jake", and got up and poured him a cup.

"Josiah, I need to talk to you if you have time."

"Okay, but let me get Buck and the boys squared away on their day's work. I'll be back in a few minutes and we can talk then. Just sit here and drink your coffee. I won't be long."

Jake was so nervous, minutes seemed like hours. After what seemed like an hour, Josiah finally came back in the house and sat down at the table with Jake. Etta poured them both more coffee and went back into the kitchen.

"What's on your mind, Jake?"

"Well, first of all, I want you to know how much I appreciate your taking me in and giving me a job and treating me like I'm one of your family," Jake said.

"You are one of the family," said Josiah. "We're all glad that you're here."

Jake took a deep breath and started telling again about how he and Eph didn't get along, and how Eph was their pa's favorite, and how he felt that he was never going to be able to get a fair shake if he had stayed at home. He kept on about how neglected he felt, and blamed Ike and Eph for the reason he left. By no means, did he tell he had stolen his brother's land and left because Eph had threatened to kill him. Doing a really good selling job on Josiah, Jake made sure he told how close he and his mother, Becky, were.

"I never had done much farm work before I came here, and I've learned to really like it. Watching you and learning from you has caused me to really admire you and want to be like you some day. I want to own a fine ranch with a lot of livestock just like you, and that brings me to why I wanted to talk to you."

"A week or so ago I met a man named Ben Green. Who incidentally thinks very highly of you, Ben had decided to move to California and was really anxious to leave. Naturally, he had to sell his farm and he talked to me about it. I hadn't even thought about buying any property, but after we talked a couple times, it was obvious he was willing to nearly give the farm away."

"I wound up buying his farm, Josiah, along with his stock. He made me such an unbelievable deal, I feel kinda like it was meant to be. The way it worked out, I was able to pay for it with the money Pa gave me."

When Josiah heard this he thought Jake was going to tell him he was quitting, and he didn't want him to quit. He was doing too much good at the J-T.

Coming up with something quick, he told Jake, "It sounds to me like you're leaving, and I hate to see that. What'll it take to make you change your mind?"

"Jake, I like what you do here and appreciate what you've accomplished. I would hate to see you quit and I think we can probably work out something if you're agreeable."

"I'm glad to hear you've bought Ben's farm. I know the place and it's nice. There should be no reason for you to leave here. You can borrow any of my slaves to help on your place whenever you need them. If you have to build something, we can help with that and anything else that you need, we can pitch in and help."

"I guess what I'm saying, Jake, is this. You can stay here and work and between the two of us, both farms will not only operate but prosper. What do you say?"

Josiah had just put himself in a vulnerable position. Now in the *catbird's seat,* Jake jumped to take advantage of it.

Based on the way Josiah was talking, Jake asked for much more.

"I'll tell you what: I'll stay and work for you and help you build up your cattle herd and sheep flock for the same wage that you're currently paying me, but I need your help on some things. I would like to borrow some of your slaves to work on the Green Farm to help with my livestock. And in the spring, when it comes time for planting, I will need help with that, too. Is that something you would consider?"

Josiah readily agreed, and they shook hands on it.

As they were walking out of the house, Jake looked at Josiah.

"Oh yeah, Josiah, there's one more thing. I want to marry your two daughters."

"Whoa," Josiah gasped. "Do you know what you're asking?"

"Yes sir, I do. The three of us have become close over the last few months, and I'd like for them to be my wives."

Josiah asked, "Why in the world do you want them both? I thought a man only married one woman. At least that's what I did."

Jake told him how much he thought of the girls, and then told him about the people he had read about in New York who married several women. It had worked out quite well for them, so that's what he wanted to do.

"I'll have to think about that, Jake. Have you talked to Leann and Raelyn about it?"

"No, but if you give your permission, I will go and talk with them."

Etta had followed the men out of the house. Jake turned to say good-bye. She looked as though she was in shock.

He whipped back around without saying anything to her and walked to the barn, mumbling all the way. *You idiot! What have you done? Why did you say anything about getting married? Man. I don't even need one woman, let alone two.*

Alone with his thoughts, he decided it might not be such a bad deal after all. Both girls knew just about everything there was to know about sheep. If he was able to establish a major flock, they would be very helpful. Besides, he was really fond of both of them.

He would go out and talk to them when he finished at the barn. As he worked, his thoughts went back and forth. They might not even want to marry him, but then again, they were marrying age. Neither one had a boyfriend, so maybe they would. It was a beautiful day, but it was going to be hot.

The way things turned out with Josiah put Jake in a good mood. He chuckled when he came up on all those hairless sheep. He saw Leann sitting under a shade tree and spotted Raelyn a little farther down, sitting on the creek bank with her feet in the water. He rode up to Leann, got off his horse and sat on the ground with her. Raelyn saw him and waved. She dried her feet, put on her shoes, and walked over to join them.

Jake told them about his talk with Josiah earlier, and they both agreed that his buying the Green Farm was a good idea. They seemed happy that he was not going to leave the J-T. Talking at length, they discussed several things that would need to happen for him to be a successful farm owner.

After a little while Jake asked, "Do you want to know what else I told Josiah?"

Together, the girls said "Yeah, tell us."

Jake said, "I told Josiah I want to marry you; both of you."

In unison, both girls cried, "You want to what?"

"I told him I want to marry both of you. He said he would have to think about it and asked if I had talked to you, and I told him no, but I would if he gave his permission. Then I decided to come and talk to you anyway. What do you think?"

Josiah wanted to know why I wanted both of you instead of just one.

"I told him that I was crazy about both of you and feel that we have become close over the last few months. Don't you agree?"

Leann said, "Yeah, we've gotten pretty close, but I don't know about getting married. I always thought I would be the only wife. I never dreamed I would have to share my husband with another wife. I just don't know."

Raelyn chimed in. "Jake I really do like you, but I feel the same way Leann does. I just don't know either. Let's say that we agree to marry you, how will that work? I sure don't want to sleep three in a bed. What are you thinking about? I don't understand how that would work."

"I've been reading about a group called Mormons up in New York, and although their church doesn't sanction it, some of the men have more than one wife. In fact, some of them have several, and it seems to work out really well for them. The husbands love all their wives, and all the wives love their husbands. They have lots of children, and with all of them pitching in to help with things, there is hardly anything they can't do as a family."

"I promise I don't want any more than the two of you, and if you will agree to marry me, I will work hard for Josiah and extra hard to make the Green Farm a big success. I don't have things worked out in my mind yet because when I got up this morning, I didn't know I was going to propose marriage today."

"Think about it, and I will, too. I promise I will work things out so you will be happy to be married to me. I'm going to ask Josiah if he will loan me some helpers to add on to the house at the Green Farm. There are two bedrooms now, but I think there needs to be more, especially if children come along at some point."

It was getting close to dinnertime, when Eddie rode up and said, "Jake, Pa wants to see you up at the barn."

Jake said good-bye to the girls and climbed on his horse. Eddie was going in for dinner, so they rode in together.

"What have you guys been doing this morning," Jake asked.

"Not much. Rounding up a few strays."

"Find any."

"A few."

When they got to the house, Eddie dismounted and went in, and Jake went to the barn to see what Josiah wanted.

"Jake. I've been thinking about what you said, and I reckon if the girls want to, then they can both marry you, but I'll be dog if I can understand why you want to marry more than one woman. But if you're set on doing it, I've got some conditions to go along with my permission. The main one is that you stay here and work for me. This doesn't mean you can't work the Green Farm, too. It just means you have to work here."

Jake interrupted, "That's fine with me; I'll do it."

Turning the conversation off Josiah's conditions, Jake asked, "Josiah, do you think I might can get some help to expand the house at the Green Farm?"

"Yeah, we can do that."

They walked toward the house while they talked about other things, and never did get back on the subject of conditions Josiah had. Inside, they sat down to one of Etta's huge, delicious dinners.

The marriage wasn't mentioned at dinner. The boys talked about having to look for strays that morning, and the girls didn't talk about much of anything. Every now and then, Jake caught Leann giving him a playful look, then, she would looked away, smiling. Raelyn pretty much just ate her dinner without any kind of outward emotion.

While they were eating Jake told Josiah, "If you've got a minute after we finish, I would like to talk to you."

"Okay."

All in all, it was just a normal dinnertime; topped off by warm peach cobbler and fresh cream.

When everyone finished dinner, all the young folks, except Jake, split up and went back to the jobs they were doing before dinner. Jake and Josiah stayed at the table while Etta gathered up the empty dishes and the leftovers. Josiah asked, "What do you want to talk about, Jake?"

"I just want you to know that I talked with Leann and Raelyn before dinner about getting married, even though you hadn't given permission yet. They didn't give me an answer yet, and I'm not going to push them for one. I just wanted you to know."

"What if just one of them wants to marry? Will you marry just one?"

Jake, fiddled with the salt and pepper shakers still on the table,

"Well I haven't thought about that, but yeah, I guess I will."

Standing up, Josiah said, I have to go into town on some business."

Jake followed Josiah out of the house, then grabbed his horse and went back to the sheep pasture to see the girls.

His mind was a muddled mess as he rode down to the where the girls were. Josiah's question was stuck in his mind and he hoped his answer would not ultimately be what happens.

Both girls were standing by the shelter when he got there and he didn't dismount. He just asked them, "Have you given any thought to what we talked about earlier?

They both said they had, but weren't ready to give an answer yet.

"That's fine. We'll talk about it tomorrow or the next day."

He said, "I've got to go. I'll see y'all later."

Jake had to go back to the barn to see about a heifer that had come into heat, and to try to get her together with one of the bulls.

At the barn, Buck and the boys had a hard time with the bull. This bull was big, contrary and mean, but the guys were finally able to get him in the corral. It got easier after Jake lead the heifer in. The breeding seemed to be successful and this is the part of Jake's job he liked best.

Later, after he finished with the cows, he stopped by the house to pick up the leftovers Etta had said she would save for him. He was going to miss her good cooking once he got married. Hoping the girls knew how to cook, he wondered how they could, since they stayed in the sheep pasture all day every day. Oh well. He shrugged his shoulders. They would figure it out if and when they reached that point.

The next day Jake went to work as usual, and checked in with Josiah first, to see what he was to do that day. After he found out he was to help with some sheep problems, he headed on down to the sheep pasture where he saw Leann. However, Raelyn wasn't there.

"Hey, Leann, it looks like you're stuck with me this morning. Where's Raelyn?"

"She said she didn't feel good, so she stayed home."

Later, Leann and Jake were working together to repair the rail around the shelter and Jake said, "You know, we make a pretty good team, don't we?"

Then Leann said, "Do you think we'll make as good a team after we're married?"

Jake stopped what he was doing and looked at her, and asked, "Does this mean?"

And before he could finish the question, Leann said, "Yes, I've decided to marry you."

"That's really good," he said. "Is Raelyn going to marry me, too?"

"I don't think so right now. She might want to wait until a little later. That's why she's not down here this morning. She hates to face you. Jake, I can make you happy by myself. I've loved you ever since you came here, and if I have to share you with Raelyn at some point, I will, but I can make you happy. I told Pa last night, and he's okay with it. Are you?"

"Yes, of course. I'm happy." He looked puzzled and said, "What do we do now?"

"We get married, silly," and she threw her arms around him, and kissed him.

It caught him off guard. He had never been kissed before, and he liked it.

"Mama will have to tell me what to do about a wedding dress? There are going to be so many things to do. I need to go talk to Mama."

"I'll see if I can get Pa to arrange for a preacher, and Jake, we need to decide on a date for the wedding, so my parents can start making arrangements,"

Leann told Ina, one of her helpers, that she was going up to the house, and she grabbed Jake's hand and said, "Come on." They walked to the house and when they got there they went in and Leann said, "Mama, Jake and me are gonna get married.

"Etta gave both of them a big hug. They told Etta, because Leann had told Josiah the night before. Josiah probably told Etta, but she acted surprised anyway.

"I guess I'd better get busy and make a dress." She began naming off a great many other things that needed doing. She and Leann started getting so taken up with all they had to do Jake thought he would be wise to get out of there.

He said to unhearing ears, "I'm gone. I'll see ya later."

Etta had saved leftovers for him, so he went to the kitchen, got them, and headed home. His mind was now a really muddled mess. He was about to get married, and about to marry a girl that he really liked, but not the one that he really loved. Leann had said "yes" to his proposal, so what else could he do? He thought to himself, *I can sure mess things up.*

He built a fire in the cook stove to heat up his leftovers and boiled some coffee, and in a few minutes it was red hot, so he warmed up his supper and went outside to eat it and drink his coffee.

He thought about all the things that were getting ready to change his life.

Since only Leann would be marrying him, he wondered how that would change things. He wouldn't need as much room for one wife as he would for two, but still wanted to add on to the Green Farm house, anyway. Raelyn might decide to come one day. If she did, then she would have a nice place to live.

Once he and Leann decided on a date, he would know what had to be done, and when. If Leann wanted to get married immediately, they would have to live at the river house until the other house was ready, and if they were going to live at the river house, some work had to be done to make it livable for a woman.

CHAPTER FIVE

When Jake got to the J-T the next morning, he went into the dining room. Only Josiah, Etta, and the girls were still there. The boys had already left. Jake sat down, and Etta poured him a cup of coffee. A short minute later, Raelyn said, "Pa, can I be excused? There's something I need to do before I go back down to the flock.

"Okay."

She left the four of them.

Leann said, "Jake, Mama and me have been talking and we don't see any reason why we should wait to get married. Will it be all right with you if we have the wedding in two weeks? Preacher Foust will be leaving in about three weeks and won't be back 'til next spring."

Jake swallowed real hard. "Yeah, that sounds fine. I guess since it's only going to be two weeks, we'll be living at the river house for a while. Is that okay with you, Leann?"

"Anywhere you want to live is okay with me."

Both she and her mother were acting a little giddy.

"Josiah, do you think it would be possible for me to get some help fixing up the river house for Leann?"

"Yeah. In fact," Josiah said, "I will have some men come to your place in the morning. You can ride out to the sawmill with me right now if you want to, and we'll decide what we'll need to dress the place up. While we're at it, we might as well add another room. I'll send enough lumber and experienced men to have the job done by next week. You'll have to have some more furniture, too, won't you?"

Jake said, "Well, I guess so. All this stuff is new to me."

It seemed there was a plan, not necessarily Jake's plan, but a plan nonetheless.

At the sawmill, Jake stood by as Josiah told his foreman what he wanted and instructed him to deliver two wagon loads of lumber to the river house the next morning.

Next, they rode out to where several slaves were working. Josiah called seven of the men away and explained what he wanted them to do.

"I want you to go to the tool shed and get what you will need to do the job. Then, I want you to take the tools and go to the sawmill early tomorrow morning and catch a ride on the lumber wagons to the river house. Leann and Jake are getting married. "They all seemed happy at the news.

Jake had noticed it before, but this time he really did notice how kind Josiah was to his slaves. He showed them respect, and they reciprocated.

Josiah had built a little community where all the slaves lived. Most of them lived in cabins, but there were three barracks-type buildings where some of the single men lived. Jake guessed there were probably two hundred or more slaves. Some had families and some were single, both men and women, but they all had jobs to do. Josiah took good care of them.

"We'll be on time, Master Josiah, and do a good job for Miss Leann and Mister Jake.

On the way back to the house Jake thanked Josiah for his help. Josiah assured him it was more for Leann than for him. "But you're welcome."

Jake took the opportunity to remind Josiah that they had talked about adding onto the Green Farm house.

"I hadn't forgot it Jake. I'll see about getting started on it when they finish the river house. Those two women aren't going to give either one of us time to breathe, so it looks like our work is cut out for us until everything gets done," he said.

When they got back to the house, Josiah didn't get off his horse. He said he had some things that needed his attention, so he left Jake there, without telling him to do anything specific.

At loose ends, he dismounted and went in the house. Leann and Etta were busy inside and talking non-stop, so he didn't interrupt. Looking for something to do, he went out to the barn. Not much was happening there, so he got his horse and rode down to the sheep pasture to see Raelyn.

"Hey," he called out before dismounting.

"Hi," she answered.

"How're you feeling? Leann said you weren't feeling good yesterday."

"I'm better. I guess I must have ate something that didn't agree with me, but I feel better now."

Jake asked, "What do you think about the wedding?"

"It's okay, I guess."

"You don't sound too happy about it."

"Yeah, I'm happy," Raelyn sighed. "I hope you're very happy."

"I think we will be and Leann seems thrilled to be getting married. I am too, but I would be even happier if you had said yes, too."

Raelyn looked up at him, "Jake, I think I really love you. If you had asked just me I would have said yes, but I just don't think I can marry you or anyone else and not be the only one. It's going to be hard to see you and Leann together knowing I'm not part of your life, but right now I just can't do it. Maybe in the future, if I haven't found a husband, and you still want me, if I can see how well it has worked for you and Leann, and if she's agreeable, then we'll talk about it. I love you, and I love my sister. Please don't be mad at me. I wish I didn't feel this way, but I do."

"I wish you didn't feel that way, too. I'm not going anywhere, Raelyn, and one day, whether you think so or not, we will be married."

Jake left Raelyn and rode back to the house. Josiah's horse was still not at the hitching rail, so he gathered some courage and went into the house. Etta and Leann were still there, still busy, still talking nonstop.. They stopped for a minute when Jake appeared in the doorway, giving him a *why are you here* look.

"Listen, Josiah's not back yet and he didn't tell me anything to do before he left. I've got everything caught up, so I'm gonna take off. I want to go over to the Green Farm to see if Ben has left yet. I'll see y'all in the morning.

"Bye," both women said, returning right back to whatever it was they were doing.

Back on his horse Jake headed to the Green Farm. It would be mid-afternoon when he got there, but he wouldn't stay long.

Ben and Tommy were outside working to get a canvas top installed on a wagon, when Jake rode up.

"Hey Jake, get down and keep us company while I try to get this cover on our traveling home for the next few months."

"Hi, Ben. I just wanted to come by to see how you're doing. It looks like you're about ready to go. Is this what some people call a prairie schooner?"

Ben said, "Yeah, that's what it is."

"How long do you figure it's going to take you to get to California?"

"Well, I hope it won't take more than about four months. It's about thirty days to my brother's in Oklahoma, and from there to where we're going in California is around fifteen hundred miles. I think we might be able to average twenty miles a day. If we can do that, we can be in California before winter sets in, but it's going to be close. It gets cold where we're going, but it doesn't snow much, so we can work all year."

"I've said good luck to you before, but I'll say it again. I really do wish the best for you."

Jake then told Ben about Josiah agreeing to help with the expansion work on the house, and asked, "Do you know Josiah's oldest girl, Leann?"

"Yeah, I know Leann; she's a fine girl."

"Well, I'm fixing to marry her."

"Get outa here. You're the one that needs good luck," Ben joked. "Seriously, I wish for you a good life and hope you're as happy as we are. When's the wedding?"

"In two weeks," Jake told him.

Ben and his wife had decided they couldn't take much of anything with them since they would be so cramped for space. The three of them needed a place to sleep in the wagon in case it rained at night, and there just wasn't enough room for much else.

They were going to take a second wagon loaded with provisions. His wife and Tommy would be taking turns driving it. It would not be a covered wagon, but rather just a wagon with a tarp covering the supplies.

"I sure hate to have to leave everything, but I'm glad you're getting it, Jake, especially since you're getting married."

He showed Jake a few things that he didn't show him before, and Jake wished him good luck again, and mounted up. Halfway down the driveway, Ben yelled, "We hope to be gone by the day after tomorrow."

Jake turned and waved, then headed back to the river house. It would be close to dark before he would get there.

***

The next morning, men and lumber arrived at the river house soon after breakfast. They jumped down off the wagons and started unloading. The man in charge was a man named Lee, and he began assigning duties to each man. Four men, including himself, were to start building the extra room. The other three were to start refurbishing the existing inside.

When each man finished his job inside he would start building some new furniture.

Lee said, "Master Josiah told me to build a new bed first, then three chests to hold clothes and things." Why they needed three chests, Jake didn't know, but he was grateful.

"When we come back tomorrow, we'll bring a load of firewood from the sawmill."

When all the men were working, Jake went to the J-T to work. There were two or three cows and a couple of heifers that he thought were coming into heat, and he wanted to try what Doctor Wells called artificial insemination. Jake had read a great deal about it and talked at length with Doc, but hadn't tried it yet.

Jake was immensely interested because he felt it was a way to jump start his own herd. And, if it worked with cattle, he could make it work with sheep as well. Since sheep didn't come in heat as often as cows did, he was working on a plan to get fifty percent more ewes impregnated, than if he just let nature take its course. Cows come into heat year-round, but sheep come in mainly from September to January, so it was important for him to be able to make this new method work.

After referring to some of his books and brushing up on notes he had made during conversations with Doc, he brought the animals into the barn. One by one, Jake performed the procedure. It was only a matter of time now, to see if it worked.

It was dinner time so Jake went to the house to eat. When everybody had finished eating and were heading back to work, Jake caught up to Leann and Raelyn. He tugged on Leann's arm to stop her.

"How're things going for you, Leann?"

"Everything's perfect. Last night at supper, Pa told me he was going to give me something very special, but he wouldn't tell me what it is. I can't imagine what it is, and I just can't wait to see it. Jake, I'm so excited and can't hardly wait for us to be married."

Raelyn continued on for several yards before she stopped and waited for Leann. A few minutes later, she turned and looked toward them, and when Jake looked at her, she gave him what looked like a forced smile.

That bothered him. He wanted Raelyn to be happy. Also, he hoped she, too, would become his wife…. someday.

"I need to get back to the barn, I've had a busy morning and the vet room is a mess. I'll see ya later, okay?"

Still thinking about Raelyn, he decided it was probably better the way things had worked. Marrying only one of them, would give him the chance to learn how to take care of a wife and what was expected of him as a husband. He was convinced Raelyn would come to him at some point and tell him she would be his other wife.

Finishing up at the barn he took off early, and stopped by the house to pick up his customary leftovers. Etta was in the kitchen.

"Hi, Etta. I came for the leftovers."

"Hi, Jake. They're right where they always are. I made some fried pies for supper and they got done early, so I put one with your stuff. I hope you like it."

"I'm sure I will. Anything you ever fix is good, I'll see ya in the morning."

"Bye, Jake."

He was really anxious to see what had been accomplished on the river house while he was at work. He ran to his horse, mounted up, and galloped all the way home. When he got there, he was surprised at how much the guys had already done.

Rafters for the roof over the new room had been put up as well as the framing on two walls. A doorway had been cut in one wall, allowing access to the new room.

The existing rooms had such large cracks in the walls the outside was visible from nearly anywhere inside the house. Some of the men had spent the day chinking those cracks.

If the weather held and they accomplished as much every day, there should be no problem finishing by next week. As soon as they finished the river house, Jake hoped they would go on over to the Green Farm and start on that house. It would be a much larger job, and he was anxious to have a nice place for Leann to live.

The rest of the week was routine. Leann and Raelyn spent most of their time in the sheep pastures, while Buck and the boys rode herd on the cattle, making sure they didn't lose too many strays. It seemed they had branding to do nearly every day, and they enlisted Jake's help when they could find him.

On Saturday afternoon Josiah caught up with Jake in the barn.

"Jake, I think it would be a good idea for you to plan to work at the river house next week to help the men finish up. I thought it would be a good idea if you spend some time at the Green Farm, too, since Ben left on Thursday. "Don't worry about coming to the J-T to work next week."

That surprised Jake because Josiah was a fairly stern taskmaster, and for him to give him time off was shocking. He guessed the reason for this act of kindness was that he was marrying his daughter, and he wanted her to live in a comfortable place. He still didn't know how afraid Josiah was of losing him, especially now that he had his own farm.

"I don't know what to say, Josiah, except thank you. I need those days off and you, being the wise man that you are, knew that. I really appreciate it."

Josiah left the barn and Jake walked out to get his horse. He mounted up and rode down to the sheep pasture to see Leann before he left.

"Hi, Lee. Whatta ya doin'?"

"Just working."

"I just came down to tell you that I won't be here for the next week. Your pa said I should stay and work on the river house so we can finish it next week. He also said I should spend some time at my farm since Ben has left and I'm gonna take him up on it."

"I'm going to my farm tomorrow after I check things out at the river house. Why don't you come and go with me? If you come to the river house first, then you can see both places."

"Okay, I will."

Jake grabbed her hand with both of his, gave it a gentle squeeze, and kissed her on the cheek. Then he mounted up and left.

Leann didn't say too much when she saw the river house, and Jake could tell she wasn't anxious to start living there, but he asked her anyway, "What do you think about all the improvements to the house, Leann?"

"It's fine. Wherever you want us to live will be okay with me," she said. "It's going to be much nicer than it was."

Jake showed her around a little more, and then they left for the Green Farm.

This was their first time being alone with each other and Jake wished he had a buggy so they could ride together. He tried to create a romantic mood, but that was next to impossible riding two horses. With his limited knowledge of romancing women, the romantic mood fell flat.

When they got to the Green farm and Leann saw the house, Jake didn't need to create a romantic mood. She acted very excited and Jake could tell that she would love living in that house, even without all the improvements and expansion that was planned for it.

She "oood" and "aahd" over everything. She put her hands on the walls and cabinets and said she just couldn't wait until it was hers. She was arranging furniture in her mind and was very excited.

As they walked through the house, it looked as though the Greens had left just about all the furniture, even the beds. Leann noticed that there were no blankets or quilts or anything like that. Those were things they would need on the trail.

They walked outside to the smokehouse. Jake was mildly disappointed when he found the Greens had taken nearly all the meat.

That would be a big help to them, in case Ben had a run of bad luck hunting game on the way. On the other hand, he might be able to shoot a buffalo, a bear, or an elk or something else big, so they shouldn't have any problem having something to eat while they traveled

In the barn there was a good supply of hay, and Leann noticed there was quite a bit of tack left. The Greens had taken most of the tack for the horses, but left some hames and half-hames, a plow, and other equipment used to work the land. All in all, Ben had left enough to almost completely set them up in housekeeping.

"Has your pa told you that he's gonna enlarge the house?"

"He said something about doing some work out here, but he didn't say what."

"Well, I don't know too much about it, myself. Josiah is planning to enlarge the house, but hasn't given me any details. I need to talk to him and try to find out what he's willing to do. I think he's planning to furnish the labor and materials, at least I hope he is."

Convincing Josiah that the project is for his daughter and his grandchildren was important, so he would come through for them. Jake would make sure Josiah knew how excited Leann was when she first saw the place so he could picture in his mind just how excited she would be after the work was done.

They spent a fun day together and hated to see it end. Leann had brought a picnic dinner and they enjoyed fried chicken down by the river. After dinner, they explored a cave that was close to where they ate.

Leann wanted to get back to the J-T before dark, so she left and went back by way of the river house.

Arriving at the house, they both dismounted and hugged. Holding hands and giving each other little pecks, it was easy to see Leann didn't want to leave. Finally, they embraced and kissed passionately.

They said goodbye there, and Leann went home.

Jake boiled some coffee and heated up some of Etta's leftovers. He sat down to think about all that was going on. After being at the Green Farm, the realization that he was in the cattle business hit him. He knew, of course, that he owned the cattle, and Josiah had agreed to loan him some people to look after them, but the impact of the responsibility had never registered. He also knew borrowed slaves wouldn't look after the cattle the way he would.

Another thing he thought about was a brand, his own brand; one that people would recognize as his. He also thought about changing the name of the farm. Since the Greens didn't live there any longer, it didn't need to be called the Green Farm. He had to think up a name.

There was so much to think about and so much to do. He was getting nervous and the wedding was only a week away.

Leann had told Jake he needed to arrange for the preacher, so on Monday morning he ate an early breakfast and left for Mercer just as the men were arriving to work on the house. Glad to have a chance to go to town, he was looking forward to seeing Doctor Wells if he was in. Also on his list of things to do in town was to see if the general mercantile store had a nice shirt suitable for the wedding.

But first things first. As soon as he got into town he went straight to the church to find the preacher. He was cleaning up after the Sunday service.

Jake said, "Howdy, I'm Jake Isaacson."

The preacher answered, "Good to see you, Jake, I'm Elmer Foust. What can I do for you?"

"Me and Leann Taylor are gonna get married next Sunday and we want you to come and perform the ceremony. It's going to be at the J-T ranch. Can you do it?"

"I'll be happy to do it. I know how to get to the J-T, so I'll see you Sunday afternoon."

As Jake was leaving the church, he heard the preacher say, "Jake, after you're married, I sure would like to see you and Leann at Church. I will be leaving in two weeks and will be gone until spring; but several laymen have said they will hold services every Sunday while I am gone."

"Thanks, I'll mention it to Leann."

Next, he went to Doc Wells' and was glad to find him there. Doc invited him to come in, and they sat down to talk for a few minutes.

After the small talk was finished, Jake said, "Doc, I've got a lot to tell you. Since I saw you last, I bought Ben Green's farm and all his cattle and Ben left for California immediately after I bought it."

"The way things worked out, I had to tell Josiah before I wanted to, but he was okay with it. In fact, he has even loaned me some men to help look after the place."

"That's good, Jake. If there's anything I can do to help, just let me know. I'll help any way I can,"

"Here's a shocker for you, Doc. Next Sunday, me and Leann are gonna get married."

"I'm thrilled, Jake. "I've known Leann all her life. In fact, I was at the J-T when she was born, and believe it or not, I helped the midwife with her birth. You're getting a good woman, Jake. I hope y'all will be happy. She should make you a fine wife."

"Would you like to come to the wedding, Doc?"

"I wouldn't miss it."

When he left Doc's place, he went to the store to buy a new shirt to get married in. He went in and Mr. Puckett wasn't there, but Mrs. Puckett was. "Mrs. Puckett, I'm getting married Sunday and I need to buy a new shirt for the wedding."

Mrs. Puckett said indignantly, "Well, I think that is the least you can do. What about the pants? Are you going to wear those that you have on now?"

"Well, yes ma'am, I guess I will. Do you not think they're proper?"

"I should say not. Now you go over there and find some pants that fit and a shirt that will go with them, and try to look nice for your bride. You don't want Leann to be ashamed of you on your wedding day, do you?"

"No ma'am,"

"Let me see those boots." Jake raised his foot up high and she said, "All right, the boots look okay, but you need to give them a good scrubbing with saddle soap. Do you have any? If you don't, there's some up at the counter"

With Mrs. Puckett's help, he found a shirt and some pants and a can of saddle soap. He paid for his purchases and left. As he walked down to the little café for dinner he mumbled under his breath, "The next time I go in there I hope Mr. Puckett will be there instead of his wife."

After dinner he rode to the Green Farm to look around again and spend some time there by himself. As he basked in the pleasure of knowing he owned this beautiful farm he was thinking of just how he could increase his herd and how he could establish a nice flock in the shortest amount of time.

When he and Leann moved there permanently, he could do much more than he could while living at the river house. He was hoping they could move in by Christmas. The way Josiah talked, they were going to do a major addition, and maybe even some slave cabins. Jake didn't own any slaves, so he couldn't understand why Josiah would want to build slave cabins, but if Josiah was willing to do that for him, he would take it.

During the rest of the afternoon there he discovered some of the things Ben had left, which he hadn't seen yet. He found a branding iron in one of the stables in the barn with a "GF" on it, and that put him to thinking again about his own brand. Maybe he would just have an "I." That would be simple. It would also be easy to alter, so he held on to that thought. What if he had "J-I?" That was too close to the "J-T" that Josiah had. He didn't have to decide right then. He had some time, and maybe Leann could help him.

The more he thought about it the more he liked the idea of having a brand similar to Josiah's. It would be easy to change into his brand if and when he found some J-T cows on his land.

It was getting late and he was getting hungry. His dinner had left him, and he couldn't wait to get home to fix supper.

All the way home he tried to think of something good to fix for supper, but the cupboard was nearly bare at the river house, so he settled on breakfast for supper.

Jake fried some streaked meat and eggs and heated up some of Etta's biscuits. The coffee he boiled actually tasted good.

Turning in early, he reviewed the long day he'd had. Most of it was related to the wedding in some form or another. Since he was about done with his part of the wedding preparations, he decided to stay home the next day and watch the men work on his house; while he caught up on some rest. He fell asleep, thinking about everything. There was a plethora of things on his young mind.

The rest of the week passed quickly. The men finished up at the river house on Thursday, and Leann just happened to be there. She was amazed at the work they had done. The outside was white-washed and it looked really nice compared to before. That pleased Jake, knowing that it pleased Leann.

On Saturday Leann went back to the river house, taking Raelyn with her. Raelyn complimented them on the house, but she didn't have a whole lot to say after that.

The main reason they came was to tell Jake where and when the wedding would be. Leann wanted it in a little grove of trees on a hill about three hundred yards from the house overlooking the sheep pasture. That was where she first saw Jake, and the view from the grove was beautiful. Besides, she thought it would be romantic.

This suited Jake just fine. "I'll be there." He gave her a peck on the cheek, and Raelyn looked away. They left and Leann said, "See ya tomorrow. Be on time."

The girls waved as they walked back to the ranch house.

CHAPTER SIX

Jake was up early on Sunday morning after a fitful sleep the night before. He built a fire in the cook stove, and then went to the springhouse to get some water to heat. He didn't bathe too often, but thought since it was his wedding day, he had better spruce up a little. He laid out his new shirt and pants and wiped off his boots. He'd used saddle soap on them last night and they were clean, but he just wanted to be sure. He was afraid Mrs. Puckett might be there, and he didn't want any comments from her.

He cooked his usual breakfast of streaked meat, eggs, and coffee. All the biscuits were gone, so he didn't have any bread this time. As soon as he finished, he washed up and got dressed. He brushed his hair the best he could by looking in the piece of mirror he had, and wondered if it was time to leave. It dawned on him that he wasn't supposed to be there until after dinner, and he'd just eaten breakfast. He took off his new clothes, put on his old ones and went outside and sat by the river.

After a while he went back into the house and got ready all over again. Jake didn't own a clock, but judging from the position of the sun, it must be close to noon, so he mounted up and headed toward the J-T to get married.

When he got there, he saw Josiah, Buck, and the other two boys standing outside the house. Josiah asked him, "Did you have dinner yet?"

"Naw, I didn't want anything."

"Well, go in the kitchen and find you something. You need something on your stomach. Etta didn't cook dinner today, but there is plenty left from last night."

"Okay."

Jake went in and found some chicken and biscuits left from the night before and he was hungrier than he thought. Sitting down at the table to eat, he could hear Leann, Etta, and Raelyn talking ninety miles an hour in the bedroom, but he didn't see them. He finished eating and went outside with the guys.

The preacher hadn't arrived, and there weren't any other people there, either. The men talked about the river house, the Green Farm, and anything else they could bring to mind to pass the time away.

In a few minutes preacher Foust arrived, and right behind him were about a dozen friends of the Taylor family, From the other direction, came the slaves who were particularly close to the family, including Miles and his family Two others; girls named Ina and Sue, were just like sisters to Leann and Raelyn. They'd been born on the ranch and were close to the same ages as the girls. Both of them helped Leann and Raelyn with the sheep. Ina was especially close to Leann and Sue was tight with Raelyn. They liked and disliked the same things. They argued and fussed and then made up just like average people. No one could ever tell Sue and Ina were slave girls.

Slave was actually a misnomer. Ina and Sue were the daughters of white indentured parents. They were considered slaves because their parents had been considered slaves. Their mothers had died when the girls were young and about six years ago their fathers were killed in a fire, trying to rescue some horses in a burning barn when the roof collapsed on them. Josiah has taken care of them ever since.

The preacher went into the house, and in a minute came right back out. "Everybody, listen up. It's time to go down to the grove for the ceremony. Just follow the path and the pretty flowers Ina and Sue scattered along the way." Most everyone walked, but a few rode either their horse or wagon.

"Jake, you need to take your buckboard," Josiah said, "so you and Leann can leave after the ceremony. You can give Etta a ride to the grove, too." As he drove the buckboard to the grove, Jake noticed somebody, probably Etta, had put lots of food and other things in the back. He had not even given food a thought and doubted if Leann had, either. This was good, though. It would fill up their larder until they could get to town and stock up on the supplies they needed.

Jake braked the buckboard, helped Etta down, and they walked to the spot in front of the preacher. Jake looked around and noticed his bride wasn't there. *Where's Leann*, he thought.

As if on cue, he turned around. Josiah was coming toward them in a buggy, and Leann was sitting beside him. Jake thought, *Boy, she's beautiful*. He was starting to realize, indeed, he was a lucky man.

Pulling the buggy into an empty spot, Josiah leaned over and spoke softly to Leann. He pulled the brake, jumped down, and walked to the other side to help her down. She took his arm and they walked toward the grove.

In his best clothes, Josiah looked nice, but Leann looked spectacular.

She had on the dress Etta had made for her. Basically, it was a plain white cotton dress. With the addition of ruffles, Etta had added just the right amount of flair. By not wearing the customary petticoats underneath, Leann's five-foot nine-inch figure was emphasized. The length was barely above the ankles—just the right length to show off the shoes Etta had found at the general mercantile. Leann's long blond hair was tied back in a pony-tail and it was no wonder Jake thought she was beautiful. She walked, with a smile on her face and a little breeze in her hair, making Jake forget all about being nervous. He had never been with a woman, and seeing the real beauty of Leann made him want to hurry and get this wedding over with, so he could leave and be with his wife.

Raelyn looked pretty, too, in a new dress Etta had made. Standing beside Leann, smiling, she stirred uncertain emotions in Jake.

Raising his hand to silence the group, the preacher said, "Leann, Jake, step forward and stand here in front of me." When they were in position, he opened his Bible. Looking at the people in attendance, "I'm happy to say I've known Leann since she was a little girl, and I think she is really a fine young lady. I only met Jake last Monday, but he seems to be a nice enough fellow, and if Leann chose to be his wife, then he must be a good man."

"Jake Cobb Isaacson, will you take this woman to be your wife?" Jake didn't say anything. He just stood there with a funny look on his face for what seemed like forever. Then the preacher whispered, "Jake, you say," I will."

Jake came out of his trance and said, "I will."

"Leigh Ann Taylor, will you take this man to be your husband?" Leann said, "I will."

The preacher then said," I now pronounce you man and wife," and it was over.

Jake thought, *Is this all there is to getting married? You answer one question? Man, I got nervous for nothing.*

After the ceremony, the people were congratulating the couple, and in a few minutes, some of the guests started to leave. Jake was glad to see Doctor Wells. They talked for a few minutes and agreed to get together in a few days. The married couple visited with a few of Leann's special friends and even talked warmly to the slaves who attended.

Sue and Ina were the last guests, still having fun talking and laughing with Leann and Raelyn.

Josiah walked over to Leann, "Honey, you know I told you I had a special gift for you."

"Yes Pa, are you going to give it to me now? What is it?"

Josiah pulled Ina and Leann away from the others. He nudged Ina toward Leann. "This is your present. I'm giving Ina to you. She has been your friend since you both were little, and I hope you will stay friends from now on. She will help you do things, and I thought this would be something you would like more than a new horse or anything else."

Leann was thrilled. "Can you believe what Pa just did? Did you know about this?"

"No, but I'm tickled that he did."

"After I spend a few days with my new husband, I'll come to the J-T to get you. Get together everything you want to keep and when I come back, I'll pick you up and we'll start our new lives together."

They hugged each other, then Leann hugged Sue, and the slave girls left.

Leann's brothers returned to the house after an obligatory hug. The preacher wished the newlyweds good luck. Leann, Jake, Raelyn, Etta, and Josiah were the only ones still in the grove.

Jake didn't say very much. It was more Leann's party than his, so he let her decide how to wind it up. She hugged and kissed her mother and daddy, then Raelyn. Jake hugged Etta, shook Josiah's hand and gave Raelyn a hug. She squeezed him extra hard, and that feeling stayed with him for several minutes.

He gave Leann a hand getting up on the buckboard. Then he got on and they headed for the river house. On the way, Jake was thinking about the hard hug Raelyn had just given him.

He parked the buckboard near the house. Leann waited for Jake to help her down, and they went inside, stopping right in front of the door. They turned and looked at each other, wondering, *What do we do now?*

Neither had ever had any experience with the opposite sex, so their uneasiness was natural.

"You sure look pretty, Leann."

"Thank you,."

"I'm really glad you married me."

They hugged, and Leann kissed him, "We had better get the stuff out of the buckboard. It won't be long before it starts getting dark."

When it was unloaded, Leann went into the new, spare bedroom and changed out of her wedding dress into her normal, everyday clothes. Jake sorted through the food her parents had sent, and took the meat, milk, and other things that needed to stay cold to the springhouse. It was always cool in there because of the cold water flowing through constantly. Anything that needed to stay cold, would keep without spoiling.

Leann had finished changing by the time he returned to the house. Again they looked at each other, trying to figure out what to do next.

In a minute Leann asked, "Are you hungry?"

"I sure am," Jake said.

"Well, let's see what Mama sent. She knew we didn't have anything in the house yet, so she sent enough food to last for a day or two. Here's some fried chicken, and here are some potatoes and greens, and other things we can fix to go with it."

"Can I help you?"

"Did you take any milk to the springhouse?"

"Yeah."

"If you'll go get it, I'll fix some gravy."

She knew how to build a fire in the stove, and she knew how to cook, so she felt very much at ease in the kitchen. She acted as though she was enjoying fixing supper for her new husband. She fixed some coffee and poured Jake a cup before they ate.

He took a sip and thought, *This sure is better than the stuff I've been fixing.*

She made biscuits, mashed potatoes, greens, and heated up the chicken Etta had cooked, and they sat down for their first meal as husband and wife.

"This is a mighty good supper, Mrs. Isaacson."

"Well, thank you, Mr. Isaacson."

"Mrs. Isaacson – that sounds good, don't it?"

"Yeah, it sure does. Jake, we're gonna spend the rest of our lives together. How does that sound?"

"It sounds real good."

The small talk continued, and they had a good time.

After supper Leann washed the dishes, and cleaned the kitchen while Jake changed clothes. They walked outside and strolled down by the river. Holding hands as they walked, they were beginning to feel more at ease with each other. In fact, they were genuinely enjoying each other's company.

They turned back when Leann suggested they go inside and make up the bed, and finish anything else that needed to be done, while they still had some daylight. Their only light was from candlelight,, and that was not very bright.

After the bed was made with the new sheets and quilt Etta had sent, and the other chores were finished, Jake and Leann sat in their two new chairs and talked. They talked about the wedding ceremony, and about the guests who had come. Then Leann started talking about Ina.

"I can't tell you how thrilled I was when Pa gave her to me. I think you're gonna be happy with her too, Jake. She's not like a slave. She's like us. I know you're gonna be glad to have her around. Me and Ina have been close since we were little, but we've really become close since her pa was killed."

Jake already knew her from being at the sheep pasture, but he didn't know her very well. Leann convinced Jake that she was going to be a very welcome addition to their new family.

It was about an hour after dark before they finally agreed that it was time to go to bed. Both were scared to death, Jake more so than Leann. While she went into the extra room and put on her nightgown, he took off his boots and shirt in the room they were to share. He left his pants on.

Leann got in bed first, and then Jake blew out the candles and slipped in beside her. The room was pitch black, and Jake was thankful there was no moon. His face was so red he was sure Leann could see it, if the moon was bright.

She turned toward him, put her arms around him, giggled. "Why do you have your pants on?" She giggled again.

Jake felt like his face was getting redder, and he mumbled, "I just do."

"Well, take 'em off. This is your wedding night."

Jake was thankful again for the darkness as he slipped off his pants. Leann pulled him toward her, and he put his arms around her. They kissed…. and enjoyed being together. The night was wonderful. They fell asleep with their arms around each other and slept that way all night.

Leann woke up before Jake the next morning and slipped out of bed. She went to the kitchen, stoked up the fire in the cook-stove, and put on a pot of coffee. After about a half-hour, Jake got up and joined Leann in the kitchen. He felt a little awkward about facing her for the first time after they slept together, but she made him feel totally relaxed the minute he saw her.

Smiling, she said, "Good morning, sunshine. Want some coffee?"

"Morning. Yeah, that sounds good."

Leann cooked breakfast with Jake's help, and they sat down to eat. Leann was giggling and playful, and Jake was laughing at and with her. After breakfast, he joked, and said he didn't get enough sleep and needed to go back to bed…. and needed her to go with him.

So back to bed they went and didn't get up until almost noon. They were typical newlyweds: happy, silly, and enjoying each other.

After dinner, they took the buckboard, stopping first at the General Mercantile store. Mr. and Mrs. Puckett were both there, and after some small talk about the wedding, Mrs. Puckett said to Leann, "Jake looked nice, didn't he?"

"Yes ma'am, he sure did."

Mrs. Puckett smiled at Jake, and gave him a little wink; then she helped Leann with the groceries and other household items. Mr. Puckett helped Jake pick out fifty Rhode Island Red baby chicks and a sack of chicken mash. Pretty soon they had nearly a wagonload. Starting from scratch as they were, meant buying a huge amount. After Jake and Mr. Puckett finished loading the wagon, the newlyweds left, deciding to go back to the river house instead of making any more stops.

They unloaded the buckboard, then went down to the riverbank to enjoy the late afternoon. Holding hands, they sat and talked about the future.

"Jake, what are you gonna do with the river house when the Green house is finished?"

"I don't know. I haven't thought about it. Maybe your pa'll buy it back. You know, Leann, I've got so many big plans for the future, my mind just spins, sometimes."

"I want to build a really large cattle herd and sheep flock. I want to buy more land sometime, and I want us to have several children. If we get big enough, we might even have to buy some slaves."

"I can't wait, especially the part about having children."

Pretty soon it was time to go in and fix supper. Jake helped, but Leann did most of it.

After supper they lit some candles inside and then went out on the porch where it was cool. Leann brought the quilt out and folded it three or four times to make a cushion. With their arms around each other, she and Jake sat on it, listening to the sound of the water. The dim light from the new moon reflected off the ripples in the river. An occasional yelp of a distant coyote, or a whippoorwill's song were the only other sounds.

For Leann and Jake, the world, and everything in it was perfect. Until they'd moved into the river house, neither knew how much they loved each other.

But Jake still had occasional thoughts of Raelyn.

"I'm cold, Jake. Why don't we go inside?"

"Okay, I'm ready. I've got a little hankering for something

sweet, so let's see what we can find."

Leann pulled out some leftover biscuits and some preserves that Etta had made, and they sat at the kitchen table enjoying the sweet treat. When they finished, Leann cleaned up the mess, then turned down the bed. She asked Jake if he was coming to bed, too, and in a minute they were in each other's arms again. This time Leann didn't change in the spare room, and Jake didn't go to bed with his pants on.

Josiah had told them that they could take a few days off after the wedding, and they took advantage of that. After three days, they were both ready to get back to work, but first, they had to come to agreement on Ina. It was assumed that when they went back to work at the J-T, they would take Ina home with them since she now belonged to Leann. However, Leann and Jake had not yet discussed where she would stay, and what her part would be in their lives once she got there.

Jake suggested they leave her at the J-T until a slave cabin could be built for her, but Leann balked at that. Ina was like her sister; not like a slave. In their culture of early America, the husband was the dominant figure in the home, with mostly passive support from the wife. Leann recognized that and didn't want to overstep her bounds, but in this case, she had to stand up to her husband. "Jake, I know you're the head of our new family, but I've got to tell you that I don't want Ina staying in any slave quarters. She's like my own sister and I want her here in the house with you and me."

"I promise she won't invade our privacy. Also, she can help cook, clean the house, look after the animals, and a lot of other things that will let me spend more time with you."

Jake thought about it for a little while. He said, "Okay," but he wasn't sure how three grownups in a little house would work out. Not only did he now understand the reason for the extra room, he now understood the reason for the three chests that Josiah had Lee build.

The next morning, they left the river house without breakfast, knowing they would eat the plentiful leftovers in Etta's kitchen. At the house, Leann hugged and kissed Josiah. Jake also kissed Etta and shook hands with Josiah. While they were eating, Josiah gave them their assignments for the day. "Doc Wells was here yesterday looking for you, Jake. He didn't say what he wanted, but said he would come back today."

"Okay. Thanks, Josiah."

In a little bit they left the house and went to work; Jake to the barn, and Leann to the sheepfold,

Leann and Raelyn were happy to see each other. "I missed you, Leann. It was lonesome here while you were gone."

"I missed you, too, sweetie, but I am really enjoying being married. Jake and I are having so much fun together."

Ina and Sue came up and interrupted them. Leann hugged them. "Ina, we've got your room ready. You're gonna be living in the house with Jake and me."

"Oh boy. When will I be going home with you?"

"Today"

Ina squealed with excitement.

"After dinner, go to the barn and get a wagon, and then go to your place and get all your stuff. You can either go straight to the river house or you can come back here and we'll go together."

"I'll come back and meet you."

As she listened to Leann and Ina, Sue was sad. She and Ina had grown up together, and had hardly ever been away from each other. But she still had Raelyn, and that helped.

Right before dinner, Doctor Wells came to the J-T, and immediately looked up Jake. He found him in the barn. "Jake, I talked to a fellow the other day who wants to sell his entire flock of sheep and I thought you might be interested in, at least, a part of them. They are a different breed than what you're familiar with. They are called Icelandic Sheep."

Then Doc said, "Hold on to your hat, Jake. The sheep are colored."

"Colored?" asked Jake.

"Yeah, and here's the good part. This man brought in a few pairs to experiment with, in hopes of building a large flock. He felt the uniqueness of colored sheep would drive the price up, and he'd really have something. Unfortunately, it didn't work that way."

"Now, here's the winner, Jake. You've become expert at animal breeding, and you understand more than most people when it comes to animal husbandry. If you can understand the books on color genetics, you can use the framework to keep color out of your flock, or you can breed for a specific trait. Genes are different colors, You can do just about anything you want with this knowledge and this breed of sheep.

This man has around three hundred and fifty head. He will sell them for two dollars a head. If you're interested, the timing is perfect since we're coming into the breeding season for sheep You can get a head start without having to wait until next year. Let me know if you're interested, and I'll tell the man. You can go look at them whenever you want to."

Jake asked, "What do you think, Doc?"

Doc said, "I think you would be smart to buy them, or at least buy a few. For two dollars, you can't go too far wrong. I think it would be a wise move."

Jake said, "Okay, Doc, I trust your judgment. Tell the man I'll come look at his flock, and if I like 'em, I'll buy 'em."

Doc said, "Okay, I'll be seeing him tomorrow. If you want to come to town on Sunday, I'll go with you to look at them. It's not far from town."

"I'll see you on Sunday then," Jake said.

After Doc left, Jake's mind was racing like crazy. He was counting sheep, and coming up with unbelievable numbers. He didn't know how many ewes were in the three hundred fifty head, but he figured if there were three hundred, he could have over eleven hundred head by next year.

He figured it this way: Eighty percent of ewes that are bred, conceive, which would give him 240 pregnant ewes. Generally a ewe gives birth to three to five lambs. Using the minimum of three lambs each, after they were born he would have 720 new lambs. Add those to the 350 in his purchase, plus the thirty-five he already had, and he came up with over 1100.

He figured a minimum of three lambs per ewe, but realistically, there should probably be an average of four, so that would add another 200 or 250.

He couldn't wait to tell Leann. *There is another good thing about this. Leann and Ina are already used to caring for sheep so I have built-in shepherds. How good is that?*

When Leann came up for dinner, Jake pulled her off to the side, quickly telling her about Doc's visit.

Returning to the house, he found Leann and Ina busy fixing supper. They were acting like two young, adolescent girls, giggling and playing, and having a good time. Jake couldn't help but smile when he saw how happy they were.

Soon, supper was ready, and they all sat down to eat. Ina wasn't used to eating with her Master, and Jake got the idea she felt slightly intimidated sitting at the table with him. For Leann's sake, he tried to make her feel comfortable.

Ina went to her room after the supper mess had been put away and Leann and Jake went out onto the porch to continue their short noontime conversation. "I didn't get to finish telling you about Doc's visit. I think I told you the part about a man wanting to sell a flock of Icelandic Sheep. Leann, you're not gonna believe this, but the sheep are colored."

"Colored?"

"Yeah, and Doc says when I learn about color genetics, I can do just about anything I want to with the flock. He's only asking two dollars a head for 'em."

"I think you ought to buy 'em if you like 'em," Leann said.

"I probably will. And here's another thing, Leann. If I buy the flock, you and Ina will more than likely have to stop working at Josiah's and stay at the Green Farm to tend them."

Surprised, Leann responded, "You think so? Well, we'll do it if we need to."

"Josiah's not paying you anything, anyway, so you might as well work for yourself."

In a little while they went inside and retired for the night.

After breakfast on Sunday, Jake left to meet Doc Wells in Mercer. From there, they rode out to Robert Miller's farm in Doc's buggy.

Jake was intrigued when he saw the colored sheep, but a little surprised to see several white sheep in the mix.

"Doc, I thought they would all be colored."

"That's what I was talking about when I told you that if you understand color genetics, you can do many different things with breeding."

Seeing the white animals cinched the deal as far as Jake was concerned because he saw unlimited possibilities for the flock.

When they got to the Miller's house, Mr. Miller came to the door and Doc introduced him to Jake. "Well, what do you think about my sheep, Jake?"

"They're interesting. I've never seen any like 'em. How much did you say you want for 'em?"

"Two dollars a head."

"Is that your rock-bottom price?"

"Yeah, that's the best I can do."

"I'll tell you what. I'll buy your flock if you will drive them to my place."

"Okay. I'll do that. When do you want 'em?"

"In a week or ten days. I have to do some things at the farm before I will be ready for 'em. If you agree, I'll pay you when you bring the flock and we can get an accurate head count."

Mr. Miller agreed and they shook on it and Jake and Doc left. All the way back to Doc's place, they talked about sheep breeding. "I've got a book I want you to read. I'll give it to you when we get to my place."

"Doc, thanks for the book and for all your help. I'll start on this book tonight."

Jake started back to the river house dreaming and calculating all the way.

He and Leann spent the rest of the afternoon outside, enjoying the pretty day. They invited Ina to come spend it with them.

***

At the J-T the next day, Jake asked Josiah, "Will you sell me some fence posts and boards to build a small corral at the Green Farm?"

"Yeah, you can get some. I'll send them out a little later. I haven't told you, but I'm sending lumber and a crew of men out there after dinner to start on the addition to the house. If you would like for us to build the corral, some of my men can do that when they get there."

"That's great. Would you care if I go meet 'em and show 'em where to build it?"

"Yeah, that'll be okay. I need for you to be there anyway because I'm going out there. I want to show you what I have planned and want to make sure you're agreeable to it."

That afternoon, about twenty men and three wagons loaded with lumber, tools, and all sorts of other supplies rolled into the Green Farm. Josiah was with them, and while the men unloaded the wagons, he and Jake walked around looking at the house, and talking about what they should do regarding the expansion.

"Maybe an extra room would be the ticket," was Jake's idea, but when Josiah started talking about what he thought was needed, the extra room grew into four extra rooms and a back porch. At that announcement, Jake was super quick to agree. With the house discussions finished, they went out back and decided where to put the corral. "The reason I want the corral is because I just bought a small flock of sheep and need someplace to put 'em when they arrive

"Well, I think you will need a shelter inside the corral, so let's add that to the list."

"Thanks, Josiah. I appreciate everything you're doing for Leann and me."

The next morning the men went back to the Green Farm with more lumber and started building according to Josiah's plans. At the

J-T, Jake didn't see Josiah. He had gone back out to the farm to supervise.

When Jake went back on Saturday, he could hardly believe the progress. The corral was already finished. At that rate, it shouldn't take more than another two weeks to finish up.

The following Monday afternoon, Robert Miller arrived at the Green Farm, driving over three hundred sheep. He had sent someone ahead to the J-T to tell Jake they were coming, so he, Leann, and Ina were there when they arrived. After they counted the sheep—342--, Jake counted out $684.00 and paid Mr. Miller.

It was a good thing Leann and Ina were there because Jake didn't have a clue what to do. Since the sheep were in a new place, Leann put the dominant ram inside the corral with a few ewes, and the rest of the flock followed. They weren't about to leave that ram. The grass inside the corral was plentiful enough to last a few days, so Leann left the flock right there until something else could be done.

"Honey, I think it's time you tell your pa you're going to have to stay here with our flock now, and you will have to quit working at the J-T. Tell him Ina can stay on and work for him for a while, but she will have to quit, too, as our flock grows."

Jake didn't worry about Leann staying at the farm by herself. Two of Josiah's men would be there looking after the cattle, and they could look out for Leann as well.

CHAPTER SEVEN

Leann, Ina, and Jake had been living at the Green Farm about three months. The house was pretty when Jake bought it, but after the four room addition and the tender loving care given by Leann and Ina, it had become a showplace.

The four rooms were all added next to the existing bedrooms, making it a rambling single story ranch house. The front porch was extended all the way across the front and down one side. A fresh coat of white paint added just the right touch.

Since mowing was difficult, the lawn was small, but the girls had planted flowers everywhere. They anticipated changes in the seasons, so before one species died, another was planted to take its place.

It was considered to be *home* now, and things were beginning to happen. The six ewes bred at the river house had all given birth, and Jake's forecast of twenty-four lambs was right on the mark. He now had thirty-four sheep from the original ten he got from Josiah. It was getting close to time for the four heifers to become fresh.

And last, but certainly not least, it looked as though Leann was with child. She was not certain yet, but should know for sure in another two or three weeks. Jake wasn't sure what he thought about that.

She couldn't wait to tell her mother. When Leann and Jake went to the J-T for the usual Sunday dinner, she told Etta the symptoms. Etta agreed that more than likely Leann was expecting, and they immediately started making plans for the new addition.

***

Jake worked every day at the J-T breeding cattle and sheep. By spring, Josiah's livestock head count should show substantial growth.

Josiah realized more and more how lucky he was to have Jake, and nearly anything Jake asked for, Josiah gave to him. Jake, of course, still didn't know Josiah felt that way, so he didn't ask for too much. If he ever found out Josiah's feelings, poor Josiah.

Most of the time, Jake had Leann ask for whatever he wanted, and she usually got it.

Getting ready for the usual Sunday dinner, Jake said, "Leann, while we're at your parents' today, I want you to tell your pa that you're gonna have to have Ina quit working for him. Now that you're expecting, you're going to need her stay here and help you."

"But Jake, I'm not that far along yet. I don't need Ina to help me."

"I know, but I don't want to take any chances. Something could happen,"

"Okay."

"There's something else I want you to do while we're there."

"What is it"

"I want you to ask Josiah for a horse for Ina. Try and convince him that if she has her own horse, she would have a way to get to the J-T if she had to come and work when she was needed."

"All right, I'll ask him, but I hate to. Are you ready?"

"Yep. I'm ready."

Leann talked to her pa at dinner. When she and Jake returned to the Green Farm, they had a pretty horse tied to the back of the buggy.

***

Just about every day, when Jake was at the J-T, he spent time with Raelyn, either at dinner or the sheep pasture. If one of them had to be away, he or she was missed by the other. There was no inappropriate behavior; just feelings on both sides, and as time went on, the feelings were growing stronger.

If Jake was at the barn most of the day, Raelyn would find some excuse to go up there, or if Raelyn had to stay at the pasture all day, Jake would find a reason to go down there. Luckily, Sue, Raelyn's helper was always in the pasture, so Raelyn could usually get up to the barn without too much trouble.

It didn't take a genius to see something was going on. Josiah had noticed she was spending more and more time at the barn with Jake, and he didn't much like it.

***

Winter was coming and the days were getting shorter. Doctor Wells came to the ranch with regularity since the season had changed, and many of Josiah's ewes were coming into heat. He and Jake were able to experiment with different breeding methods and to practice techniques they had only read about.

Jake took advantage of Doc's visits. Every time he came to the J-T, Jake had him go to the Green Farm and do some work there, too.

Doc's services were expensive, but Jake managed to show Doc's invoices were solely for work done on the J-T herd or flocks.

Doc and Jake were in the barn when one of the cowhands looking after Jake's cattle came galloping up. "Mister Jake, one of your cows just had twins."

"Really? I knew it was getting close to time. Doc, three more of my original six are ready, too."

"That's good, Jake. You've also got some heifers in Ben's herd that are expecting, too, don't you?"

"Yeah. I don't know exactly how many, but some are. Doc, my herd should start showing some growth from now on, don't you think?"

"You're right", Doc said. "Within the next year or two, you should see a big difference."

Jake had already decided that after the sheep-mating season was over, he was going to ask Josiah for some time off, so he and Doc Wells could work on his herd. Since Jake didn't have a large crew like Josiah, it was necessary to plan carefully. More and more, Jake and Leann thought they might have to buy some slaves.

***

Etta was in the yard when a stranger rode up to the house. "Ma'am, is a fellow named Jake Isaacson here?"

Etta pointed him to the barn where Jake was working. Jake didn't see him come in, and from just inside the barn door, the man said in a loud voice, "Jake Isaacson, what in the world are you doing?"

Jake whirled around. Recognizing the man, he yelled back, "Dewitt Bishop. I don't believe it. I wouldn't have thought of you coming here for a hundred dollars. What are you doing all the way over here from Cana?"

They shook hands and hugged, telling each other how glad they were to see each other. Dewitt's family and Jake's family were friends in Cana. Jake had never gone out much when he was at home, so Dewitt was not really a friend, but they knew and liked each other.

"What are doing over this way, Dewitt?"

"I'm on my way to Tennessee and when your mama found out I was coming this way, she asked me to bring this letter to you."

He gave Jake the letter, but before he opened it he asked, "What's been happening in Cana? You know, it's been over a year since I was there."

Dewitt told some of the everyday happenings in Cana, then they went up on the front porch and sat down while Dewitt continued to fill him in on the latest news from home.

Etta heard them and came out of the house. The men stood up and Jake introduced her to Dewitt. "It's nice to meet you Mrs. Taylor."

"Nice to meet you, too, Dewitt. You've come a long way. Would you like to stay for dinner?"

"I'd like that very much. Thank you."

Etta returned to the kitchen, and they sat back down.

"I guess you know this is Mama's cousin Josiah Taylor's farm. Well, I'm married to Josiah's oldest girl and she has just found out for sure she's gonna have a baby. Be sure and tell Mama when you see her."

"You might see her before I do, Jake. If I like it in Tennessee, I might stay there."

When Josiah, Raelyn, and the boys came to dinner, Jake introduced Dewitt all around. Conversation was light as Etta served up a feast, and everybody stuffed themselves.

When they finished, Dewitt said, "Folks, I had better be going. It was nice meeting y'all, and Mrs. Taylor, the dinner was delicious. Thank you. Jake, I'm glad I got to see you again. Congratulations on the baby."

When he left, Jake opened the letter.

My dearest Jake,

How lonesome it is here without you. I miss you so much and wish daily for you to come home, but it's not possible yet because Eph still has hard feelings toward you. They may have mellowed some in this past year, but for your safety, you should stay with Cousin Josiah for a little while longer.

Your pa is well, and he misses you as I do. He and Eph work every day, and they had a real good crop this year. He said we would have plenty to eat this winter. They also put lots of meat in the smoke house.

Do you remember hearing Eph talk about Maggie Thompson from Sparta? She is now your sister-in-law. She and Eph got married two months ago, and Eph and her papa are partners in some kind of big land thing. I don't know much about it, but Eph says they can make a lot of money, and your pa agrees.

Please tell Josiah how I would love to see him. Give him my thanks for taking you in when you needed him. He is a good man.

Sweet Jake, I long to see you, and know that I will some day, but in the meantime, please take care of yourself and pray for your family.

Your loving Mother

Tears came to Jake's eyes. He loved his mother so much. Busy working since he'd arrived, marrying Leann, and now expecting a child, there had not been much time to think about his mother and daddy. He looked at the letter again and remembered home in a special way.

CHAPTER EIGHT

TWO YEARS LATER

In slang terms, Jake was boring with a big auger. He had become the father of two fine boys: Raymond was eighteen months, and Peter was three months old. They were the lights in their daddy's eyes.

His new-found profession as a breeder was unbelievably successful. Everything seemed to be going his way.

The sheep and cattle had had two seasons of breeding, and it appeared Jake had the magic touch when it came to increasing the livestock population for his farm, as well as for the J-T. Josiah treated him like a king.

Josiah's boys were jealous. Josiah knew it, and made sure they didn't harm Jake, or interfere with his work. With Doctor Wells help, Jake had increased Josiah's herd and flock by more than 30 percent, a significant number considering the hundreds of heads he had.

Jake wasn't shy about taking credit for it. Although Doc Wells was a major player in the breeding program, Josiah thought Jake was mainly responsible for the good results. That was just the way Jake wanted it. In his good old straight-forward, semi-honest way, Jake had worked things out so Josiah paid all of Doc Wells' fees, including the fees incurred at the Green Farm. With the huge successes they were having, almost everyone was happy…. especially Jake.

Doc Wells had kept his eyes open for deals on livestock he thought would interest Jake, and Jake had increased his herd quite a bit. Between buying more head and his knack with breeding methods, he had around four hundred head of cattle and fifteen hundred head of sheep.

He was looking at the possibility of buying some more land. His herd had outgrown the Green Farm and was already using some of the free-range land bordering his, but he didn't want to continue with that. There was a bigger chance of getting hit by rustlers on free-range land.

Josiah had talked to somebody in the Territorial Land Management Department about selling some of the free-range land to Jake, but people connected to the government didn't ever get in a hurry, so he would just have to wait.

**

Jake's day at the J-T was pretty calm, so he rode down to the sheep pasture to visit Raelyn. Over the last few months, they had been getting closer. A day didn't seem complete without the two of them being with each other, at least for part of the day.

He dismounted and walked over to her. "Hi, Rae. Whatta ya say?"

Raelyn smiled. "Not much. Whatta you say?"

"Well, I've been doing a lot of thinking about you and me, and I think we need to talk."

"Okay, what about?"

"Do you remember before Leann and I were married, I asked both of you to marry me, and you said you didn't feel right about not being my only wife?"

She frowned at him. "Yeah, I remember. Why?"

Jake stepped closer, "Well, you know what a nice family I have. I love Leann and Raymond, and Peter more than life itself, and Ina has become like one of us, but it just seems like my family isn't complete without you in it. I know you're my sister-in law, but I want you to be my wife. Have you ever thought about this since Leann and I married?"

"Not at first, but I have thought about it since we have become such close friends."

"Well, Raelyn, would you consider being my wife now?"

"Have you talked to Leann about this?"

Jake looked away. "No I haven't." He looked back at Raelyn. "But I will if you're interested."

"Jake, I love you, and you know I love Leann. After all, she's my big sister. And I love little Raymond and Peter. I think I would like to marry you, but I won't unless Leann agrees to it. I won't be a party to destroying the marriage and the family you have now."

"Does that mean you'll marry me if Leann is okay with it?"

Taking Jakes hand, she lifts it up and places it against her cheek. "Yes."

"All right then, I'll talk to Leann, and if she agrees, I'll talk to your pa again. You know he agreed the first time I asked you, so I hope he will again. If I can, I'll talk to Leann tonight. I love you, Raelyn."

With that he mounted up and was about to leave when he overheard Sue tell Raelyn, "I was afraid you were going to say "no".

You've been mad at yourself for more than two years because you didn't marry him the first time he asked. I'm just glad he asked you again. Maybe if you get married, you won't be so hard to get along with."

"Shush. He can hear you."

Jake acted as though he didn't hear and smiled as he rode away. He was praying things would work out. Raelyn was his first choice when he began thinking about marriage.

***

After supper, which was a veritable feast, Jake went into the living room and played with the kids while Leann and Ina washed the dishes and cleaned up the kitchen and dining room. Before long Leann stood in the doorway watching. "Okay guys, it's bedtime."

Jake said, "You heard mama. Pick up your things and let's go."

They carried the boys to their room and put them down for the night. After they finished hugging and kissing each one, they quietly went back to the living room and sat down.

"Anything interesting happen today?" Jake asked.

"Same old thing;watching those two *wild men,* cleaning a little, cooking a little. How about you?"

"Just a normal day. You know, I've been thinking about the time I asked you and Raelyn to marry me. Do you remember that?"

"Of course I do," she said.

"What did you think when I asked you both?"

"Well, at first I thought you were crazy, then I thought Raelyn and I had always been together and still would be, but there would be a lot of changes in our lives if we married you. Neither of us had any idea how two women married to one man would work."

"I know I told you I wanted to think about it before giving you an answer, but I knew as soon as you asked me I was going to say yes. Raelyn was not so sure, and that's why she said no.

Over the last three years, sometimes when I'm with Raelyn, I get the distinct impression she is sorry she said no, and wishes she had said yes."

Sensing the opening he was looking for, Jake asked, "How do you feel about that?"

"I don't know. I love my sister and miss being with her every day, but having her in the house as another wife is something I would have to think long and hard about. I think you and I have a good marriage, and probably don't need anybody else to interfere with it."

The look on Leann's face showed she was serious.

"Well, I was down at the sheep pasture today talking to Raelyn about this very thing. You're right. She does wish now she had said yes. I asked her if she would like to marry me now, and she said yes, but only if you agreed to it. She loves me, but she loves you, too, and doesn't want to do anything that will be against your wishes. After all, you're her big sister."

"I told her I would talk to you and see how you felt about it. If you are agreeable to it, I will talk to your pa."

"Leann, you know I love you and don't want to do anything to hurt you. I love the kids and hope we can have more. You also know how I've felt about you and Raelyn ever since I came to the J-T. I don't feel Raelyn would seriously affect my marriage to you. In fact, it can help it. You know how I want a big family. Well, this can help with that. You won't have to be pregnant all the time. Raelyn can take some of that pressure off of you."

"Think about it and let me know when you're ready. Just remember that I love you. I don't think bringing Raelyn in would harm our marriage, but it will have to be your decision. This is the only way Raelyn will consent to it."

"Okay, I'll think about it," Leann said coldly. Standing up and looking Jake straight in the eye, "But I've already told you how I feel. I think you and I have a good marriage without any outside interference. But you're the head of this family, and if you think you need another wife, then I guess that's what you'll have to do. I love Raelyn and hope this won't change our feelings for each other or the feelings between you and me. Do what you feel you have to do, Jake. I'm going to bed and I'll see you in the morning."

With a coolness Jake had not seen before, Leann went to their room and closed the door.

A minute or two later, she opened the door and said, "By the way Jake, I think I'm going to have another baby." Then she slammed the door shut.

Jake sat up thinking for a long time before going to bed. The thought of having Raelyn as his wife excited him. But he knew how Leann was feeling, and that made him feel depressed.

Finally deciding to go to bed, he slipped into the bedroom, got undressed and eased into bed next to Leann. He turned toward her thinking she would turn his way and put her arms around him as always, but he was dead wrong.

She stayed on her side of the bed facing away from him, and wouldn't roll over, even though he gently tugged on her, encouraging her to turn and embrace him.

He soon gave up. Rolling over, Jake faced away from Leann and went to sleep.

The next morning he was up early before either Leann or Ina, adding kindling to the hot coals in the stove, so he could make coffee. When it was ready, he poured a cup and sat down at the table. With his head in his hand, he drank the coffee.

Pretty soon Ina came in and poured herself a cup of coffee.

"Where's Leann?"

"She's not up yet."

"She's always up by this time. Do you think she's sick?"

Bringing her coffee to the table, she sat down with Jake. "Do you think I need to check on her?"

"Naw. I don't think she's sick. She's upset with me. We had a talk last night and I told her I wanted to ask Raelyn to marry me. She got mad and stormed off to bed."

Ina knew then what was wrong. "I'm only an unimportant slave girl, but I really love Leann and I have grown to love you too, Jake. I also love Raelyn and would really enjoy having her here, but are you sure this is the right thing to do? It's not my place to say anything, and I'm sure you have thought this through, but are you sure?"

"Yep, I'm sure. I've thought this through completely and I know it's the right thing to do."

Ina got up and started cooking breakfast. Just as she was about to serve Jake, Leann came into the room carrying little Peter, while she nursed him. She spoke to Ina and sat down with Peter, ignoring Jake.

"Good morning." Jake smiled at them.

Leann just sort of grunted.

His smile turned to a frown, and he went on with his breakfast. Smart enough to take things easy, he let them unfold without too much static.

In a few minutes he spoke to Leann again.

"Are you sure you're going to have another baby, Leann?"

"I'm pretty sure. Things are just like they were before I had the other two."

"I'm really happy to hear it and, Leann, I'll be there for you the same way I was for the other two. Maybe it'll be another boy."

At that point, although he hadn't said a word about Raelyn, he wanted to, but thought it would be better to wait until the atmosphere relaxed a little.

Ina and Leann talked between themselves, and soon Leann finished nursing Peter. Ina took him to his room to dress him, and put him down to play. When Ina left the room, Jake thought this would be the time to talk to Leann.

"You seemed upset last night. Are you better this morning?"

"I'm okay"

"Have you thought about what we talked about last night?"

"Yeah, I thought about it all night, and my feelings are the same as I told you. I don't think we need anybody else in our marriage, but since you are the head of this family, I feel I have no choice but to go along with what you say. I'm only thankful it's my sister you're bringing in, instead of some stranger. That's all I'm going to say about it."

Jake assured her, "I'll make things work out. You'll be glad to have Raelyn with us."

He left for the J-T and went straight to the sheep pasture with the news that he had everything worked out with Leann.

"Do you mean it?" Raelyn asked smiling from ear to ear. Her blue eyes dancing and her cute dimples emphasizing the excitement on her face.

"Yeah, it's all worked out."

"Is Leann all right with it?"

"Yeah. She was a little hesitant at first, but she's okay with it now."

She ran over and put her arms around him. "When can we get married, Jake?"

"Well, first, I have to talk to your pa. If he says it's okay, then we'll have to work out the plans with both your parents. I'm going up to see Josiah right now. I feel sure he'll say it's okay."

Seeing them entwined, Sue ran up and gave Jake a hug. "I'm really glad you two are finally getting together."

Jake nodded, then, mounted up to go see Josiah.

He found Josiah at the barn. "Josiah, have you got a minute? We need to talk."

"Okay. Let's go to the house and get a cup of coffee. I need a break, anyway."

"Josiah, I know you can't understand, but I want to marry Raelyn. She's ready now, and we want your blessing. You gave your permission nearly three years ago, and we hope you will again."

Josiah knew Jake had made a good home for Leann and the kids, and he knew how rich Jake was making him, so it didn't take but a minute for him to give Jake his permission.

"I still don't understand why you would want more than one woman, but if you're man enough to handle two of them, then have at it. I won't stand in your way."

Josiah sent one of his men to the sheep pasture to fetch Raelyn, and when she got to the house, he called Etta to come into where they were. "Mama, Jake and Raelyn wanna get married and I told them they could. Do we still have some of that cider Bobby brought us?"

"Yeah, we've got some."

"Good. Go get it and let's celebrate."

They all had a small celebration right there in the dining room. Raelyn asked, "Pa, when Leann married, you let her take Ina with her. Can I take Sue when I get married?"

"If you want her, child, then you can have her."

That surprised Jake, but he didn't say anything.

Immediately, conversation spun around choosing a wedding date. Two weeks from Sunday was decided on.

Jake and Raelyn went back to work.

After dinner, Jake rode to the church in Mercer to find Rev. Elmer Foust. He was shocked at what Brother Foust told him. Brother Foust told Jake he was happy to marry him and Leann, but he believed a marriage was something between one man and one woman. He said his beliefs would not let him perform the ceremony between him and a second woman, even though he knew Raelyn was a fine woman.

This was like hitting Jake right between the eyes, and he didn't know what to do. "Do you know anybody who might do it for us?"

"No I don't, Jake. Sorry."

The only other person Jake really knew in town was Doc Wells, so he went to his place. When Doc answered his door, Jake explained why he had come to town, and that Rev. Foust refused to perform the wedding ceremony.

"Doc, can you think of anybody I can get to do the ceremony?"

"Not really, Jake, but here's an idea. I know a man who lives up on White Oak Road who is a Mormon. Since you have shown an interest in the Mormons, maybe he can tell you something that will help. He might be able to tell you somebody that would do the ceremony. Do you want to talk to him? I'll go with you if you want me to."

"That would be real good, Doc. I'll try anything at this point."

They rode up to the man's ranch, and Doc introduced Jake to Robert Hiatt. "Robert, Jake has something he wants to talk to you about."

"Mr. Hiatt, I'm not a Mormon yet, but I've been reading a lot in the *Book of Mormon* and studying the Mormon's ways. I admire their customs a lot.

I'm wanting to marry a second wife like many of the Mormons do, but the only preacher I know won't do the ceremony, and I'm wondering if you know anybody that would."

Robert smiled at Jake and told him, "Since you're adopting the Mormon ways, a Mormon Deacon can perform the wedding."

"I don't know any, do you?"

Robert smiled. "Yeah, I know one."

"Does he live anywhere close by?"

"Yeah"

In frustration, Jake asked, "Well who is he, and where can I find him?"

Robert just smiled again, and told Jake, "I'm a Deacon, and I'll be happy to perform your wedding ceremony. When and where is it to be?"

Jake told him, and they worked out the details. He and Doc left, and rode back to town. Once again, Doc came through for Jake.

When he got back to the J-T, Jake explained everything he had run into, but was happy to tell them things were all worked out. When he mentioned Robert Hiatt's name, Josiah nodded.

"I know Robert. He's a good man."

"Josiah, I got to thinking on the way back from Robert's about my farm house. What would you think about adding some rooms, since there's going to be more people living there?

I think it would be good to add some more rooms. Tell you what. I'll have some men and materials sent over in a day or two."

"Thanks, Josiah."

Josiah seldom joked, but today he couldn't resist. "Now let me get this straight, Jake. Do you want the men to build a double sized room with a huge bed, so you and both wives can be in it at the same time, or do you want them to build you a room with doors going into adjoining rooms on either side, so you can take turns shuttling your wives in and out?"

Jake didn't think any of it was funny, and when Josiah saw he was irritating him, he stopped with the wise cracks.

"Jake, I'm sorry. I was just joshing you, but I do want to know one thing and I'm serious. How is this going to work? Will the wives come to your bed when you select one, or will you go to the selected one's bed?"

Josiah really wanted to know, but Jake didn't answer. He hadn't figured it out yet.

CHAPTER NINE

The next two weeks were very hectic. Between trying to keep up his responsibilities at the J-T and the Green Farm and trying to spend as much time as possible with Raelyn and at home with Leann, Jake was exhausted. On top of that, he was being subjected to something he never dreamed about.

When he had told Robert Hiatt about reading the *Book of Mormon* and studying the Mormon ways, and admiring their customs, Robert had interpreted that as meaning Jake wanted to become a Mormon.

The day after he and Doc Wells went to Robert Hiatt's, Robert came to the J-T to see Jake, and told him he needed to do certain things he was not prepared to do.

Robert instructed Jake on talking to other people about converting to Mormonism, how to get a group together, and a host of other things regarding the Mormon religion.

From then on, he came to see Jake every day or two.

Jake didn't like it. However, he had to act as if he was going along with Robert's teachings, at least until the wedding was over. If he didn't, he was afraid Robert might back out of doing the ceremony.

Finally, Jake had had enough. When Robert arrived at the J-T again Jake was just leaving the main house. He hurried to him before Robert could dismount from his horse.

"How ya doin' Robert?"

"Fine, thank you."

"Listen, I thank you for making all these trips to help me get started with the Mormon things, but Robert, I am so busy right now, I think I'm gonna have to wait 'til after my wedding to do the things you want me to do."

"Josiah is overseeing the construction of a large addition to my house. Etta and the other women are really busy making dresses and all the things women do at a time like this. I'm real busy, trying to look after my job at the J-T, as well as looking after my own farm."

Robert seemed to understand. "I can see what you mean, Jake. I won't bother you anymore until after the wedding. It looks like your plate is pretty full."

"Thank you Robert. I knew you'd understand. Will you excuse

me? I've got to go somewhere."

Jake mounted up and went to the sheep pasture to see Raelyn.

***

He took his time going back to the Green Farm that evening. Thinking about all that was going on in his life, it suddenly hit him: what were the sleeping arrangements going to be? Of course, he knew he would be with two wives, but it hadn't dawned on him that something would have to be decided on a night-by-night basis. *How can I be with one without the other getting mad? Who will decide who will sleep with me? Have I made a foolish decision by wanting to marry two women?* These were questions he thought about as he made his way home.

Maybe Robert could give him some pointers. Robert had only one wife, but he knew people who had more than one, so Jake decided to ask for suggestions the next time he saw him.

***

Leann was starting to come around a little since she saw that Jake was definitely going to marry Raelyn. Deep down she was actually feeling a little excited about having her little sister coming to live with her and Jake.

She was glad, too, that Sue was coming. Leann, Raelyn, Ina, and Sue had always been close. To think about all four of them in the same house was exciting. Though they were like sisters, Ina and Sue had always lived in slave quarters, so this was going to be quite different. Leann wondered how Jake was going to handle living in a house with four women, one of them pregnant. She found out the day before that she was definitely pregnant. Soon, there would be three children.

***

Three days before the wedding, Jake decided he had better get some new clothes. Hoping Mr. Puckett would be at the store, he rode into town. He didn't want to go through the same ordeal with Mrs. Puckett.

Mr. Puckett stood just inside the door as Jake stepped into the store. As soon as he got inside. He breathed a deep sigh of relief.

"Hi, Jake. What are you doing in town on a Thursday?"

"Hi, Mr. Puckett. I came in to buy some new clothes suitable for a wedding. Me and Raelyn are getting married Sunday."

"Well, congratulations, Jake. My wife is much better at picking out clothes for special occasions than I am." He turned and called out, "Lavinia, Jake's getting married. Come help him pick out some nice clothes."

He was trapped. The friendship between the Puckett and Taylor families was strong, so once again, he had to endure the experience with Mrs. Puckett. As it turned out, it wasn't too bad. Either he had learned some things, or Mrs. Puckett was easier to get along with than last time. Whichever it was, he got his new clothes and left without being traumatized.

Two days later, Jake went to see Raelyn. He had important questions that needed answers. "Rae, would you like to stay at the river house for a couple of days before going to the Green Farm, or would you rather just move on in to the Green Farm?"

"I don't care as long as I'm with you. We'll do whatever you want to do."

"I think I might like for us to stay at the river house for a while, but I'll let you know at the ceremony tomorrow."

He gave her a little peck on the cheek and left for Robert Hiatt's place to ask some questions.

When he reached Robert's front yard, Robert saw him and called from the barn, "Hey Jake, I'm out here. Tie your horse up and come out here."

When Jake walked into the barn he said, "Hi Robert."

"Hi Jake, What brings you out this way?"

"Well, I've got a couple of questions that I don't know the answer to and I was hoping to might be able help me."

"Well sure, if I can. Whatta ya need?"

"You know I'm getting married to a second wife. I don't know what to do about the sleeping arrangements and I'm hoping you can tell me what people with more than one wife do."

"I don't know first-hand, Jake, but I've heard some people talking who have multiple wives. They said the wives were the ones who decided who would be sleeping with the husband on a day-to-day basis."

That seemed strange to Jake, but he nodded anyway, and asked Robert a few more questions. "Thanks for the information, Robert. I'll see you tomorrow."

He mounted his horse and left.

Actually, he was somewhat relieved. He would turn the decision over to Leann and Raelyn, and not have to worry about making one of them mad. The more he thought about it, the better he liked it.

He decided that he and Raelyn would definitely stay a few days at the river house. It would give him time to talk to both women about his decision on the sleeping arrangements. Having finally made that decision, he felt much better.

The day of the wedding, Jake and Leann got up and had coffee like any other day, but it wasn't like any other day. In a few hours, Jake was going to cut his relationship with Leann in half by marrying someone else, and giving her the other half of the relationship. Even though Raelyn was Leann's sister, and their love for each other was deep, there was an unwanted, helpless, feeling of resentment in Leann that she couldn't shake. Trying to act as if everything was normal, she hoped Jake didn't notice it. She didn't know how long she could put on a front. They were all going to be together all the time. She prayed for help.

Soon, Ina and the boys were up. Jake put Raymond in the high chair. Leann nursed Peter while Ina fixed breakfast. She was flitting around like a silly kid, so anxious for Raelyn and Sue to get there. After breakfast Ina took the children to dress them. Jake and Leann went to their room to get ready. They dressed pretty much in silence. Jake was trying to be overly nice, and Leann was trying to be supportive, but the atmosphere was still somewhat strained.

When everybody was ready, they piled onto the wagon for the trip to the J-T.

They went to the house first. Leann, Ina, and the kids went inside while Jake stopped for a few minutes to visit with Leann's brothers, who were sitting on the front porch.

In a few minutes, Doctor Wells, and Mr. And Mrs. Puckett came. Then Robert Hiatt and his family drove up. As before, several of the slaves, who were close to the family, came.

Not nearly as many friends came as had come for the first wedding. Most of the Taylor's friends were Christians, and couldn't support a polygamist wedding. This bothered Etta and Josiah, but Jake didn't care. All he wanted was to marry Raelyn. Later, he would try to win everyone's approval.

Leann and Ina, each with a child in her arms, walked outside with Etta and down to the grove where Leann and Jake's wedding had taken place. Leann's brothers, the guests, and Jake followed. As before, Josiah and the bride came last, riding in a buggy.

Jake took his place and turned around to face the guests. Looking at Raelyn in the dress Etta had made for her, he couldn't believe how beautiful she was.

The dress was similar to the one Etta had made for Leann's wedding, except it was made of white muslin. The design was the same...just different fabric. It was ankle length and Etta had sewn ruffles around the bottom.

This must be what an angel looks like, he thought. He couldn't take his eyes off her, even after she stepped close to him. He looked over at Leann and she, too, looked gorgeous. *How lucky can a man get? Nobody, nowhere can possibly have a wife as beautiful as either of mine.*

The ceremony was pretty much the same as the one performed by Elmer Foust, but Robert asked the couple a few more questions. Jake didn't know for sure why he was asking, but answered the way Robert instructed, as did Raelyn.

Robert pronounced Jake and Raelyn married, and as before, guests and family stood around visiting and congratulating the newly married couple. Pretty soon the group started to dwindle, and only the family was left. It wasn't but a few minutes later when Raelyn's brothers disappeared.

Raelyn, Leann, and Etta crowded into the buggy and rode to the house, while the others walked.

Before long, Leann, Ina, and the children left for home. To Jake's surprise, Leann kissed him good-bye, and kissed Raelyn as well. It made him happy, but he felt an instant pang of guilt.

The guilt quickly disappeared when he looked at Raelyn. She had changed out of her wedding dress, but was still a vision, and Jake could hardly believe she was his. In the years he had known her, he had never really realized just how beautiful she was.

Before they left for the river house, Raelyn took Sue by the hand and walked down toward the barn. "Sue, Jake and me are gonna stay at the river house for two or three days before we go to the Green Farm. After that we'll be going to the Green Farm to live and I'll come get you and take you with us. Get everything together that you want to take with you because when you leave, you won't be back here to stay anymore."

Sue hugged her. "I love you Raelyn."

"I love you, too."

They walked back to the house where Jake had everything about ready to leave. The buckboard was full. Etta had cooked a big batch of food to take with them to the river house. They wouldn't have to go to the store to buy groceries. She knew they would be going to the Green Farm and just wanted to help until they got "home"

Raelyn hugged her parents, and Jake hugged Etta and shook Josiah's hand. He helped Raelyn up on the buckboard; then he got up, and they left for their private time at the river house.

As soon as they were out of sight of the J-T house, Raelyn was all over Jake, hugging and kissing him so much he had a hard time driving the buckboard. In fact, she caused him to drop the reins one time, and it was a good thing the horses obeyed Jake's voice command to "Whoa."

So amorous was Raelyn that Jake could hardly get down off the buckboard to pick up the reins.

After they got on their way again, she slowed down a little, and it wasn't long until the river house came into sight.

Jake thought back to the time when he and Leann had gone there after they were married, and he assumed it would be the same with Raelyn. They would unload the wagon. He would put the perishables in the springhouse, come back to the house, and the two of them would walk around, go outside, sit on the porch, and kill time until supper. Then, after supper they would go to bed.

But that was not what Raelyn had in mind.

As soon as they pulled up to the house and got down from the buckboard, she grabbed Jake's hand and pulled him into the house, into the bedroom, and onto the bed. Jake didn't even have time to say a word. Raelyn undressed them both, and finally, they melted into each other.

It was Raelyn's first time to sleep with a man. Jake, of course, had been with Leann many times, but it was indescribable with Raelyn. He knew immediately he had made a good decision by marrying the two sisters. They were going to make his life a pure pleasure.

An hour or so later, Jake sort of came to his senses and started to get up, but before he did, he propped up on one elbow. "Wow, Raelyn, you're really something. You know, we can love each other like this for the rest of our lives. I sure am glad you married me."

"I hate to get up, but we have things to do before it gets dark."

"Whatta we have to do?"

"To start with, we have to unload the buckboard. We have to put some of the food in the springhouse and we have to build a fire in the cook-stove as well as some other things."

"All right, but I think you're mean."

With a flushed face and a naughty look, she got up and halfway got dressed, and helped him.

He had to swing wide around her in order to get anything done.

She kept trying to drag him back to the bedroom. After three or four trips to the springhouse, he had finally put all the meat, milk and other perishables away.

Pouting the whole time, Raelyn managed to empty the rest of the buckboard.

She coaxed him back into bed one more time before supper, and it wasn't long before he ran out of steam. "Rae, we've got to get up. It's gonna be dark before long and the only light we have is candles. We need to start thinking about supper and doing other things that have to be done before dark. We'll be together all night, okay?"

She calmly got up from the bed, dressed and started doing things around the house.

Jake built a fire in the cook stove and helped Raelyn prepare supper. After they ate, they walked down to see the livestock, and then settled onto the bench he had made that sat by the river.

A full moon had come up early, and its' reflection in the water created a beautiful and peaceful scene. Jar-flies were serenading each other in the trees and everything together made for a very romantic moment.

The couple sat there, holding hands and enjoying each other.

After it got dark, they went into the house, and Jake built a fire in the fireplace. Although it wasn't cold, the fire made it cozy. They settled in chairs and began to talk.

"Raelyn, this might not be the best time to bring this up, but it's something that needs to be understood before we move in the Green Farm house permanently. I want you and Leann to be the ones to decide on the sleeping arrangements each night, and I think it will be a good idea if we go to the Green Farm tomorrow, and talk to Leann about it. That's one reason I decided to stay here for a couple of nights."

"Why don't you decide who you're gonna sleep with?"

"Cause anything I decide will make one of you mad."

"I guess you're right"

"Rae, I sure am glad that you're now part of my family. I want us to have lots of kids and one day I want a much larger ranch with thousands of head of stock. If we all work together, we'll be rich someday."

"That sounds good, Jake."

A few days after Jake moved Raelyn to the Green Farm, Robert Hiatt started pushing him again to get people together to talk about becoming Mormons. Each time he came over, Jake came up with an excuse not to do it. After a while, he quit coming so often.

Jake ran into Robert a couple months later at the store in Mercer. While Jake was getting his supplies together, Robert started talking about having a get-together.

"Robert, I've been doing a lot of thinking lately, and I've decided that I don't want to become a Mormon after all. My pa and grandpa have always wanted me to be a part of their religion and I've decided to do it. I appreciate all your interest, though."

Visibly upset, Robert turned and walked away without acknowledging Jake's words. Jake never saw him again.

CHAPTER TEN

ONE YEAR LATER

The addition to the house that Josiah had been so generous in giving was finished. He had added a second floor, with four additional bedrooms, giving Jake and his family more room than they knew what to do with.

Adding the second floor made it necessary to change the downstairs slightly. A staircase was required to get upstairs and they located it in the main hallway downstairs. The main hallway runs all the way from the front to the back of the house with a secondary hall branching off to the right and running all the way to the end of the house. Three bedrooms are on each side of that hall. The living room, dining room, and kitchen were on the other side of the main hall.

Three hundred yards from the main house, Josiah also built ten slave cabins, and two barracks buildings for future use. Six of the cabins had two bedrooms and four had one bedroom. Each one had a kitchen, dining, and living area combined. The barracks were designed to house twelve people. Furnishings would be added as slaves were brought in to occupy them.

Jake decided on a sleeping arrangement that made all the women in the house unhappy. Now that they had ten bedrooms, he thought it would be best if he had his bedroom on the first floor, and the four women had theirs on the second floor. The other three wouldn't be able to hear what went on in his room, when he had one of the wives with him.

The children would have their rooms on the first floor, next to his. He figured since he was the man of the house, and head of the family, there wasn't any way the women would defy him.

However, they vowed to keep after him, until he came around to their wishes. When four women who want the same thing get together, defiance comes in different forms. Jake's arrangement was by no means final.

Since Jake changed the name of the Green Farm to The J-I Ranch and was beginning to get recognition from a variety of people, from the average person to large landowners, and ranchers. Jake could work wonders with new breeding methods, and they were anxious to find out what he did. But he was very careful not to divulge any information that might create competition for his ranch. Although he worked for the J-T, not even Josiah, or his sons knew just how Jake did those wondrous things.

Six months after Raelyn and Sue moved in, Leann was at the sheep pasture with Raelyn and while there a terrific pain hit her. She doubled over and it scared Raelyn. "What can I do, Leann?"

"I think I'm having this baby. Have somebody get the midwife. Hurry!"

Raelyn ran to where Jess was working and told him what was happening and sent him for the midwife.

Leann managed to get to the house and pretty soon, Jess arrived with the midwife, whose name was Virginia.

Delivering babies was old hat to Virginia. She had been doing it for years.

After about two hours, Leann had another little boy, whom they named Lewis. This was the third child for Leann, and Jake was really proud to have three sons.

Raelyn had wanted to get pregnant right away, but so far it had not happened. She was starting to get discouraged, but Jake kept insisting she would soon have success.

***

Josiah had spoken with some people at the Territorial Land Management Department months earlier, about selling some free-range land to Jake, but nothing had ever come of it

Several weeks after Lewis was born, a man with the TLM came to see Jake. "Mr. Isaacson, my name is Bill Cox and I work for the TLM. Word reached our office that you would like to buy some free-range land if any came available. Is that correct?"

"Yes, it is."

"Well Mr. Isaacson, the TLM is willing to sell you six hundred acres if you want it."

Jake jumped at the chance. "You bet I want it. What do I do?"

Bill explained the details, including the cost and Jake agreed to everything. Jake walked with him to his horse and they shook hands.

The next morning, Jake went to the TLM office and finalized the sale.

"If any more land becomes available I would like first refusal if you don't mind."

"Mr. Isaacson, we'll see that you get it."

When all was said and done, Jake's purchase increased the J-I

Ranch to one thousand acres.

***

With the additional land, Jake focused on increasing the size of his cattle herd, and his sheep flock, it quickly became apparent he needed more help. He needed slaves.

Jake had never purchased a slave, but Josiah would know just what to do. When Jake asked for help, Josiah agreed to go with him to a slave sale.

The first Saturday of the next month, they took the wagon to Dayton where the sale was being held. Dayton was only five hours from the J-T, so it wasn't a back-breaking trip. After an early breakfast at Josiah's, they left, and reached Dayton around noon. Etta had packed a box-dinner for the guys, so they didn't have to stop.

Just before they got there, Josiah said, "Jake, if you see any slaves you want to buy, you should be prepared to treat them kindly. Not only is it the right thing to do, but if you're good to them, they will produce much better for you."

"Yeah. I've noticed that with you and your slaves."

They drove straight to the courthouse. The sale was already underway when they arrived. Several slaves in shackles were standing on a platform, or a box-like surface that had been set up on the lawn. People – mostly men - were looking them over. If a man liked what he saw, he bid on the slave. If nobody bid, or if a slave had any sign of an attitude, he was put in wagons with tops and bars and sent down south to what were called "nigger traders." This was a rough life for those people. The slaves were treated as if they were animals.

In a few minutes, Josiah spotted one he thought would be good for Jake. Jake's high bid of $200 won the slave. The same number that had been given to Jake as a bidder was pinned on the slave's shirt and he was placed in a separate area with others who had been purchased. He would stay there until the sale was over.

As the day wore on, Jake bought three more men. He and Josiah decided it was enough, for that trip. Jake paid for his slaves and led them to the wagon.

It was getting late. Josiah didn't want to camp on the way home because they would have to keep the men in shackles. With the slaves in the back of the wagon, Jake drove to the sheriff's office, where Josiah arranged for the men to spend the night in a couple of cells. There, the slaves would at least have a bed to sleep on; not the most comfortable, but a bed nonetheless. Josiah paid the Sheriff for whatever food the men would be given for supper that evening

Jake and Josiah stayed at the little hotel across from the courthouse, where they ate supper and breakfast the next morning. When the waitress poured Josiah a second cup of coffee, he ordered four extra meals for the new men. The fare at the jail wouldn't be nearly enough to fill up the slaves.

When they finished they got their team out of the livery stable. After picking the men up from the jail they started toward Mercer.

As soon as they were away from Dayton, Josiah untied the hands of the slaves, so they could eat while they rode. The shackles stayed on their legs. Jake and Josiah had no way of knowing yet what kind of men they had, and didn't want to take a chance on any of them running away. After all, Jake had paid handsomely for each one.

The trip back to Mercer provided time to get acquainted with the men and see what kind of character each had. On the way, Jake and Josiah talked to the men, found out something of their pasts, and tried to show them they were good people, who would not mistreat them. The slaves were offered fruit on the way and at dinner, Jake offered them what he and Josiah were eating. While they were eating dinner, Josiah asked, "Jake what do you think about taking their shackles off?"

"I think that's a good idea."

Jake unlocked the shackles and the men seemed to appreciate it. They began to appear a little less wary and tense.

Josiah had been thoughtful ever since dinner. As they drew near to Mercer he had a suggestion. "Jake let's go by my ranch and pick up Lee. He's one of my best and favorite slaves. You can take him to your place to stay with the new men for a couple of nights to help them get situated."

"That's a great idea. Josiah. Thank you."

When they picked up Lee, Josiah stayed home. Jake and the five slaves went on to Jake's ranch.

The women of the J-I didn't know when Jake would arrive or who to expect for supper, so they didn't plan a big meal. Hearing the wagon drive up, Leann went outside to meet Jake. The other three soon followed. "Girls, I've brought five extra mouths to feed tonight. I don't know if you have enough fixed or not so if you don't you need to rustle up something. We're all hungry."

Jake followed them into the house and Lee led the men to the slave barracks.

They got busy cooking and when it was ready, Ina and Sue took supper to the slaves. Of course it was delicious. The new men were astounded. They had never been treated so well.

***

After breakfast the next morning, Jake met with Lee in the barn. "Good morning, Lee."

"Good morning, Mr. Jake."

"How did you guys do last night? Any problems?"

"No problems, sir. All of them talked about the good supper they had."

"That's good. Lee, here's what I want you to do. I want you to talk to each one of the new men and try your best to find out just how much each one knows about farming. I want to know who knows about livestock, who knows about growing crops, and anything else helpful in operating a ranch. The women pretty much have the sheep operation under control, at least temporarily, but other than that, the ranch needs help in just about every area."

"Okay, Mr. Jake, I'll see what I can do."

Jake got on his horse and went to the J-T to work. On the way, he was thinking big. In his mind, he could see a ranch and staff many times larger than what he already had.

He spent a routine day at the J-T and was anxious to get back home.

After supper, Jake settled in the living room. When the dishes were done and put away, the four women joined him. Leann busied herself with a baby blanket that was nearly finished. Ina and Sue worked on a quilt they were making, while Raelyn just sat watching.

Before long, Leann put the children to bed. She put the two youngest in the bedroom next to Jake's. Standing in the living room door, she stretched and yawned. "Good night, everybody. I'm going to bed." She turned and headed upstairs. In a little while the other women turned in, leaving Jake alone. Finally, he gave up and retired, too.

Somewhere around midnight, first one, then another of the children started crying. They cried and cried, but no one came to check on them.

Jake was getting aggravated. He'd been awakened by the crying and it wasn't being attended to. Finally, he threw back the covers, grabbed a robe off the end of his bed, and stomped upstairs to Leann's room. "Leann", he yelled. "Can't you hear those kids crying? Get up and go down there and tend to 'em." He turned from the doorway and didn't notice she was already awake.

She quickly grabbed a cover-up and followed Jake downstairs. In front of her, he didn't notice the slight smirk on her face. "I'm sorry, Jake. I didn't hear 'em. It's hard to hear things down here from upstairs." She got them quiet and went back to bed.

About three a.m. the baby started crying again and Jake woke up again. *I'll never be able to sleep with this going on.* He lay there awake, waiting for someone to check on the crying child. No one came.

Jake went to Leann's room again. With a stronger yell, "Leann, Leann, wake up. Get downstairs and stop the kid from crying."

Again, with a slight smirk, she went down, calmed the baby, and again apologized. "I'm sorry Jake. I just can't hear the children from my room." She smiled and returned to her room.

In Jake's addled mind, he told himself, *something's gotta be done about this. I've got to get some sleep.* then he went back to bed, and Leann went back upstairs.

The next morning, Jake had a hard time getting up. In fact, Ina had to wake him when it was time for breakfast. With his elbow on the table and his head in his hand, he thought, *Every night can't be like last night. I'll have to figure out something because I have to have plenty of sleep in order to work at both jobs.*

After finishing his breakfast he went to get a report on the new slaves. Lee told him, "Mr. Jake, you and Master Josiah did a real good job pickin' them boys because they all have a lot of sense. They're all mid-forties and pretty settled. On top of that, they're all familiar with livestock and growing different crops."

This pleased Jake, especially about the crops. He was going to need good help when it came time to plant. Finally, fully awake, he left Lee and rode to the J-T to work.

About mid-morning, Virgil, the town's blacksmith came to the J-T to repair some things that had broken. While he was there, Jake told him, "Hey Virgil, when you finish with Josiah's stuff, how about looking me up. I want you to help me decide on a brand for my ranch."

"That afternoon, he and Jake got their heads together and worked on a design. It wasn't a coincidence the J I brand looked very similar to the J-T brand. Just something else hatched out of Jake's sneaky mind.

Jake had helped Buck and the boys with branding, but by no means was he an expert. Before leaving for the day, he met up with Josiah. "Would you mind sending somebody out to the J-I Ranch next week to show my men how to brand? My herd is getting pretty large. Actually, the branding is probably overdue."

"Yeah, I can do that. How about Monday morning?"

ANOTHER YEAR LATER

Time moved swiftly at the J I Ranch. The children were growing by leaps and bounds. Raymond, the oldest son was now six years old. And the family was growing. Leann had her fourth son, naming him Joel. She, Jake, Ina, and Sue doted over the children.

But Raelyn was a little distant. She and Jake had been married for over two years, and she still wasn't pregnant. This really worked on her emotions. She was jealous of Leann, which caused Leann to have a superior attitude toward Raelyn.

The Territorial Land Management Department offered Jake the opportunity to buy another eight hundred acres, and, of course, he'd jumped at it, making his ranch eighteen hundred acres. This additional land adjoined Josiah's, and Jake planned to use that to his advantage. He was by no means in the same class as Josiah, who had fourteen *thousand* acres, but in the short time he'd been ranching, Jake was satisfied with his progress.

He and Josiah went back to Dayton, and bought more slaves. Two married couples, plus two additional single men brought the total slaves owned by Jake, to eight men and two women. He didn't count Ina and Sue. To him, they were family.

He was well pleased with the four original slaves. From their first day, they plowed and planted money crops. Food crops for the family and slaves, plus plenty of corn and hay for the cattle. And all but one rode herd on the cattle helped with the branding, and worked around the barn when necessary.

To reward them for their good work and their loyalty to him, Jake had bought each of them a pillow for their bunk and a warmer blanket. Living in such comfort, he felt guilty for the way the slaves had to live.

Due to Jake's expertise, his number of cattle increased, which created an increase in the need for branding. Sometimes strays with the J-T brand wandered over from Josiah's land. The J I brand was so similar it was no trouble to brand over the J-T brand. Once rebranded, no one could tell the difference.

Buck and the boys kept a pretty good eye on their stock, so it didn't happen very often, but if they did slip up, it was "good-bye stray." To do the right and honest thing and return the cows never entered Jake's mind.

With the birth of his fourth child, Jake was once again losing sleep due to the kids' crying in the middle of the night. Leann's continued claim that she couldn't hear them from upstairs, forced him to make a change in the bedroom arrangement. His bedroom and the children's room stayed where they were, but Leann moved into the room next to the children, and Raelyn moved next to Leann. The children's room created a buffer between Jake's and either wife's room.

Jake had had zero experience with women before he married Leann, and now, he had four women in the house. He was often amazed at their different moods and attitudes. Leann stayed exhausted from looking after four children, and Raelyn was depressed because she couldn't get pregnant. The other two were so crabby when their hormones were raging no one could get along with them. Neither had a man, and they acted pretty frisky around Jake, especially when Leann and Raelyn weren't around.

Raelyn was desperate to have a child. Sheep-mating season was getting near and one day when Jake was at the sheep pasture, Raelyn said she wanted to talk to him.

Walking away from the others, "Jake, I love you so much. I just want you to know how ashamed and embarrassed I am because I haven't been able to get pregnant. After agonizing over it for long time, I've reached a decision."

"I've noticed how Sue looks and acts toward you and I know she's crazy about you. Therefore, if you would like to sleep with Sue and get her pregnant, I'll give my permission. It's not right for Leann to have all the children, and since Sue belongs to me, I'll just consider any children conceived by the two of you to be partly mine."

"I've already talked to Sue, and she is all for it."

"Boy, Rae, that's some decision that you've made, but I'm gonna have to think about it. I don't know if it would be right or not, since I'm married to you."

"All right, Jake. You think about it."

Knowing instantly what his answer would be, Jake couldn't wait to tell Raelyn that he would do it, but thought it best if he waited a respectable amount of time. He didn't want to appear too anxious. He thought Sue was very desirable, and he would love sleeping with her.

A respectable amount of time turned out to be the afternoon of the next day. "Raelyn, I've thought a lot about what we talked about and if you really want me to do it, I'll try to get Sue pregnant. I don't know if I can do it the first time. It might take several times to be sure."

"That will be okay, Jake. I just want you to do it."

He thought, *Man you talk about a win, win situation; I get to sleep with a good looking, desirable girl and have my wife's blessings, too. What a deal.*

After Jake married Raelyn, she and Leann had decided each one would sleep with him every other night. Since that was working out pretty well, it was decided Sue would replace Raelyn on her night.

On the advice of the midwife, they waited until Sue's most fertile time, then Jake slept with her three times that week, hoping she conceived. Raelyn resumed her nights with Jake the next week. But all were not happy.

From the time Jake first slept with Sue, the household at the J I ranch had become like a powder-keg; ready to blow up at any time.

The four boys were taking a toll on Leann's nerves. Between nursing and changing the younger ones and Raymond picking on all three of his younger brothers, she was about to go crazy. Jake was at work all day, so he was no help.

At the sheep pasture, two more women were unhappy. "I don't see why they picked just you to sleep with Jake," Ina told Sue one day. "I can probably get pregnant easier than you can."

"Why do you think so?"

"'Cause I'm older and more mature than you are."

"No you're not. I'll get pregnant. You just wait and see."

"Both of you shut up," Raelyn sobbed, as she turned and ran away. Depression had become a constant in Raelyn's life while Sue's anticipation of pregnancy was keeping her spirits up.

Bickering, between Ina and Sue, went on for the next three months. When it was obvious that Sue was not pregnant, Raelyn told Jake he needed to sleep with her again.

Once again, Jake and Sue slept together three times, to get her pregnant. Jake didn't care if she did or not. He enjoyed just trying; and so did Sue.

Once again, Raelyn took her rightful nights with Jake and the household returned to normal.

Two months later, it was pretty definite Sue was expecting.

***

Shearing time was especially difficult. Josiah's flock had

increased in number, and Jake had two flocks because he kept his Icelandic sheep separate.

Miles was still in charge at Josiah's. Actually, moving back and forth between ranches, he was also in charge at Jake's ranch. As his flock grew Jake had had platforms built each year for shearing. Having no way to determine if he had enough, only time would tell.

It took fifty men three weeks to finish the job at both ranches. As it turned out, Jake could have used more platforms, but the shearers didn't complain.

After the shearing and bundling, Josiah's wool was taken to market first, then Jake's. Although he did well, Jake wasn't happy with the price his Icelandic wool brought. He could see he was going to have to educate some people on the fine points of colored wool, but overall, he was satisfied with the year's wool production.

Of course, he would push for more next year.

Sheep-mating season was in full swing, and Jake had his hands full trying to keep up with all the ewes in heat at the J-T as well as the J I Ranch.

Early on, he'd realized two of his original slaves, Thomas and Asa, could be fully trusted. He met them at the barn first thing after breakfast each morning, teaching them some of the breeding methods he knew. They were starting to take some of the workload, giving him the chance to experiment with some experimental breeding ideas he had been hoping to try.

Doc Wells was still playing a major role in the development of the herds and flocks of both ranches and helped Jake with the experimentation. Jake was always thinking of how to get ahead, so while they took sperm from some of his Icelandic rams, he was thinking of horses. He needed more.

"Doc, how 'bout keeping your eyes open for some good horses at a good price?"

"What are you looking for?"

"I want ten or so that have already been broken. I don't know how to break one and I don't wanna learn. While you're at it, Doc, I need about a dozen good mules for plowing."

"All right, I'll keep my eyes open. It shouldn't be too hard to find some good ones."

When enough sperm had been collected, Doc left and Jake injected it in some of Josiah's pure white ewes. Careful to mark each donor and recipient, he was anxious to see if the results were what he expected. In about five months he would know.

The doctor was well compensated for the hours he spent at the two ranches. Jake was still fooling Josiah to pay for not only his own bill, but most of Jake's, too. Lucky for Jake, Josiah was still unaware of it.

A few weeks later, Doc found the animals Jake wanted at a nearby farm and rode to the J I to tell Jake.

"Jake, I think I've found the horses and mules you're looking for."

"Good, where are they?"

"Not too far from here. Bill Snow has them and is trying to sell most of his stock. I'll go with you to look at them if you want me to."

"Good, when do you want to go?"

"How 'bout right now?"

"Okay, Let's go."

After a short ride of about an hour, they reached the Snow farm. When Jake saw the animals, he decided to buy them and he and Doc drove them back to the J I ranch.

After bringing them to the ranch, he noticed one was particularly gentle, so he gave it to Raymond. He was almost ten years old, and he took this to mean his pa considered him to be a man.

***

Two weeks before Sue was due to give birth, she started having pains. No one knew what was wrong, but Leann sent for the midwife, anyway. It was a good thing. Sue's baby boy was born an hour after the midwife arrived.

Rushing home after receiving word that Sue was possibly in labor, Jake arrived a few minutes after she gave birth. He jumped off his horse and without tying it up ran into the house and into Sue's room.

"Jake, we have a little boy."

"I know, and I'm real proud of you, Sue."

"Jake, I'd like to name him Daniel, if you don't care. We can call him Danny."

"Then that's what we'll name him. Daniel Isaacson; that's a fine name."

"Sue, I'm so proud of you. Our little boy is beautiful," Raelyn said. "I'm gonna help you while you're recovering, so don't worry about a thing. I'll take care of anything you need. I feel almost like I just gave birth. This is wonderful."

"Thank you, Raelyn."

Jake was acting the part of the proud papa, and everyone seemed thrilled at the birth of Danny, with the possible exception of Leann.

"Jake looked at Leann. "We have a new baby boy. Isn't this great?

"Yeah, I guess."

"You don't act too happy about it."

With sad eyes she said, "Yeah, I'm happy.

It had been two years since she had been pregnant, and she was starting to get concerned she wouldn't conceive again.

And even though Raelyn considered Danny hers as much as Sue's, she still wanted to have a baby.

***

One day, as Jake was getting home from a ride with Raymond, a man named Ed McGee, from North Carolina, approached him and asked if he would sell the J I ranch. It took Jake completely by surprise and he said he would have to think about it.

Jake and Ed talked three more times, but they couldn't get together on a price, so he didn't sell it, but a seed had been planted. It stirred up the idea of going home. He thought he would put the ranch up for sale, and go back to Cana, whenever he sold it.

The next morning, Jake filled Josiah in on his decision. "Josiah, I don't know how to tell you what I'm going to tell you, except to just come out and say it. I've been doing a lot of thinking and have decided that me and my family are going to sell out and move to Cana."

Josiah was horrified at the thought of Jake leaving. He knew he would be losing his "cash cow," and also his two daughters.

He was much sorrier to lose Jake than his daughters. "What'll it take to keep you here, Jake? I'll do just about anything within reason to keep you from leaving. You and me have got a good thing going, and I hate to see you break that up."

Jake sensed something different in Josiah's demeanor. "You know how hard I've been working to build my own flocks and herds, and also how successful I've been at building yours. Even though my flocks and herds have increased, they are just a small fraction of what you have, but I'll stay if you'll do what I'm about to ask you to do."

"I want you to go through your flocks, and cull all the sheep that are not white and give them to me. Then give me any sheep that are born not white from this point forward. This way you will know all the white sheep are yours, and the imperfect ones are mine. Also, I would like for you to round up all the newborn calves and their mothers and give them to me. If you'll do those things, I'll stay and work for you."

"Okay, I'll agree on the sheep, but before I agree on the cows, tell me this. Does this apply to calves born on an ongoing basis?"

"No. It only applies to the calves on the ground now."

"Okay, Jake. I'll agree to it."

Jake looked right at Josiah, "You know that I keep my white sheep away from my colored ones. The sheep you give me, won't be put with the white ones. You are welcome to count my white sheep, and keep track of their newborn, so you'll know I'm not taking any of yours that I'm not supposed to have."

Josiah nodded and said, "Okay."

He turned and walked away from Jake to find Buck and the other two boys.

That very day, Josiah and his three sons culled the non-white sheep from his flock. They also rounded up the calves and mothers and drove the sheep and cattle to Jake's ranch.

This increased the amount of Jake's livestock by a large percentage, but Jake still had some ideas about how to get more from Josiah without Josiah knowing it. He found out earlier about artificial insemination, and how well it worked with his Icelandic sheep and Josiah's white sheep. This was typical of the way Jake thought. It didn't matter how good someone was to him, he would still screw them if he could. Since he made the agreement with Josiah, he decided not to put the ranch up for sale.

Jake stayed on and worked for Josiah, while he worked his own ranch, and as before, both ranches were thriving. The cattle herds were increasing, and each sheep breeding season was amazing. Jake was inseminating many of Josiah's white sheep with Icelandic sperm, so Jake's flock was growing at almost the same rate as Josiah's much larger flock. By using this method, Jake could keep his word to Josiah to not mix any of Josiah's white sheep with his. The flock at Jake's ranch was also growing by leaps and bounds. He and Josiah were getting richer and richer, and Jake kept having to buy more slaves.

CHAPTER ELEVEN

SEVEN YEARS LATER

The railroad became a reality, and it was going to pass through the edge of Jake's property. It would have missed him had he not bought the last tract. Now he owned over 5000 acres.

The negotiations for the right of way and the price had not taken place yet, but the railroad assured Jake he could continue growing grain right up almost to the tracks..

Jake continued to work both ranches, and both operations had really grown and flourished. His hard work surely hadn't hurt his fertility. Sue had had another little boy named Nat.

Leann still had not gotten pregnant, so Ina slept with Jake. She gave birth twice, naming her sons Gene and Ashton.

While Ina was pregnant with Ashton, Leann got pregnant. Ten months after Ashton was born, she had Jed. Eighteen months later, she had Ike, whom they named after Jake's dad. Then, twenty months later, she finally had a little girl. They named her Kitty.

Believe it or not, after all those years of trying, Raelyn got pregnant. When her time came she had a little boy whom they named Joseph, but called him Joey. Since Raelyn had always been Jake's favorite and Joey was hers, he was truly the apple of Jake's eye, and his favorite.

Raymond was almost eighteen, and quite a character. He was a very handsome young man, with an eye-stopping, muscular build. He didn't get out in public very often, but when he did, the girls couldn't take their eyes off him. He was a big help on the ranch, and spent a lot of time at the sheep pasture.

When Sue was not looking after Danny and Nat she spent most of her time there, pining away for a man. Raelyn still let her sleep with Jake occasionally, but not enough to keep her desire for the opposite sex satisfied.

One day, when no one was at the pasture except Sue and Raymond, the two of them were trying to get a thorn out of a lamb's foot. The thorn was in a hard to reach place and it caused the two to brush against each other repeatedly. They finally removed the thorn, but continued their contact. "Raymond, your hand brushed my chest."

"No it didn't"

"Yes it did and you did it on purpose."

"It must have been an accident. How did I do it, like this?", and he put his arms around her from the back and grabbed both breasts.

Sue turned to face Raymond and put her arms around him and they kissed. Hormones took over, and they found themselves on a mat on the floor of the shelter.

After that, it became natural for them, and they looked for every chance to be alone at the shelter. This went on until one day, Jake found out about it, and things really exploded. Jake actually looked at Sue as a wife, even though she wasn't. He saw her as an extension of Raelyn, and she was, of course, the mother of two of his children. This conduct could not go unpunished. At some point in the future, Raymond would feel Jake's wrath, but since women were subservient to men, it was unlikely anything would be done to Sue.

One day, a man named Gridley Watson came to see Jake, and after introducing himself, he said, Mr. Isaacson, I'm president of the Intercontinental Railroad. I've been in the area for a little while, checking on the progress of the surveying, and have noticed just how beautiful the J I Ranch is. I live in the East, but I want to establish two or three homes across the country to use when I travel. I also want to use them as vacation homes to get away from the "rat race" of big business life. Mr. Isaacson, would you be willing to sell the J I Ranch?"

He appeared to Jake to be really interested in it.

"I don't know. I'm gonna have to think about it and see what would be involved."

"I'm going to be in Mercer for another week, so you can more than likely find me at the rooming house in town. If I'm not there, you can leave word with the lady who owns it and I'll come back out here to see you. I hope you'll decide to sell because I really like what I see."

I'll think hard on it and make a decision before you leave to go back."

They shook hands and Mr. Watson left.

Wheels started turning in Jake's head as he tried to decide what would be the best thing for him to do.

That night, he sat down with his four women, and told them about Mr. Watson's visit. He didn't need their approval, but he wanted to know what they thought. He had learned life was so much better when the women were happy.

He had a strong desire to see his mother even though it had been twenty-one years since he last saw her. *Surely Eph has forgiven me by now. I wonder if Cana has changed much since I left.* He had several things to consider; and one of the main things was how much Mr. Watson was willing to pay for the ranch. He had to decide if he was going to sell all the livestock with the ranch, if he was going to sell the slaves with it, and a great many other things before making a commitment to Mr. Watson. He was hoping the women would give him their opinions and thereby help with the decision, but he knew the burden to make it was on him.

After a restless night, Jake went to the J-T to work. Still undecided about selling his ranch, he would consider things until the next day, and then go see Mr. Watson with his decision, whatever it might be.

Then, something pivotal happened to make his decision easier.

He stopped by the house to speak to Etta and have his usual cup of coffee, then went to the barn to see what Josiah had for him to do. Josiah wasn't there, but Buck, Ray, and Eddie were, and after some uncomfortable small talk, the three of them started making accusations that shocked and scared Jake. They had been jealous of him for a long time, and Josiah had kept things under control. Now, things were coming out in the open, and it was a very uncomfortable situation. Josiah wasn't there to defend him, and Jake feared for his safety because the boys were really getting worked up. They accused him of rigging the outcome of the sheep and cattle breeding in order to increase his herd and flock, while showing minimal results for Josiah's. They didn't know how he did it, but they knew he did. They said they knew, for sure, that he was catching some of their strays and putting his brand on them. They accused him of marrying their sisters just to get in good with their pa and take their place with him. They even accused him of trying to replace them in their mother's eyes. They were pulling out all stops, but the main thing to which they kept referring was how he was cheating their pa. They accused him of using strange breeding methods to his advantage and Josiah's disadvantage. Jake thought they were about ready to beat him up when Josiah came in. "What's going on?" then they hushed up.

"We've got to go."

Jake breathed a big sigh of relief, and warmly, but shakily welcomed Josiah, but Josiah's demeanor wasn't the same. Instead of smiling and talkative, he was very aloof, and said only what he had to say.

Jake was pretty sure the boys had been talking to their pa and had poisoned his mind against him. If Josiah's attitude had changed, it would be best to sell out and leave this part of the country.

When he got back to his ranch, he told the women what happened at the barn.

Leann said, "I think it would be best to leave."

"Me too," Raelyn said. "Pa never did have much to do with us, other than use us as shepherds."

Leann said. "Ever since we quit working at Pa's ranch, he hadn't hardly even spoke to us. I'll miss Mama, but we're mothers ourselves now, and our place is with you, Jake, so we're ready to leave."

Jake said, "Okay. I'll go to town tomorrow, and talk to Mr. Watson.

The next day, Jake rode into Mercer, to the little rooming house where he'd stayed when he first came to Josiah's, and where Mr. Watson was staying for the next few days. He went in and asked, "Is Mr. Gridley Watson here?"

The lady pointed over Jake's shoulder and said, "There he is in the dining room."

Jake turned around, and Mr. Watson saw him. "Come in and have a cup of coffee," so Jake joined him.

"Jake, is it all right if I call you Jake?"

"Jake, I hope you've come to tell me you're ready to sell me your ranch."

"Well, Mr. Watson, I've come to at least talk about it."

"Jake, I'd appreciate it if you'd call me Gridley. Mister is too formal and stiff"

"Okay, Gridley."

"What have you decided, Jake?"

"Nothing, up to this point." Jake wanted to find out what Gridley had in mind before he did too much talking.

"I need to know what you're wantin' to buy. Do you wanna buy the livestock, the slaves, and all the farm equipment, or just the ranch?"

"That depends on whether you want to sell it or not. I'll buy the farm with or without all the other."

Jake asked, "Do you own any slaves?"

"Yes I do. Why?"

"What kinda place do they stay in, and what kinda beds do they sleep in?"

Gridley seemed surprised at the questions. "My slaves live like most all slaves. They stay in a large rectangular building with a fireplace at each end for heat, and each man has a mat to sleep on."

Jake asked, "On the floor?"

"Yes."

"Well Gridley, if I sell you my ranch, I'll take my slaves with me. okay?"

Even with all of Jake's shortcomings, he didn't want to see people get mistreated. He had learned this from Josiah.

He may have made a mistake by telling Gridley he would take the slaves with him because at this point he had no idea where he was going, other than to Cana. He didn't know if he would be able to get another ranch, and he just committed to keeping over a hundred slaves. He thought if he couldn't get a fair sized ranch when they got to Cana, he might just give some, if not all of them, their freedom, but they would cross that bridge when they came to it.

Jake then asked Gridley, "If I say I'll sell my ranch to you, what are you prepared to pay for it?"

Gridley replied, "I don't normally do business this way, Jake, but you have something I want, and I'm prepared to pay for it. How many acres did you say you have?"

"Five thousand, two hundred."

"Jake, I know I'm crazy, but if you will sell me your ranch, I'll pay you five dollars an acre. How does that sound?"

Jake nearly swallowed his tongue. He was so shocked he couldn't say a word for several seconds.

Gridley asked again, "Does that sound okay, Jake?"

Jake cleared his throat. "Yeah, that sounds pretty good, but that price has to be for the land and buildings only. Any livestock has to be a separate deal, okay?"

"Okay," Gridley smiled. "Now Jake, I made you the offer for the land, so you tell me what you want for the livestock."

Jake was thinking big. "I'll take twenty dollars a head for the cattle and ten dollars for the sheep."

Gridley burst out laughing. "Come on, Jake. I may look dumb, but I'm not stupid. There aren't any cows or sheep in this country worth those prices." The smile left his face. "You must not want to sell them."

A slightly sheepish smirk covered Jake's face, "All right, I'll sell you the cattle for fifteen dollars, the white sheep for seven, and the Icelandic sheep for eight. But I'll want to pick out a few head of each to take with me to use as brood stock, in case I'm able to find a place, when I get to Cana."

"So you know where you're going from here?"

"Yeah, I'm going back home. I've been gone for twenty-one years, and I just hope my parents are still living."

Gridley was surprised. "What a coincidence. Our railroad is going to pass close to Cana, so maybe we'll see each other there sometime."

"That would be good."

Gridley got down to business once again. "Okay Jake, I'll take your farm and livestock, but here's the deal. I don't want to take possession for ninety days. I'll pay you half the amount this week, and the rest when I take possession. Since you're going to be in Cana, I can just bring the balance over there. Is that agreeable?"

"Yeah, that'll be okay."

"We'll need a lawyer, Jake. Do you have one, or should we use one of the railroad's lawyers?"

Jake was skeptical about using the railroad's lawyer. "I'll use one of our local lawyers."

Even though Jake didn't know any lawyers, he figured Doc Wells would because Doc knew just about everybody in the area.

They finished their business, and decided to have another cup of coffee.

"Jake, are you familiar with the Homestead Act?"

"No. What is that?"

"It might be a good way for you to get some free land when you get to Cana."

Jake's ears perked up at the words "free land".

"Can you tell me something about it? It sounds like something I would be interested in."

"The bill is in the United States Congress now. It's designed to encourage people to move to the West, and will give one hundred and sixty acres of land free to anyone who applied for it, providing the applicants are over twenty-one years old, head of a household, and a citizen, or applicant for citizenship."

Ideas started to spin like a top in Jake's head as he thought about how he could take advantage of that, and get much more than one hundred sixty acres. He would sit down and devise a plan when he got home.

When they finished their coffee, they shook hands and agreed to meet there in two days, and go together to the lawyer's office.

"By the way," Jake said, as they were parting, "I may not have time to get an accurate count of all the livestock before we meet again, but I know an approximate number. If I can't get all of them counted, will you be willing to use my estimate? Then we can settle up when the final payment is made. Can we do that?"

Gridley agreed, and they shook hands again.

Jake left the rooming house and went directly to Doctor Wells' office to see if Doc could give him the name of a lawyer. Luckily, he could.

"The lawyer's right here in Mercer. He's good, but I caution you to watch out for him. He has the reputation of being somewhat of a shyster, and one who doesn't mind bending the rules occasionally. What you need done should not be a problem.

Jake thought, *This guy is right up my alley.*

Doc said, "Come on, and I'll walk you down to his office and introduce you."

The lawyer's office was just a few doors down from Doc's. He looked up from the papers he was reading when they entered. Doc introduced him. "Jake, I'd like for you to meet Homer Green. Homer is a cousin of Ben Green, the man who sold you your farm."

They shook hands, and Jake told him, "I have a confidential matter I want to discuss with you."

Doc excused himself and left.

Homer pointed to the chair in front of the desk. "Won't you please sit down?"

Jake took the offered chair and explained what he wanted done.

The two-day deadline was not a problem, but he needed information about the sale price, terms, and any other specific details that should be included.

Jake filled him in on the details of the sale, which they discussed at length.

Finished with the business he came to do, Jake stood up and shook Homer's hand. "Thanks for your help. I might have some other business for you a little later on." He left then and headed back to the ranch.

Jake seemed to do some of his most constructive thinking while riding. His mind was consumed with thoughts of the Homestead Act, and how he could take advantage of it.

When he got home, Raelyn was the only one there. It was so hot the other three women had taken all the kids to the creek to cool off, but she wasn't feeling well. He told her about the sale, and she immediately started asking questions about when they would leave and where would they go. She peppered him with questions.

Jake answered a few, but would fill all the women in on what was going to happen, when the others returned. Raelyn was anxious about the move. She was pregnant again and was afraid of what a move might do to her.

Jake started thinking. *I can't just pull up stakes and lead approximately one hundred and forty people, fifteen or twenty cattle, and fifteen or twenty sheep to Cana. I have no idea where we'll go when we get there. I need to make a trip to Cana and buy some land before I can move my family, slaves, and livestock.*

Remembering the hairy experience he had on his way to Mercer, he felt it would be good to have someone with him.

When work was finished for the evening, he went to Thomas and Asa's cabin. Thomas answered Jake's knock. He stepped outside and Jake asked, "Where's Asa?"

"He's inside. Let me call him."

"Asa, Master Jake's here. Come out here."

When they were both outside, Jake told them, "Men, unless something happens, I'm going to Cana on Sunday and I'm gonna take you all with me. Since coloreds aren't allowed to stay in a hotel or rooming house, we'll have to camp every night while we're on the road and we'll need to take provisions with us. More than likely we'll be gone at least three weeks, maybe a month. Tomorrow, I want you to kill and butcher a cow and a sheep, and salt the meat down really good. That will be part of our provisions."

Excited, Thomas and Asa said, "Yes sir, Master Jake. Thank you, Master Jake."

Everybody had returned from the creek by the time Jake went back to the house. He sent the older kids outside to play, then, told the women what his plan was.

"Me and Thomas and Asa are leaving for Cana Sunday and will be gone three weeks, maybe more. We will all be leaving in about three months. Whatever you do, do not breathe a word of this to Josiah or any of the family. I don't want any of them to know about it until it happens."

"I'll tell Josiah that I got word my pa is really sick and I want to see him before he dies. If any of Josiah's family asks any questions, tell them Dewitt Bishop came through with a letter from Becky, and that is why I went home."

The next morning, Jake caught Josiah at the house. Etta poured him a cup of coffee as he sat down at the table. "Do you remember a few years ago when Dewitt Bishop came through from Cana?"

They nodded.

"Dewitt has been living in Tennessee, but went back to Cana to visit. Ma asked him to deliver a message on his way back to Tennessee. My pa is sick and wants to see me before he dies.

Etta looked at Jake with tears in her eyes. "We're sorry to hear that, Jake." Josiah nodded his agreement.

"Thanks. I would like to leave Sunday. I'll be back just as soon as I can, but will more than likely be gone at least three weeks, maybe a month. I'm taking Asa and Thomas because three people are safer than one."

Josiah agreed. "That's a good idea. Go and have a safe trip. Be sure to give your mother my love.

"I sure will."

***

Jake met Gridley at the rooming house at ten o'clock Thursday morning. They walked together to Homer Green's office, where they were to sign the papers for the sale of the J I Ranch.

"Morning, Homer. This is Gridley Watson."

"It's a pleasure to meet you, Homer."

"My pleasure, Gridley."

Homer handed each of then a copy and kept one for himself. "Please read your copy and note any corrections that might be necessary."

Jake and Gridley each read their copy carefully and neither found any errors.

Jake signed all three copies as seller, Gridley signed as buyer, and Homer signed as witness. Gridley had estimated how much money he would need for the transaction and had gone to the bank to withdraw the funds in gold, but the local bank didn't have enough. They telegraphed the bank in Dayton and had some gold sent over from there.

Fortunately, he got enough and weighed out thirty-one thousand, eight hundred and fifty dollars and handed it to Jake. Banks were having trouble with paper money, and everybody wanted to use gold, especially for land purchases.

Homer then explained, "The papers you have just signed will serve as the ninety-day note since everything is spelled out in the papers. Is that agreeable to you gentlemen?"

They agreed.

"Jake, how about meeting me at the railroad construction office in Sparta in ninety days? I can pay you the other half then. Will that work for you?"

"Yeah, I should be in Cana by then and Sparta's not too far. That'll work."

They shook hands. "How about some dinner, men? I'm buying."

"Sounds good to me," Jake said.

Homer said he had an appointment and couldn't, but thanked Gridley.

Jake and Gridley went to the rooming house and ate a big steak.

Finishing their dinner Jake said, "I've got to get back to the ranch."

"I sure am glad I got to know you, Jake. I look forward to seeing you again."

They shook hands, and Jake left for the ranch, feeling like a wealthy man.

***

The next day he worked half the day at the J-T and then went home to get ready for his trip. Each man would ride a horse and carry some things in the saddle bags, but they would also take a wagon.

The wagon was necessary in order to carry enough supplies for the three of them for three or four weeks, so he put the bed rolls and things like that in it. He pulled out a rifle and scabbard to carry on his horse, plus two more rifles that he would cover up, and put in the wagon, just in case they ran into trouble. The meat Thomas and Asa were processing, would take up most of the room in the wagon, so he couldn't put too much more into it.

The three would take turns driving the wagon with their horse tied behind.

The whole time he was working to get his stuff together, Raelyn was right with him. "I sure am gonna miss you, Jake. I wish I could go with you, but of course, I know I can't."

"I know, Rae. I wish you could go, too, but the road is no place for a woman unless she's with a group. Besides, you've got to stay here and look after my boy, Joey."

***

Jake's devious mind was always working, and he had conjured up an idea. He went to Mercer to talk to Homer Green about it. He cut straight to the chase when he sat down in Homer's office. "Homer, I wanna discuss the Homestead Act. Do you know much about it?

"What do you want to know?"

"I've got eleven sons and one hundred twenty-one men slaves. I want to know if there would be a way that all of them could be declared heads of households, and each get a hundred and sixty acres."

"If you can make this work, I'll pay you fifty cents an acre."

Homer answered, "I've never had anyone come to me with an idea like this. How did you come up with it?"

Jake said, "I don't know. The idea just came to me, and I thought it just might work. It won't be for any land around here. As you know, I'm leaving Mercer and going west. I just hope I'm going far enough west to qualify since that's the purpose of the Act. If I can get all my sons and men declared heads of household, it will amount to over twenty-one thousand acres. If you can make this happen, I'll pay you more than ten thousand dollars. I'm leaving Sunday for Cana and will be gone three or four weeks I hope you can have this worked out by the time I get back. Oh, I want the land somewhere near the Cana area."

"I'll see what I can do. I think maybe I can make it work."

Jake left with a good feeling about it and thought how great it would be if he could get several thousand acres for free.

He went back to the ranch and finished loading up. He wanted to get an early start in the morning. As he watched Asa and Thomas put their one change of clothes in the wagon. Jake thought, *Maybe I can buy them another pair of pants and a shirt when we get on down the road. Buffalo Creek would be a good place to do that.*

After all, they were traveling with him, and were more like friends than slaves. He bet they would appreciate some new clothes.

Thinking about Buffalo Creek, he wondered how Mrs. Perkins would feel about the three of them staying at her rooming house.... but didn't know if he had the courage to ask her. It would surely be better than sleeping on the ground. He might just go by to speak to Mrs. Perkins, and if somebody was staying there, he wouldn't say anything, but if there was nobody there, he might just ask her. She was a really nice lady and just might welcome three travelers overnight, even though two of them were colored.

After supper, the older children disappeared, going their own way. The younger children headed to the living room for one last hour of play, and the adult members of Jake's family sat around the kitchen table talking about his upcoming trip.

Leann asked, "Where are you gonna stay when you get there, Jake?"

"At my parents' house. Pa has a bunkhouse that I hope he'll let Asa and Thomas stay in."

"Does your mama look anything like Pa?" Raelyn asked.

"You know, I've never thought about that. Maybe a little. Before long, you can see for yourself."

Soon it was time for the smaller children to go to bed. The women gathered up the kids and took them upstairs. Jake remained seated at the table as he listened to the nighttime sounds his family made while preparing for bed.

Although not all the children were upstairs, Jake reflected on each of his twelve kids and realized how fortunate he was to have such a wonderful family.

Soon, three of the women called down to him, saying they were tired and going to go to bed.

Jake called back up, "Good night. I'll see you in the morning."

Only Raelyn had not said good night.

Jake was excited about the trip. He wasn't sleepy, but went to bed, anyway. Since Raelyn was depressed about him leaving for so long, he had invited her to sleep with him.

When she came to him, they lay in bed for a long time with their arms around each other. In low voices, each told how much they loved the other. Soon, snores and soft sniffles were the only sounds coming from the room.

Ina was up earlier than usual the next morning, so she could fix Jake's breakfast and pack a dinner for him.

Jake was up early, too. "Honey, fix some extra. I'm gonna bring Thomas and Asa up here to eat with me and they'll need a dinner, too. She looked at him oddly, then added more water to the gravy.

He went down to the slave cabins and knocked on the door of Asa and Thomas's cabin. When Asa answered, Jake said, "If you all haven't eat yet, come on up to my house and eat breakfast with me."

They gave each other a puzzled look, but did what Jake told them, following him back to the house. Inside, they took places at Jake's table and ate until they were full.

Jake and his two slaves left the kitchen and checked their gear and wagon one more time. Finding everything okay, they were getting ready to mount up, when the whole family came out to tell Jake goodbye. Raelyn had tears in her eyes, and when she put her arms around him, she didn't want to let go.

Trying to ignore the lengthy hug, Leann said, "Turn loose, Raelyn, I want to hug him, too."

She gave him a big hug and whispered in his ear, "Be careful and hurry back. I love you."

Ina and Sue gave him a "token" hug. They both loved Jake, but couldn't let Leann or Raelyn see too much emotion toward him. They were still slave girls.

But Jake didn't look on them as slaves any longer. They were the mothers of four of his children.

After the good-byes, the three men mounted up and started for Cana. Asa took the first turn driving the wagon. As they passed through Mercer, Jake stopped at Mr. Puckett's store and bought a big bag of hard candy, splitting it three ways when he went back outside.

"We ain't never had nobody treat us good like you, Master Jake," Asa said and Thomas added, "Thank you Master Jake. We sure do thank you." They were totally surprised, but gladly accepted the candy. Smiling at Jake, they each put several pieces in their pockets, then put the rest in the closest saddlebag. It was like traveling with a friend instead of a Master, and they were grateful for Jake's kindness.

By late afternoon they reached Buffalo Creek. Jake was glad the general store was still open. He went in, and a few minutes later he stuck his head out the door. "You two come in here." When they did, he said, "Each one of you pick out a pair of pants, two shirts, and a pair of boots."

This floored the two slaves.

"Master Jake, we ain't never had no new clothes before. Thank you so much." Thomas told him.

Asa asked Thomas, "Whatta ya reckon's goin' on?"

"I don't know, but let's enjoy it while we can."

After Asa and Thomas had made their selections, Jake paid for the purchases and they went to Mrs. Perkin's rooming house. Jake went in by himself, under the pretense he just wanted to say hello. It had been several years since he was through the town.

Mrs. Perkins remembered him, believe it or not, and gave him a cup of coffee that was just as good as he remembered. "Mrs. Perkins, it's been twenty-one years since I was through here and your coffee is just as good as it was then. I've remembered it all that time."

"Since I last saw you, I got into ranching and became pretty successful. Now, I'm getting ready to go back to where I came from."

Looking around, Jake concluded there were no other tenants in the house, so he mustered up his courage. Taking a deep breath, he asked, "Mrs. Perkins, would you consider letting me and my two colored "friends" have a room for the night."

Staring at him, she didn't answer for a minute. Then, she shook her head and said, "Well, I don't usually let colored people in here, but since I don't have anybody else and since you seem to be such a nice man, and they're friends of yours, I'm going to make an exception and let them stay. But you go outside and take them around to the back and come in that way."

Jake nodded his thanks. "My friends can stay in the same room."

"Okay."

Jake did as she had told him to do. When Asa and Thomas were in the house, he introduced them to Mrs. Perkins. They were extremely polite. They both thanked her for letting them stay there and assured her they wouldn't be any bother.

Mrs. Perkins wasn't quite as anxious as she was before. "Your room is number 202 and your friends are in 204."Their room was next to Jake's, and soon they were all settled.

When they were all in their rooms, Jake left and took the horses and wagon to the livery. For Mrs. Perkins' sake, he didn't want people to see two colored men coming or going from the rooming house.

After he finished with that, he went to the little café that was still there and took a seat at an empty table, and ordered three steaks and potatoes when the waitress appeared. "My friends and I are staying with Mrs. Perkins. I drew the short straw to come and get food. If it's okay with you, I'll bring the plates back after we've finished our supper."

"That'll be okay."

Fifteen minutes later, Jake paid for the dinners, took the wrapped up meals back to the rooming house, and enjoyed a big steak supper with his two "friends".

The next morning, Jake went back to the café and got three plates of ham, eggs, grits, and potatoes and brought them back to Mrs. Perkins'. Mrs. Perkins furnished the coffee, and the second day was off to a great start.

After breakfast, all three men thanked Mrs. Perkins for her hospitality and headed for the livery stable. The horses had already been fed and after checking the wagon, they were off.

Asa and Thomas didn't even look like themselves in their new clothes. They were fairly nice looking, as far as colored folks went. Their new clothes made them look like something other than common slaves.

It was what Jake wanted. He didn't want people to see him as a white man, and them as his two slaves. You could never tell who or what kind of people you might run into, and what their intentions might be.

Jake figured that by the end of the next day, they'd be pretty close to Cana, and he was starting to get anxious to see his mother, but scared of what Eph might do.

They rode all day, but still five or six miles away from Ike's place, they stopped and set up camp for another night.

Disappointed that they were still not in Cana, Jake was still excited, just knowing they were close to his mama. "Asa, how about picking up some of those dead limbs over there and build us a fire. Thomas, take this bucket down to that little creek and get some water and I'll get the food out of the wagon. This will probably be the last time we'll have to cook out 'til we head back to Mercer."

Over supper, Jake said, "Boys, we're in familiar in territory. I know this country and I think we'll be at my family's place before noon tomorrow."

When morning came, Jake did some extra primping as he prepared to see his mother, and made sure Asa and Thomas were in their new clothes and boots. He wanted everything to have a positive impact on his family.

"Men, I need to tell you something about my family. Many years ago I did something bad to my brother and had to leave home. I haven't been back since then," he told Asa and Thomas as they dismantled the camp. "I hope Eph has forgiven me while I've been gone, but just in case he hasn't, you two to be prepared to step in and defend me in the event something happens.

Remembering what his ma had said in her letter; that Eph had gotten married,Jake felt relief. He figured his brother was probably at his own place, instead of Ike's. He'd have to see Eph sooner or later, but would just as soon it would be later.

Finished breaking camp, they mounted up and rode toward Ike's. Landmarks were looking more familiar, and pretty soon the house was in sight.

One look was all it took. He spurred his horse into a gallop, reaching the house in a few minutes. He hopped off his horse, ran up on the porch and banged on the door.

A feminine voice from inside said, "Come in,"

Jake opened the door and saw his mother standing at the stove.

She turned at his entrance and saw him…. and couldn't say anything for a minute; then she shouted, "Jake, Jake, Jake. Is that you, Jake?"

"Yes Mama, it's me."

She ran to him. Putting her arms around him, she kissed and kissed and kissed him.

She looked up like she was looking to the heavens. "Lord, you can have me now because my baby boy has come home."

She hugged and kissed him again and again.

When she had her fill of hugs and kisses for the moment, Becky ran outside on the porch and yelled at the top of her voice, "Ike, Ike, come quick. Jake's here."

Ike came running. The first thing he saw was Asa and Thomas standing beside the wagon. He thought to himself, *That's not Jake.,*

He ignored them, continued on into the house, and there was Jake. They hugged, shook hands and hugged again. Then Ike asked, "What made you decide to come home, son?"

They sat around the table and Becky poured coffee while Jake explained why he was there. "Mama, Pa, after I went to Josiah's I was able to buy a few acres on the edge of his ranch, and due to a lot of real good luck, I was able to build a pretty large ranch. I found I had a knack for different kinds of breeding methods and was able to build up a large herd of cattle as well as a large flock of sheep. By doing all these things, I have become very successful."

"I'm selling my ranch in Mercer, and when the sale is finalized, I'm planning to move back to this area. The reason I'm here now is to try to find some land to buy, so I can move my family and workers in about three months."

"The two colored men outside are ranch hands I brought with me for security on the road."

"You might be interested to know that you have twelve grandchildren and another one on the way."

Becky squealed with excitement. "I can't wait to see 'em."

Jake felt he'd talked enough about himself, and asked, "What about Eph?"

Ike said, "He is living over in Bradon, on a farm he bought from Gerald Hall before Gerald died about four years ago. You remember, Jake. Gerald was the man who bought Eph's land from you before you left for Mercer."

"I remember him, Pa. It hurts, but I remember him. Did Eph ever get over it?"

Looking over at Becky, Ike said, "It took a long time, but he did. In fact, one time I heard him say he missed you, and would like to see you. It was hard on him. You hurt him bad, Jake, but he's over it now.

How long do you think you'll be here? If you have time, I'll send somebody over there tomorrow to tell him you're here."

"That would be fine, Pa.

When they finished talking, they went outside to walk around the place. Jake had forgotten Asa and Thomas were still outside and introduced them to Becky and Ike. Suddenly realizing they would need a place to sleep, Jake asked, "Pa can my men sleep in the bunkhouse? Will it bother any of your hands?"

"I don't think so, but I'll talk to 'em when they came in from the fields."

"Pa, is it okay if we put most of our stuff in the barn? We've also got some salted meat that needs to be put in the smokehouse. Is that okay?

"Son, you know it's okay. You don't need to ask about such things."

"Thanks, Pa."

"Thomas, Asa, you can unload the wagon now. Put my clothes up on the porch and I'll take 'em in later. Take the meat to the smokehouse and put the rest of the stuff in the barn. You can put your things inside the door of the bunkhouse until a little later."

Leaving them to their task, he, Becky and Ike walked around the farm. Jake was glad to see the place was pretty much the way he remembered it. He noticed the old target Eph had made and used to practice with his bow and arrows was still nailed to the wall on the shed.

"Remember how you could never get the hang of shooting a bow and arrow?"

Yeah, I remember and I remember how good Eph was, too. Does he still hunt a lot?"

"Not like he used to. He's too busy. Every now and then he'll bring me a mess of venison, but everybody is too busy anymore."

Walking back in the direction of the house, "Pa, do you know of any land for sale?"

"Yeah. There are quite a few farms for sale right now. A lot of families are going to California, to try to strike it rich in the gold fields."

"Do you have any suggestions?"

"How many acres do you want?"

"It depends on the price, but I would like to buy four or five thousand."

"Wow"

Ike thought for a minute and then said, "Here's a thought: Bob Merritt and Sam Evans have already gone, and their farms are for sale. They adjoin each other. Between the two, they make about six thousand acres. Is that too much?"

Jake shook his head and said, "Not if the price is right."

"I think it will be right because they have both been gone for a long time and really need to sell their places. I suggest you go to town in the morning and talk to banker Earl Marler."

When they reached the house, Ike's hands had come in from the fields. Ike went in to talk to them about Asa and Thomas and came out and said there was no problem.

Jake told the two they could stay there and to put their clothes where they were told.

The next morning, Jake went to the bank in Cana. Walking up to the teller's window, he asked to see Earl Marler and was pointed in the direction of the banker's desk behind a spindled half wall.

Mr. Marler was a nice looking, middle aged man. He was maybe six feet tall, medium build, and nearly bald. He stood and shook Jake's hand. "What can I do for you Mr., what did you say your name is?"

"Jake Isaacson, sir. I'm interested in the Merritt and Evans farms that might be for sale."

"Well have a seat and let's talk."

Jake sat in the chair in front of the banker's desk and listened as Mr. Marler told him that both farms were on the market for two dollars an acre, and the price included the houses and outbuildings. Jake wanted to look at them immediately.

"I've already sold my ranch in Mercer and I'm planning to move my family and workers here when I find some property to buy. Cana is my home and I'm anxious to get back here."

"Well I'm afraid it's going to be tomorrow before I can show you the farms. I'm going to be in meetings all afternoon."

"That'll be fine. I'll be back first thing in the morning."

They shook hands and Jake rode back to Ike's.

He told Ike about it and asked, "Do you know of any other places like those two, Pa?"

"I'm not sure about adjoining farms, but I know of some that are fairly close to each other."

"Pa, do you know anything about the free-range land that would be involved if people claimed some of it by using the Homestead Act? Do you know how close that land is to Cana?"

"I don't know, but Earl probably does. Ask him when you see him in the morning."

That afternoon, Eph came to see Jake, and while Jake was very uneasy, Eph acted like he was genuinely glad to see him. He hugged him, and didn't show any sign of hostility. "Why'd you come back, Jake? What are your plans now that you're here? What have you been doing for the last twenty-one years?"

He seemed genuinely interested in everything about Jake's life.

He was surprised to find out he had eleven nephews and a niece and said he was anxious to meet them. After Jake had answered all of Eph's questions, he asked Eph several about his life. He said he had married Maggie Thompson, and they had two sons and lived just outside Bradon.

While it was good to catch up, pretty soon they ran out of things to talk about, and an uncomfortable silence filled the room. After three or four minutes of staring at the floor or glancing at each other, Eph said, "I guess I had better be going."

Becky asked him to stay for supper, but he said he had to get back. Maggie and the boys were expecting him. He told Jake if he didn't get back before he had to leave, he would see him when he moved back to Cana.

CHAPTER TWELVE

Jake got up early and had coffee with his mother. While she fixed him a good breakfast, they did some more catching up before he left for town.

"Thanks for breakfast, Ma. I've gotta get goin'. I've got an appointment with Mr. Marler at the bank. I'll see you later."

When he got to town, Mr. Marler was ready and they immediately left the bank for the farms that were for sale.

On the way to the first one, Jake asked, "Mr. Marler, do you know of any others for sale?"

"Yes, I know of several for sale and I'll be glad to show them to you, if you want to see them."

"I might want to, but I want to see these two first."

When they arrived at the Evans farm, Jake walked around, looking at the buildings. The house was nice. The whole place reminded him very much of the Green Farm the first time he saw it.

They left the Evans farm and rode to the Merritt farm, which was equally as acceptable but different. The house on the Merritt farm was larger, but the Evans house was nicer. Both houses were plenty nice enough for Jake's family, but neither was large enough. Whichever house he chose to live in would have to be enlarged.

As Jake walked around the Merritt farm, he paid attention to the way the farms were laid out. A road ran right down the middle separating the two properties. Both property lines were smack in the middle of the road where they adjoined each other.. The Merritt farm had 2800 acres, and the Evans farm had 3600. Jake really did like both farms and told Mr. Marler he was interested in both places.

It was mid-afternoon by the time they returned to town and went directly to the bank. Sitting down in front of Mr. Marler's desk, Jake said "Earl, I hope it's okay if I call you Earl…I'll tell you what I'll do; I'll give each one of the owners a dollar and a half an acre for their farms."

Earl said, Jake, I've been authorized to drop the price to a dollar seventy-five an acre, but I'll have to wire Mr. Evans and Mr. Merritt with your offer to see if either or both will accept."

Jake nodded, "Go ahead and do it and let me know what they say."

Next, he wanted to know when Earl could show him some other

farms and asked several questions about the free-range land.

Earl had a wealth of information about everything Jake asked him, the most important being there were about three and a half million acres of free-range land in the area ripe for homesteaders.

Jake instantly thought, *If I can do a selling job on the right people, and pull a few strings, I can become owner of a large part of that land.* Large landowners were in the catbird's seat when it came to appropriating government lands, so the first thing to do was buy 10,000 acres to make himself a large landowner.

When Gridley Watson paid for the other half of the J I Ranch, Jake would have nearly $65,000. That would be enough to buy a huge amount of land, as well as several head of livestock, plus money left over to pad the pockets of some of the influential people with whom he would be dealing.

The next morning Earl showed him 8000 acres about four miles from the Sam Evans farm and then 2500 acres that bordered the Evans and Merritt farms.

As they were riding back toward town, Jake asked the price and Earl said, "They are priced the same as the Merritt and Evans farms."

"I'll make the same offer on these two; a dollar and a half per acre," Jake told him.

Earl frowned, "I can accept the offer for the 2500 acres, but I'll have to wire William Ewton, the man who owns the larger farm."

Jake sighed, "Okay, but I don't want the 2500 acres unless I can get the others."

"Earl do you know anything about livestock prices?"

"Yes I do."

"Well, if I get the farms, I will want to buy some cattle, sheep, horses, and hogs."

Earl said, "So many people are leaving for California and needing to sell just about all their belongings, you can get some really good buys on livestock. I know of several thousand head for sale at a good price right now, so maybe we can work some things out. Since the farmers had to leave their farms before they sold their stock, most of them left their animals, and hired people to check on them from time to time, hoping they would be sold before winter sets in, when they to have to be fed."

"I guess you noticed all the stock on the Evans and Merritt farms; they're all for sale."

Jake nodded. "I might consider making an offer if I get the farms."

If he bought the land, he would need several buildings to house his workers. His workers might be able to build what he needed, or he might have to hire carpenters, but either way, he would definitely need to buy some lumber.

"Earl, where do you recommend I buy lumber?"

"I can think of two. One is out on Mountain Creek road and the other one is fairly close to the Evans farm on Morrison Springs road. Either one of those would be fine.

"Jake, why don't you set up your own sawmill? You've got plenty of timber to choose from. Your farms are at least fifty percent in timber and maybe more than that."

Jake hadn't thought of it before, but after Earl made the sawmill suggestion, he thought to himself, *Why not? Why not go into the lumber business? There is a lot of money to be made there.*

"Earl, I've got to get back to Mercer. How long do you think it will be before you get answers to your wires?"

"I should hear within a couple of days. It's been two days since I wired Messrs. Evans and Merritt."

Jake hoped their answers would be there tomorrow, but he doubted if he would hear anything from Mr. Ewton by tomorrow, since Earl was only wiring him today to tell him about the offer.

Jake decided to wait and leave for home the day after tomorrow. Maybe he would know about all four farms by then.

"Earl, if you don't have the answers before I leave, wire me at the new Western Union office in Mercer. It will take me a week to get home, but I'll check with them when I get there."

***

Becky had planned a family get-together for Jake's last full day. Eph and Maggie and their two boys were coming. It was going to be good to have an old-fashioned get together with plenty of food. Becky had fried two chickens, made potato salad, and baked two pies… one apple and one cherry. Maggie brought a covered dish as well, so there was a lot of food. Nearly everybody ate so much, they didn't have room for the watermelon.

As they were getting ready for pie, Eph and one of his boys noticed a rider coming. Soon he was close enough to recognize Earl Marler. He dismounted and joined the group.

"I apologize for interrupting, folks, but I wanted to bring Jake some good news. I just got answers from all three landowners and they have all three accepted your offer. And they would like to sell you their livestock."

"They left the selling price on the stock up to me since they know I'll do my best to get a fair price for them."

Earl, I want to spend the rest of the day with my family. Since this news came up, I'll postpone leaving for one more day. I'll come to your office tomorrow if you can get the papers drawn up for the farms. We'll talk about the livestock prices when I get there."

"I think we can get the papers ready, and I'm pretty sure the livestock prices will be to your liking."

Becky interrupted and offered Earl a glass of cider, and he stayed for a little while, visiting with the family.

While they were visiting, Jake asked Earl, "What do you guess will be the asking price for the stock?"

"I think the cattle will probably be somewhere around ten dollars, the sheep, six, the horses, twenty, and the hogs, three."

"I'll think about it overnight and let you know in the morning, but they sound a little high to me."

"They're fair prices, Jake, but if you would be willing to buy all of them, then we can do a little dealing."

"It depends on how many head there are, but we'll see."

***

Earl had the papers ready when Jake arrived at the bank.

"Good morning, Jake."

"Good morning."

"Jake, the papers are ready, but before you sign, let's see if we can agree on livestock prices. If we can, I can have my secretary include addendums to include the livestock with the farms, and it will save a great deal of time and paperwork."

"I know what you told me yesterday, but here's what I'm prepared to do. You estimated there were two thousand cows, six hundred sheep, seventy-five horses, and sixty hogs between the four farms. Those figures sound a little low to me, but I'll buy all of them if you will let them go for seven-fifty a head for the cattle, four dollars for the sheep, twelve-fifty for the horses and one dollar for the hogs. If there are more, then I'll take whatever the amount, and I'll take all four farms."

"I have about twenty thousand dollars in gold with me, which is not enough to pay for everything, so you decide what you want to do. I'll pay cash for the four farms right now if I forget the livestock. I'd prefer to buy the farms and all the livestock and pay half right now and the balance in ninety days. I have sold my ranch to the owner of the Intercontinental Railroad and those are the terms I gave him. You know he is good for the money just as I am good for the money. You can make a note, and I'll sign it. You will still have the farms and livestock as collateral."

"I won't be taking over fully for about sixty days. If you accept the offer, I want your permission to send people in to build several cabins and barracks for my workers, so the buildings will be ready when we get here. I will probably have to come back to set things up before I move my family for good. What do you say? Do you need more time to think about it?"

Earl said, "No, Jake. I don't need any more time. I think you're beating these folks up pretty bad on their livestock, but since you're willing to take everything on all four farms, I will accept your offer on their behalf. The terms of half now and half in ninety days should not be a problem if you are willing to sign the note to my bank instead of the four landowners. I will advance the other half to them with your one-half down payment, then, you can just pay us. Will that work for you?"

"That'll work. Now how're we gonna reconcile the actual count of the animals?"

"I suggest that when you move, we make an actual count and settle up then."

"Sounds good to me."

"Let me get these numbers to my secretary."

Earl went to his outer office, and in a few minutes came back. "Jake, can you possibly wait until tomorrow morning to sign the papers? It doesn't look like my secretary is going to be able to complete everything before we close. I'm sorry."

"Aw man. I guess I'll have to. I just need to get started back to Mercer."

This was going to delay him for at least a half a day, but he was so happy with the coup he had made, he was more than willing to do it. This would also let him spend more time with his mother.

***

When Jake got to the bank right before dinner the next day, the papers were ready. Jake set the saddlebag he'd carried into the bank on the floor, signed the papers, and passed them back to Earl. He and his secretary signed as witnesses. Retrieving the bag of gold from the saddlebag, Jake handed it to Earl and watched as he weighed out eighteen thousand dollars in gold.

When they finished, they shook hands. Earl invited Jake to dinner and he accepted. He thought *I've lost so much time already another half hour won't make any difference.* They went to the café across from the bank and had a big steak and potato and were stuffed by the time they finished. Earl said, "I feel like going back to the bank and take a nap."

"Me too, but I can't. I've got to go back to Pa's farm to say good-bye, and get my men and start for Mercer."

They wouldn't get too far before dark, but he didn't think they could wait any longer to leave.

***

The next week's travel was uneventful, and Jake found he enjoyed traveling with Asa and Thomas. They had become like buddies, and Jake was looking forward to more time associating with them.

When they got within sight of the house at the ranch, some of the kids saw them coming. They started screaming, "Pa, Pa, Mama, here comes Pa," and ran toward them. They stopped and the kids hopped on the wagon. Jake pulled Joey up in his lap.

When they got to the house, Jake told Asa and Thomas he would see them in the morning.

All the women happened to be at the house when Jake arrived and they ran out in the yard to greet him. Three slaves had been left to look after the sheep.

Then he had a warm homecoming with his big family. He couldn't help but notice Sue and Raymond were right together, and if one moved, the other would move to the same place. Nothing out of place happened, but it looked suspicious to Jake, especially after what had happened between the two previously.

After a few minutes the homecoming began to wind down. The smaller children went back to play and the older kids excused themselves. The women hung around while Jake filled them in on what happened on his trip.

It had been a long trip and Jake was tired. It was Leann's night to sleep with him, but he begged off, saying he thought he would just go to bed and go to sleep, alone.

The three weeks absence had put Jake behind in his work. Several heifers on his and Josiah's farms needed to be bred. But before he took care of that, he went to town to see if Homer Green had found a way for Jake to take claim of lands using the Homestead

Act.

Homer was excited to see him. "Hi, Jake. Boy, am I glad to see you. Did ya have a good trip?

"Yeah, it was fine. Have you been able to do anything about what I asked you to look into before I left?"

Homer, ignoring the question, excitedly asked Jake, "Jake, have you ever heard of the Midwest Ordinance?"

Jake frowned. He didn't like his question being ignored. "No."

"Well, the ordinance was passed back in seventeen eighty-seven to establish a system for creating new states out of the public domain as the population moved westward. The largest groups of federal land recipients are the states, but railroads, war veterans and large entrepreneurs have also been able to get large grants. The United States has already given away around two hundred eighty-eight million acres and still has millions available for *the right people;* those who can show they can improve the land and set up vast acreages of agriculture."

"My brother, Jess, is the administrator of the ordinance, and can make things happen. He was here visiting one of our sick relatives while you were gone and I talked to him about it. He wants to talk to you. I thought what he said was scary. But if you're prepared to take a big chance, you could become the owner of more land than you ever dreamed of."

"The way Jess talked, things might can be worked out for you to become the owner of around eight hundred and fifty thousand acres. If you want our help, you would have to "sell off" about a hundred thousand acres to Jess and me, but you would net around seven hundred and fifty thousand acres. That will be the second largest ranch in the country. What do you think?"

Jake was flabbergasted. "What do I have to do?"

"Nothing. Just be prepared to sign some papers and swear to certain things. The government is very lax in handling these land deals so there's not much risk. But there is some, and you need to know it. If we get caught, it could mean prison time, but Jess is comfortable with his plan and with his knowledge of these things. If he's comfortable, then I'm comfortable. Are you in, Jake?"

"I don't know. Why are you fellows interested in me getting all that land and you all only getting a small part? That doesn't make much sense to me."

Homer looked at Jake anxiously, "Because I'm a lawyer and Jess is a government worker. You are already a large landowner, so it's much easier for you to get a huge land grant than it is for either one of us. Besides, we don't want or need such a large amount of land. So whatta you say?"

Jake shook his head in wonder. "I'm gonna have to think about it. I would like to have the land, but I sure don't want to go to jail. What does your brother think the chances of success are?"

"He thinks they are one hundred percent or else he wouldn't be willing to put his neck on the line. He has almost complete control over who gets what from the ordinance. With almost three hundred million acres available, who is going to notice a few hundred thousand? I think you would be a fool to pass up this deal. It can set you up for life, and the beauty of it is you can get the land over in the area where you're going to move. The fact of the matter is, just about the whole area where you're going can be yours. You can own more land than some states have, so you need to think hard on this Jake. I need to let Jess know, so he can get started on making it happen. It will take about six months, so the sooner you make up your mind, the better."

Jake nodded. "I'll let you know tomorrow."

He stayed up nearly all night thinking about the deal.

When Raelyn realized he was up, she went in the front room and sat down beside him. "Are you all right?"

"Yeah. I just have some things to think about."

She didn't ask any more questions. She just sat with him, keeping him company.

***

The next morning he went to Homer's office. "Homer, go ahead and have Jess get started, but I'm not going to sign any letters of intent or anything else for that matter If the deal works, then naturally I'll sign whatever has to be signed for the transfer of the property, but until then, I will deny knowing anything is being done on my behalf by anybody connected to the Midwest Ordinance."

"That will be okay. Go ahead with your move and whatever else you have planned. If and when the deal works out, Jess and I will come to Cana to finalize it, or you can come back to Mercer, whichever is best at that time."

CHAPTER THIRTEEN

Jake tried to dismiss the ordinance deal from his mind and concentrate on catching up with his work at the J I Ranch and the J-T. He met with Josiah the day after his return. "Morning."

Etta poured Jake a cup of coffee and left the men to talk.

"I got back yesterday. Pa's some better and the doctor says he might still live for a good while, so I decided to come back to work and to my family. I'll probably wanna go back in about a month or so. Is something wrong, Josiah?"

"No. Why?"

"You don't act like yourself. I just thought there might be something wrong."

Things were still strained between him, and Josiah and the boys, but Etta was still her old sweet self toward him. He loved Etta and was going to miss her.

On his second day back at work at the J-T, Josiah's boys cornered him in the barn the way they did before, accusing him of everything under the sun.

"Jake, why'd you come back?"

"I work here. Why?"

Ray said, "We don't want you here. Ever since you came, you've been a problem for us."

"What kind of problem?"

"Well, first of all, you came riding in here full of all kinds of crazy ideas and turned our pa's head," Buck told him. Then you married our sisters. Who, but a crazy man would marry two women? You've tried to influence our ma and pa to favor you over us, and you've stole Pa's cattle."

"Whatta ya mean, stole his cattle?"

"You've caught some of our strays and put your brand on 'em."

"I have not."

"Well, we're a fixin' to give you a lesson," and all three crowded around Jake with clenched fists.

Josiah happened in again just like before, and Jake decided he had had enough.

"Josiah, I quit. Your boys have made it impossible for me to work here any longer. They've accused me of everything under the sun and there's no telling what they've told you. I've worked my butt off for you and you've got to admit that I've been a big part of making the J-T the success it has become over the last twenty years. Buck, Ray, and Eddie have been jealous of me ever since I got here and you're the only the reason they haven't run me off before. But now it looks like they've influenced you by things they've told you, so I'm leaving."

"I've got to say, Josiah, I owe you a lot for taking me in when I needed your help and I won't forget it and I thank you for that. I hate to leave you, but I just can't work under these conditions any longer."

"The J I Ranch has gotten pretty big now, so it's time I start spending all my time over there anyway. You're welcome to come over and see your girls and your grandchildren whenever you want to, but I won't be back here."

Stunned, Josiah asked, "Are you sure you know what you're doing, Jake?"

"Yeah I'm sure. From now on, you can get your three smart boys to build your herd for you. I wish you luck, Josiah, but I'm through."

Ray nudged Buck and all three smirked.

Walking away, Jake turned and asked Josiah, "By the way, do you want to buy the river house back?"

"No, I don't want it."

"Okay, I'll try to sell it to somebody else". And with that, Jake jumped on his horse and left.

On his way down the long driveway, he ran into Doc Wells. "Hi, Doc."

"Hi, Jake. I was just coming to see you."

"Doc, I can't talk right now. I just quit the J-T. A lot has been going on and I just felt I had to leave, but I hope that won't make any difference about me and you working together. Please feel free to come to my ranch whenever you want to and hopefully you'll keep on helping me with the breeding methods we've been working on."

"I consider you a good friend, Doc, and I don't want my leaving Josiah to change things between me and you."

"I don't know what happened here, but nothing will change between us. Will it be all right if I come to your place tomorrow?"

"It sure will."

When Jake got home, he got the women together and told them he quit the J-T. Flabbergasted, nobody said anything for a minute, then Raelyn broke the silence. "I don't blame you. I'm glad you quit. Pa never did appreciate all the things you did over there. I'm glad you quit."

Leann said, "Me too."

Then Ina made a fresh pot of coffee, and they sat around talking about what would happen next.

"I'm gonna have to go back to Cana in a couple of weeks to start building some places for the slaves to live and I'll probably take ten or twelve men with me. You know, the way time is flying, it's only a little over two months 'til we have to be off the ranch."

"What if you wait 'til we move to build the cabins and things? Couldn't they camp out while their places are being built?" asked Raelyn. "I don't want you to have to leave us again."

"No, I've gotta get that done before we move. By the time I go back and get the cabins and barracks built, and get back here, it's gonna be almost time to move."

"I wanna caution you again to not let Josiah, Etta, or anyone else know what we're getting ready to do – not even Doc."

A week later, Jake thought he should go ahead and take a crew back to Cana and build the quarters for the slaves. In the interest of time, he decided to buy the lumber when he got there instead of milling it himself. That would speed things up.

He sent for Asa and Thomas. "Boys, I want you to pick out eight trustworthy men that you feel can do the amount of building in Cana that we have to do and they need to be ready to leave in two days."

"In the meantime, I want you to get some help and kill, butcher and salt three cows and six sheep and wrap them for traveling."

The men nodded and turned to leave.

"Wait a minute,"

"Sir?"

"We've got to take enough provisions to last about a month for eleven hungry men, so you had better kill about five cows and six sheep."

"Yes sir,"

"Tell the men to bring whatever they have to make into a bedroll. We'll take two wagons, but there won't be room for mattresses; pillows maybe, but no mattresses."

"This trip will be a little different from the last one. A group of ten colored men and one white man will probably make people a little uncomfortable when they see us, so we'll stay clear of towns and just mind our own business."

Thomas and Asa went back to their area where they would pick the men and get started on the slaughtering.

***

Jake sent Leann and Ina into town the next day to see if Mr. Puckett had enough clothes to outfit the eight extra slaves. He wanted to buy them the same things he bought Asa and Thomas on their first trip-- a pair of pants, two shirts, and a pair of boots.

Leann was also to buy some extra skillets and two extra coffee pots, all the fatback Mr. Puckett had, plus coffee, flour, and other foodstuffs Jake and the slaves would need for the trip.

The women bought nearly all the men's clothing Mr. Puckett had in the store, but it wasn't enough. They were short two pairs of boots and six shirts. At least all eight slaves would have at least one new shirt and only two would be without new boots.

Jake would try to find the other stuff on the way or maybe in Cana when they got there.

He left the women to unload the wagon and went to the barn alone. Taking the box of gold out from where it was hidden he guessed he got about ten thousand dollars to buy lumber, some tools, roof tin, and other things they would need to construct the buildings. It wasn't enough to build as many cabins and barracks that would be needed, but enough to build shelters for all the slaves temporarily.

After taking out what he thought he needed, he put the rest back in its' hiding place and returned to the house.

As Jake was trying to plan the trip to be as efficient as possible, he thought, *When I get to Cana, I'll go by my parents' place to see if they might know of a lady who I can hire to come and cook for us while we're there. That'll eliminate taking one or two men off the job to cook for the others. Too, I wanna see if Pa'll loan me some tools and maybe an extra wagon that I can haul lumber in. This'll save me from having to buy all the tools we'll need. I'll take 'em back when I finish with them.*

***

Raelyn accepted Jake's second trip to Cana better than the first one, but she still hated to see him go. She was now over seven months pregnant and wasn't feeling well at all. She hoped the baby would be born before she had to leave for Cana. In her condition, a long trip on the road would be really hard.

The whole family was up to see Jake and the men off.

Raymond stood as tall as he could. "Can I go with you Pa?"

"Son, I wish I could take you. You'd be a big help, but I need for you to stay here and be the man in charge while I'm gone." Jake knew Raymond was capable of running the ranch, and felt comfortable leaving him in charge.

"Raymond, while I'm gone I want you to keep your distance from Sue, okay?"

Raymond's face turned bright red. He didn't say anything and just looked at the ground.

The good-byes were brief. Jake hugged and kissed Leann and Raelyn, but only gave Sue and Ina a peck on the cheek. He said, "I'll see ya," and they were off. Two slaves drove the wagons and everyone else was on horseback.

Although there were eleven men on this trip, they made pretty good time. Having made the trip once already, Jake knew where to camp overnight. He chose the same places except for the night spent in Buffalo Creek. This time they camped outside of town.

After a week on the road, they arrived in Cana. As Jake had planned, they stopped at Ike's first.

Becky was outside, washing clothes and saw the group coming. She yelled at Ike to come there, and they greeted Jake and his group when they reached the house. Jake hugged them and left Asa and Thomas in charge, while he and his parents went into the house. It had been so many years since Jake lived in Cana, he had forgotten just about everything he knew about the area, so he had to ask his parents for suggestions about different things.

"Pa, I've got to buy a lot of lumber. Where do you suggest I go to get it?"

"Well, I guess the closest place would be Jennings sawmill. It's not too far from here and it's on the way to the Ewton farm."

"Thanks Pa. I'll go by there."

"Ma, we're going to need someone to do the cooking. Do you know where I might find somebody?"

"Ike said, Ma, what would you think about Nancy?"

"Yeah, she would be perfect if she would do it. Since her husband died I'm sure she needs to make some extra money. I'll go see her when I finish washing."

"If she's interested, Ma, bring her with you when you come out."

"Ma, we can't stay. We've got to get out to the Ewton farm and get started. There's a tremendous amount to do and a short time to do it. I'll see you after a while when you come out."

He kissed her and he and his group left for the Ewton farm, stopping at the Jennings sawmill on the way. He bought the first load of lumber there, and continued on to the farm.

That afternoon Becky rode out to the farm, taking Nancy with her. Jake really liked her. She seemed to be a very nice lady. Her appearance was that of a typical farm wife, used to hard work all her life.

"Miz Nancy, how 'bout looking over what food we have and the utensils and pans and so forth. When you figure out what you need, I'll give you some money and you can go to town and stock up. I'll have Asa go with you."

"I don't know, Jake. Maybe I'd better go by myself."

Realizing Nancy was hesitant about riding with a colored man, Becky said, "Come on Nancy, I'll go with you."

"Jake it looks like you need a good supply of firewood for the stove, if Nancy's goin' to do much cookin'.

"Ma, while you're in town, will you look for two pairs of boots and six shirts for some of my men? Here's some money."

"I'll see if I can find 'em."

Becky, Nancy, and Asa left for town, and Jake got one of the men busy splitting firewood.

The rest of the afternoon was spent unloading the wagons and deciding where the cabins would be built. Becky, Nancy, and Asa hadn't returned yet, so Jake's crew piled into a wagon, and he drove them down to a large creek at the foot of the hill from the site. They loaded it up with good-sized stones to serve as footings to keep the buildings off the ground. Jake pitched right in and loaded rocks just like the others and a couple of the men changed their attitudes toward him. By the time they hauled the wagon back up the hill, and to the farm, Becky and the others had returned.

Nancy went right to work fixing supper. When it was ready, she told Jake and he yelled for everybody to come and eat. Nancy and Jake ate at the kitchen table, while the slaves ate where ever they could find a spot to sit. Most ate outside on the ground, but a few sat on the floor in the house.

The meal was delicious, and all the men stuffed themselves.

Becky found the shirts and boots Jake had asked for, and after supper, he presented the new boots to the two slaves who'd gone without on the trip. Finally, he was able to give all the slaves a second shirt.

Work was finished for the day. Jake found Nancy in the kitchen finishing up the dishes.

"Miz Nancy, if you're ready to go home, I'll send somebody to escort you."

"If I can have my own private room, I'm prepared to stay if you want me to."

"That'll be real good."

"But I want your promise that I won't be bothered by any of your men."

"I promise. You'll be safe here."

"Would you mind having someone get my bag off the wagon?"

Jake got it himself and showed her to a room right off the kitchen that would be a good room for her. She seemed pleased with it.

Jake's room was also on the first floor. Asa and Thomas brought their bedrolls in and chose corners on the first floor to be at the beck and call of their Master.

Since there were no slave quarters yet, Jake directed the men to get their bedrolls and find spots on the floor upstairs where they would sleep for the next week or two. They needed to be a distance from Nancy.

Jake had decided it would be easier to build barracks than cabins. They were simple rectangular structures with no interior walls and would go up in a hurry. Until more could be built, four barracks buildings would hold up to twelve men each. For the married people, five two-bedroom cabins would be built. By doubling up, two families could live in one cabin until others were built. All this would be a temporary fix until he could move his family and finish the rest of the buildings they would need.

As in all small towns, word spread fast that Jake Isaacson had bought the Ewton farm as well as three others, and that he had a crew building houses for his workers. By mid-morning the next day, people started coming out to see what was going on. Some knew Jake when he lived there as a boy, and some were just curious. Some even picked up hammers and saws and pitched in to help.

Almost from the start they fell behind schedule. Jake should have known inexperienced help couldn't do the job as well as experienced help. He realized rather quickly if the temporary quarters were going to be finished, he needed experienced help.

He laid out instructions to Asa and Thomas and went into town to see if he could find some help.

Jake went to the bank to see Earl Marler. Earl's secretary recognized him and led him to Earl's desk. "Hi, Jake. What can I do for you?"

"Earl, I'm in a bind. I brought a group of men out here to build quarters for my workers and since they're all inexperienced, I'm afraid we're not going to be able to do the building, and I've got to get back to Mercer. Do you know of any good carpenters I can hire?"

"I know some men who can probably help you. I'll go see if I can find them and Jake, you should put out the word at the General Store because sooner or later, everybody in town comes through there."

"Earl, can I leave some money with you to pay wages if I'm able to find the men I need to do the building?"

"I'll be happy to pay the men."

The next morning, seven men came to the farm, ready to go to work. All of them were experienced carpenters.

Now he thought maybe they could even get enough built to be more than temporary quarters. Maybe they could get all the buildings done that he needed, but if not, they could come close. He hired all seven. They all had brought their own tools, which helped. He told them if they knew anybody else who wanted a job, to have them come out. He thought if he could find eight or ten more men, he would only stay for maybe one more week because his ten men weren't getting that much done.

The next day four more came and the following day only one, but the day after that, there were six more, making the total number of experienced hands eighteen.

Jake had been watching the men as they worked, and picked out a man named Harold and made him foreman. Perhaps in his mid-fifties, Harold exhibited leadership, and seemed to know more about building than the others. He told Jake he had been a carpenter most of his life, and was happy to help out as foreman.

When the men were returning to work after dinner, Jake called to Harold, "Wait up, Harold. I want to talk to you."

Harold stopped, turned, and walked toward Jake, meeting him half-way. "Whatta ya need, Boss?"

"We need to spend some time planning out the work to be done, and you need to know quite a few things about the job."

"I'm gonna be leaving tomorrow. If you're able to find more men and want to hire 'em, do it. I don't care how many you hire as long as you have all the buildings finished in six weeks. That's when me and my people will be here for good."

"Do you know Earl Marler at the bank?"

"Yes sir."

"Well, Earl has the money for your all's pay. When you need lumber, go to Jennings' mill. Earl has the money for that, too. In fact, Earl has the money for everything you will need. If you need anything else, you can go see my pa, Ike Isaacson, and he will help you."

"This is going to be a really large project. Do you think you can handle it?"

"Yes sir. I've done large projects over in Sparta, and I know I can do this."

"Okay, so let's look at what is to be done. I want a total of six barracks buildings that will hold sixteen men, and here are the measurements. I want twelve, two-bedroom cabins and twelve, one-bedroom cabins, and here are the drawings and the dimensions for them. I may need more later, but those will be my needs when we first get back. Do you still think you can do this?

"Yes sir. I won't let you down."

When Jake finished with Harold, he told Asa and Thomas, "You guys look after my men, and I'll see ya later. I wanna go see my parents and tell them good-bye. We'll be leaving in the morning. Have all the men get their stuff together, and be ready to travel after breakfast tomorrow morning."

Then he remembered to tell Nancy that he and his men were leaving after breakfast the next morning, and she would not be needed after that. She was disappointed but understood. He said he would ask his mama to take her home.

The trip from Cana to Mercer was tiring, but everyone was glad to be going back home, even though it was only for five to six weeks.

They'd traveled in only one wagon, leaving the other one for the carpenters to haul lumber and tin and other building supplies.

With all the things on Jake's mind, he forgot he would need his second wagon to haul wool after the sheep shearing, which would take place before his family and workers left the ranch for good. It had taken his wagons plus Josiah's to haul the wool to market the year before.

No longer having access to Josiah's wagons, he would buy another one. His ranch in Cana was much larger, and he would soon need to haul more stuff.

Jake rode into town and went straight to the carriage shop. He might need more than one extra wagon, but right now, he would only buy one. While he was in town, he went ahead and bought the supplies they would need for the shearing.

After a quick dinner with Doc, he tied his horse to the back of the wagon and drove home, hoping he hadn't forgotten anything.

***

The platforms were set up and ready for the shearing to start on Monday. Josiah and Miles weren't there with their expertise, but they wouldn't be in Cana either. It felt strange without them. Jake would handle it on his own. After all, he'd been a part of the shearing for several years, and he thought he knew everything he needed to know in order to get it done.

For the next two weeks Jake's workers sheared sheep as fast as they could and finally finished. Jake tied up the bales with paper twine the way he had been taught, and he kept up with the shearers most of the time. It was a back-breaking job, and he was spent when he finished. Every night, as soon as supper was over, he went to bed and went to sleep.

This didn't please his wives, but he was simply too tired for anything else. Raelyn did sleep with him three or four times, just to be near him. She slipped into his bed after he was asleep. Eight months pregnant, she just wanted to be close to him.

The last sheep was sheared on the afternoon of the sixteenth day, and Jake's wagons were loaded up with wool.

It took more trips than usual to get all the wool to market. Finally finished up after three and a half days of hauling. Jake was anxious to see how well he did. While the market cashiers were figuring up what they owed him, he went to visit with Doc Wells. Jake still didn't tell him he was leaving Mercer.

The visit was a short one. Jake went back to the market to collect for his wool, and he was well pleased with the amount. He ran into Josiah and they spoke, and made a little small talk, but the strain was still there. Josiah's boys were with him, but they didn't speak. They just glared at Jake

That's all right with him. In two more weeks, he wouldn't be around to worry about them.

***

Jake thought of himself as an efficient planner, but it dawned on him a few days later the move of his family and workers had not been planned very well. *How in the world did I expect to move everything and everybody on two wagons?*

He would have to buy more wagons, maybe as many as five or six. When moving nearly a hundred and fifty people, something had to carry them.

Jake was being very careful not to let anyone know he and his family were leaving, and he worried the wagon man would think it strange to buy so many wagons so he made up a story.

The next day he rode to town and to the carriage shop. "Howdy,

John."

"Hi, Jake. What brings you back so soon?"

"John, I've decided to get in the lumber business. Whatta you think about that?"

"That's probably a good idea. You've got plenty of timber on your place that's not doing you any good."

"I know, and that's why I've got to have more wagons—probably five. I need 'em to carry logs from the woods to the sawmill to the lumberyard."

That seemed feasible and practical to John, and no questions were asked. Nothing seemed out of the ordinary. He only had four in stock, but three more would be finished within the week, so Jake bought the four and told him he would send drivers to pick them up and might be back for the others.

Over the next week, Jake and some of his men cut out the cattle they would take for breeding stock and picked out ten white and ten Icelandic sheep they would take for the same purpose.

They also culled forty cows and thirty sheep to be slaughtered for the long trip to Cana. There would have to be at least forty cows and thirty sheep because when figuring twenty-one meals for a hundred and fifty people, a huge amount of food would be needed.

Leann and Ina killed several chickens and went ahead and fried them. They would stay good for quite a while if they were cooked. Raelyn and Sue baked a large amount of bread and biscuits. Those would stay good for a long while, and with fatback, streaked meat, or bacon would make a good snack along the way if the women or children got hungry between meals. A good bit of flour, sugar, potatoes, coffee, and other foodstuffs were packed in the wagons. The day before leaving, vegetables that would not spoil or rot before eaten would be pulled from the garden.

Jake wanted to take more than they would need rather than come up short. With only a few towns between Mercer and Cana it would be hard to buy food on the road. Also, they might not reach Cana in a week.

If they had food left over, they would eat it when they got to the farm in Cana. If not, they would go to the store and buy more.

At the end of the week Jake rode into town at mid-morning to see Homer Green. As he walked in Homer's office, Homer looked up. "Morning, Jake. How you doin?"

"Fine. Listen, we got ready early, so I decided that we would go ahead and leave, but I needed to see you first. When Gridley Watson comes to pay for the balance of the ranch, tell him I will be in Cana at what's known as the Ewton farm."

"Tell him there is plenty of grass, so the cattle and sheep will be okay, but if he's more than another week or two coming, you might need to hire someone to go out to the ranch to be sure the sheep haven't scattered."

"I also wanted to touch base with you about the government land deal and ask if you ever tried to find out about the Homestead Act and my one hundred thirty-four *heads of household.*

"I haven't done anything about it since this thing with Jess came up, but I will still check into it if you want me to. I just assumed you wouldn't want to take a chance on that if you got all that land through the ordinance."

"I still want you to pursue the Homestead Act possibilities. That could mean a lot of free land, and that would be in addition to the ordinance land."

"Talking about the ordinance land, I want to remind you, Homer, that I don't want my name connected to it in any way until it's ready to finalize. Okay?"

"Okay Jake."

Next, he walked up the street to see Doc. Over cups of coffee, they visited for a little while, and then Jake eased into the subject of his leaving the Mercer area for Cana.

"Doc, I've been wanting to tell you something for a pretty good while, but just couldn't take the chance that something might slip out before it should. This will probably come as a shock, but I've sold the ranch and we're all moving to Cana."

"I've already bought land over there, in fact, I have more already than Josiah has, and he's been building his all his life. The land is really, really beautiful and Doc, I'll be able to see my parents whenever I want to, and they can be a part of seeing their grandchildren grow up. Since things went sour with Josiah, I think I've made the right decision, and the girls think so, too."

"You probably have, Jake, and I wish you the best of luck. I'm disappointed, though, that you felt you couldn't trust me enough to tell me before now. You should have known I would not have told anybody, especially Josiah."

"Doc, I feel real bad about that, but I just couldn't take the chance that something might slip out by mistake somewhere. It was just too important to keep it secret. Josiah still doesn't know, and won't until we're already gone"

"Doc, there's something in the works right now that is really big, and if it comes to pass, I'm going to need at least one full-time vet and I would like to have you if you think you would be interested."

"Well, let's stay in touch, and we'll talk about it."

"Let's do that." Jake shook Doc's hand, gave him a hug, told him good-bye, and left.

***

As luck would have it, soon after Jake got home, a stranger rode up and asked if this was the J I Ranch and asked if Mr. Isaacson was there.

Lewis ran into the house and yelled, "Pa, there's a man outside who wants to see you."

Jake went outside and introduced himself.

The man introduced himself as Tom Beavers. "I'm Mr. Gridley Watson's property manager. I came by to see when Mr. Watson can take over ownership of the ranch."

"Tomorrow. We're planning to leave early in the morning. I told Homer Green, our lawyer, that we are leaving and told Homer to get in touch with Gridley to tell him where I will be. You probably know, he still owes for half the ranch."

"Yes sir, I know that and Mr. Watson wanted me to tell you that he will meet you at the Intercontinental Railroad office in Sparta two weeks from today to pay you what he owes you."

"That will be fine." Then, they went over things he should know about the livestock.

When they finished, Tom said, "I'll spend the night in town tonight."

"Okay. I assure you we will be gone first thing in the morning."

Tom wished him good luck and left.

***

After dinner, Leann and Raelyn put on their happy faces and made a trip to the J-BAR-T to see their mother. It was probably the last time they would see her.

Etta was so glad to see them. She fixed her usual feast for supper and wouldn't hear of the girls leaving until they had eaten. "Besides, your pa and brothers will want to see you, You haven't been here in a good while."

So Leann and Raelyn stayed and ate supper and visited a little bit with Josiah.

The brothers got up and left just as soon as they ate, but the girls enjoyed being with their parents, especially their mother. After a little while, Josiah stood up. "I'll be leaving you ladies to your conversation. I have to pack for a trip to Dayton."

The girls stood and hugged him, each one saying, "Goodbye, Pa."

About dusk, they told Etta they had to go home, and they both hugged her with an extra amount of squeezing and both had tears in their eyes. Etta said, "I don't understand why this goodbye is different from any other."

And Raelyn said, "It must be because I'm about ready to deliver. Leann said, "I guess I'm just so glad to see you since it's been so long." and those explanations seemed to satisfy Etta.

CHAPTER FOURTEEN

Since Tom Beavers had said Gridley would meet him in two weeks, Jake decided to not take the ten cows to Cana. Fearing they would slow down the caravan and he wouldn't be in Cana in time to meet Gridley, he had Thomas select ten more Icelandic sheep. *Having all sheep should speed us up a little.*

Jake felt pretty safe with the slaves, but just in case, the last thing he packed was his rifle. It went in his horse scabbard. He armed Asa and Thomas as well, confident he could count on them if anything happened.

When that was done, they were ready to go.

***

Almost from the start, Jake wished he had not planned to leave until after Raelyn's baby was born. The road was rough, and the ride in a wagon especially so. She was having a hard time. Leann and Sue tried to make her as comfortable as possible, but they were fighting a losing battle.

Late in the afternoon they came to a river surrounded by plenty of grass for the animals to graze. They stopped and the men set up camp. Some gathered wood for a fire, while others watered the stock and brought water to the camp.

The women immediately started preparing supper.

The attitudes of the slaves were a pleasant surprise. They acted like regular people out for an adventure. The men were getting along really well with Jake and the boys, and the women were acting like good friends to his women. Things worked out pretty well the first night.

***

After three days, Jake figured they were a half day behind schedule. Considering so many were inexperienced travelers and about a third of those had to walk, it was good time.

Raelyn was holding her own and getting more miserable every mile they went, but she was a trooper and tried not to complain. Jake gave her as much attention as he could.

On the fourth night, as they were getting ready to eat, somebody yelled, "Riders coming."

"Asa, Thomas, grab your rifles. Come over here and stand with me."

In a few minutes he could make out the riders.; Josiah and his sons. They rode into camp as if they were ready to whip everybody.

Jake stood tall with his rifle pointed to the ground. "What's your problem, Josiah?"

He dismounted. "I don't appreciate your leaving the way you did. First, you didn't tell anybody you were leaving. Second, you have taken my two daughters and all my grandchildren. And third, you stole all the formulas and writings having to do with the methods you used when breeding my livestock, and I want them back."

The whole time Josiah was talking, his three sons looked as though they were just itching for a fight.

"You just calm down, Josiah. I didn't steal anything from you. Most of the techniques I used in the breeding are stored in my head. Very little was written down, and what was written down was left in the barn where I used it. Your sons have been so intent on running me off, I wouldn't be surprised if they stole it. As far as your daughters and grandchildren are concerned, they all wanted to leave because of the way your boys and later, you, treated me."

"I'll say this Josiah, and I've said this before; you were good to me for several years, and you took me in when I needed help, and I'll always be grateful to you for that, but now, thanks to your boys, things are different. We are on our way to Cana, and we plan to settle there. If you and Etta should ever want to come see your daughters and grandchildren, you can come, but you will have to have a better attitude."

"Now, get out of our camp. We're getting ready to eat." Jake turned his back on Josiah and walked over to where his wives were and started eating supper.

Josiah and the boys were shocked at the way Jake had stood up to them and had no immediate response. After a minute or so, Josiah asked sheepishly, "Jake, would you mind if I say goodbye to my daughters and grandchildren?"

"Yeah, that will be all right."

He hugged and kissed not only Raelyn and Leann, but Ina and Sue as well. All four had been raised together, and Josiah looked at all four as daughters. When he finished saying goodbye, he mounted up. Spurring their horses, Josiah and his sons galloped away.

About two hours before setting up camp for the fifth time, Raelyn started having terrific pains. Jake stopped the caravan and called for one of the slave women to come up there and help Raelyn. She knew a little about being a midwife.

While Raelyn labored, Jake put Asa in charge and camp was set up. Food was prepared and stock taken care of. Jake paced nervously away from Raelyn's wagon.

Along with the sort-of midwife slave, Leann stayed with Raelyn, giving help and support until the baby was born. "Jake you have another son."

Jake raced to the wagon. The trip had taken a toll on Raelyn, and she was in a bad way. He cradled her in his arms.

She looked up at him. "My sweet Jake, I'm so proud to be able to give you another son. I would like to name him Ben, if that's all right with you. I wish I could go on to Cana with you, but I'm afraid I won't be able to. Just remember how much I love you."

Then she closed her eyes and stopped breathing.

Jake was brokenhearted. He held her and cried. Big tears ran down his face. The others in the camp left Jake alone with his grief.

Raelyn's boy, Joey, took his mother's death hard, clinging to Ina. Those closest to Raelyn; Leann, Ina, Sue and all the other children were torn up over Raelyn's death. As best they could, the women comforted the children while grieving for their lost sister.

Thinking little Benny was hungry, Leann tried to nurse him, but had no milk. *How in the world are we goin' to feed this child without milk?*

As if on cue, Asa approached Leann. "Miss Leann, can I talk to you?"

"Yes Asa, what is it?"

"Miss Leann, do you know one of our women named Carrie?"

"Yeah, I know who she is. Why?"

"Well Miss Leann, Carrie lost a baby giving it birth three or four weeks ago. She's worried 'bout how you're gonna feed the new one since his ma died. She said if you want her to, she will nurse it 'til we get to someplace where they got milk."

"Thank you, Asa. Let me talk to Jake about it."

Leann talked to Jake and he emphatically said "No. I'm not gonna have a colored woman nursing my child."

"But Jake, if you don't, what are you going to do? Without milk, Benny will die."

Jake paused and thought for several seconds. "Well, I don't guess we have any choice. Tell Carrie she can nurse him."

Asa called for Carrie and she came to Leann's wagon and nursed the baby. Benny took to her like she was his mama.

But it was tough country, and they couldn't do anything but forge ahead. Two of the men dug a grave, Jake wrapped Raelyn's body in a blanket, and she was buried. Jake found a large stone with rounded edges in a nearby creek and stood it up at the head of the grave, vowing to come back sometime, to visit her.

When they resumed their trek, Carrie rode in the wagon with Leann and the baby and nursed him every time her got hungry. Jake had seen Carrie before. He bought her. But until she began nursing his child, he hadn't noticed how desirable she was.

***

They reached the Ewton farm on the ninth day and let out a loud collective cheer. More to celebrate was that all the buildings were finished.

The very first thing Jake did was assign the slaves to their quarters, so they could put up their stuff as it was unloaded.

Next, Jake and Leann went into the house and assigned bedrooms. Ina and Sue each got their own. As the oldest, Raymond got his own room, but the others had to share.

Once those assignments were finished, the wagons were unloaded and things put away. Supper was a small cold affair, and everyone turned in shortly thereafter, exhausted from the trip.

The next morning Jake took Leann and all thirteen children to see Becky and Ike. Leann carried little Ben.

When they first got there, Jake lined the children up according to age. "Tell Grandma and Grandpa your name and how old you are. Raymond, you start."

The kids did as Jake told them and it was a wonderful gathering. Ike and Becky were so happy to meet Jake's family and Jake was happy they were all together. Being a genius in the kitchen, Becky managed to feed his family and the visit continued around the table. Still tired from the long trip. Several children started getting silly. Jake soaked up the laughter and happiness. He was still mourning for Raelyn, but his family was helping make it easier to accept.

After a day of frivolity with his family, Jake knew it was time to get down to business. He went to the bank the next morning to see how things stood in regard to settling up on the four farms and the materials and wages for the carpenters who built the buildings. "Hi, Earl. I'm back."

"Good to see you Jake. Are you here for good now?"

"Yep, I'm here for good. Earl, the reason I came in is to tell you that I'm to meet Gridley Watson in Sparta in three days to collect the balance due on my Mercer ranch. I might want to deposit some of that money in your bank."

"Thank you Jake. I welcome that idea, and I would very much like to continue working with you."

"Before we settle up on the four farms we need to get an actual head count of the livestock. I think it will probably take at least two days, and I'd like to get it done as soon as possible so we can finalize these four transactions."

"Look, I've got four sons old enough to help, and if there are six of us, it might not take as long."

"I agree", Earl said. "I'm tied up the rest of today, but if you and your boys want to go ahead and start counting, I'll take your word for the accuracy if you'll guarantee it. I'll be able to help tomorrow."

"All right. That's what we'll do."

They settled up on the money for the construction, and Jake went back to the farm. He called Raymond, Peter, Lewis and Joel together. "After dinner you four will be going with me to start counting the livestock. Raymond, take Joel with you and start counting on the Ewton farm and I'll take Peter and Lewis and go to the Freeland farm." The smaller farm and fewer head would give Peter and Lewis good experience on how to count stock.

They all came in at suppertime, hootin' and hollerin'. The four boys had counted stock for the first time and were feeling exuberant. In their pa's eyes they were grown up enough to do what he called *honest to goodness* business work.

Supper was a noisy affair as each boy had a story to tell.

Jake had decided that when all four farms were his, he would name it the J I Ranch, the same as he did in Mercer. Instead of 5500 acres, he would have 16,000, and that was a pretty big ranch. If things worked out on the Homestead Act, he could more than double that acreage. If by chance the ordinance thing worked out, his acreage would increase by fifty times or more.

With the extra hand, the livestock count was finished the next afternoon and Jake followed Earl back to the bank. His secretary started working on the papers as soon as she received the numbers that would finalize the sale of the four farms which would become the J I Ranch.

"Earl, I'm supposed to meet Gridley Watson in two days at the railroad office in Sparta to get the money for my Mercer ranch, and I'll come back the day after that to settle up with you."

"That'll be fine, Jake. So tell me what your plans are for all this land." They spent the rest of the day brainstorming on the future of the J I Ranch.

All went as planned. Gridley paid Jake, and Jake paid Earl, but Jake had spent most of his money on the farms. He needed quite a number of things to get his new ranch started and little cash with which to buy them.

However, he had seven hundred and twelve head of sheep on his new ranch. Shearing them and selling the wool would give him some instant cash. It wouldn't be a staggering amount, but enough to buy quite a few things.

The thought had been planted in his mind earlier, and he decided to go into the lumber business, and let Raymond and Peter run it. He would spend some of the wool money on a large mill saw and several crosscut saws to get started. Lewis, Joel, and Danny were old enough to start helping, so he would put them to work at the sawmill with Raymond and Peter. It could prove to be a good cash crop, especially with winter just around the corner.

Too late to plant much, Jake had most of his slaves plowing and planting winter grain crops as food for his animals. They also planted turnips, collards, and other things that would provide food during the winter. All in all, things were off to a good start at their new home, and the future really looked bright.

***

Everything six-year-old Joey did and said was perfect in Jake's eyes, but he was beginning to be a little irritating to his brothers. Joey was so obviously Jake's favorite, even the boys who were grown, or almost grown had a big problem with it.

Jake bought Joey a gentle little horse and took him nearly everywhere he went. The other kids couldn't understand why their pa wouldn't take them to the places he took Joey. Leann and Sue and Ina couldn't understand why he showed so much partially to Joey and not to any of their children.

This began to be a problem within the whole family.

Seven months later

While Jake was branding cattle one day, a rider came galloping up with a message from the telegraph office. It was from Homer Green.

Everything worked out STOP Come to Mercer immediately STOP Please reply STOP.

The message nearly scared the life out of Jake. After several shaky moments, he reasoned if Jess had it worked out, then it must be worked out.

Jake turned the telegram over and wrote *Return one week STOP Secure housing for 3 men Stop.* He handed the paper to the messenger. "Wire this back to Mr. Homer Green."

The man galloped off, and Jake hightailed it to the house. He sent Nat to find Asa and Thomas, and he had them come to the house. Jake paced as he waited.

When the men knocked on the door, Jake opened it and hauled them inside. "We're going to Mercer tomorrow. Come here and have breakfast with me in the morning. We'll leave from here. Now go get ready."

"Yes sir, Master Jake," they answered at the same time, then turned and hustled to their quarters to pack.

They weren't the only ones hustling. Jake moved madly from one place to another taking meat from the smokehouse and potatoes left over from the trip to Cana. He sent Danny to the store in town to buy several slabs of streaked meat and bacon. He wanted to take a bunch of eggs, but couldn't figure out a way to carry them without all of them breaking since they would be carrying everything on a couple packhorses. He sent word to Thomas for a couple slave women to make a good many biscuits, and he had Ina make several as well. Streaked meat and biscuits with their coffee would make a mighty fine breakfast.

While he was getting his stuff together, Leann came into the house and noticed all the foodstuffs packed up. "Going somewhere?"

"Yeah. I've got to go to Mercer in the morning. There's some business I have to do with Homer Green."

"How long will you be gone?"

"I'll only be there one day, so just as long as it takes to get there and back plus that day. I'll tell you all about it when I get back."

***

As usual, he carried his rifle and gave one to Asa and Thomas just in case they ran into trouble. They'd left the house right after breakfast and made good time. By riding late and starting early every day, they got to Mercer a whole day sooner than Jake expected. He didn't know where Homer lived, so he couldn't see him until the next day at his office, but he did go by Doc Wells' and visited with him for a little while. Asa and Thomas waited outside.

When they got ready to leave, Jake stood to leave. "It was good to see you, Doc."

"Where y' all staying?"

"We're gonna camp just outside of town."

"Nonsense. You're gonna stay right here."

"But Doc, I've got Asa and Thomas with me."

"So what? They're welcome, too."

"That's mighty nice, Doc. If you're sure it's not too much trouble, we'll stay."

Doc was brave, letting two colored men stay at his house. What would the town folks say?

***

The next morning Jake was at Homer's office bright and early. He wanted to get their business done, so he could get started back to Cana.

When Homer came in, he had a big smile on his face. "Good morning, King Jake."

"What do you mean? Why did you call me king?"

Homer grinned. "Because as soon as you sign some papers, you will own a kingdom."

"Are you sure?"

"Jess had sent the papers by special messenger the day I sent you the telegram, and the letter he enclosed gave detailed instructions on just what to do. The deal is pretty much *cut and dried*.

"Jess signed everywhere he was required to sign, and has an 'X' in the places where you are to sign. Everything has been approved from Jess on up the line; now it's just a matter of signing the papers."

The contract showed that the government was awarding a grant of 1330 sections to Mr. Jacob Isaacson to be used for the development of agricultural homesteads. A section was 640 acres.

Before Homer would let Jake sign, he showed him two contracts showing that Jake was *selling* eighty sections to Homer Green and eighty sections to Jess Green—51,200 acres apiece. After *selling* the land, Jake was left with 1170 sections or 748,880 acres. Homer was right; that was a kingdom.

Jake didn't know until Homer told him that 1170 sections was 1170 square miles or roughly thirty-four miles in one direction and thirty-five miles in the other direction. That was a huge land acquisition.

Jake was overwhelmed. "Do you have a map or something to show the boundaries of the property?"

"I do. Jess sent it with the papers, and he marked in red the one hundred sixty sections that you *sold* us."

"Jake, you now own the largest ranch in this part of the country, and it should make you very rich, if you work it properly. You're going to need a great many people to work it, and more than likely you will have to buy more slaves. It's good you have twelve sons. As they get older, they can be a real asset to your operation. I know your first love is animal husbandry, and you can just go crazy with that. I suggest you contact a land-use expert to get advice on the different kinds of crops you will want to produce."

They talked until dinnertime and then went to the café and had something to eat. After dinner, they went back to Homer's office, so Jake could get his papers.

"Good luck, Jake. I don't guess you want me to pursue the Homestead Act now, do you?"

"Why not? We may as well see how far we can go. Just don't take any chances. Stay in touch, and you're welcome in Cana anytime. See ya later."

From Homer's office, Jake went straight to Doc's where he started speaking the minute Doc opened the door. "Doc, do you remember when I came to say goodbye before I went to Cana, and told you that something really big might happen, and if it did, I would be needing a full time Veterinarian? Well, it happened, and I'm definitely going to need one. You said we would talk about it, so I'm here to talk."

Doc was surprised and didn't know how to immediately respond, but managed to ask Jake inside to tell him about it. Settling into chairs at the table, Jake began. "Well, first of all, when I moved to Cana, I was able to buy almost seventeen thousand acres and over three thousand head of livestock. That alone is more than Josiah owns after nearly a lifetime of work."

"Now, the reason I came to Mercer on this trip was to sign off on a huge land grant I was able to get that consists of more than seven hundred thousand acres. Actually, when you add my Cana land to this land grant, I now own almost eight hundred thousand acres. I'm totally overwhelmed by it and don't have any idea how to go about organizing an operation this big. I know I'm going to need at least two vets and maybe more working full time."

"I want to increase the cattle herd to maybe fifty thousand head, the sheep to maybe ten thousand head with a good portion of those being Icelandics, and Doc, I want to start raising horses. I need a month or so to get my feet on the ground, but I'm going to have to start finding people within a couple of months. If you think you might be interested, then I won't look for a vet. I think I'll need at least two, so if you come with me, you can hire your assistant."

"Jake, this sounds very interesting, but as you know, I've been in Mercer for a long time and it would be hard to leave, but let me think about it. I've never been to Cana and have wanted to go for a long time, so let me have a coupla weeks to think it over, and I'll come to your place in Cana with my answer. I'm not saying I will come to work for you, but I'll come to Cana and give you my answer, yes or no. Is that okay with you?"

Jake nodded. "You bet it is. The family will be glad to see you. I don't guess you know it, but Raelyn died in childbirth on the way to Cana when we were moving and I sure do miss her."

"I'm sure sorry to hear that, Jake. She was a fine young woman."

"Are my two traveling companions out back? I need to get them and get on the road. There's so much to be done. Think hard about this, Doc. I would sure like to be working with you again. I'll see you in Cana." And with that, Jake went around to the back and got Asa and Thomas, and they started toward home.

The two slaves noticed that Jake was in an unusually good mood, but didn't think it proper to ask why.

As they traveled farther away from Mercer, Jake told them he'd had some very good luck, and when they got back home, they were going to have a big celebration. They hurried and made it home in six days.

***

Jake gave everybody the next day off for a big celebration. Three hogs and a calf were butchered and barbequed over an open fire. Jake's whole household;family and slaves participated. During the festivities, Jake had Raymond pull a wagon to the middle of the gathering and he got on it and whistled to get everybody's attention. When they got quiet, he told them about the land acquisition, and tried to explain just how big the ranch was now.

He told them there would be many changes, and he would be adding quite a few more people. Things were so up in the air at this point, and he hadn't decided just how things would be yet, but asked everyone to cooperate, and if they did a good job, they would be rewarded. That's about all he said, then they got back to eating and having a good time.

Jake jumped down and signaled to Asa and Thomas to join him at the wagon. "You two wait here after everybody leaves. I want to talk to you."

In a couple hours the crowd started to thin out, and when everyone had gone, Jake sat Asa and Thomas down under the big sycamore.

"Fellas, now that the ranch has gotten so big, I'm going to need a great deal of help in running it, and I hope I can count on you both to help me. You were the first slaves I ever bought, remember? From the start I always tried to treat you good and show you respect. Do you agree with that?"

"Yes sir, Master Jake. You sure did," they said in unison.

"You remember our first trip from Mercer to Cana? I didn't know what to expect from either of you, but you both proved to be trustworthy gentlemen and I started to look at you as friends instead of slaves."

"Thank you for that Master Jake", Thomas said.

"Now here's the reason I want to talk to you men. I have been thinking about this for a pretty good while, and I came to this decision while we were on the last trip to Mercer. As of this minute, you are both free men. I'm giving you your freedom."

The two were shocked. Neither could speak, but managed to give high fives to each other. Jake went on.

"This means you are free to leave the ranch whenever you want to, but I have a proposition for you, and you should listen carefully to it."

"We are going to have to buy two or three hundred more slaves to work the ranch, and I would like for you two to be in charge of them. The ranch is about thirty-five miles in each direction, so the work force will be spread out, meaning you two will no longer be together. I may have to get a couple more people to look after the slaves because it will be really hard for just two of you to supervise people on that much land. If you feel that any of your friends, who we already have, can be foremen, tell me, and I'll consider them for jobs just like yours. I probably won't give them their freedom, at least not yet, but I would like to talk to them"

"There's another thing; I think I can pull some strings and get you a homestead parcel. When we decide where you will be working and if you will want to do it, you can go off the edge of my land and find some land that you like and if it's free-range, I may be able to get each of you one hundred and sixty acres that will be yours free and clear. It may be at least a month before we can make these things work because of all there is to do to get organized, but I assure you, these things will happen."

"Finally, if you decide to stay with me, you will be paid a fair wage for your labor."

"Also, I know neither of you has a woman and will have a hard time finding one of your kind in this part of the country, so what if I go to the sale and find one for each of you, buy her, and give her her freedom, so she can marry you. Are you interested?"

"Yes sir, Master Jake, I sure am," Asa said.

Thomas said, "Me too."

Jake looked at each man. "Okay, then it's a deal?"

Both men said, "Yes sir," and couldn't thank him enough.

"One more thing; you don't have to call me Master anymore, okay?"

All three just grinned.

***

At the bank the next morning, Jake told Earl about the land grant. "With all this additional land I'm going to need many things. I'm land rich and cash poor at the moment. Would something around eight hundred thousand acres stand good as collateral if I need to borrow some money?"

Earl was amazed at Jake's good fortune and began to think of Jake as a very good client. "Of course, how much do you think you will need?"

"I don't have any idea, but I know I'm going to need quite a bit. I have to buy at least two to three hundred more slaves to start with. Plus wagons, plows, mules and just about everything anyone would need to run a farm, only this one is a hundred times bigger than the average farm. We're going to have to build several more buildings, and I'll need the names of the carpenters who built the ones we have."

Earl squirmed in his chair a little. "Jake, of course I'll do what I can, but you may be talking about more money than our bank has. We may have to bring in another bank and maybe two to meet your requirements."

"That will be okay and rather than give me all that money, just give me a bank letter of credit that would allow me to buy things as I need them and pay as I go along."

"Sounds good. I'm going to ride over to Sparta and Bradon to see if I can get their banks involved."

"Earl, do you know where I might find a land-use expert to advise on what crops to raise and how much of each."

"As a matter of fact, there's such a man in Bradon. If you want to ride over there with me tomorrow, I'll welcome the company."

"Good deal. I'll see ya in the morning."

He went back to the ranch and gathered Leann, Ina, Sue, and his six oldest boys together to start outlining what would be needed from each one of them. Looking on it as an adventure, each was willing to do whatever was necessary.

***

Jake sat down with the land-use man and showed him the drawing of his ranch.

The man was very impressed. He suggested Jake divide his ranch into five sections. Turn so many acres over to the livestock for pasture, so many acres be used to grow cash crops like cotton, rice, sorghum, wheat and so many for orchards. Much more acreage would be needed for food crops for the livestock; corn, milo, and soybeans and good grass would be needed for grazing.

It might take more than five hundred people to plant that much acreage with that many crops. It would be a huge undertaking. He gave Jake a target number to shoot for, but wasn't sure if even that many would be enough.

Jake knew what he had to do now, and needed to get started. He thanked the land-use man and went to meet Earl.

CHAPTER FIFTEEN

Ten years later

Doc Wells had moved to the ranch shortly after Jake had moved his family, and was in charge of three other veterinarians. In addition, Doc and each vet had an assistant. Jake was not a veterinarian, but he knew quite a bit about it, so he counted himself as the fifth vet. When he was working with the animals, Leann was his assistant.

Since the time Jake had promoted Asa and Thomas to foremen, they'd urged him to promote two other slaves. Joshua and Michael had proved to be very valuable to the operation. Jake had split the ranch into four sections and each foreman was responsible for the slaves in a section. Asa had the northwest; Thomas, the northeast; Joshua had the southeast; and Michael, the southwest.

As Jake had promised, he'd secured one hundred and sixty acres of land apiece for Asa and Thomas to homestead. He went to the sale and found a woman for Asa right away. It took a long time to find one for Thomas, but finally, he found the right one. After watching and working with Joshua and Michael, he later went and found a woman for each of them. All four of Jake's foremen had families of their own, and they all loved Jake dearly.

***

Jake's children weren't children anymore. Ben, the youngest, was now fifteen years old, and Raymond, the old man of the group was twenty-eight. They all worked for their pa, except for Joey, and he didn't do much of anything except be his pa's pet. His official duties were to act as messenger between Jake and the sons, but there wasn't much of that to do.

To fill up his time, he would keep his eyes open for things his brothers would do wrong and then go tell his pa and get the wrongdoer in trouble. The spoiled brat was always bragging about how much better he could do things and what their pa was going to do for him or give him.

One day, Joey's brothers were in the south pasture. He rode out to where they were, riding in a brand new saddle with silver ornaments on it. He reined in and proudly said, "Look what Pa bought me."

Pete asked, "Why did Pa buy it for you?"

Joey shrugged. "I guess because I deserve it."

Another time he told his brothers he was sure their pa was going to turn the whole ranch over to him when he got a little older, and then he would be their boss.

He was such a thorn in their flesh, sometimes they just wanted to do away with him.

They were fed up with it. When the brothers came in from the fields one evening, they went to the barn to put up their horses and were talking among themselves about what to do with *that spoiled, little shit, Joey*. Pete and Lewis, the two meanest in the bunch, said they wanted to kill him.

Raymond, the oldest and one of only two or three voices of reason, said, "No, that would break Pa's heart,"

The others overruled him, and went about making plans to kill Joey when he rode out to where they were, sometime within the next few days. If he didn't ride out soon, they would find him somewhere and take care of him.

Joey was in one of the stalls, rubbing down his horse and heard them talking. He knelt down so they wouldn't see him and listened to everything they said. Scared to death, he decided to run away. He stayed in the barn until after his brothers went into the house.

As soon as the coast was clear, Joey raced out of the barn and went directly to where Jake was. Being near his Pa would be safe.

Nobody seemed to notice Joey was in deep thought during supper. With so many people at the table, his lack of conversation wasn't remarked by anyone. In his room after supper, he got his things ready to run away from home. Into his saddlebag he packed some clothes and the little money Jake had given him. After everybody else went to bed, he packed up some leftovers from supper, took the bag to the barn, and put it next to his saddle. His plan was to leave the next morning.

Sleep came hard. He tossed and turned most of the night, finally getting up way before daylight. In the dark, he dressed quickly and slipped down the stairs quietly so as not to wake anyone. Hurrying to the barn to saddle up, his horse nickered a welcome. Glad to see his saddlebag right where he left it, Joey slung the saddle over the horse and tightened the cinch. He picked up the saddlebag, hung it over the horse's rump, and led the horse away from the house on foot. A hundred yards down the drive, he mounted up and galloped away as fast as he could.

About mid-morning he needed a break and something to eat. Tired of riding, he found a shady spot under a tree. He dismounted, grabbed a biscuit from his saddlebag and his canteen, and sat, leaning against the trunk of the tree. After a while, he noticed a group of people riding toward him.

As they got closer, Joey could see a man on horseback riding alongside a wagon with two other men seated in it, driven by a fourth man. They stopped when they reached him, and the man on the horse spoke to the man driving the wagon, then both men got down. They were terrible looking men. Both had guns strapped to their hips, and looked as though they had used them before.

Standing over Joey, Horse Man growled, "Whatchu doin' out here, boy?"

Joey stood and made up a story. "I'm going to see someone; probably not anyone you know."

Without any warning, they grabbed him. Wagon Man sneered. "You're gonna have to wait. You're goin' with us."

Joey fought as much as he could, but the men soon overpowered him and threw him in the wagon with the other two men. They slapped his horse and it took off running.

That afternoon, Joey's horse came galloping into the compound without him, Jake was the first to see it and immediately became frantic. He ordered everybody to spread out and look for Joey, but of course, they didn't find him.

***

For thirty days and nights, the two men and their three captives were   on the road heading south. Joey and the others were given very little to eat and drink. He overheard their captors talking, and the word *Mexico* was mentioned several times, so he figured that was where they were headed.

On the thirty-first day, they came to a town filled with people. They called to each other and stood on the street talking. Joey couldn't understand a word anybody was saying. He figured they had reached Mexico.

They rode up to a place that looked like a market and stopped. Horse Man dismounted and walked over to talk to someone. He came back to the wagon and jerked Joey and the other two men to their feet, then dragged them to a line where other tied-up men and some women were standing.

Joey noticed that each one would get up on a platform, and

people standing in front of the platform would say some things. When the conversation ended, someone would take the man or woman down off the platform and the person who spoke last would lead him or her away. Then the next one in line would get up on the platform, and the same thing would happen.

It didn't take Joey long to realize he was about to be sold as a slave. He was terrified.

When it came Joey's time to get on the platform, he noticed one man standing out front dressed in a fancy uniform. The man conducting the sale said something, then the man in the uniform said something, held up two fingers and nobody else said a word. Joey figured no one would bid against the uniformed man, so after a few seconds, he was led off the platform. The uniformed man took him by the arm, and they left the platform area.

The man put Joey in a funny looking buggy, and they rode for about twenty minutes, stopping at what Joey imagined a palace would look like. He was astonished. Keeping his feelings to himself, he followed the man inside.

He surprised Joey by speaking to him in English. "I am General Antonio de Lopez de Santa Diega. What is your name?"

"Joey."

The General asked, "Is your name Joseph?"

"Yes."

"What is your father's name?"

Joey spoke proudly. "Jake."

"Is it Jacob?"

"Yes."

"From this moment on, you will be known as Joseph Jacobson, and we will call you Joseph. I bought you for the purpose of being my houseboy, and you are to do whatever my wife or I tell you to do. Do you understand?"

"Yes."

At that moment a very pretty lady came into the room. She was five feet two inches tall with an olive colored complexion. Her teeth were beautiful and her shiny black hair fell almost to her waist.

The General smiled at her. "Darling, this is Joseph. He is our new houseboy. Joseph, this is my wife Lorena Santa Diega."

Joey said, "Hi"

Lorena nodded. "Hello, Joseph."

The General turned to Joey. "You will address me as General and my wife as Ma'am. Do you understand, Joseph?"

"Yes."

"Good. Come with me. The General led Joey to a room on the first floor, not too far from the kitchen. "This is your room, and you should be comfortable here. You are to stay in here until my wife or I tell you to do something that requires you to come out. We have guards stationed around the house, and if you should try to run away, you will be shot, otherwise you will not be guarded. Now wash yourself and come to the main room to meet me. I'm going to take you out and buy you some clothes that will be suitable for this home."

Joey did as he was told, and when they got to the store, the General bought him several pairs of pants, several shirts, underwear, and shoes. On the way back to the mansion, the General looked over to Joey. "I hope you like it here. You will be treated well and fed well. All you have to do is what you're told."

Joey clung to his new things and simply nodded.

Terribly depressed, he desperately missed his pa, but he wasn't so afraid anymore. He'd met his new Master and saw the lavish surroundings in which he would be living.

His first meal in his new home was supper. The General came to his room and told him the chef would set him a place at a table in the kitchen, and that's where he would take all his meals.

The chef was a middle-aged woman who couldn't speak English, but seemed to want to please Joey. They had a heck of a time trying to communicate. Using hand signs and all sorts of signals each tried to get the other to understand what they were saying. At times, they both laughed.

Joey was an extremely handsome young man like all his brothers. It was very easy to look at him, and that probably helped with the chef. She was not flirty, but it was easy to see she liked to look at him.

Joey pointed to himself. "Joseph,"

The chef did the same. "Isabella."

They smiled and nodded again, and then Isabella fixed Joey a plate. He ate as if he hadn't eaten in days. Actually, he hadn't had much since he was kidnapped, and this food tasted so good. It was very different from what he was used to.

Wanting to know what it was, he pointed to an item on his plate and held his palms up and shrugged. and Isabella would say, "Tortilla" or "Frijoles", or whatever he was pointing to.

Joey rubbed his stomach. "Good."

They got along great from the start, and Joey was glad to have a friend.

At the J I Ranch, Jake was also very, very depressed. Joey's disappearance weighed heavily on him. Joey was his favorite. Everybody in his family knew it and tried to empathize with him, but sometimes, deep down, it was hard to do. Jake stayed in the house most of the time, and allowed Raymond to take charge of the ranch's day-to-day operation.

***

Three months had passed since his kidnapping and Joey, or Joseph as he was known, was faring remarkably well. He had plenty of time to think about why he was in this situation, concluding that if he hadn't been such a horses butt with his brothers, they wouldn't have planned to kill him, and he wouldn't have had to run away from home. The fault was his, and he decided to make the best of a bad situation.

He and Isabella had become really good buddies She was teaching him how to speak Spanish, and he was trying to teach her some English. The General was very pleased with him and his work ethic; something he'd never had before. He was given minor responsibilities and no longer had to stay in his room all the time as when he first got there.

One thing caused Joseph a little discomfort. He didn't know what to make of Lorena. She seemed to be a little too friendly sometimes.

***

Poor Jake resigned himself to the fact that Joey wouldn't be back and dedicated himself to the animal husbandry part of his ranch. He and Doc Wells began working together the way they used to, and it really helped Jake. It forced him out of the house to take more interest in his ranch. He began to realize that although Raymond had taken over quite a bit of the day-to-day operation, he was having a hard time because of the interference from some of his brothers.

Jake realized something had to be done. He was thinking about assigning each one a piece of the ranch and moving them closer to their responsibilities. At the same time, it would get them out of his and Raymond's hair

Before he could set up the meeting with the boys, Kitty, his only daughter, was involved in something bad. She liked to visit the town of Sparta, and to get there she had to go through the community of Falling Water. It seemed every time she went to Sparta, she got sidetracked by Dave Roberts, the son of Mac Roberts, who owned a spread there. Dave was a fine looking young man and Kitty was attracted to him. She often traveled slowly through the community hoping to flirt with him.

On one of her trips to Sparta, Dave caught up with her. Flirting wildly, he talked her into going to the barn with him. After much smoozing, they had a good rumble in the hay. It was Kitty's first time and afterwards she panicked, fearing she was pregnant. She went home and told her brothers she was raped by Dave, and that set up a tragedy of gigantic proportions.

***

The next day, Dave and Mac Roberts rode up to the J I Ranch to see Jake, but Jake wasn't there, so they asked for Raymond, since he was the oldest son, but Raymond had gone with Jake. Going down the line from the oldest, they talked to Pete, and Lewis happened to be there with him.

"Pete, I don't know if Kitty told you or not, but we've been sweet on each other for a while. I'm in love with her and I rode over here to ask your pa for her hand in marriage. I don't have a ranch or wealth to compare to yours, but me and Pa have worked real hard and have built our ranch to the point that it's providing us with a fine living. I can easily support Kitty and give her a good life with just about anything she wants."

Mac verified that, and let the boys know he was in favor of the marriage.

Pete told Dave, "I'll have to talk to Pa before an answer can be given. I'll talk to him tonight and come to your place tomorrow and tell you what his answer is, but it'll probably be favorable."

Of course, he didn't talk to Jake about it, and wondered why, if Dave had raped Kitty, he would come asking for her hand. This didn't make sense to him, but since his sister said she had been raped, he believed her, and told Lewis they needed to do the honorable thing. They were full brothers to Kitty and were probably more protective than the half-brothers would be.

The next day the two of them rode over to Falling Water to the Roberts farm and called Dave out. He and Mac both came out expecting an answer about the marriage, but Pete and Lewis drew their pistols and shot them dead on the spot.

"That'll teach you to rape our sister," Pete said, and they calmly turned around and rode off.

When the bodies of Dave and Mac were discovered, word got around and the people were outraged. Most figured who'd done it. Dave had told some of his friends that he had asked Pete for Kitty's hand and was expecting the answer when he came over.

A few brave souls got together and decided the meanness had to be stopped. Figuring Jake was the most influential person around, they went to see him right after the killings and told him of their suspicions. He thanked them for reporting it to him, and pledged to get to the bottom of the situation, but nothing was ever done about it, and the furor eventually died down.

Jake realized he had to exercise more control over his sons before total chaos broke out over the whole region. A new sense of urgency gripped him as he thought about each son, and where would they be best suited. Before he made a decision on most of them, he went ahead and set Raymond up.

Raymond had gained quite a bit of experience over the last several years, and could handle the operations of the entire ranch if he had to. Jake had a house built about a quarter of a mile from the main house, where he could be available to Jake on a daily basis, but away from the main house.

CHAPTER SIXTEEN

Joey continued to gain favor with the General. He'd proved himself trustworthy. Not a threat to run away, accompanying Isabella to the market was an every-day task. Amazing the people most closely associated with him, he'd quickly grasped the language, and after two years in the General's service spoke fluent Spanish. Honest and capable, he was running the General's household quite frequently.

Other things about Joey amazed people who knew him, especially his psychic abilities.

Joey didn't know how he did these things, concluding it must be a gift from God. He had learned a little about God from the priest at the Church where the General took him every week and had also heard about God from his grandfather, Ike, and occasionally from Jake.

As an example, the child of one of the General's junior officers' had been missing for two days before Joey heard about it. In his mind, he saw a particular abandoned house. As it was not appropriate for him to address the General directly, he told Isabella to tell the General to have the searchers look there and they would find the boy. Although Joey had never been to the area where the house was located, the boy was found there and was reunited with his parents. He had done something wrong, and his mother threatened punishment when his father got back in town. Afraid of his father, the boy ran away to avoid the punishment.

The General wanted to know how Isabella knew the boy was in that house. She told him what Joseph had told her. Impressed with Joey's ability to see things, the General did not forget it.

***

Mexico had been shaken for more than thirty years by struggles for power among selfish, ambitious military men. Political power shifted from the Gachupines to the Criollos. The Mestizos and Indians had little or no voice in the government. General Santa Diega was the leading political and military figure during this period. Ruling as a dictator, he proclaimed himself president or was elected three times. Groups fighting for power overthrew him each time.

Joey knew the General was a powerful man, and was soon to learn just how powerful.

Unbeknownst to Joey, one of the General's political enemies was conspiring with a group of sympathizers to assassinate him. Joey had not heard anything about it, but he began having visions of the General in danger

Bothered by the visions, he asked Isabella, "Will you ask the General if I can speak to him?"

She did, and the General agreed to see him.

In the General's office, Joey told him what he saw in his mind. Remembering how he knew where to find the missing child earlier, the General acted on Joey's tip. He got some of his soldiers together and caught the men in a planning session. After roughing them up, the men confessed and were put into the military prison to await trial.

Grateful for the warning, the General decided to reward Joey for saving his life. He knew for sure Joseph, as he called him, was ready for a much larger job.

The next day the General called all his employees together. He told them about the conspiracy, how Joseph had sensed danger and as a result had saved his life.

The employees all responded with applause and shouts of "Atta boy, Joseph."

The General held up his hand and asked for quiet, then announced, "Because of his insight I am promoting him. Effective immediately, Joseph will be Chief of Staff of this household. He will be second only to me in authority and responsibility."

The staff applauded and quickly gathered around Joseph, offering their congratulations, before returning to their jobs.

Lorena smiled as she watched, hoping Joseph would no longer resist her flirtations and advances the way he had previously. He'd been promoted to a high position within the household. His feelings of inferiority were no longer an excuse. She was so hot for Joseph she could hardly wait until she could get him alone. The General was scheduled to go out of town for an extended stay in about a week and that would be even better.

Joey took over the General's office in the mansion. From there he would run the business of the estate.

He was also given a bigger room to live in; in fact, it was actually a suite, which included a small living area off a large bedroom. He was thankful for the larger space, but missed being so close to Isabella. It wasn't as easy to see her every day.

She had taken him under her wing and was as protective as she dared to be. Many times she warned him to be very careful of Mrs. Santa Diega. She called her an evil woman.

One of the first things Isabella did after Joey was promoted was caution him again to be really careful.

Joey settled into his new job as if he had been doing it for years. Almost every day Ma'am, the General's wife stopped by to see him. Sometimes the visit would be a normal kind of visit, without any importance, but other times her visits seemed solely for the purpose of seducing him. Joey was still not much more than a kid, but he handled himself beautifully, resisting her without causing a problem. He even managed to keep her at a distance when the General was out of town.

One time Joey had gone to his bedroom for something when he felt some feminine arms go around him from the back. He knew instantly what was happening, and he grabbed Lorena's arms and backed away from her. "With all due respect Ma'am, we can't do this. Your husband has put me in a position of trust and is depending on me to look after his interests. Besides, you're married."

"It's all right, Joseph. My husband doesn't have to know about anything. Your quarters are private and no one will ever know. I know you like me and want me as much as I want you. Kiss me."

"No Ma'am. I can't. It wouldn't be right. Stop it Ma'am. I'm not going to betray the General. Ma'am, you need to get away from me."

She made another attempt to grab him. "Kiss me, Joseph. I know you want to."

Joey grabbed her arms and pushed her away, making marks on her arms. All at once, she ripped her dress and screamed at the top of her voice, "Help, help. Guards, help me."

Two guards rushed into the room. "Arrest this man. He tried to rape me. Arrest him."

Lorena then ran to her quarters crying, but nobody noticed that there were no tears in her eyes.

That afternoon, when the General came home, she told him, "Darling, I hate to tell you this since you're so fond of him, but Joseph tried to rape me this morning. Look at these marks he made on my arms."

"I can't believe Joseph would do something like this. What happened?"

"I don't know. I was just walking in the hallway by his room when he grabbed me and forced himself on me. I screamed for the guards and they came in and arrested him. Darling, it was awful."

The General was furious. He went to the jail to see Joey, and nothing Joey could say would convince him he was innocent. The General was much older than Lorena, and because of their age difference, he was very paranoid about her, always thinking some other man would take advantage of her. This was why he wouldn't listen to Joey's side of the story. The General told the police to hold him for trial.

***

Joey's trial was a farce. His defense attorney was a weakling, obviously under the thumb of the General. With the General acting as prosecutor it was over quickly. The five-man jury were uniformed men under the General's command. The trial only lasted a little over one hour, and they found Joey guilty of attempted rape. He was sentenced to the military prison for an indefinite period.

Isabella and the rest of the General's staff were very sad. They all knew Lorena was an evil person and prayed she would get her just reward.

Joey was put in prison under the charge of Warden Hector Rodriguez, and from the start, he had a friend. Warden Rodriguez knew Lorena, and was sure Joey had been railroaded. Exercising his authority, he made Joey as comfortable as possible by keeping him separate from the general prison population.

Joey expressed his gratitude to Warden Rodriguez over and over and assured him he would not cause any trouble. He told him he was totally innocent of the rape charge, but felt he was in prison for a reason.

Two months after his imprisonment, Warden Rodriguez made Joey a trustee. The title provided quite a bit of freedom to move about the prison, and he got to know many of the older, political prisoners put there by General Santa Diega. The more Joey talked to them the more they noticed he had something different, something special. He came to be trusted by the inmates and several confided in him, confident that what they told him would not go any further.

Life in the prison continued day to day, until a conspiracy was discovered in the seat of government and two of the conspirators were   thrown into the prison to await trial. As usual, Joey went to visit the men, to see if there was anything he could do for them. Jose Hernandez, Minister of the Army and Juan Diaz, Minister of Internal Security was here. To say they were scared would be a gross understatement. The charge of conspiracy to overthrow the government was a capital offense and carried the death penalty if convicted.

***

Having established rapport throughout the month awaiting trial, Joey went to talk with the men in the cell they shared the day before their trial. After they started talking, each of the men confided in Joey certain things and asked his opinion on several other things. They were confiding in him because they knew he had been General Santa Diega's Chief of Staff, and was familiar with how the higher ups thought and acted.

Toward the end of their conversation, Joey told the men what he was seeing in his mind.

"Juan, "I believe you're going to be found innocent, and in three days you will be offered your job back,"

"But Jose, I'm afraid I don't see the same thing for you. I hope I'm wrong, but I think you're going to be found guilty."

They didn't take him too seriously. He was not much more than a kid and couldn't know what was going to happen. Still, Juan felt a little more confident and Jose was a wreck.

"Juan, if the trial goes the way I see it and you are found innocent and get your job back, will you do me the favor of telling the president about me and how I foretold your fate. You see, I was kidnapped from my family and brought down here and sold as a slave. Now I'm in this prison for something I didn't do."

"Indeed I will. I just pray that in my case you're right."

"You do answer directly to the president, don't you?"

"Yes I do."

Joey shook hands with both men and left.

***

The trial of Juan and Jose seemed a little fairer than Joey's. The witnesses and the defense attorneys were not as wimpy. A defense was actually presented, but unfortunately for Jose, the evidence against him was too overwhelming. The verdict was guilty for Jose and not guilty for Juan. The judge sentenced Jose to death by hanging and told Juan he was free to go.

After the trial, Joey hoped someone would come and release him or at least give him a new trial, but day after day, nothing happened.

Juan had forgotten to tell the President.

CHAPTER SEVENTEEN

Jake had picked up the nickname *"Big Jake."* Even though he was the largest land owner in the whole region and had gotten most of his land by questionable means, he still couldn't get the Homestead Act out of his head. He wanted to go to Mercer again to see Homer Green. If he could get 160 acres for each one of his 500 slaves, it would add considerably to the J I Ranch. In round figures it would add about 82,000 acres and raise his total acreage to around 900,000 acres.

Jake was by far the wealthiest man in the region and near the top of the list of wealthy men in the whole country. Even that didn't seem to curb his greed. He couldn't get enough land, livestock, or any other belongings to satisfy him. Oil had been found on some of his land as well as rich mineral deposits, which increased his wealth by several percentage points every day. He was so greedy that when he went to the general store, he would bargain with the store owner to get a better price. The store owner was just a poor man trying to make a living. Jake could buy a hundred stores like his, but still he wanted to beat the man down on price.

The more he thought about more land, the more he wanted to talk to Homer. He got Raymond, Pete and Lewis together. "Guys, I have to go to Mercer and I want you to go with me. I wanna leave the day after tomorrow so you'll have all day tomorrow to get things ready. We'll need to take some supplies, but not nearly as many as we did when I went over there with some slaves. This time, we'll eat when we come to a town instead of having to eat on the trail. We'll have to take supplies, but not too many. We'll have to camp some nights and will need to eat, but we can make do with bacon, streaked meat, coffee and flour. Lewis, you're a good cook, and you can make us some biscuits if you need to."

They all packed guns, both rifles and handguns in case of trouble. There had been problems with Indians in some areas, and they surely didn't want to run into that. Only one pack horse would be taken, so if some mean people saw them, it would look like there was probably not enough to make it worthwhile to try to rob them.

***

Many things had changed on the road from Cana to Mercer since Jake had last traveled it. Buffalo Creek had two or three new businesses, including a new café, and a complete town was being built midway between Cana and Buffalo Creek. The railroad was coming through that area, and a couple businessmen had seen a chance to turn a modest investment into something really big.

The new hotel in Mercer was owned by Homer Green. He had made a successful ranch out of the land he got in the deal involving him, his brother and Jake, and built the hotel with profits from the ranch.

When Jake and the boys got there, they registered at the new hotel. The boys hadn't been to Mercer since they moved away several years ago and Raymond told the others, "Let's ride over to Level Cross to see if we can find any of our old buddies." The others thought it was a good idea and told Jake they would see him before supper.

Jake agreed and went to see Homer. After the small talk was finished, Jake got right to the point. "Homer, are people still getting land through the Homestead Act? I've got over 500 slaves now, including about 75 women, and I'd still like to do the same kind of deal I asked you to look into before I moved to Cana. Why did I not ever hear from you on that?"

"Well, about the time you first asked me to look into the Homestead Act, the ordinance thing came up, and since we did the deal with the ordinance, I was afraid if we got too greedy, it would raise a red flag in front of the wrong people."

"You may be right, but I'd like to pursue it again. Are you interested in trying to do it?

"I don't know, Jake. I'll have to think about it. Things are running so smoothly for me right now I don't know if I want to get involved with any questionable activities. I'm getting older and thinking about retiring. I have plenty of money. If I retire from my law practice, my ranch, the hotel and some other investments will provide me with a good, steady income. Jake, why do you want to do something like that? Don't you have enough land?"

"You never have enough land, just like you never have enough money."

Homer promised he would think about it, but was not leaning that way. "Jake, are you gonna be in town tomorrow?"

"Yeah, I'll be here."

"Let me sleep on it Jake. Come back in the morning and I'll give you my answer."

"Okay. I'll see ya in the morning." Jake left to go back to the hotel.

The next morning, he and his boys made a trip out to the J-T to see Etta and Josiah. Jake really didn't want to go, but they were his sons' grandparents, and he thought it was the only decent thing to do since they were that close. Etta just went on over the boys, and they loved it. "I've thought a lot about you boys and how I've missed you. You're still my little boys." She kissed each one on the cheek and ruffled their hair and then hugged them again.

"I made some apricot turnovers this morning. You want one?"

"Yes ma'am," each one replied.

"Jake, how 'bout you?"

"That sounds mighty good."

They had always loved Etta. Josiah was gracious, and acted thrilled to see them, but it wasn't the same as the way Etta marveled over them. They loved Josiah, too, but differently than they did Etta.

Josiah turned his attention to Jake. "Jake we've been holding our own since you left, but I've got to admit the ranch isn't as prosperous as it was when you were here. How're things goin' for you?"

"Well, actually we're just managing to get by. You know, it takes a lot to feed a crowd like I've got."

He didn't think Josiah knew about the large land grant he got and didn't want to tell him.

Etta invited them to stay and eat dinner, and they did. They continued to catch up on what had been going on with each family. "It didn't dawn on me 'til just now, but I guess you don't know that we lost Raelyn."

The news devastated both Etta and Josiah. Josiah sat there with a shocked look on his face and Etta went to pieces. "Oh Lord. My baby's gone. What happened, Jake?"

"Well Ma, Raelyn died after giving birth to a beautiful little boy she named Benny. There wasn't anything anybody could do. It was just something that happened."

"I've got to tell you some more bad news. Do you remember Joey, Raelyn's boy?"

"Don't tell us he died, too."

"No ma'am, but he disappeared and we haven't seen him for a long time."

That upset them, but not like the death of Raelyn.

Josiah's three sons listened to the conversation, but showed absolutely no emotion whatsoever when they heard the news of the death of their sister, reinforcing Jake's low opinion of them. They did act mildly interested when Jake was telling about Joey's disappearance, but said nothing.

After dinner Jake pushed away from the table and stood up. "Folks, we've got to be goin'. It was good to see you again and if you ever get over to Cana, we'd like for you to come stay with us. Everybody would like to see you."

They said they would love to come. Jake and his boys shook hands with Josiah and hugged Etta and left for town.

***

Jake had high hopes when he walked into Homer Green's office, but his hopes were soon shot down.

"Jake, I thought seriously about the Homestead deal last night. Considering where my life is right now, I don't think it would be the right thing for me to do. I pretty much let you know yesterday where I stand on the subject, but agreed to think about it overnight. Approaching the subject from every angle, it brought me back to the *no* answer. I advise you not to pursue it any further. The government is tightening up on grants and there is a definite risk involved if you decide to continue with it. You may be able to find a lawyer somewhere who will try to do the deal, but as a friend, I strongly advise against it."

Jake was very disappointed, but he knew in his heart that Homer was right. "Looks like I came all the way here for nothing. But I thank you for the advice."

They shook hands, and Jake went back to the hotel and met his boys. They would get an early start in the morning for Cana.

***

The next morning, Jake was up early. He went into the parlor to have a cup of coffee with Mrs. Perkins while the boys went to the livery to get the horses ready for travel. In a little bit, they were on the road to Cana.

They saw smoke in the distance one afternoon and wondered about it, but dismissed it as a brush fire. When they got into town, people were talking about how Indians had attacked a family's ranch and burned their house and barn. There was no word about the fate of the family who lived there. Other than that, the trip was uneventful.

***

When Jake got home, a welcoming party of Leann, Ina, and Sue ran out to meet him. Leann and Ina gave Jake a big hug, but Sue held back. Leann hugged her boys, then they took the horses to the barn.

The women led Jake into the house and sat him down at the kitchen table while Ina poured him a glass of lemonade. They wanted to know all the details about how the trip went.

"Me and the boys went to see your Ma and Pa."

"Really? How're they doin'?"

"Fine. I told 'em about Raelyn and Joey and that tore 'em up, but they're doin' pretty good."

After catching up, things got back to normal and everybody went back to their own activities.

CHAPTER EIGHTEEN

In prison for over three years, Joey was beginning to feel he would spend the rest of his life there. The General had visited the prison on occasion, acting toward him the same way he did all the other prisoners, but he hadn't seen the General for quite some time. Rumors spreading around the prison had it that he'd fled the country for political reasons.

***

Miles away, at the presidential palace, the president was in a meeting with his cabinet. Juan Diaz, the Minister of Interior Security, noticed that the president looked terribly sick. When they took a break, he asked him, "Mr. President, are you all right?"

President Ruiz told him, " No, Juan, I'm not all right."

"Is there anything I can do for you Mr. President?"

"No, I don't think so. I am tormented. The political situation is almost unsolvable, and I don't know whether I'm going to survive as president or not. General Santa Diega had been one of my bitterest enemies, but now that he has fled to Jamaica, I don't know what the situation is going to be until the next session of Congress."

Juan sensed that something else was troubling the president. "Is there more that concerns you?"

President Ruiz hesitated, debating with himself whether to answer the question, " I have talked to everyone I can think of who might be able to help me, but nobody seems able to ease my mind." He took a deep breath and blurted, "I fear I'm going insane. I need help, but I just don't know where else to go."

The memory of Joey came to Juan's mind as the president talked. "Mr. President, would you mind if I make a suggestion?"

"What is it?"

"Do you remember when Jose Hernandez and I were arrested and put in jail to await trial?"

"Yes, I remember."

Juan told him how Joey told him and Jose exactly what was going to happen without ever having heard of either of them before. "I believe this young man might be able to help you, Mr. President."

"He may still be in prison. Warden Rodriguez had made him a

trustee and placed him over certain prisoners. This was how I came to know him. He asked me to remember him to you after you reinstated me to my job, and I'm ashamed to say that I forgot it until this very minute."

The break was over. People were coming back into the room to reconvene the cabinet meeting. President Ruiz pulled aside an aide and told him to go, or have someone go, to the military prison and bring prisoner Joseph Jacobson back to the palace.

The cabinet meeting was over by the time Joey arrived at the presidential palace, and he was taken to President Ruiz without delay. Upon entering the meeting room, Joey didn't know whether to bow or shake hands or what. He stood self-consciously just inside the doorway.

Pointing to the chair right across from him, the president immediately put Joey at ease. "Please have a seat," he said in English.

Joey sat in the chair and waited for the president to tell him why he was there.

"Tell me about yourself. How did you come to end up in a Mexican prison?"

Joey had learned a little about protocol when he worked for the General. He began with, "Mr. President," and started from the time he was kidnapped.

My real name is Joey Isaacson, and I'm the eleventh of twelve sons. My father is a rancher in America. I was kidnapped from the ranch and brought to Mexico and put up for sale as a slave. General Santa Diega bought me and took me to his home, changing my name to Joseph Jacobson because my given name is Joseph and my father's name is Jacob. I answer to the name Joseph Jacobson now and don't mind being called that. Later, he made me his Chief of Staff. I was falsely accused of raping the General's wife and put into prison where I've been for over three years."

"Did Lorena try to seduce you when you were there?"

"Yes sir."

"Did she try it more than once."

"Yes sir."

The President looked at him intently, "That's what I figured."

Feeling it was safe to tell the story, Joey continued. "She tried to force herself on me. She put her arms around me, and I had to grab her arms to push her away. It made red marks on her arms. Then she tore her clothes and screamed for the guards, saying I had tried to rape her, and demanded that they arrest me. I had a short trial where I was found guilty, and I've been in prison ever since."

"Well, Joseph, that's not why I called for you. My Minister of Interior Security tells me you can see things in the future and can analyze thoughts. I need your input on some things I'm currently going through. If you can correctly diagnose my problem, I may be able to get you out of that jail. How does that sound?"

"That sounds wonderful, Mr. President. Do you want to tell me what your problem is?"

The President stood up, and started pacing. As he paced he talked. "Joseph, you're not of this country, so you probably don't know how our politics work, but I am a member of the liberal party and was elected president over your former boss, General Antonio de Lopez de Santa Diega, a member of the conservative party. He has either declared himself president or has been elected president three different times, and overthrown each time. After the last overthrow, he fled to Jamaica and is there now."

"Here's my problem. The conservatives are trying their best to overthrow my administration because they think we are not doing the best job for the country, and want to bring back the General. Santa Diega is a ruthless tyrant who should never be allowed to hold public office. My goodness, he's been overthrown three times. What does that tell you? On top of that, Napoleon and the French are threatening war against us.

But my political problems are only a part of what is bothering me. Something else is just eating on me. It's constantly in my subconscious. I can't sleep, and when I do go to sleep, I have nightmares about it, and I'm afraid it's going to take my sanity."

"Are you able to tell me about your nightmares, Mr. President?"

The president stopped pacing and looked directly at Joey. "Every time I go to sleep I see the same thing I see in my mind when I'm awake. I'm walking in the countryside and while I look healthy, everyone I see is emaciated. There is no grain in the fields and dead animals are lying everywhere. What used to be a flowing stream is now just a trickle, and dead fish are lying on the banks. Then, when I come back home, my family and staff are beginning to get sick, but I am still healthy. Joseph, this is what's tormenting me."

You think about this, and when you have an answer, tell Warden Rodriguez to bring you back to see me, and I hope it won't be long."

"Mr. President, I don't have to think about it; I can tell you what you want to know right now."

"Really? Tell me what you think, Joseph."

"Mr. President, before I tell you what I'm about to tell you, it's important to understand that I feel God has given me the gift which allows me to see certain things that other people can't see or foretell."

"The fields with no grain, the emaciated people, the dead animals and fish are what is going to happen in this country, as the result of a terrible drought that is coming. You have six or seven years to prepare for it. If you prepare well, your people will be spared and your political enemies will come to your side. They will see that you love your country and its people. Napoleon and the French will not attack, seeing that your people have rallied around you, and you're too strong for them to defeat."

"My suggestion is appoint someone to be in charge of the preparations, and immediately start building a large system of mammoth-sized cisterns. You will probably still lose a sizeable amount of livestock, but you should be able to save all your people and that's what's important."

"Your people should be able to live quite well during the years before the drought. The good rains that will come before the drought will fill the cisterns and produce twenty-five to thirty percent more crops than usual."

"The government should require each farmer to take twenty percent of his grain crops to granaries that will be built. Even with this tax, the people should still be able to put back enough savings to buy what they need from America when the drought comes."

"Many of the streams will dry up, but the larger streams and rivers can be used for washing and watering the livestock. In the last year before the drought starts, the people should slaughter most of their livestock and cure the meat to carry them through the hard times ahead. This will also help conserve water by not having to share it with the animals. It will be necessary for you to ration drinking water to the people until the drought ends."

"Mr. President, if you will do these things, your country should survive, and you and your people will not be sickly, but healthy."

Joey had been speaking quite a few minutes. He stopped and swallowed, wishing he had a glass of water. Confident in his interpretation of the president's nightmares, he continued. "Mr. President, this is what I think will happen and if I'm right, you should not have any more nightmares about it. Hopefully, you will sleep well tonight."

Joey stood. "With your leave Mr. President, I'm ready to go back to my job at the prison now."

The President summoned his aide to escort Joey back to the

prison. "Put him in the charge of Warden Rodriguez."

About mid-morning the next day, Joey was summoned back to the palace. Fearful that what he had said was not what the president had wanted to hear, he thought he was in deep trouble.

When he walked into the president's office, he was greeted with a hug. Shocked, he stepped back, managing a small smile. "Good morning, Mr. President. Did you sleep well?"

The President answered with a resounding, "Yes! Last night was the first night I have slept well in weeks, and I want to thank you, my son."

Then he told Joey the shocker of all shockers.

"Joseph, I arose early this morning with many things on my mind and have come to what may be a controversial decision. Based on what you told me about the future of our country and your confidence in its accuracy, and the fact that my nightmares stopped when you interpreted them, I believe my decision is the right one."

"Son, I'm calling a meeting of my cabinet later today and announcing that I am creating a new office that will be held by you, the new prime minister; that someone you mentioned to be in charge of building the cisterns and other conservation measures. You will answer to me and me only. An office near mine is being set up for you, so if you need anything from me, you will be close by.

"Incidentally, you will not have to go back to prison. I met with Warden Rodriguez early this morning and told him of my decision. He agrees that I made the right choice. He thinks you're an outstanding young man."

"And oh yes, I'm giving you the home, or palace as you call it, that belonged to General Santa Diega."

"Mr. President, I don't know what to say."

Let's have dinner, then get you settled in your office, and then, I want to know what you have in mind about those cisterns you talked about. Then, if we get through in time, you should go to you "palace", he said with a smile and see what you need to do to make it your new home."

"Mr. President, do you know if the chef, Isabella, is still there?"

"I don't know. Is that important to you?"

"Yes sir. She was my first and only friend when I came here. She helped me a great deal, and played a big part in my learning this language. I would like very much for her to be a part of my staff."

"Done. If she's still here, fine, and if not, we'll find her and bring her to you."

"I don't want to force her to work for me, but if she's so inclined,

I would like for her to be with me because I can trust her."

Dinner was something Joey had never seen before, served in a magnificent dining room. Neither had to ask for anything. If they so much as looked like they needed something, one of the many servants would get it for them.

Joey thought, *Man, this is really going to be something.*

***

Joey took a minute to look around his new office, then sat down across from the president. "What is it you want to know about cisterns?"

"I know what a cistern is, Joseph. I know people who have them in their yards or near their barns, but I can't imagine anything like you're proposing. Tell me what you have planned."

Joey gave the question some thought before replying. "I'm amazed at how things turn out when you don't even know the stage is being set for important events. I was just an average farm boy who was taken from his family and sold as a slave hundreds of miles away. My Master liked me and elevated me to the position of Chief of Staff of his large home and estate. Then I was put in prison for something I didn't do. During this time, I remembered the God my father and especially my grandfather and grandmother told me about. Apparently He's been working for me to save your country and your people."

"To answer your question, I was allowed to read the books in General Santa Diega's library. I remember reading some books about cisterns that were used in ancient times by the Egyptians, then the Romans and Greeks. In some parts of the world, they are still being used."

"The ones I plan to build here in Mexico are similar to the Egyptian's. It was said that some of theirs were as large as a cathedral. This is what I want to do for the larger towns. Other towns will have smaller ones."

If your engineers can interpret the pictures and drawings in the General's books, I'm confident we can store enough water to last until the drought is over. In some cases, I think we can tunnel several miles to tap into the water remaining in a river. Mr. President, I don't have all the details worked out yet, but with God's help and the brilliance of your engineers, we should be able to make this work."

"Very good, Joseph. Now go on to your new home and get settled, and I'll see you here in the morning."

"Thank you, Mr. President. I hope you get a good night's rest again tonight. I'll be here in the morning."

***

Joey pushed open the heavy entrance door and gasped. All the servants were lined up in the foyer. He stepped inside. The aide assigned to him hurried to his side and explained that he had prepared the servants for Joey's arrival. They were waiting to give him their names and identify their jobs.

Joey walked down the line, listening to each, feeling a bit like an officer inspecting his troops. At the end of the line, his heart jumped with joy. There was Isabella. Breaking protocol, he gave her a big hug and kissed her on the cheek. Hugging her again, he whispered in her ear, "I want to talk to you later." Tears welled up in his eyes as he remembered how good she'd been to him when he first came there. She looked like an angel standing there waiting for his orders.

He dismissed the line of servants back to their jobs, and spent the rest of the afternoon getting settled. He moved into what had been the General's and Lorena's suite of rooms and thought, *What if my Pa could see me now. Not even Big Jake has anything this nice. My brothers would probably be really envious of me now.*

Isabella called him to supper a few hours later. She had fixed enchiladas the way she knew he liked them. Rice, guacamole, avocados, frijoles and a delicious strawberry dessert completed the meal. He ate in silence, then said to her, "Pour yourself something to drink and come sit with me for a few minutes.

She ignored the part about pouring herself something to drink and sat in a chair across the table from him.

He smiled and shook his head at her. "What have you been doing since I left for prison?"

"After you left, the General made sure things were like they were before you came. He watched all of us closely to make sure we didn't show any signs of missing you. It was hard because we all missed you, but finally, things got back to normal. We never did know what happened, but one day the General left and didn't come back. After that, things turned bad for us."

"Joseph, I'm so happy to see you again, and for what you have become. I am hoping things will be better for me now. We were told the estate was going to be closed, and we would no longer have jobs, but now that you're here, maybe everything will be all right. I didn't know what I was going to do because, as you know, I have to support my old mama and papa."

Joey nodded and asked her an odd question. "Do you have an assistant in the kitchen?"

"Yes. She's very good and an excellent chef."

"Good. I want you to be in charge of running the house. You will supervise the maids, butlers, the grounds keepers and all the household staff as well as the chef. Except for buying food and other things needed to run the house, you will not be in charge of the business of the household. For the time being, I will take care of the business end of the estate." He smiled and said, "I have experience doing that, remember?"

Isabella smiled back. and said she did. Then she said again, "I'm so happy you're back, Joseph, or should I call you something else?"

"Joseph will be just fine."

He looked out the window. It was still daylight, so he excused himself and walked around the grounds. Joey imagined no one in all of Mexico had anything to compare with it, including President Ruiz.

He returned to the hacienda and went straight to his suite. It had been a long day, and much had happened. He crawled into the General's big bed, intending to think over all that had occurred that day, but was soon sound asleep.

***

The next morning Joey called an impromptu staff meeting and invited the president to sit in. "Three days hence, I will hold a meeting in this office for civil engineers from all nearby towns. As soon as you can get an itinerary put together, I want messengers sent to engineers in the towns that are   farther away to announce my coming to meet with them in central locations at various times outlined in the itinerary."

"While you're working on the itinerary, I need to find a top-notch man I can depend on to do the job that I will outline. The man will need to find others to supervise the excavating and building of the cisterns in their respective areas. He must be willing and able to travel anywhere in the country. Anybody have any suggestions?"

They came up with a few names. One name, Miguel Hidalgo, came up more than the others, so Joey sent a staff member to get him and ended the meeting.

***

Miguel was a pleasant man in his mid-fifties and well educated.

He'd served a four-year apprenticeship in Mexico City before going out on his own twenty-four years ago. In the forefront of building some of the largest and most beautiful buildings in Mexico, he was also well traveled. Only recently, had he returned to his hometown.

Thinking Miguel was the right one for the job, Joey explained the gigantic excavating and construction project that would need to be finished in six years. "Would you be interested in heading up the project? And if so, would you be able to find some others you would be comfortable working with?"

"I'm very flattered that I would even be considered for such a project and am honored to be asked. Yes, Mr. Prime Minister, I would love to head up the project, and yes, I feel that I can fill the other positions with responsible people."

He and Joey shook hands on the deal and went to dinner.

The conversation was basically a get-acquainted session, with each asking questions about the other. Joey felt it was necessary for them to like each other if they were going to work together successfully.

Back in Joey's office after dinner, they made some preliminary plans and then agreed to meet again in the morning. Miguel left for his own office.

President Ruiz stopped by late in the afternoon to see how he was progressing.

Joey grinned. "I'm happy to say that Miguel Hidalgo agreed to be the lead engineer for the total project. Things seem to be falling into place very well."

President Ruiz nodded, then changed the subject. "How old are you, son?"

"Almost twenty-five years old, sir."

"Have you ever had a sweetheart?"

"No sir. I was only seventeen when I was kidnapped from my family. Since I've been in captivity, I have never had the opportunity to meet or court any girls."

"Well, if you had the chance to meet a nice young lady, would you be interested?"

"Yes, sir. I have dreamed many times about marrying a beautiful woman and having several children."

"Well, you come to the palace for supper tomorrow night. There's someone I want you to meet. Will you be able to come?"

"Yes, sir. I'll be there."

***

Joey left his office a little early. He'd never met a girl other than friends of his family's and he was nervous. He'd been just a boy and certainly none of those had been for courting purposes. He was jittery about it, but thought the President had steered him in the right direction so far. It should be okay.

He bathed and changed clothes. He stopped by the kitchen for a word of advice from Isabella, then allowed his appointed driver to drop him off at the front door of the palace. *What a life*, he thought as he exited the fancy carriage.

A butler welcomed him and took him into a huge room where several people stood around sipping from tiny glasses.

The President glanced up from across the room. In a few strides, he was next to Joseph, clapping him on the back. "Welcome, Joseph."

Then turned to everyone in the room and in English said in a fairly loud voice, "Everyone, this is Joseph Jacobson, the newly appointed Prime Minister of Mexico and who, I believe, is the savior of our country. Joseph will be dining with us this evening, so each one of you please introduce yourself to Joseph and make him feel welcome."

A polite applause followed the introduction.

"Come with me." President Ruiz took Joey across the room, stopping in front of the most beautiful young woman he had ever seen. "Joseph, I'd like for you to meet Miss Juliana Rivera. Juliana, this is Joseph Jacobson."

Joey took her hand and kissed it. "It's a pleasure to meet you, Miss Rivera."

"It's nice to meet you, too."

The president excused himself to make the rounds in the room, leaving the two of them to get acquainted. They talked for quite a while, partly because they were the only young people in the room, but mainly because they were immediately attracted to each other. Soon, the call to supper was made, and *due to a strange coincidence*, Joey and Juliana were seated next to each other. They flirted all through supper, barely paying attention to what they were eating.

The evening ended entirely too soon for Joey, but he managed one last question before she left. "Juliana, can I see you again?"

"Yes,"

"Will you have supper with me tomorrow night?"

"Yes"

"I'll tell you what. I'll have my driver pick you up around five thirty and we'll have supper at my place. Is that all right with you?"

"That sounds like fun. I'll see you then. Good night." She gathered her cloak around her and left..

The love bug had bitten Joey. He had a hard time sleeping that night for thinking about her. He wondered how such a beautiful woman could possibly be attracted to a slave like himself.

Her father was a member of President Ruiz' cabinet. Like all cabinet members, he'd been appointed by the president. Joey wondered how Juliana's father could possibly permit her to see him again.

He just simply didn't realize the power and prominence that had suddenly been thrust upon him. He didn't realize he was the *golden boy* who belonged to everyone, including Juliana's father. If President Ruiz approved of the courtship, politician Senor Rivera certainly wasn't going to object.

***

Joey opened the meeting he'd termed "Cistern meeting," welcoming the fourteen engineers sitting in his office, and quickly turned it over to Miguel.

He had taken Joey's ideas and translated them into engineering methods. His voice droned on as he outlined the details of how each cistern was to be built.

Joey tuned him out. He couldn't wait for the meeting to be over. Actually, he couldn't wait for the whole day to be over, so he could get home and prepare for his date with Juliana.

The scraping of chairs brought him back to reality. Finally, the meeting was over. He stood and thanked the men for coming.

He had another meeting with Miguel and then one with President Ruiz. Those two meetings would fill his afternoon before he would be free to leave.

At the end of the late afternoon meeting, President Ruiz asked him, "How did things go with you and Juliana last night?"

"Just fine, sir. She's coming to my place for supper tonight."

"Good boy. Have a good time. She's a great catch,"

"Thank you, sir. I will." He walked out of his office with the president and raced home, anxious to have every detail perfect for Juliana.

***

That evening was the beginning of a very special relationship.

Isabella and her assistant had prepared a feast fit for a king. Flowers had been placed all through the visiting areas of the palace, adding to the romantic mood. The couple sat at the table and talked for a long time, learning about each other.

When Joey told her about his life experiences, she was amazed and very proud of him. She was actually in awe of someone who could have lived through what Joey had.

Juliana's background was typical of the daughter of a well-to-do family. She had studied in America with hopes of one day becoming a teacher. That accounted for her fluent English. She had had all the advantages of affluence, but she didn't appear to be spoiled like so many rich girls were. She was a down-to-earth girl, and Joey loved that about her. Actually, he loved everything about her.

They moved from the dining room to the parlor and continued getting to know each other. The night passed faster than the night they met, and somewhere around midnight, Juliana said she had to go home. Joey had the buggy brought around, and he drove her home, himself.

She snuggled close to him on the drive.

Joey stopped the buggy in front of her home. He turned to her. "I have to go out of town next week and will be gone for a month or more. Can I see you every night until I leave?"

"Yes," She was disappointed that he was going to be gone so long.

"Juliana, I really hate that I have to go, but I've got a very important job to do. You've probably heard your father talking about it."

"I know, Joseph. It's just that I like being with you so much."

"I promise it's for the good of the country. I'll be real busy and if you will stay busy, maybe the time will go by quickly."

"I'll stay real busy."

Joey had four nights before he had to leave and wanted to make every minute count, so he arranged to have Juliana picked up at her home every afternoon and taken to his place, to be there when he got home from the office.

On the fourth night he'd asked Isabella's staff prepare the most romantic meal they could imagine. It was to be a special night, and he wanted everything to be perfect. Good old Isabella had gone the extra mile by having musicians play while Joey and Juliana dined. Isabella had come close to making it so.

After dessert, the couple went out on the back veranda and sat in a comfortable love seat and looked up at the sky. Every star in the heavens seemed to be right over the palace, and the mood could not have been more perfect.

Finished marveling at the beautiful sky, the wonderful meal, and all the other things that had been so perfect, Joey took Juliana's hand. "You know, I'm just a plain farm boy that has been blessed somehow through misfortune, and I'm certain God is going to continue blessing me, but I'm still lacking something. Juliana, we have only known each other a few days, but the first time I saw you, I knew you were meant to be mine. I love you and believe you love me. I'm asking you to be my wife. Will you do me the great honor of marrying me?"

"My sweet Joseph, I, too, knew as soon as I saw you that we were meant to be together. I love you dearly and would love to be your wife."

They hugged and kissed passionately. Several minutes later they decided they had better go tell her parents.

Ecstatic at the news, Senor and Senora Rivera called Juliana's brothers in to share the news with them. The rest of the night was filled with excitement. It didn't take long for questions to pop up about when and where the wedding would take place. It would surely be the event of the year and certainly require much planning. Joey was very happy to leave that up to Juliana's parents.

"Folks, as bad as I hate to, I've got to go. I have to get up early and meet with the President before leaving town in the morning. Juliana, I'll stop by and tell you goodbye before I leave."

She walked him out to his buggy and kissed him goodnight, then kissed him again. "I love you." She whispered, then turned and went into the house.

***

Morning came early and Joey was at the office soon after sunrise. He had much to do and a long way to go. The President came in soon after, and they went over details of what was happening with the cistern program.

Finished with their discussion, Joey pushed aside the papers. "Mr. President, I asked Juliana to marry me last night, and she said yes. I will   probably be gone for about a month meeting with engineers, but I hope we can marry soon after I get back. I'm going to her house on the way out to tell her goodbye, and I'm going to suggest it to her parents."

"And oh yes, Mr. President, will you stand with me when I marry Juliana?"

"You bet I will. I'm very happy for you both."

* * *

At Juliana's house, he was in a rush to get started on his trip, but had to outline some things to her parents. He wanted the wedding to be held at his mansion. A multitude of people would be invited, and his place would hold more than the Church they attended.

They agreed and it was decided the wedding would be in six weeks.

Relieved that his suggestions were accepted so easily, Joey walked out of the house with Juliana. He kissed her resoundingly, and climbed into his buggy and left.

The itinerary was so well planned that Joey and his traveling companions would be in a town to sleep each night.

CHAPTER NINETEEN

After almost five weeks and a steady schedule of meetings, Joey finally got back home. He had met with almost every civil engineer in Mexico and explained to them what needed to happen in the next six years. He also set up follow up meetings between those engineers and Miguel, so Miguel was really going to be a busy man for the next few years.

Joey was aching to see Juliana, but he had to see the President and then meet with Miguel before he could see her.

He had sent an aide to get Miguel, so when he finished with the President, Miguel was waiting outside his office for him. "Come in Miguel, It's good to see you after so many weeks."

"It's good to see you, too, Mr. Prime Minister."

"Miguel, I'm not certain what the protocol is, but when you and I are working together, how about calling me Joseph? When we're in the company of others, you can call me Mr. Prime Minister, but I prefer to be called just Joseph, okay?"

"Okay, Mr. Prime Min, uh… Joseph."

"Miguel, I set up meetings all across the state between you and area engineers and we'll get into that later, but today I need to talk to you about something different."

"What is it, Joseph?"

"Miguel, in addition to the cistern project, there will be an equally large construction project. We're going to need huge warehouses built across the country to hold grain and other crops harvested during the upcoming good times and this is why I called for you."

"You're going to have your hands full just looking after the cisterns and I'm hoping you might know of someone who could handle such a building project. He would be your counterpart and you both will report to me."

"Joseph, I think I can come up with someone, but will you give me until tomorrow for an answer?"

"Tomorrow will be fine, Miguel, we'll talk more later. I'm gonna get outa here and go see my girl."

"Okay, Mr. Pr…uh, Joseph."

Joey ran to his buggy and told the driver to take him home, and to hurry.

Reaching the hacienda, he ran to Isabella's office. "Hey, I'm back."

Before she could say a word, he ran to his room, cleaned up and changed clothes, then ran back to Isabella's office. "Isabella, I'm on my way to pick up Juliana. I'm going to bring her back for supper, Fix us something real nice, okay?"

He was in and out so fast that Isabella hardly had time to say anything except, "Okay."

He had a stable boy saddle his horse, and took off for Juliana's like a streak. Arriving at the house, he slid off his horse, tied it to the rail, ran up on the porch and knocked on the door.

Mrs. Rivera opened it and was surprised to see him. "Joseph, we didn't know you were back. Come in and I'll get Juliana."

"Where is she,"

"Out in the kitchen."

"Let me get her," Joey tiptoed through the dining room and there she was.

It was the first time he had seen her when she wasn't dressed up, and he just loved the way she looked. She had on a plain housedress with her hair tied up, and she looked gorgeous. She turned around and saw him and screamed as she ran to put her arms around him. They hugged tightly, but only gave each other a little peck because Juliana's mother had followed Joey to the kitchen. A serious kiss would have to wait.

"I'm going out and saddle your horse. I want you to come and eat with me, "Joey told her.

"Okay, but I'll have to change clothes and try to make myself look a little more presentable."

"You look beautiful to me. Why do you have to change?"

"Well, okay, but I've got to brush my hair. It won't take long."

While she got ready, Joey saddled her horse and then they rode leisurely to Joey's house. They talked non-stop on the twenty-minute ride.

Supper wouldn't be served for at least an hour, so they stabled their horses and sat outside to enjoy more of the beautiful day. Joey took her hand in his. "Tell me what plans have been made for the wedding."

"Okay. First, the wedding will take place next Saturday, and the ceremony will be performed by Father Ricardo Feliciano, the Priest at Our Mother of Mercy Catholic Church. Father Feliciano has known me all my life and it's only natural that he be contacted to do the wedding."

"I'm not familiar with the Catholic religion, other than having gone to Church with the General several times, but it's all right with me to have Father Feliciano."

"I've asked several of my girlfriends to be my attendants. Who are you going to ask to be yours?"

"I don't know many people except prisoners and I don't want to ask them. Do you have any suggestions? I did ask the President and he said he would, but I haven't asked anyone else. I guess I could ask Miguel and Warden Rodriguez, but I don't know who else to ask."

"You need to think of at least three more and I suggest you ask my two brothers. I've also got a cousin that I feel would be willing to be a part of the wedding."

"Fine, let's talk to them."

Mariana, the woman who replaced Isabella as chef, called them to supper and as usual the food was delicious.

"When I come here to live, I'll probably get as fat as a pig."

"I don't care, just as long as you're here with me."

Finishing supper, Juliana wanted to see the whole house. "I've only seen the visitors' area and the dining room. I'm anxious to see where I'll be living."

The hacienda or palace as Joey called it was absolutely spectacular. It was possibly the largest house on the North American continent with 135,000 square feet, 192 rooms with 51 fireplaces. Thousands of original furnishings decorated the rooms, and there were many original pieces of art from different Masters. It had magnificent sixteenth century tapestries as well as about 40 bronze sculptures. A well-established library held nearly 10,000 volumes. Room after room was filled with art and luxury including a banquet hall with a seventy-foot ceiling.

When Joey showed her his bedroom, she was flabbergasted. "Wow! I've never seen anything so magnificent, and I just can't believe it's soon going to be mine. This whole house is totally amazing, and I can't wait to move in."

"I can't wait for you to move in either. I just wish it was tonight."

They returned to the sitting room and spent the rest of the evening just being together. From time to time, Juliana would talk about things that still had to be done for the wedding.

Due to his position and the standing of Juliana's family, it was going to be a really big deal, but Joey wished it didn't have to be. The whole thing was foreign to him, so he went along with whatever Juliana and her mother decided. He just wanted it to be over.

As usual, the evening ended too fast, and Juliana had to go home. Joey tied her horse to the back of the buggy, and drove her home.

***

The following day was spent in meetings, and Joey's time was no longer his. It started with a meeting with Miguel that lasted until dinner. Miguel gave him the name of a builder he felt would be good to fill the position of general superintendent. Pedro Castrale had a long list of well-known buildings that he had constructed.

Joey sent for him and managed a quick meeting with the president while he waited for Pedro.

When the builder arrived, time was spent explaining what Joey wanted, and Pedro asking questions about what was expected. The discussion was lengthy, continuing until nearly suppertime. As they talked, Joey's confidence in Pedro grew, and he offered him the job, and Pedro said "Yes." With Miguel and Pedro on board, the rest of the organization should fall into place without too much problem, allowing Joey to spend most of his time with administrative duties.

While Joey was in meetings, Juliana stopped by his office and left word with his assistant that she wouldn't be able to see him that evening. She was getting together after supper with her mother and her attendants. It had something to do with the dresses.

Joey missed seeing her, but he was tired and welcomed a night alone. He ate supper and went to bed early.

The next few days flew. The wedding was only two days away. Busy at the office, Joey hardly had time to think about it. When it did cross his mind, he wished he could just bring Juliana home. Since he couldn't do that, he made the best of it. Besides, he enjoyed watching Juliana's excitement.

***

During the rehearsal the night before the ceremony, Joey didn't know what to think about the funny signs people were making, touching their heads, then the middle of their chest, and then touching their chest on each side. The priest said some things Joey couldn't understand, but with some coaching from the president, he made it through the rehearsal.

***

Joey had no idea how many people were invited to the wedding, but he thought all of Mexico must have been by the way so many people were coming into the Church. At exactly five o'clock, the ceremony started.

Joey and his groomsmen entered the front of the Church. One by one, Juliana's attendants walked down the aisle and stood to the side. Then Juliana and her father entered the back of the Church.

In all of his life, Joey had never seen anyone as beautiful as Juliana. His heart raced as he watched her glide down the aisle on the arm of her father.

The priest started talking to the crowd a little bit, and then he spoke in a foreign language Joey didn't understand. He spoke to Joey and Juliana in Spanish, which they understood. At different times the people made those funny signs, and every now and then, everybody knelt. Joey had never seen anything like it. *Do they do that at all weddings or just ours?*

A few minutes later the priest said, " I now pronounce you man and wife" and after an awkward pause, the priest said, "Joseph, you may kiss your bride now."

Joey smiled down at Juliana. He wanted to kiss her, just not in front of all those people. But since he was told to do it, he gave her just a tiny bit more than a peck, and Juliana looked up at him and smiled. He offered her his arm, and they walked down the aisle, directly to the big reception room. It had been beautifully decorated by his staff, and received guests for what seemed like forever. The celebration lasted for hours.

Finally, Joey was alone with Juliana. They never had a chance to eat supper and were starving, so the first place they went was to the kitchen, where they grabbed some leftovers and acted silly the way newlyweds did.

Leaving their dishes in the sink, they tiptoed to the bedroom for the night, so to not awaken the staff. Juliana went into a dressing room and came out wearing a pale blue gown and peignoir with her long, coal-black hair cascading down over her back and right shoulder. Joey was overwhelmed again by her beauty and had a hard time containing himself. They talked for a while, played for a while, and then went to bed.

The night was even more special than Joey had imagined it would be. Juliana was profoundly tender and passionate and soon they went to sleep in each other's arms.

***

Joey and Juliana awoke at the same time. They got up, brushed their teeth, and did a couple other things and Joey asked. "Wanna go back to bed?" Juliana didn't answer. She ran across the room and leaped into Joey's arms. They kissed and Joey laid her on the bed while they were still kissing. They stayed in bed for about an hour, just hugging and kissing and loving. When they got up, Juliana's face was red from Joey's whiskers. She looked in the mirror and was embarrassed, but Joey thought she looked cute.

About mid-morning Mariana knocked on the door and asked if they wanted breakfast.

While they were eating, Juliana asked Joey, "Would you like to go to mass?"

"Go to what?"

"That's what they call the Church service in the Catholic Church. I usually go every Sunday."

Joey thought, *That must be what the General took me to when I was with him.*

"I don't want to go today. I just want to spend the day with my new wife."

"I want to spend the day with you, too."

After a late dinner, the pair rode over to the Rivera's to see Juliana's parents and spent a relaxing afternoon with them. It was sort of a lazy Sunday afternoon, and they all enjoyed doing nothing, just visiting with each other. Mr. Rivera was interested in Joey's plans. He was also interested in just how he was going to pull off such a huge program, and they talked about that. Then they talked about other things, and Joey filled them in on his life, beginning with the death of Raelyn and coming forward to this very minute. He capped it off by saying how thankful he was to have found Juliana, and he promised that he would make her very happy.

Mrs. Rivera asked them to stay for supper, which they did, and it was just a nice family day spent together. In addition to the four of them, Juliana's brothers, Don and Pablo, joined them. Joey liked her brothers, especially Don. After supper they visited a while longer, and Juliana said they must go. They hugged, and as they were leaving, the Riveras told Joey how glad they were to have him in their family.

The next three days just flew by.

***

Returning to work, Joey found a large backup of things that had to be done almost immediately, and he got right to it. Nearly seven weeks had passed since President Ruiz put him in charge of the project, and while seven weeks didn't seem like a long time, relative to six years, Joey wanted to get it done as quickly as possible.

***

Six months later. Joey was well-entrenched in the business of trying to save the country. Cisterns were being dug and warehouses were being built. Notices had been sent to every community in the country announcing that twenty percent of all grain crops would be required to be turned in as a livelihood security measure--no exceptions.

Several of the farmers wanted to know where this gringo got off taking their crops, but they realized they had no choice in the matter.

Joey was a happy man. His project was moving along nicely and he was going to be a father in four months. He and Juliana were hoping for a boy.

***

Nat, son of Jake and Sue and Joey's half- brother, had migrated to Mexico several years ago, bought some land and was now a successful rancher. His ranch was a long way from the capital, but he saw the bulletins and government notices that seemed to be coming in nearly every day. There was something about the name of the new gringo prime minister that caught his attention. It had to be a coincidence that this new prime minister was an American named Joseph Jacobson and his brother who disappeared was named Joseph and a son of Jacob. Every time Nat saw a notice signed by the prime minister, he thought about it. He was well aware that his brother's name was Joseph Isaacson, but still, he wondered.

Having received yet another notice, he told his wife that someday they needed to go to the Capital city and try to meet this man.

FIVE YEARS LATER

All the cisterns were finished and were being filled. Most of them were trenched or tunneled to creeks or rivers, but some were depending on rain to fill them up. There had been an abundance of rain over the last few years, and farmers had harvested more than they ever had before. The smart ones put back all they could, just in case the forecast was correct.

Most of the warehouses were finished as well. Many were already full of grain, that was collected from the twenty percent of the harvests.

With almost a year to go before the six-year target date, it was time for the hard part: slaughtering the animals. Notices went out to everyone who had livestock that they needed to slaughter the animals and cure the meat to sustain them during the upcoming drought. Most did this, but some didn't believe a drought was coming. They had enjoyed too much prosperity over the past five or six years.

Two sons had been born to Joey and Juliana. Michael was the oldest and Stephen was *the live wire*. They were very happy as a family, but Joey was starting to get a little anxious about the drought he believed was coming. What if he just *thought* God told him those things and there would be no drought? What if they had built all these things and had taxed the people twenty percent of their crops and the rains continued? What would become of him? He prayed about it, but no revelation came to him. He continued to work as hard as he could to get ready for what he thought would surely happen.

***

When the harvest was finished at the end of the seventh year, the rains stopped abruptly. People didn't think much about it. They already had their food laid up for the winter and wouldn't be preparing the soil or planting for several months.

***

A few years ago Jake decided to go into the hog business. Already a sizeable operation with cattle, sheep and horses, he thought he needed to capture the market on pork as well.

Since the grain and vegetable harvests were over and the weather was getting cold, it was time to kill hogs. He had established a reputation for having some of the best hams around and he planned to kill around 1800 hogs. The market for smoked hams had increased several fold over the last few years. The thousands of people moving west wanted to buy good food on the trail. Of course, ham was not the only thing coming from a hog. Lard was a major product, and of course, shoulders, ribs, and pigs feet were in large demand. Jake had found a large market for the rest of the hog and was determined to satisfy it.

It took quite a bit of time to complete everything in order to market the hams and other pork products. The curing took most of the time. Hams had to smoke for several months to get the best flavor, so Jake didn't plan to sell very many until spring, when they would put out most of the crops.

***

Spring had finally arrived, and the J I Ranch was a busy place. Plowing fields, picking up rocks, planting corn, wheat, cotton, soybeans and all the other grain and vegetable crops took up the time of the farmers. After the planting, they were blessed with favorable rains and warm weather and the plants started peeping through the ground in short order. It looked as if it was going to be a good year.

CHAPTER TWENTY

South of the border, things were not looking as promising. The weather in Mexico was warmer than in America, farmers planted crops earlier, except it hadn't rained at all, except for a few sprinkles and there was hardly any growth. The ground still had a little bit of moisture, but it needed rain. With little measurable rainfall in about two months, some of the streams and creeks were starting to get low.

Joey and the President were meeting on a regular basis trying to determine if the drought Joey had predicted had actually started or if it was just an abnormally dry spell.

Deciding it was the start of the drought, Joey sent directives to every town and community.

Starting immediately, each person will be allowed only four gallons of water per day. It can come from private wells, cisterns, or any other private source. Water from any streams that might flow through the property can be used as needed as long as the stream is flowing. Any violations of this order will bring severe consequences.

Included in the directive were addresses for the national cisterns and the national granaries and the requirements for using them. In the event that people would have to use the granaries, there would be a cost per pound charge and a possible limit of the amount, depending on the length and severity of the drought. The directive was signed by Joseph Jacobson, Prime Minister, Republic de Mexico.

Joey was trying very hard not to let the oncoming drought affect his family life. He kept Juliana informed about most things, but he didn't tell her how serious it might get later on. He wanted her bubbly personality and charm to continue without any worries.

Over the course of the past year, she had been after him to grow a beard. "Joseph, you're a handsome man. So is Antonio Fuentes," she'd say. "And his beard is so becoming. Why don't you grow one?" The next time, she'd mention Carlos Giron or Cesar Gutierres or another of their friends.

Joey didn't want to grow one, but finally succumbed to her wishes; just to please her. He figured he could always shave it off.

In the years he and Juliana had been married, Joey had become very close to her parents. He'd lost his mother at a young age and was taken from his father as a teen and looked upon the Riveras as his own mother and father. and they returned the feeling. He determined that if and when the drought got extreme, he would take care of them just as he would Juliana and the children.

The President was beginning to get flack from some of the politicians, both friend and foe, and he referred them all to Joey.

Firmly believing in what he was doing, Joey felt the warnings and instructions had come from a higher power. He got pretty hard-nosed, and set the complainants straight. Not so gently, he reminded them that they had been warned to prepare for the drought for the past seven or more years.

They couldn't argue with that, and realized they had come up against the wrong man if they wanted favors or sympathy. Joey had no political axe to grind, no favors to pass out or request, By handling everything himself, the President was kept out of it.

***

For three years, hardly enough rain fell to wet the ground. Using the cisterns had become a way of life for many. Some people still had meat they had cured, and some fruits and vegetables they had put up, but more and more often, the granaries. The situation had become critical.

Joey sent notices to several cities and towns in America advertising Mexico's need for food:

Mexico needs fruit, vegetables, livestock. Follow routes along Conchos, Fuerte, Sonora, Yaqui rivers or perish in desert, Grass availability depends on water flow. Mexican government pays top dollar. No limit. Corrals available. Capitol Center, Torreon, Mexico.

Jake was at the table, drinking his last cup of coffee when Raymond walked in. "Pa"

"In here, Raymond."

"Pa, I was in town and saw an ad posted on the board at the store saying Mexico wants to buy just about anything that can be eaten. The ad says they will buy any quantity and will pay top dollar for it."

"That's interesting. Why don't we look into it? Raymond, send someone to fetch Joel, Danny, and Gene and let's talk about this. It's too late for them to come today, so tell 'em to come in the morning.".

Raymond stayed for a while and they discussed the pros and cons of the Mexican market. Raymond seemed a little hesitant, but Jake couldn't see anything but dollar signs.

The days were getting longer, the flowers were starting to bloom and the honeysuckles smelled so good everyone wanted to be outside, Raymond included. He stayed for supper and immediately afterwards headed straight to the backyard to enjoy the beautiful springtime.

Leann sat with him for a while after the dishes were done, and in a few minutes, Sue came out. They visited for about half an hour, then, Leann got up. "I've got some things to do before bedtime, so I'm gonna go in and get 'em done."

"I'll see ya, Ma."

"Sue, I'm getting ready to go home. You reckon there's any way you can get out later and come to my place?"

"I don't know. The only way will be for me to wait 'til after Jake and Leann go to sleep, but I'll try."

She and Raymond went in. Raymond kissed his mother, thanked her for supper and went home.

***

Sue got home about five o'clock the next morning and went straight to the kitchen and made coffee. Leann came in a few minutes later. "Good morning. Sue. You're up early this morning."

"I know. I didn't sleep good and just got up."

They didn't have much to do until later in the day, so they just relaxed over their coffee.

In about an hour Raymond came in, looked at Sue and winked. "Something smells good. Am I too late for breakfast?"

"No, I'm getting ready to fix it right now. How many eggs you want"?" Leann asked.

"Three." Raymond had breakfast with the two of them. Ina had come in earlier, but just had coffee.

After they finished, Raymond excused himself and went to work.

Jake was starting to get some age on him and didn't get up as early as he used to. He slept until nearly eight o'clock. The women had gone about their business, but Ina went back to the kitchen and fixed his breakfast.

The other brothers arrived at the ranch about mid-morning. After the usual greeting and brotherly horsing around, Jake told them about the ad Raymond saw. "I want us to look at this from different angles and then hear your opinions of what we should do."

Joel looked at Raymond. "Is what you saw on the ad all you know?"

"It is."

Gene frowned, "Why do we want to go all the way to Mexico? We don't have any trouble selling our cattle here?"

Jake interjected, "Because we can probably get fifteen dollars a head down there, and ten dollars is the best we can do up here."

Gene leaned back in his chair, "Yeah, but we don't have to spend weeks on the trail if we sell them up here, besides that, I hear they're having an awful time down there. It hasn't rained in I don't know how long. How could we keep a herd alive without grass?"

Raymond said, "The ad talks as if there is grass along the rivers, and if we make the drive along a river, there shouldn't be a problem. I figure if we drive down on the east side of the Rio Conchos, we can make it okay."

"How far is it to where we will have to go?, Danny asked.

Jake said, "I figure about five hundred miles."

Joel whistled. "Boy, that will be a tall order. It will take almost two months just to get them down there, and then we'll have to come all the way back. I don't think we should do it." He looked at his pa. "How many head are you thinking about, anyway?"

Jake smiled, "I'm thinking two thousand head. Look, I thought about this for most of last night, and I think you can break the herd up into smaller units, maybe no more than five hundred head, and increase the miles you can go each day. Instead of the usual ten miles, you might go as many as fifteen. That should take thirty to thirty-five days. I figure you can move five hundred head with only twenty men, which is a lot less than the fifty needed to move a thousand. I would like to try it, and if it works out as well as I think it can, we might be able to make two runs down there before it gets cold weather."

Joel looked around at his brothers. "Well, if we do this, who will look after the ranch?"

Jake answered before anyone else could respond. "You all have foremen you can trust don't you?"

Joel nodded "Well yeah, but that's a long time to leave them in charge. It's a long time to be away from our families, too."

"I'm for doing it." Danny said. "Cattle prices here keep going down, and if we can get fifteen dollars a head in Mexico that's quite a bit of extra money we can make. Think about it. The difference between ten and fifteen dollars on two thousand head is ten thousand dollars. That's a lot of money. I say let's go for it. Besides, I've never been to Mexico."

Jake had been hoping for a unanimous vote. "We don't have to make a decision today. You boys think about it, and we'll get together tomorrow and decide for sure what we're going to do, okay?"

***

Before going to bed, Jake talked to Leann about the meeting with the boys and the opportunity to sell livestock to Mexico. "What did the boys say?"

"Well, some wanted to do it and some didn't. I hope they will decide to do it because of all that extra money. In fact, with luck, we might be able to make two trips before winter sets in."

"Jake, honey, whatever they decide, I think you're getting a little too old to go on a two-month cattle drive."

"It won't be two months."

"Jake, it's too far for you to go." He didn't have an argument for that and didn't say anything.

After Leann went to bed, he sat at the kitchen table figuring the pros and cons of different scenarios to get the cattle to Mexico. Leann had put a damper on his thoughts of going. After trying every way he could think of to make it possible for him to go, he knew she was right. Deep down, he'd known from the beginning it wasn't a trip he could handle. Begrudgingly, he did not include himself on the drive.

***

None of the boys had changed their mind overnight. Joel and Gene still weren't for it. Raymond and Danny were. Jake was for it, and that made the difference. Sitting outside on the porch they made plans to leave the following week. It was now Tuesday and Jake set next Monday as the day they would leave.

Since Pete and Lewis were more involved with the cattle than the others, he sent instructions for them to separate four herds of five hundred head each. They were told to include any animals that might have health problems, but problems not bad enough to keep them from making the five hundred miles. Then he told them to stock a chuck wagon for each herd, plus a wagon filled with tubs of water for drinking. If they stayed close to the river, the cows could drink from the river.

As Jake looked at the four sons, he realized he wanted all his sons, except Benny, to work the cattle drive. The first herd will leave early Monday morning with Raymond and Pete in charge. The second one should leave two hours later with Joel and Lewis in charge. Danny and Ashton will lead the third and leave early

Tuesday morning. The fourth herd will be led by Gene, Ike, and Jed and will leave two hours after that." Ike was a real good cowhand, but wouldn't be much help if they ran into a fight.

"Be sure each cowboy has a rifle, pistol and plenty of ammunition for both. Y'all probably won't be bothered by Indians, but you could possibly run into some gangs of bandits along the way. Don't fool with 'em. If you're approached by bandits, kill 'em."

He told the four, "I want each of you to pick twenty of your best cowhands and explain in detail what we're going to do. Tell 'em to plan carefully for the trip. Tell 'em to be sure to take what they need, but to not overdo it."

Each son who was there was told to go tell their brothers that were closest to where they lived, except he would not be sending Benny. Benny would stay and help him.

The boys continued the plans with a few questions and answers. Finally satisfied, they stood up to leave.

"Bye, Pa."

"See ya Monday."

"Meet ya at the departure point."

"Sure ya can't go?"

***

The departure point was fairly close to Peter's home. Pete had married his sister, Kitty shortly after killing Dave and Mac Roberts. Considered *soiled* after sleeping with Dave, she wasn't expected to find a husband and had insisted Peter marry her since he had killed her future husband. Jake had voiced his objections but had no control over the situation.

Jake was anxious. He wanted to be a part of the cattle drive. By spending the night at Peter and Kitty's. he could watch the first herd leave the next morning. It was the first time Leann had spent the night with them. She enjoyed their hospitality and playing with her many grandchildren.

After the children were put to bed, Jake and Leann retired, too. "You know what, Leann? The first herd won't even be off J I Ranch property the first night. Would you like to go along on the drive for the first day? We could camp with them and go home on Tuesday."

"That sounds like a lotta fun. Let's do it."

Awake early the next morning, they rode to the departure point with Peter. The other boys weren't too surprised to see their pa, but quite surprised to learn their ma was riding with them for the day.

***

It took the first herd eleven days to reach the Mexican border. They had hardly crossed into Mexico when the greenery started to disappear. With each mile, the ground was drier. Close to the river for maybe two or three hundred yards there was grass. Any farther away, the ground was like powder. With at least three more weeks on the trail, they hoped the grass wouldn't run out before they got to Capitol Center in Torreon?

***

Joey was busier than ever. People were coming into the capital in droves looking for food. He'd had to set up additional offices to handle the crowd. Each person was given a ration of grain, which was then milled. Mixed with their allotment of water, they could make bread called tortillas and sometimes other dishes. Many of the people still had meat they had slaughtered and cured, so with the tortillas, they could make some pretty good meals.

Michael and Stephen were getting big enough to really enjoy, and Juliana had just recently given birth to Jeffrey, their third son. Except for the dry spell, and the problems the people were having, Joey's life was just about perfect.

President Ruiz didn't have any children of his own. He'd treated Juliana as a daughter long before he introduced her to Joey, and since their marriage, the president often acted as if he was their father. He'd *adopted* their children as his grandchildren. Invited to Joey's home often, he spent a lot of time with the boys.

***

Four days into Mexico, Raymond and Peter stopped the first herd for the night, knowing Joel and Lewis were a couple of miles behind them. The cattle drank from the river and grazed on the limited grass, while the cook prepared supper as usual. Eating it was a quiet affair. The cowboys were getting weary.

Things settled down quickly after supper. Guards were set, and several cowboys rode the perimeter of the herd to keep cattle from straying, alternating every two hours. On the third shift, one of the riders caught a glimpse of rustlers stealing some of their cattle, and he yelled an alarm.

Raymond, Peter and the others grabbed their guns, jumped on their horses, and rushed to the herd where they heard gun-fire. One of the rustlers had shot twice at the cowboy who raised the alarm.

More than twenty cowboys was no match for the rustlers. They gave up the plan to steal cattle and took off, riding away as fast as they could. Raymond pulled up, but Peter and a few gave chase, catching up and killing them all. Five rustlers would rustle no more.

Peter said, "You men take their horses, guns, and anything else of theirs that you want. Don't bury them. Maybe it'll serve as a lesson to other thieves who see 'em.

When that was done, the men returned to camp. It was a long time before they settled down again.

The events of the night wore heavy on the minds of most of the cowboys. Raymond was sick about the killing of the five men, feeling sorry for their families. Probably so desperate, he figured they had resorted to stealing in order to feed their children.

Peter, on the other hand, was such a calloused individual, it didn't bother him at all. He even joked about it.

When Joel and Lewis rode by later that morning with the herd and saw the corpses, they could only imagine what had happened. The herd pushed on, Joel and Lewis hoping their brothers were still alive and okay. Since they didn't see any of their men's corpses, they assumed everybody was all right

***

Raymond figured they had about eighteen more days before they reached the capital, and he could hardly wait. They had already been on the trail for fifteen days, and it wasn't getting any easier. *My imagination must be playing tricks on me. It looks like the water level in the river is getting lower. What if it dries up after we get there? How will we get home?*

He didn't dare mention this to any of the men. They might panic and head back, then the rest of them would be in real trouble. He kept his thoughts to himself.

Strangely enough, when they stopped for the night, Peter pulled him away from the rest. "Does the river look like it's getting lower to you?"

"I was thinking the same thing, but don't mention it to any of the men." Raymond's caution was unnecessary. Some of them had already noticed the same thing. "We need to get to the capital as soon as possible."

Peter agreed. "Think we can drive a couple more hours a day? Maybe leave an hour earlier in the mornings and stop an hour later. How much quicker will that get us there?"

Raymond calculated. "Maybe three days,"

They told the rest of the cowboys and told one man to stay back until the second herd got to him and tell Joel and Lewis of the change in plans. He could catch up during the day. The third and fourth herds were at least a day behind, so they nailed a sign to a pole and drove it in the ground and hoped they would see it when they got there.

The extra two hours driving per day paid off in terms of time savings. It cost them in terms of weight loss for the cattle, but since they were   going to sell them per head instead of by weight, they really didn't care. They smelled the corrals long before they saw them. Located on the north side of Torreon, it made perfect sense. Cattle would be arriving from America.

Raymond rode ahead and made arrangements for the corrals. Pete and the others drove the cattle in, where a vaquero directed them to put the cattle in two of them, then waited on the second herd before going to find out who to see about buying them.

Joel and Lewis and their herd came in a few hours later and put their cattle in two of the corrals. The four brothers met and decided they couldn't do much until the next two herds got there the next day.

They went into town to try to find a place for nearly a hundred men to spend the night. The city had several hotels, but none with enough rooms to accommodate all of the J I people, so they had to split up into three different groups. Only half the group was there the first night, so they reserved the additional rooms for the next night. The city had all the hotels due to its being the seat of government, and when congress was in session, there were many people in town.

By mid-afternoon the next day, the other herds were in and put up in their corrals. The nine brothers rode into town to find the prime minister's office and were given the directions. By the time they found it, the line in front of the entrance was long and the hour late, so they decided to come back first thing in the morning, giving the ones just off the trail a chance to clean up and make a more favorable appearance when they addressed the government officials.

Before they all went to their hotels, Raymond assigned two men to stand guard at each of the four corrals. He picked eight more to relieve them in three hours and eight more to relieve those three hours later. He then picked sixteen men to have an early breakfast and relieve the last eight. He thought it was a good idea to have four per corral after it got daylight.

CHAPTER TWENTY ONE

After breakfast, the brothers headed over to the Capitol Center to see the prime minister and collect their money. They were anxious to get on the road to home.

The line was short so early in the morning, and soon they were escorted into the outer office of the prime minister. A few minutes later, an aide approached and led them to the office.

The brothers had no idea whom they were meeting. It had been years since they saw Joey and would not have recognized him had he been clean-shaven. With the beard, he was a total stranger to them.

Not so for Joey. He recognized his brothers right away, nearly going into shock when he saw them. Making up some story, he excused himself for a couple of minutes to regain his composure. Not exactly sure how he was going to play it, he considered several ideas before deciding to play with them for a while without their knowing who he was.

He returned to his office and asked in Spanish, "Who's in charge here?"

The brothers looked at each other in confusion. They hadn't considered the language difference. Raymond knew just enough Spanish to say *"No comprende."*

Joey then asked in English, "Are you Americans?"

"Yes sir"

"Very well, I'll speak to you in your language. Who's in charge here?"

And Raymond said, "I am, sir."

"What is it that you want?"

Raymond explained that he had seen an ad in America saying the Mexican government wanted to buy all kinds of livestock, fruits and vegetables. "Me and my brothers have brought two thousand head of cattle to sell."

Joey acknowledged the bounty. "That will go a long way in feeding the people." He looked at each of his brothers, then asked, "Who are you and where do you come from?"

Raymond replied, "Our name is Isaacson and we are nine of twelve sons of our father, Jake Isaacson. One brother now lives in your country, the youngest is at home with our father and one is dead. Our father owns a very large ranch in America and we all work for him. Due to concerns that Mexico needs the cattle, he decided to help you by sending two thousand head here instead of selling them to his regular customers. To help you out, our father will take a loss and sell the cattle to you for eighteen dollars a head."

Joey stood up. "He will take a loss and sell them to me for eighteen dollars a head? I am buying them every day for twelve. Where do you get off trying to take advantage of us because we are in trouble? You take your two thousand head of cattle and go back to where you came from."

Raymond stood up across from him. "Sir, it took us more than a month to get here, and if we have to take the cattle back, it will take another month and many will die on the way since they have already walked this far. If we go back to our father without having sold his cattle, it will greatly disappoint him and bring shame on all of us. Will you consider paying fifteen dollars for our cattle? If you will, we might be able to save face with our father and we'll be sure to tell him what a kind man you are."

Joey put his hands in his pockets and sprung an unexpected obstacle on them. He said, "Mr. Isaacson, I can only deal with the owner of these cattle. Did you bring any kind of power of attorney from your father giving you authorization to do business in his place?"

"No sir."

"Well then, if you want to go home and get your father and bring him here to deal with me, I will pay him fifteen dollars a head for the cattle. Due to the drought we're having, we can't keep the cattle alive. They will have to be slaughtered, but I'll still pay your father for them when he gets here… if you want to go get him. If this is not agreeable, then I want you and your brothers to have them out of our corrals by noon tomorrow."

Raymond didn't back off, nor did he lose his temper. "Sir, can my brothers and I have until tomorrow morning to give you an answer? We need to talk about this among ourselves. If you will give us this time, we will be here first thing in the morning."

"Very well. That will be fine."

The Isaacson brothers stood and followed Raymond out of Joey's office.

Joey watched them leave, then walked to the window and watched as they mounted up. He paid particular attention to which horse belonged to Peter and quickly called his aide into his office. "See that man riding the roan horse? The one wearing the brown jacket?"

The aide nodded..

Joey slipped the gold cross and chain from around his neck, holding it carefully. Juliana had given it to him when they got married and he treasured it more than anything else he had. Gently, he placed it in the hand of his aide. "Follow them. When you can, slip this into that man's saddlebag. Let me know when it is done.

The aide nodded again, and left Joey's office, returning a short while later. "What you asked has been accomplished."

***

The brothers loitered around town for a little while, sampling Mexican fare at the market and laughing over beers at a cantina. Their responsibilities were basically over, and a little free time was welcome.

As they left the cantina a squad of *policias* approached them and all of a sudden, they got a terrible shock. "Lay down your guns and prepare to be searched."

Indignant, Peter said, "What for? What did we do? We didn't do nothing."

With guns drawn, the policemen issued their command again. "Lay down your guns. A valuable gold cross was stolen from the prime minister's office, and he believes one of you took it."

They all dropped their guns to the ground, and the police started searching their things. They had been the only vendors at Joey's office, so it didn't take but a couple minutes to find the cross in Peter's saddlebag. He was arrested immediately.

"Sir, you've made a mistake. I didn't steal that cross. Somebody must have put it in my bag. I swear. I didn't steal it."

The officer ignored his plea and those of his brothers, leading him to the prime minister's office.

The brothers followed until they were stopped by a guard at the outer office. Peter was taken inside to stand before the prime minister. Facing Peter, Joey told the policeman to take him to the military prison and lock him up.

As they watched their brother led away, they determined to do their best to get him released. They tried to go back and see Joey, but were told he was too busy to talk to them. They would have to come back in the morning.

***

As ordered by Joey, Peter was brought to the government offices and held in detainment until the brothers arrived about eight o'clock the next morning. A guard took Peter to the prime minister's office where his brothers were waiting in the hallway. The guard knocked, and Joey said,

"Come in."

The guard opened the door and escorted the brothers into the inner office.

Joey dismissed the guard. "Shut the door behind you and stand guard outside the door. Do not let anyone come in." He turned his attention to the brothers all standing at attention, not knowing what to expect. They knew he was a powerful man and could do anything he wanted to them.

He looked each man over carefully, causing each to feel more nervous and afraid. When the perusals were finished, he took a deep breath and let it out slowly. "Relax, gentlemen. Nothing bad is going to happen to you. Men, I know you don't recognize me, but I'm your brother, Joey, the one you wanted to kill."

The brothers were flabbergasted ... and a little uneasy. Joey held all that power.

"You didn't have the chance because I was kidnapped, brought down here, and sold as a slave. In the years since then, I have become convinced that God caused these things to happen, and He has used me as an instrument to help save the people of this country."

Joey started with Raymond. With tears in his eyes, he hugged him and kissed him on the cheek. "I forgive you."

Next was Peter. Joey hugged him and kissed him on the cheek. "I forgive you."

Right down the line he went, giving each brother a hug and a kiss on the cheek, telling them they were forgiven. By the time Joey got to the end, some of the brothers were crying, too.

As any important government official can do, he called an aide and told him to have the state dining room set up for dinner. Joey looked at Raymond. "How many cowboys do you have with you?"

"Eighty"

He told the aide, "Set up for a hundred hungry men."

"Raymond, go get your men. We'll celebrate our reunion."

***

At dinner, the brothers still weren't sure everything was okay with Joey, but as the dinner continued, they became more relaxed.

Joey told them what had happened to him since he left home and reiterated that he believed he had been used as an instrument to help the people of Mexico. "Nobody had an inkling that a devastating drought would come, but I saw it in my mind about seven years before it happened. How else could I have known about it unless a higher power told me?"

The brothers had no answer for that.

"I want to see Pa and Benny. I need your word that you will go back home and bring them down here." Peter started to argue about it.

"We can't do that. It takes more than a month to get there and we've already been gone longer than that. I just don't see how we can do what you ask."

Joey, remembering that Peter was the one who wanted to kill him, said, "Peter, you were the one who wanted to kill me. If you don't give your word, I will put you in jail and hold you until Pa and Benny are here. I have the legal right to do it. The police found my gold cross in your saddlebag, remember?"

Peter quickly changed his tune and gave his word. Knowing Joey had the authority to do as he said, the others promised to bring Jake to see him.

They all made the promise, but remembering Ashton's honesty, Joey singled him out. "Ashton, do you swear you will bring my father back to see me?"

Ashton said, "I swear."

"Good. My own mother died when I was little, Leann pretty much raised me, and I would really like for her to come with Pa. It would be great if Ina and Sue would come with them, too. But I especially want to see Pa, Benny, and Leann."

They broke up shortly after dinner, and Joey pulled Raymond aside. "I've given more thought to this situation and I will pay you half for the cattle now, and pay the balance when Pa gets here. You can go to the Disbursements Office in the morning and get your money. Not quite sure he believed they would bring his pa and the others, Joey wanted to hold some kind of collateral. He thought a fifteen thousand dollar balance for the cattle ought to do it.

Before his brothers departed, he invited them to his house for supper. "Please come and meet my family."

"Be in front of the Gomez Palacio Hotel at five-thirty. I'll have someone there to meet you and escort you to my place.

The President of Mexico will be invited to meet you, so be on your best behavior.

The brothers absolutely could not believe what they were seeing. Their pa had a fine place at the J I Ranch, but it didn't remotely compare to Joey's home.

Joey met them at the door. "Welcome. Please come in." He led them into the family room where Juliana and the children waited. She stood when they entered and he wrapped his arm around her waist. "Brothers, this is my beautiful wife Juliana"—he nodded at the children—"and my sons, Michael, Stephen, and Jeffrey."

After they got there and met Juliana and the children, they took a walk around the grounds and were amazed at the lush beauty of the place. None of them had ever seen anything like it. They all seemed to enjoy meeting Joey's family.

The president finally arrived and was introduced to Joey's brothers, graciously putting them at ease immediately. The call to supper was made soon thereafter. The children's nanny collected the boys for their own supper in the kitchen.

Juliana was the perfect hostess, going from brother to brother, making them feel welcome and telling them how happy she was to get to know them. She said she could hardly wait to meet their father.

***

The brothers picked up their money the next morning, then went to Joey's office to tell him goodbye. A few tears were shed, and all in all, they were glad to have found each other. Raymond said, "I don't know how many of us will come back with Pa, but some of us will. I don't want Pa and Leann to come all that way without some protection."

"When y'all come back, you can stay with me." That was incentive enough to make them want to come back.

One by one, the brothers said good-bye and left the office. When they all returned to the street, they rode together to the corrals where the cowboys were waiting with the chuck wagons and the five horses they took from the bandits.

Joey had had some provisions put in the chuck wagons that morning without Raymond and the boys knowing it. They surely were glad to see it. Full bellies would make the trip back home more pleasurable.

Some of the hired men had been with Jake since before Joey disappeared, but most of them didn't know the story. Once on the trail, quite a bit of conversation about him flew back and forth.

The brothers still found it almost impossible to comprehend.

They were anxious to get back home, so they could tell Jake. Raymond said, "I'll come back with Pa. Who wants to come with us?" Gene said, "I'll come." Joel, Ashton, and Jed also volunteered. Raymond thought the five of them would be enough. Jake and Benny would make seven. It was unlikely anybody would bother a group of seven armed men.

***

It took a full thirty days to make the trip because the chuck wagons slowed them down so much. The closer they got to home, the harder Raymond pushed them. Finally they reached the J I Ranch land, which meant only one more day on the trail.

The next day, they got to Jake's ranch, whooping and hollering as they pulled in. When they got there, the hired men all split up and went to their homes, but the brothers all stayed together until they got to Jake's house.

Gene, the most excitable of the bunch, ran into the house yelling, "Pa, Pa, guess what? You'll never believe what we're going to tell you."

Jake was in the kitchen pouring himself a cup of coffee. "Hey, you're back. How was the…what are you talking about?"

Raymond entered the room, "Pa, we found Joey. He's alive."

Jake's knees gave away and he had to sit down. "What are you telling me?"

Raymond sat down next to Jake. "Honest, Pa, Joey is alive… and is the second biggest man in the whole country of Mexico. He's the one who bought your cattle, and he wants us to take you down there to see him. We swore to him that we would. Pa, you ought to see where he lives. None of us have ever seen anything like it. We ate supper with him, and the President of Mexico was there and he treated Joey like he was his son. Joey has a beautiful wife and three children, and Pa, we have so much to tell you."

Leann came into the room and saw all the excitement. "What's going on?" Dirty and trail weary as he was, Ike hugged his mother.

"Eeww. You stink." Leann gave him a very quick hug. "Tell me."

"Ma, we saw Joey. He's alive." Leann had to sit down. "How's this possible?" She and Jake both wanted to know more about it.

Raymond started telling them, but Peter interrupted with a smile and said, "Ma. he put me in jail," and then Raymond explained that part to them.

Every couple of minutes, he told them that Joey insisted they come to see him and to bring Benny with them. He also said he would like to see Ina and Sue, too, if they wanted to come.

Gathering his wits, Jake asked Leann, "How long will it take you to get ready?"

"I can be ready tomorrow."

"Raymond, on your way home, go by Benny's and tell him to come here."

"Raymond told Jake, "Pa, five of us are going with you and can be ready whenever you want to leave, but we're all tired and would like to have at least one day to rest before we leave to go back. Some want to spend a day with their families."

"Okay, but I want to leave just as soon as possible."

Then he asked Raymond, "What would you say if we all took our wives? They can all hold their own in camp, and they shouldn't slow us down, so why don't we take them? I'm sure they would like to see Joey."

"That will be fine if they want to go, but it might take a little longer to get everything ready if they go."

"That'll be okay. Today's Tuesday, so let's plan to leave Friday."

***

Gene, Ashton, Jed, and Benny's wives were all going, but Joel's wife decided to stay home and look after their twins. Ina and Sue were going, so since there was going to be fourteen of them, Jake decided to take a chuck wagon and a cook, which made fifteen.

Friday morning, Jake told everybody, "Make sure you have everything you need. We can't turn back to get what you might have forgotten." Everyone said they had everything. "Do you have your guns and plenty of ammo?" They said they had it all.

The women's rifles went in their horse scabbards, and their pistols were in the chuck wagon, so they were ready to go.

They made a little better time since they didn't have two thousand head of cattle to look after, and they'd chosen the fastest horse to pull the chuck wagon. Raymond was hoping they could beat thirty days.

Crossing into Mexico, the brothers realized the river level was even lower than it had been just a few days ago. Raymond rode up to Jake. "Pa, the grass along the trail is patchy and the water level low. We will need to pick our places to camp carefully."

***

Every few nights after everyone went to sleep, Sue would slip over and get under Raymond's bedroll with him. They didn't think anyone saw them, and really didn't care as long as Jake didn't. He was the only one they really worried about.

***

On the thirtieth day they arrived at the corrals of the capital. After parking the chuck wagon there, Jake and his family went straight to Joey's office, but were told the prime minister had left for the day.

Raymond remembered how to get to Joey's, so they rode out there.

Jake was nervous as a cat. So was Leann. Like the boys, they were absolutely overwhelmed when they first saw Joey's home. They rode up the drive and dismounted, but Raymond was the one who went to the door and knocked.

The butler came to the door. He remembered Raymond and nodded, then motioned him inside. Leaving him in the foyer, the butler went to notify Joey of Raymond's presence.

It wasn't long until Joey came running to the front door. Hi, Raymond. Is Pa here?"

Not waiting for an answer, Joey flew out the door and threw his arms around Jake almost squeezing the breath out of him. Jake squeezed him back. They stood with their arms around each other until Leann pulled Jake away and put her arms around Joey. Everybody, including the chuck wagon cook, was crying.

Joey turned to Benny. "You're my little brother. We share the same dear mother." With that, Benny was the recipient of another great big hug.

Juliana, having heard the commotion, stepped outside, saw what was going on, and hugged and cried with them. When the tears had stopped, she invited everyone inside.

Joey told his butler. "Go get Isabella."

When she came into the room, Joey introduced her. "This is Isabella, the very first friend I made in Mexico. She fed me and taught me to speak Spanish." He looked at her. "Isabella, this is my family." He pointed to Jake. "This is my Pa." He pointed at Leann. "This is Pa's wife and the woman who raised me after my own mother died. You've met my brothers. These women are their wives." Then he pointed at the only non-member of Jake's family; their cook

Isabella nodded.

"The whole crowd will be staying here so rooms need to be prepared.. Have Mariana fix supper for them.

In a few minutes, a lady brought Joey's three children in.

Joey picked up Jeffrey and carried him to Jake. "These are your grandchildren." He handed the baby to Jake and said, "This is Jeffrey"—"and these big boys are Michael and Stephen." He pulled the boys closer. Boys, this is your grandfather.

Michael asked, "Is he like grandpa Rivera?"

Juliana knelt beside him. "Yes, except this is your father's father. Grandpa Rivera is my father,"

Michael said, "Oh."

After the initial conversation, everybody in Jake's household except Jake, Benny, and Leann went to their rooms to rest. It had been a very tiring trip.

Juliana excused herself, taking the children with her and leaving Joey to get reacquainted with his family.

So much to talk about, but nobody knew where to start. After a few moments of awkward silence, Jake asked Joey to bring them up to date on his life since he disappeared.

Joey began where the men kidnapped him and sold him to General Santa Diega and how the General changed his name from Isaacson to Jacobson. He didn't tell him why he ran away from home in the first place. It wasn't necessary for Jake to know his other sons had plotted to kill him. Jake, Leann, and Benny were totally enthralled with Joey's story and were so proud of the way he had become such a success.

Isabella interrupted to ask something about the supper menu. When Joey had answered her question, he told her," Send someone to ask President Ruiz if he would like to come for supper and meet my father."

An hour later, a carriage drove up and the very distinguished President Benito Ruiz stepped out and walked right into the house as if he lived there. No knock or bell was needed. He was that close to Joey and his family.

Joey introduced him to Jake and Leann and by that time, the others had finished resting and were back downstairs. "This is my youngest brother, Benny." He then introduced the President to his brothers' wives, then Sue and Ina and finally, Tom, the cook.

Joey reminded him that he had already met his brothers, and they all shook hands. The President was so down to earth he made everyone feel as though they had known him for years; or maybe even like a relative.

Jake and the President enjoyed each other's company. Interested in Jake's life and how he came to be such an important and wealthy man in America, the president asked many questions. Jake filled him in on the high points of his life—leaving out the specifics-- and then told him about the lowest point: the disappearance of Joey.

"I can understand how Joseph's disappearance could be your lowest point, but the way things have worked out, it was my and Mexico's high point. If not for Joseph, the drought would have been catastrophic. Joseph saw it in his mind and warned us. His plan ultimately saved millions of lives. So you see, your low point turned into Mexico's high point."

"That makes me feel a whole lot better."

"How long are you planning to stay, Jake."

"I haven't decided yet, but I hope to see you again before I leave to go back home."

"You definitely will. Jake, I have to go and I really enjoyed meeting everyone. Maybe I'll see them tomorrow."

***

It was getting late and everybody went to bed but Jake and Joey. They couldn't get enough of each other, so they stayed up later, and talked until Joey's eyes got heavy. "I've got to go to bed, Pa." They stood and hugged once more. "Good night, Pa. It's so good to see you again."

"Good night, son."

Joey had breakfast and went to work before anyone else got up the next morning. Hours later, the rest of the group started to straggle into the dining room, one or two at a time. Mariana poured coffee as they came in and took their orders for breakfast. When everybody was finally in the dining room, Isabella came in and said Joseph was sending four carriages to pick them up and take them to the Capitol Center. He wanted to show them around the center. Then he was going to have someone take them around and show them some of the area where he lived. Then they would be brought back to the center where they would have dinner in the state dining room. After dinner they would be brought back to the mansion to have a free afternoon. Joseph would join them later for appetizers and supper.

The group had been at Joey's for three days and some of them were ready to go home. They mentioned it to Jake and Joey, which started quite a conversation.

Joey asked. "Pa, when do you want to leave?

"I'm in no hurry."

After much discussion, it boiled down to whoever wanted to go back home, could go; and whoever wanted to stay, could stay. Everybody decided to go back except Jake, Leann, and Ina.

"Raymond, do you think you can run the whole ranch?"

"Yes sir, I can."

"Then me and your ma will stay with Joey for two or three months if you and two or three of your brothers will come to get us."

"We'll do that, Pa."

Word got to them before they left that the water level in the Rio Conchos had gotten seriously low, and they were advised to take the Rio Fuerte route after it joined the Rio Conchos about thirty miles north of the capital. There was still water in the Conchos, but the grass along the side was getting thinner and thinner. It was thought there was more grass for the horses along the Rio Fuerte.

They spent one more day with Joey and all but Jake, Leann, and Ina left for the J I Ranch the next morning. Raymond took the advice and led his brothers, their wives, Sue and the cook along the Rio Fuerte route.

Ina and Juliana were becoming very good friends. Ina felt so much at home she thought she might not ever want to leave. Leann was becoming close to Mrs. Rivera, giving Jake time to spend with Joey and his new best friend, President Ruiz. Jake sat in on some of the encounters Joey had with citizens needing help and his calloused attitude began to soften. He began to feel sorry for those people. Some of them would come to Joey for grain and wouldn't have enough money to pay for it. That got to Jake. The more he heard of the hardships, the more empathy he developed. It weighed heavy on his heart, and finally, he decided to do something to help. After all, he could afford it.

That night, while they were eating supper, Jake asked Joey, "Son, do you know of anything I can do to help these people?"

" I'll have to think about it, pa."

"How many people who come to you for help don't have enough money to pay for their supplies?"

Joey said, "About one in three."

"You know you owe me fifteen thousand dollars for half the cost of the herd that I sold you, which you withheld."

Joey acknowledged he did indeed owe him fifteen thousand dollars.

"Son, I'd like for you to take that fifteen thousand dollars and put it in a special fund, and when someone comes for food and doesn't have enough money to pay for it, take the cost out of the special fund."

At that moment, Joey felt extremely proud of his pa. "Are you sure?"

Jake nodded.

"Okay, I'll do it."

CHAPTER TWENTY TWO

Jake was at Joey's office when President Ruiz came in and asked Joey, "Are you familiar with what is known as the Gonzales Ranch, about two miles west of town?"

"No sir, I'm not."

"It was owned by a man named Juan Gonzales who died several years ago. Mrs. Gonzales died soon after and there was no other family, so the state took over the ranch for taxes. It's a beautiful place; four hundred and twenty five acres and a beautiful home the state has been keeping in good repair. It is fully furnished and ready for someone to move into. Joey, take your father out there this afternoon and show it to him. If he likes it, give it to him. This might help make up for some of those lost years that you were away from him."

Jake turned to the president. "But Mr. President, I have not even thought about moving down here. I have a large place in America and responsibilities there. While I would love to be near my son, I don't see how I could even consider moving here permanently."

President Ruiz ignored Jake, "Joseph, take your father out to the Gonzales Ranch and show it to him. He may change his mind after he sees it. It's beautiful."

"Yes sir. I would like to see it too."

The president nodded, turned and left. Joey sent an aide to his house to pick up Leann and Ina to bring them to his office. They would leave from there to see the ranch.

The ranch turned out to be a pretty place. The house had four bedrooms and a large back porch facing east. Sitting out there in the afternoon, the sun would not be blinding. The view from just about anywhere in the house, especially the back porch, was breathtaking and during normal times, it overlooked a lake of about ten acres.

It's gorgeous, Jake thought, *And they want to give this to me, free*? He asked Leann and Ina, "What do you think about this?" They both loved everything about it.

"Jake, it's beautiful."

"Would you like to live in Mexico?"

Leann said, "I'd have to think about that."

Ina said, "I wouldn't have to think about it. I'd love to live here."

Jake looked at Leann, then Ina. "Do you like the ranch well

enough to move here?"

"They both said, "Yes."

"President Ruiz told Joey to give this place to me."

They said, "Take it, Jake."

Joey walked up about that time and asked basically the same questions Jake had just asked. Then he asked Jake, "What do you think, Pa?"

"It's beautiful."

Joey gave a few more incentives to convince Jake. "If you decide you want the ranch, you won't ever have to do any work on it. The government will do all the upkeep and maintenance on the place. You can even learn to fish, when the lake fills up again."

"I'll have to think about it. I'll talk a good bit more to Leann and Ina about it, too."

"I hope you'll decide to move here, Pa, because I love you. Juliana and the kids love you, and we love Leann and Ina. We think you would be happy down here with us. Please think hard about it. I want you here with me. Raymond and the other boys can run your ranch for you. Besides, you're plenty old enough to retire. You have plenty of money, so why not come down here and enjoy the rest of your life?"

***

Jake spent more and more time at the office with Joey as he dealt with the many people coming in to get help. Each day, more people needed grain, but had a hard time paying for it. The situation truly bothered Jake. He had to figure out some way to help these people. He had already given fifteen thousand dollars and that helped, but there was so much more that needed to be done.

Leann could hardly believe the change in Jake. For most of his life it was, *Do to others before they do to you.* She couldn't recall a time when he ever had concern for anybody, except himself and his family. He lied, cheated, and did whatever he had to do to make money. Since spending time with Joey, he seemed like a new man and she loved him even more for it.

Ina had noticed the change, too, and she was glad he included her in his life, because she loved Jake deeply.

***

Lying awake, thinking, something came over Jake, unlike

anything he had ever experienced. More than just a thought, it was like a command he must obey. A revelation telling him what he was to do. Initially, it shocked him. He struggled, then finally acquiesced to do what he must to help the people of Mexico. Immediately, he was at peace and went right to sleep.

He woke up the next morning and did something he may have never done before; he got on his knees and prayed. "God, was that you last night? I believe it was, Lord, and I just want you to know that I'm going to do what you told me to do."

At breakfast, he sat down with Leann and Ina. "I want to talk to you for a moment. Do you remember looking at the Gonzales Ranch? I asked if you would like to live in Mexico and live on that ranch? You both said you would. Leann, have you thought about it? Have you?"

"A little."

Then Jake said, "Well I hope you thought about it more than a little and decided you would like to live here because I think we're going to move."

"What made you decide to do that?" Leann asked.

Jake told them about the experience he had last night. "It was like a vision. I've never had anything like it before. I think maybe it was God, telling me what I have to do to help these people. I could probably live at the J I Ranch and do the same thing, but I feel strongly that I should be here and I hope you two will agree to do it."

"Ina, since you and I are not technically married, you don't have to, but I hope you will,"

"I would like to move here with you. I love you and Leann, and I want to spend my life with you."

"What about you Leann?"

"If this is what you want, then I do too."

"Great. I'm going to talk to Joey and President Ruiz this morning. When I get back, I'll tell you what I have decided to do, so please don't go anywhere until then."

He asked Isabella to have his horse saddled or a carriage brought around. Either would do. He had to go to Joey's office right away.

***

Jake raced up the stairs to Joey's office. "Son, will you please ask President Ruiz to come in here. I have to talk to both of you about something very important."

Joey didn't question Jake and left immediately to find the

President. As soon as they were back to Joey's office, Jake began. "I'm pretty sure God appeared to me last night, telling me what I must do."

"First of all, Leann, Ina and I are going to accept your offer of the Gonzales Ranch and move down here."

The president was pleased. "Wonderful!"

"I plan to go home next week and hope you will send two or three guards with me as escorts. When I get home, I'm going to get my sons together and tell them I'm moving and what I want to do with my ranch. I'm going to retain ownership of the J I Ranch and will put my oldest son, Raymond, in charge of running it."

"I have seen how hard it is for some people to get grain and necessities because they have no money. The fifteen thousand dollars I gave has helped, but not enough, so I will give you twenty-five thousand head of cattle, five thousand head of sheep, one thousand hogs, and fifty percent of our vegetable crops from the upcoming harvest."

"This is what I need for you to do. I don't have the manpower or the equipment necessary to make a move of this magnitude, and it will be up to you to provide that. We can spend a little time figuring what it will take, but if that's acceptable to you, we need to set the plan in action. The main thing that scares me is the lack of grass for all those animals to graze on during the drive."

Joey leaned forward. "Could the animals be killed and butchered and salted before they get down here? Then the only animals needing grass would be the horses pulling the wagons. Pa, how many butchered cows do you think will go on a wagon?"

"I don't know. Aren't there still some people that have cured meat?"

"Yes."

"Well, let's go to somebody who has meat and see how much we can get on a wagon and then we'll know a little more about it."

President Ruiz was dumbfounded. "Jake I don't know what to say. First Joseph foretold this horrible drought and then through some kind of divine intervention, you were brought into our situation. Your son saved our people by predicting the drought years ahead of time, so we had time to prepare, and you have come offering more than anyone could ever imagine, saving countless more lives. Joseph told me when I first met him that he believed God was responsible for his being able to see the drought in his mind. Coming when you did must be part of that plan, too."

"I have been a good Catholic since I was a child, but I have never had any first-hand experience with God until He sent Joseph and you. Because of you two, from now on, I plan to be a much, much better person."

"From the bottom of my heart, Jake, I say thank you, and when my people learn of your generosity, they will revere you just as they do your son. Thank you, my friend."

Jake had more. "There is something else I'm going to do. It doesn't have anything to do with you or your country, but right now, I own more than five hundred slaves, both men and women. After the upcoming harvest is over, I have decided to give all of them their freedom. They can stay on the ranch as hired employees or they can move away, but if they decide to stay on as hired hands, I will give each single man one hundred acres and each married couple one hundred and fifty acres to do with as they see fit. This is something I should have done several years ago because right now I don't believe one person should own another person."

"All these things came to me like a lightning bolt last night when I couldn't sleep, and I believe it has changed my life. Now that I've told you these things, I think we should get busy planning how best to get things started from my ranch to your country."

"You will have to decide how many people you can send to do the slaughtering, butchering, curing, and hauling the animals. I'm going to guess that when we check how many butchered cows will fit into a wagon, we'll see it will be about eight. If my calculations are close, thirty-five to forty wagons per day can haul around three hundred butchered cows, and at that rate it will take about three months. This does not take into account the five thousand sheep and the thousand hogs and all the vegetables, so this might be a bigger program than you're capable of handling. I suggest you get your people together, discuss it, and see if you can work it out."

"As I said in the beginning, I want to go home next week. If you're able to do the program, start sending wagons to my place one week later, along with the people to do the slaughtering, and so forth. After I get home, I will wait ten days before leaving to come back, and if no wagons show up by then, I will assume you couldn't get things worked out. I'll come on back down here and become your newest citizen, but I truly hope you can do it."

The President said, "Jake, we'll do it one way or the other."

Jake finished up by saying, "Joey, I want you to swear to me right now, in front of President Ruiz, that if I die while living down here, you will take me back to Cana to be buried. I want to be buried on top of that tallest hill overlooking the main house. Will you do that?"

"Yes, sir."

"Thank you." Jake left them, feeling as if a huge load had been lifted off his shoulders. He felt free. For the first time in memory, he wasn't thinking about how he could take advantage of someone or some situation in order to make a profit.

Jake Isaacson was a completely changed man.

***

Jake sat down with Leann and Ina and told them everything he told Joey and the President. Leann came over and kissed him, then Ina gave him a big hug.

Smiling, Ina asked, "Jake, does this mean I'm going to be free and get a hundred acres?"

Jake smiled. "You crazy girl. I might just put you out on the street without anything. How would you like that?"

Ina, still smiling, "Well, that will be okay, but I won't have anymore of your children. I guess I'll just have somebody else's."

Then Jake said more seriously, "Child, as long as you are with Leann and me, you don't need a hundred acres"

"I know Jake. I was just kidding. I'm perfectly contented with you two."

***

Jake, Leann, Ina, four soldiers and three pack mules left Joey's, heading north, following the Rio Conchos. The sparse grass would be enough for the ten animals. Only one of the soldiers spoke English, so all communications between the soldiers and the others had to be interpreted by him.

They had a minor scare the first night, and it reminded Jake of the first time he went from Cana to Mercer. Sitting around the fire eating supper, some of the horses sensed danger and whinnied. The soldiers got up and went to see who or what it was. It turned out to be two men looking for Jake.

The soldiers questioned the men, but they insisted on talking directly to Jake. The English speaking soldier asked Jake if he would talk to them, and he said he would. They brought the men to the fire where Jake and the women were sitting.

Jake asked the men what they wanted. With the soldier interpreting for him, one man said he and the other man had gone to the Capitol Center that morning to get supplies.

"We didn't have enough money to pay for all of them, but we were given the supplies anyway. They told us the prime minister's father had given the money to pay for them, and we wanted to thank you. They told us you had just left for America."

"We found a friend to take the supplies home for us, and we rode hard to catch up with you, so we could thank you in person for your kindness."

Jake told them they were welcome and asked if they had had supper. When they said no, he invited them to stay and eat with them. At supper they got acquainted, and Jake told them he was thinking about moving to Mexico to be close to his son. They both told him that if he did move, they hoped if he ever needed anything, he would call on them for help. After they ate, they thanked Jake again and left to go back home.

It took the usual thirty days to make the trip. Raymond was at the house when they rode up the drive, and was surprised to see Jake and Leann. Sue was there, too, and acted sort of like a kid who got caught with her hand in the cookie jar.

After the welcoming home had subsided, Leann took the four soldiers upstairs and showed them to their rooms while Jake pulled Raymond aside. "I want all the boys to come to the main house as soon as they can get here…no more than three days. Get some help and go tell each one of your brothers."

"What's going on, Pa?"

"I'll tell you when your brothers get here."

Jake went to his office to see what had been going on since he left, and to his amazement, everything seemed to have run smoothly. *I must have taught Raymond well.*

Finished in the office, he decided to go see Doc Wells. "Jake, you old rascal, it's really good to see you."

"It's good to see you, too, Doc. What's been going on while I've been away?"

"Same old same old," Doc said. "Everything has been going well. The cattle, sheep, pigs, and horses are all increasing in numbers and the quarterly figures should reflect this. Things are going well, Jake, but it's not the same without you and Leann."

As Doc talked, Jake had a sudden thought. He needed to do something to guarantee Doc's long-term security after he moved to Mexico.

Doc had been Jake's biggest help since before he ever owned any land at all, except for the river house at Josiah's. Doc taught him much of what he had learned about animal husbandry. Jake felt obligated to him, so he would come up with something before they left. It would be great if Doc would move to Mexico with them, but he didn't know if he would even consider going.

***

Joey was interviewing people who were seeking help when four gringos came in. He immediately excused himself and came back five minutes later with four armed guards. "Seize these men and disarm them."

It happened so quickly, the men didn't put up any resistance.

"Put them in shackles," he ordered.

After they were secure, he pointed to two of them. "Remember me?"

One of them said, "No, why should we?"

"Do you remember kidnapping a young boy near Cana, in America, about twenty years ago, bringing him and some other men down here and selling them at the slave market?"

They protested. "We've never been here before. You've got the wrong men."

"It wasn't us."

But Joey said, "I spent a month with you, night and day. I endured your inhumane treatment during that time, and I could never forget your ugly faces. I'm going to turn your two friends loose because they weren't with you, but I'm holding the two of you until court resumes in the fall. At your trial, I intend to testify against you, and I feel sure you two low-life dogs will spend the rest of your sorry lives in prison."

He ordered the two to be taken to jail and he released the other two.

***

The sons started arriving at the main house on Friday, and it was really good to see them. It had been over two months since Jake had seen most of them. He wasn't used to going that long without seeing at least some of them.

They all had a good time while they waited on the others to come the next day. They laughed and horsed around the way brothers do. A couple had some funny stories about things that had happened in their areas.

Since Nat lived in Mexico, he wouldn't be there, but all the others should be.

That afternoon Jake got Sue off to herself and told her everything. "Your situation is the same as Ina's. Do you want to go to Mexico with me, Leann, and Ina? You don't have to, but I hope you do."

"Let me think about it, Jake. If Danny wants me to, I might stay and live with him and his family. Can I let you know tomorrow? I'm really surprised that you're moving away."

***

Jake called the boys together under the big box elder tree that shaded the west side of the house. They found places to sit on the benches surrounding the picnic tables.

He started by telling them of his offer to Joey and President Ruiz. "Fellows, while I was at your brother Joey's, I witnessed unbelievable hardships being suffered by the people down there. I was so touched I felt I had to do something."

He told them about his revelation.

"After that experience, what I had to do came to me clearly. I met with Joey and President Ruiz and offered to give them twenty five thousand head of cattle, five thousand head of sheep, one thousand hogs, and half of our vegetable crops in the upcoming harvest. They are to furnish all the manpower and transportation and the first group of wagons and men should be arriving any day now. I told Joey I would wait ten days, and if they aren't beginning to get here by then, I will assume they can't do it."

Jake looked down at the ground, then back up to his sons. "Now, this will probably shock most of you, but I wanted to tell all of you at one time. I am leaving the J I Ranch and moving to Mexico."

Jake held up his hand to silence their protests. "President Ruiz has offered to give me the most beautiful ranch you have ever seen. It has four hundred and twenty-five acres and a gorgeous home that is completely furnished. The best part is I won't have to do any of the maintenance or upkeep on it. The Mexican government will take care of all that."

"Oh, by the way, the four Mexican soldiers you have seen around here are waiting to escort me back down there. Leann and Ina will be going with me and Sue is going to let me know today whether or not she's going."

"I will retain ownership of the ranch, and everything should stay pretty much like it is except I'm putting Raymond in complete charge of the day-to-day operation." Once again, Jake raised his hands as the boys began to make comments.

He continued when he had their attention again. "Finally, the subject of the slaves. We have around five hundred, both men and women, and at the end of the upcoming harvest, I plan to give every one of them their freedom. After they're free, they can leave if they want to, or they can stay on as hired employees. If they stay, I will give each single man one hundred acres or to each married couple, one hundred and fifty acres. It will be their land to do with as they wish. There will be only one condition: If they ever leave the J I Ranch, their land must be given back, and each one must sign a contract to that effect. That's what I wanted to say to you, and I hope you will all be happy for me."

Of course, everyone was surprised. They milled around Jake, asking questions and offering opinions. Jake listened to all, but didn't change his mind on anything.

Later that day, Sue found Jake in the ranch office. "Jake, I talked to Danny and he wants me to stay here and live with him. If it's all right with you, I would like to do that."

"I'll sure miss you, but if that's what you want to do, it's okay with me."

They hugged. "I love you, Jake."

"I love you, too."

***

On the eighth day, men and wagons started arriving and for a while it was mass confusion. They didn't know where to go, what to do, or who to see for instructions. Wagons were getting backed up, some of the men were getting irritable with each other, only three or four could speak English, and it was a major mess!

Jake had them go to a specific area and wait until they were called. He turned to Raymond. "You're in charge. Take over."

He did just that, suggesting how things should work.

The first thing was to set up the slaughterhouse and curing barn closer to the southern border of the ranch. That would save at least a day of travel each way, and two days could be critical in some cases.

The vegetable crops wouldn't be in for a couple of months, so the only thing they had to worry about was the slaughtering.

Raymond picked Joel, Gene, Danny, and Ashton to help ramrod the operation. He didn't want Pete or Lewis to be around because they were so mean, especially Pete. Soon, things started to smooth out.

The entire first day was just getting things set up and ready to start killing. Late in the afternoon, a few cows were brought in, which was enough to start with the next morning.

***

The butchering process started out rather slowly, but as they got used to doing it, they picked up speed.

The first four wagons were sent out early the following morning. When those first four left, all the Mexicans stopped work and cheered.

***

When things finally started running smoothly with the slaughtering and shipping, Jake thought it was time for him and the girls to leave for the Gonzales Ranch. He had already told the boys good-bye when they were up last weekend, so he didn't have to do that. He and the girls just had to get their things ready.

"Girls, I think it's time to go. Start getting your things together and start packing. I'd like to leave tomorrow, okay?"

"Okay, Jake."

He met with Raymond in the ranch office. "Son, me and the girls are gonna leave tomorrow. We're gonna have to take a wagon and maybe two to hold all our stuff. Be sure the wheels have plenty of grease. The dry, dusty trail in Mexico can be rough on dry axles and cause them to seize up and we sure don't want that."

Jake truly had mixed emotions about leaving. He had worked hard and spent years building his businesses to the point where they were very profitable, and he hated to leave that. He would miss the challenges he had so enjoyed, but the opportunity to spend time with Joey was just too good to pass up. He had missed close to twenty years of Joey's life that couldn't be made up, but he could surely try.

After Raymond found out his pa, ma, and Ina were leaving the next day, he sent word to his brothers, and all but Peter and Lewis came back to say good-bye again. They either couldn't come or didn't want to, but that was all right with Jake. He saw them last weekend. They all hugged and kissed and said goodbye.

Jake, Leann, Ina and their crew started the long trip toward Mexico. Jake drove the wagon with Leann sitting next to him. Their horses were tied behind. Two soldiers rode in front of the wagon and two rode behind. Ina took turns riding along side them, first in front, then behind.

As the days passed, Jake occasionally let Leann and Ina drive or gave the soldiers a turn with the wagon while he rode his horse. The soldiers had become friendly in the month and a half they had been with them. Jake enjoyed talking with them, although he couldn't understand much of what they said. He learned their names. Pedro, Luiz, Pablo and Jose told him their last names, too, but he could never pronounce them... nor remember them.

It was a very relaxed trip, and they were eagerly looking forward to their new life.

***

Arriving in the capital, Jake, Leann, and Ina went to Joey's office first, to let him know they were back. After hugs all around, Joey dropped the keys to their new house in Jake's hand.

"I want y'all to eat supper with me, okay? I'll send a carriage for you and when you arrive, the Riveras and President Ruiz will be there to welcome you home."

"That sounds good, son."

They really enjoyed visiting with those folks and at supper, President Ruiz raised his glass and made a toast to the newcomers. "Here's to good health and happiness on your new ranch."

***

The drought continued with no relief in sight. Jake often went to Joey's office, and felt really good every time someone came in and left with some of the meat he had provided. The vegetable crops were beginning to come in and a few wagons were beginning to show up in the capital with beans, grains, tomatoes and other produce. The people who either didn't pay attention to or believe the warnings—thousands of them-- were the ones most happy to receive the donated fare.

The drought continued for another fifteen months, but Jake and the girls were okay. They used the prolific spring near their house for drinking water and cooking. Joey made sure they had plenty of meat and vegetables. The horses drank from the fairly large creek not too far from the house that still had some flow.

Jake was at Joey's the morning two staffers came running into the office shouting, "Come quick, come quick."

Following them outside, the two men saw people standing in the street, pointing to the west, shouting, "Look, look, it's going to rain!"

Sure enough, dark, threatening clouds and an occasional bolt of lightning could be seen in the distance. Young and old alike were dancing in the street, and people could be heard saying, "Thank you God, thank you."

Enthralled, they watched the clouds get closer. Soon they could hear the thunder after the lightning, and it was only a few more minutes until it started to sprinkle. Then the rain got harder and soon leveled off to just a good, steady rain. It was what they had needed for a long time.

Nobody offered to go inside. It had been years since the people had seen rain, and they weren't about to miss any of it. Soon everybody in the square was drenched. They shook hands with strangers and patted each other on the back.

Already soaked, Jake headed home to be with Leann and Ina during the memorable event. The girls were outside celebrating just like everybody in town. He got off his horse and celebrated with them.

***

It rained for three days. The streams started to fill up, as well as some wells and personal cisterns. The lake in front of Jake's house had a few inches of water in it.

Suddenly the rain stopped and for two days the sun beat down. People looked at the sky, wondering if the drought was going to continue, hoping it was not.

During the night of the second day, it started raining again and rained off and on for several days. It was the perfect kind of rain, just right for the earth to soak it up. It looked as though the drought was finally over.

Winter was just around the corner, but if the rains continued, it would make for a healthy spring. A few winter crops were planted, but for the most part, the people needed to keep doing the way they were doing during the drought, except water was no longer rationed. Food was still in short supply, and Joey was still having to dole out meat and grain.

***

Court had resumed from its summer hiatus, and the men who kidnapped Joey were found guilty and sentenced to life in prison.

Joey had mixed emotions about the verdict. On one hand he felt good they were being punished. On the other hand, he believed all that had happened to him, including the kidnapping, had been part of a bigger plan. It had had a purpose.

***

Jake was beloved by the people of Mexico for all he had done during the drought and was occasionally interviewed. He mentioned to a reporter that his son, Joseph, had encouraged him to learn to fish, but there were no fish in the lake in front of his house. It had filled with water, but the fish had all died when the water evaporated from the lake.

The day after the paper came out with the story, Jake noticed people coming to the lake and pouring something from buckets into the water. Then they left.

Intrigued, he made it a point to be at the lake when someone came with a bucket. He confronted the man and found out those people were stocking his lake with the fish they had caught in other places. Soon there was almost a steady parade of people with buckets. Sometimes a wagon loaded with washtubs full of water and fish came to the lake.

The love the people had for Jake was heartwarming.

CHAPTER TWENTY THREE

FIVE YEARS LATER

With all that Joey and Jake had done for the country and for the people, they were true national heroes. Congress wanted to honor them as such. Statues of both were built and placed in the outer court of the Capitol Center. They were larger than life-sized, and the resemblance to both men was incredible.

Jake had lived in Mexico more than seven years and felt at home. He'd enjoyed being with Joey and watching his children grow and become young men, but missed his other sons. He had been able to go back to the J I Ranch about once a year and some of the boys came to see him, but it wasn't like seeing them nearly every day.

Each time he made the trip, it got a little harder. When a man reached Jake's age, riding a horse for thirty days or more at a time was pretty hard.

The last trip he made was not a planned trip. It was a sad time for Jake. Leann had been sick for several months and finally passed away. The mortician was able to preserve the body long enough to travel from Mexico to Cana and Jake buried her on the hill at the J I Ranch next to the spot he had picked out for his own burial.

Jake and Joey's family had the best time together. From when they were young, Michael, Stephen, and Jeffrey had their grandpa wrapped around their thumbs, and it was ridiculous how much Jake spoiled them. Michael and Stephen were teenagers now, and Jeffrey thought he was. They had busy lives of their own, but they still had time to fish with their grandpa.

Joey thoroughly enjoyed having his father there, too. The years they were separated were becoming just a memory.

Ina was now Jake's only companion since Leann died, and the two fit together like a hand in a glove. Jake loved Ina and she loved him.

As his grandchildren had gotten older, so had Jake. He spent much of his time thinking about his ranch, his sons, and what would happen if he should become disabled. He decided he should make a will and read it to everybody concerned while he was alive. By doing it this way there would not be any questions about what would happen to the ranch and his businesses when he died, so he started putting thoughts together. He had specific ideas for part of the ranch, but didn't know what he wanted to do with a large portion of it. He had thought he wouldn't give anything to some of his sons because of the way they had lived, but was about to change his mind on that.

His holdings were so vast and his family so large he knew it would likely take months to do the will.

He told Joey what he was doing. "I want to see your brothers when it gets warm. I don't feel well enough to make the long trip home. How do you suggest I get word to all of them?"

Joey agreed that Jake shouldn't make the trip. "I'll send messengers to the ranch and even to Nat's. He's been living in Mexico for several years, but should be included in this."

"I want Doc Wells to come with the boys, if he's able. Make sure you get word to him, too."

They set a date in late spring; one that would not interfere with the spring planting.

"I'll go ahead and send the messengers now, so the men can make plans, even though it is several months away." Jake said, "Tell them to bring their families if they can, and plan to stay and visit for several days, if possible."

***

Jake set the fifteenth of May as the day he wanted them all to come. They started trickling in on May tenth.

The first one was Nat and Jake was really glad to see him. He had been living about two hundred miles from the capital and could have come before, but he didn't know Jake was there. He also didn't know Prime Minister Jacobson, was his brother. It had been many years since Jake last saw Nat and his family. It was a really nice reunion and they did a great deal of catching up.

Next came Raymond, Gene, Benny, Ashton, and Doc Wells. It was great to see them and especially good to see Doc. He hadn't been there before, so Jake wanted him to stay at his house to give them a chance to talk. The rest of the guys would be staying with Joey since he had plenty of room for everybody. His house was larger than a hotel.

Jake pulled Raymond aside before the group broke up. "Who did you leave in charge of the ranch?"

Raymond nodded. "I knew you would ask me that. Asa and Thomas."

"Good choice"

Over the next couple of days the rest of the boys arrived. Jake was glad to see Sue and Kitty. Some of the boys brought their families. It was good to have them all together and good for Joey's boys to meet some of their cousins.

President Ruiz came to supper at Joey's and was amazed at how many people were there. Jake smiled. "Ah, my friend, there are several more who didn't come."

"There are enough to start your own country," the president joked.

Jake grinned. "Yeah, and I've got enough land to do it, too, so you had better watch out."

They both laughed and continued their visiting.

Before he left, Jake asked Joey, "Would you mind if I read the will here, since there's more room at the *palace* than I have?"

"I'll be glad for you to."

On the thirteenth, Jake decided that since everyone was there, he would go ahead and read his will to them. After dinner they all gathered in the big room where Joey had parties and receptions.

Jake stood up and addressed his sons. "You were all raised on the J I Ranch and have been a big part of it from its beginning. You have all played a big part in making it as successful as it is, and I appreciate all your contributions. Some of you have contributed more than others and I'll talk about that in a minute."

"I want you to know I love you and will be leaving each one of you a part of the ranch, but some of you won't get as much as some of the others because of your lifestyles and deeds, and I hope you will understand that. This does not reflect my love for you. I just feel that some deeds are evil and carry a big price. I have agonized for months over how to split things up, and I think I have finally come to the right decisions."

"It has taken me nearly all winter to draw up this will, and after I decided on how much land to give each one of you, I drew the approximate boundaries of your inherited land on a makeshift map I created. This will serve until it can be surveyed, which will take several years."

He began with the oldest, Raymond, and went right down the line to Benny, the youngest.

"Raymond, you are my oldest and as such, you should have set an example for your younger brothers. Instead, you dishonored me by sleeping with my wife, and the cost of these deeds is half of your inheritance. Therefore, you will get thirty thousand acres."

Next, he spoke to Peter and Lewis. "You two are my second and third sons and I love you, but your lives have been one disgrace after another. You have bullied people all your lives and have even killed some without even being remorseful. Therefore, I'm going to leave each of you fifteen thousand acres."

Joel and Danny were next. "Boys, I'm very proud of you. You have lived good lives, and I'm leaving each of you a full share of sixty thousand acres."

Jake turned to Nat. "Nat, you chose to leave the ranch and move away. I don't hold that against you, but for all the years you were gone, you weren't contributing to the success of the ranch. For this reason, you will get thirty thousand acres with the condition that if you never return to the ranch, your share will revert to your brothers in the same proportion as their bequests. The time limit to return will be twenty-five years."

Gene, Ashton, Jed, and Ike were lumped together. Jake told them what he told Joel and Danny: that he was proud of them. They had all lived good lives and each would get a full share of sixty thousand acres.

Then he addressed Benny. "Benny, you are my youngest son and I love you dearly, and I guess I'm guilty of spoiling you. You turned into a mean and aggressive person and have caused many problems for me; therefore, your share will be thirty thousand acres."

Jake turned to Joey last. "Joey, my son, you were dead, and now you're alive. Through no fault of your own, I missed many years of happiness watching you grow up. You have become part of my life again, and the last few years here in Mexico have been wonderful. You have made a successful life here. It's doubtful you will ever return to the J I Ranch to claim any inheritance I would leave to you. Therefore, I'm leaving your part to Michael, Stephen, and Jeffrey, in hopes that they, one day, will claim title to your share. I'm leaving each one of your sons forty thousand acres."

With that, there was some mumbling among the brothers.

Jake raised his hand to stop the complaining. "The same conditions apply that I gave Nat. If they never move to the J I Ranch, their portion will be divided among the sons in the same proportion as their bequests. Instead of the twenty-five year time-limit I gave Nat, I give your three sons thirty-five years, due to their young age."

He talked to Sue and Ina next. He reminded them that he found them when they were just young slave girls and had moved them into his home because of the love Leann and Raelyn had for them. Later, they became the mothers of four of his sons, and he grew to love them both. They had stuck by him all these years. Ina was still with him, and for the last seven years or so, Sue had been with her son, Danny. Because of their relationships, he told them he was leaving each one of them tracts of land.

"Ina, because you chose to stay with me all the way, I'm leaving you the main house and sixty thousand acres. Sue, you stayed with me, too, except you did wrong by sleeping with Raymond. Therefore, I'm going to leave you fifteen thousand acres. Y'all can keep the tracts separate or if you choose to live together, you can have seventy-five thousand acres together. Your tracts will be adjoining."

Finally, he came to Doc Wells. "Doc, you are my oldest and dearest friend. We became friends before I knew any of these people except for Sue and Ina. You taught me most of what I know about breeding animals and animal husbandry in general. You helped me find land to buy, animals to buy and many other things that helped me greatly in my rise to success. Since you have been such a valuable part of my life and such a good friend, I'm leaving you fifty thousand acres. This should let you retire in comfort whenever you decide to. I love you Doc."

Doc got up and hugged Jake, "Thank you, my friend. I love you too."

After he got through with the will, he told them, "Guys, I hope business will go on as usual. I remind you that the ranch is very profitable, and the financial experts we have hired are doing a really good job allowing our business interests to grow by leaps and bounds. I caution you against upsetting any of that. Now, in addition to the land you are getting, you will participate in the profits of the ranch in proportion to the land you will own."

"There is one exception: that will be Raymond's share of the profits. Raymond will only inherit one-half a share of the land, but as the general manager of the ranch, he is to receive a full share of the profits plus ten percent."

When Jake finished with the will, everybody stood around and talked except Peter and Lewis. Peter got Kitty and they went upstairs and packed their clothes and the three of them left in a huff.

Ashton asked, "What's wrong with them?"

"They're mad because they didn't get a full share," Benny said.

When Jake heard that, he said, "I just might change my mind and decide not to leave either one of them anything."

***

With the exception of Peter, Kitty, and Lewis, everybody stayed on for several more days. They all assured Jake they would be back in the fall. "I'll be back before then. I know people in high places and wouldn't be at all surprised if the prime minister invited me to stay at his mansion," Nat joked. He seemed to be truly glad his father and brother were only about ten days from him, and he promised to come every three or four months.

"I might be able to come see you too, Nat, since a ten day trip's not nearly as hard as one that takes thirty days."

***

Finally, it came time for everybody to go home, and although Jake was exhausted and tired of company, he hated to see them leave. He and Joey had had a house full for nearly two weeks, and it was time for things to get back to normal.

***

Since Leann's death, Ina had stepped up and had become the companion that Jake needed. Over the years he had truly come to love her, and he was so thankful she was there and the feeling was mutual. For the next eight years, they lived dream lives. They had a beautiful ranch and were close to Jake's favorite son and his family. They were in touch nearly every day and things just couldn't be better, except for Jake's health. In front of everybody he acted as if he felt great, but Ina had noticed him holding his chest sometimes when he thought no one was around. He got out of breath easily and had to rest often. She knew something was wrong, but didn't know what. Jake refused to see a doctor.

***

Jake woke Ina in the middle of the night. "Ina, I don't feel very good."

She took one look at him, grabbed her robe, and ran to the room off the kitchen. She woke their house-boy and told him, "Go get Joseph as fast as you can."

Ina ran back to the bedroom. Jake was really in a bad way.

In a little while Joey and his family came rushing in. Jake was barely conscious, but was still able to talk a little. He knew he was dying and wanted to tell everyone goodbye.

Joey held Jake's hand. Jake gripped it as best he could. "Son, you just can't know how proud I am of you and how much I love you."

He took a shallow breath. "I'm asking you to please take care of Ina. She has been here for me ever since... your ma died... and I love her."

"I promise I will, Pa"

He then talked to Joey's three sons. "I am really proud to have you three as my grandsons and I love you." He gave a slight smile, "I have one more request; whenever you think of me... just remember who caught the biggest fish." He reached out to touch each of them and gave them a nod.

Jake motioned for Juliana to come closer. "My sweet Juliana, I have grown to love you as much as if you were my own daughter, and I thank you for making such a happy home for Joey. I love you, dear."

Then he took Ina's hand and held it over his heart. "I love you, Ina. Please love Joey and his family just as if they are yours and you'll be happy. I love you."

She bent over his bed and kissed him. "I love you, too, Jake."

Jake talked to them for a few more minutes, then took some deep breaths and passed away.

Joey threw himself over Jake's body, crying, and telling him, "I love you, pa. Please don't leave me."

After a few minutes, he stood up and composed himself somewhat, and wrapped his arms around Juliana and Ina. They stayed with Jake until daylight.

When it got daylight, Joey sent Jake's house-boy into town to get the undertaker to come out and get Jake's body. After the undertaker left, Joey and his family left to go home to get dressed properly. They told Ina they would come back to get her in a little while.

Later, when they got to town, Joey went to President Ruiz' office and told him about Jake's death and asked for some time off. The President told him to take as much as he needed.

When they went to the undertaker's parlor, they discussed how Jake's funeral would be handled. Joey said he had promised his father he would take him back to America and bury him at his home place. He explained that it would take over thirty days to get there and asked if they could preserve Jake's body for that length of time. The undertaker told him they had ways to preserve bodies for over six months, and they could preserve Jake's body for that length of time, but it would take about three weeks to do the job. He asked if that would be a problem?

Joey said, "No, if you're sure we can get to America without any problems."

The undertaker said he was sure. Joey told him to go ahead and do it. Then he went back to President Ruiz' office.

He asked the President if he remembered his pa making them swear that his body would be taken back home to be buried. The President said he remembered. Joey told him about how it was going to take three weeks to embalm him, so he wouldn't be leaving for America until after that.

***

The President said, "I'm going to declare a national time of mourning to start tomorrow. All flags will fly at half-staff for thirty days. Joseph, be sure and let me know the date you will be leaving with Jake's body. I want to send a delegation to the funeral and I will try to go myself."

When word got out that Jake had died, people were mourning and crying in the streets. Many of the people took flowers and notes and laid them at the foot of Jake's statue at the Capitol Center. When Joey finished his business with the President and the undertaker, they went back to Jake's house where they stayed until nearly suppertime; then they went to Joey's to eat.

The next morning Joey sent one messenger to the J I Ranch and one to Nat's, telling of Jake's death. The message said the funeral would be at the J I Ranch in Cana on Saturday, October twenty-ninth. He said to please notify all the relatives and friends and he would be coming with the body. Joey told them there would be a large contingent coming from Mexico, including the President, so prepare for a very large crowd.

***

The huge caravan escorting Jake's body arrived at the ranch on the afternoon of October 26. It was no small task finding a place for everybody to camp without interfering with things at the ranch.

Joey and his family, Ina, the president, and the Riveras would stay at the main house and some of the dignitaries would be staying in private homes. Most of the others would be camping out. Jake's sons and their families would have places to stay at the main house. Raymond's house, Benny's house, and a couple of friends' homes would also be available for family members.

It was three days until the funeral, and already there were more people than had ever been to Cana. People were pouring in from

Mexico and hundreds of people from nearby towns who didn't know Jake, except by reputation, had come to see the spectacle. The J I Ranch and the village of Cana were full to overflowing.

***

Finally, it was time.

Jake's body was carried to the graveside by Raymond, Joel, Danny, Gene, Ashton, Jed, Ike, and Benny—all Jake's sons except Peter, Lewis, Nat, and Joey. The family and VIP's followed, then moved to a roped off area nearby. From there, selected guests would stand and say nice things about Jake.

President Ruiz stepped forward and spoke to the huge crowd in his broken English. "I have been a politician my whole adult life and have risen to the office of President of Mexico through good luck, being politically correct, and being a member of a popular political party. Like most politicians, I have had difficulties and at one point I became tormented. I was haunted with troubling thoughts and nightmares and was sure I was going insane until I met Joseph, Jake Isaacson's son."

"At our first meeting, Joseph foretold disaster for my country and proposed steps to take which could save the country and its people. We implemented those steps and thanks to God, they worked."

"Somehow, through guidance by a higher power, Jake had come to Mexico to be reunited with Joseph, and after witnessing the hardships of my people, he made unbelievable contributions. He gave thousands of heads of livestock, dozens of wagon loads of fruit and vegetables and large sums of money. Without these gifts from Jake, many people would have died."

"My friends, great men like Jake Isaacson don't come along very often. Most people don't see even one man like this in their entire lifetime, but you are lucky. You knew him. To have sired a son like Joseph, and to have given all he gave to save an entire population is a legacy that can never be forgotten."

"I will close by saying, Jake, thank you, thank you. My people and I will never forget you. Rest in peace, my friend."

As tears rolled down his face, President Ruiz turned to face Jake's casket, saluted, and stepped back to his spot.

A small choir sang, "Blessed Assurance, Jesus is Mine" and the preacher from Sparta spoke briefly. After the preacher finished, the singers sang "Amazing Grace," a new song written by a slave trader named John Newton. This was fitting because both he and Jake had owned many slaves before turning to God.

The pallbearers carried Jake's casket to the grave and with the use of ropes, let the casket down slowly into the grave. The preacher said a few more words and said a prayer.

Family members and a few close friends walked by the casket, and each one put a shovel of dirt on it.

Slowly, the crowd started to thin out, but it was a good two hours before everyone except the family left. While everybody was still standing around talking, Raymond had some men fill the grave with dirt and put a cross with Jake's name on it at the head. The family started to thin out, and all the sons finally left, except Joey.

He and Juliana and Ina stayed at the grave for maybe an hour after everyone else had gone, talking about Joey's life and what he had missed in the years he was gone, and how glad he was to have found Jake when he did. He talked about what a great man he thought his father was.

As they were getting ready to leave, Joey took something out of his pocket. It was a miniature of his father's statue that was at the Capitol Center.

He laid it at the head of Jake's grave., "Pa, my people created a large statue like this to honor you, and I have brought this to your resting place to honor you here, and to remind others just how great you were. I know you have gone to a better place, and one day you and I will be reunited, as we were before. In the meantime, rest well, my father."

Joey turned and left Jake until they would meet again.